BLUE ARROW ISLAND

BRENDA ROTHERT

Cover by Damonza.com

Editorial consultant: Jenn Sommersby, Plumfield Editing

Line editing: Rose Puls, Fairy Proofmother

PART ONE

1

There's a cost to what I do. It's too heavy at times. But I've brought that cost on others, so I suppose the least I can do is bear it, even if it eventually crushes me.

Excerpt from the journal of Dr. Randall McClain

I'm alive. At least, I think so. Surely the afterlife doesn't smell like diesel fumes and salt water. It's been a long time since I breathed in anything but the musty decay of a prison cell.

I shift and raise my fingertips to my cracked lips, a bolt of pain zinging through one of my shoulders. When I open my eyes, overpowering light makes me squeeze them shut again. I've been in the dark for weeks; my eyes can't handle the brightness.

Something nudges my leg. I ignore it, gently running

my fingers over my wrists. I'm not tied up anymore. The welts left behind by the binds ache, but it's nothing compared to my raging headache.

"Wake up," someone whispers urgently, nudging my leg again.

I squint against the sunlight that floods my eyes, getting into a sitting position. A gust of thick, humid air blasts my ripe, unwashed scent straight into my nostrils.

I'm on the dingy white fiberglass deck of a boat, one of about two dozen people. Some of them are still sleeping.

No, not sleeping. The last thing I remember is guzzling the jug of water guards brought to my cell. My painful, swollen lips and intense thirst tell me I haven't had water in a long time, and I'm groggy. I was unconscious. And the other people lying on the deck are too.

"We're here," the person who nudged me whispers.

I turn to look at the woman sitting next to me, my eyes starting to adjust. Her black, shoulder-length hair has dried blood crusted in it and I can feel the dread in her golden-brown eyes. She glances down at my wrists, and I assume she's looking at my rope burns.

Then I see them in clear light for the first time—the thick black X tattoos that stretch from knuckles to wrist on the backs of both of my hands. It's been several weeks since I was branded with the marks, but I couldn't see them in the darkness. It's like I'm looking at someone else's hands, the skin familiar but the ink foreign.

She holds out her wrist, bearing the same tattoo. "I'm Amira."

"Briar."

"They're taking us to an island."

I fight to swallow against the dryness in my throat. I had no choice really, between exile and death for my so-called crime, but I thought exile meant a remote prison where I could plan an escape. How the hell will I escape from an island?

"Get up!" a deep male voice booms. "You shit sacks are jumping off this rig in about two minutes. Stand up so we can get a good look at you."

I count the guards, all men wearing dark uniforms with the New America flag emblazoned on a large patch on the shoulder. The flag's stripes are vertical now, the resemblance to a cell a fitting metaphor. The guards are a motley mixture of big and small, shaven and unshaven, fastidious and disheveled, because there are only two qualifications to serve in President Soren Whitman's rapidly growing empire: be male and believe in Whitman's brutal reshaping of society to serve his twisted biblical agenda.

There are eight of them, all strapped with multiple weapons. One of them, a bulky man with his finger casually resting on the hilt of a dagger sheathed at his waist, studies several of us and calls out, "I'll do a hundred credits on the biter."

I force myself to look down and appear demure, though it's a little late for that. He's talking about me—I bit the thumb of one of the guards so hard he had to get it stitched up. He was trying to carry a girl out of our cell, and there's only one reason guards come alone to cells late at night.

I'm sure that same guard, or maybe a different one, got that girl another time. But not that night. That night, she was safe.

"Fifty on that little Hispanic one," another guard says, leering at Amira.

"I'm fucking Egyptian," she says under her breath.

"Don't," I caution her.

Whitman's soldiers take extra glee in being cruel to women, and we can't give them a reason to quietly cut our throats out here, where no one will ever know.

While one guard finishes taking bets, another walks around, kicking the people still lying motionless. Two of them groan and move. Six don't. He kicks them again, pulling his foot back farther this time to inflict more pain.

"Six dead," he says flatly. "You want us to throw them over?"

Why are six prisoners dead? What the hell did they do to us?

"Yeah, I'm not burying those fucks," another guard says. "Toss 'em."

I keep my expression neutral as guards grunt from the weight of the bodies they're dragging across the deck. One guard has his hand wrapped around a woman's ponytail. He pulls her to the edge of the deck and shoves her body into the water, rubbing his palm on the thigh of his pants to wipe off the grease from her hair.

What used to be cruel is now commonplace, and staying impassive to it is how I survive.

We're approaching a large island, the shoreline ringed with pristine sand the shade of bone dust. A mountain looms on the island's far side, an ominous sentinel overlooking a thick jungle.

"Can you swim?" Amira asks me in a hushed tone.

I flick a glance at the gently lapping teal waves. "Yeah. You?"

"Well enough."

Nineteen prisoners remain on the deck—eleven men and eight women. If we work together, we have a better chance of finding safe water to drink and setting up a camp to protect ourselves from whatever's in that jungle.

One of the guards holds binoculars to his eyes to gaze at the shoreline. "I see 'em. The locals are waiting to welcome you."

His tone is amused. I close my eyes, take a deep breath in and let it out. Even though I'm weak and dehydrated, I'm only twenty-four years old and in good physical shape. I can make the swim.

I've beaten the odds in the six years since the virus hit. Life in New America is brutal for women, and that brutality has sharpened my will into a deadly point.

And as long as Lochlan Murphy lives, so do I.

The head guard gestures to the driver at the helm, and we immediately speed up. I steady my feet as a nearby prisoner falls and knocks another one to the ground.

"On our own or with the others?" Amira murmurs.

"Let's try the others."

She nods. We both study the shoreline, looking for the "locals" the guard mentioned.

"Shit," a man close by mutters.

It takes me a few more seconds to see what he does. My heart falls into my stomach when I make out a person nocking an arrow on a bow. A figure next to him is holding what looks like a spear.

"Who are they?" a prisoner asks from the other side of the deck, cupping a hand over his brows to shield against the sunlight.

"Welcome to Blue Arrow Island," the head guard says. "Our great leader tried to take care of you fucks and you spit in his face. So now you get to play a little game."

I cut my gaze back to the island, seeing more people with bows and arrows. Many more. Panic catches in my throat and I have to force myself to breathe.

"We're dead," Amira whispers.

But it doesn't make sense. Why would they bring us here to die when they could have just shot us back in Carson City, where we were imprisoned?

Scanning the entire shoreline, I search for options. Rock formations I can swim to for cover. A quick entrance into the jungle.

"Wait ..."

Two people are fighting on the beach. One has a spear and the other is using her fists. A swift right hook drops the spear holder to the ground, and he doesn't get back up. The woman retrieves his spear and drives it into him, more than a foot of the weapon sinking into his stomach. Then she yanks the spear out of him and walks toward a group of people, unfazed by the murder she just committed.

That's one hell of a strong woman. I couldn't drive a spear into someone that deep and then pull it back out like it's a toothpick in a glazed meatball.

At the other end of the beach, people are yelling and gesturing angrily. I think it's because of the man who was just killed.

"There are two different groups," I say in a low tone meant only for Amira.

"Are they prisoners, like us?"

"I don't know."

If everyone on that beach is united in trying to kill us, we don't stand a chance. There are a lot more of them than there are of us, and we don't have any weapons. But if they're also fighting each other ... that wouldn't be a bad thing.

The roar of the boat's engine cuts off, the vessel rocking in the water. From its sleek design, I can tell this was someone's prized yacht before the virus. Now it's a charter, transporting people to their deaths. A guard pushes a button, the links of a massive chain clanking as he lowers the anchor.

I look between the two groups on the beach again. A tall, broad man with dark hair stands at the front of the first group, his hand wrapped around a spear.

There's a woman at the front of the other group, her blond hair blowing behind her in the breeze. She doesn't have a weapon, but many of the people behind her are holding primitive wooden spears.

A choice between groups led by a man and a woman is an easy one for me. I consider telling Amira which group looks safest, but I stop myself. She seems nice, but it's always best to share as little as possible. I have to take care of myself; assuming anyone else will could be a death sentence.

Something arcs through the air, drawing my gaze up to the pale-blue sky. It's an arrow, fired toward the boat by someone on the beach. The guards don't even acknowledge it. It plunks into the water, out of range.

"Inmates, you have thirty seconds to get off this boat before we start removing you," the head guard says.

Amira jolts forward and I instinctively put my fingertips on her arm to stop her. Her eyes bulge with worry.

"We have to jump," she whisper-hisses.

"Wait."

I don't want to be one of the first inmates to reach that shoreline. If we hang back, maybe we'll be able to see what's going on before we get there.

Someone murmurs a prayer and the thunking splashes of people plunging into the water begin. Amira takes deep breaths as we approach the boat's edge, nearing the gaps where a protective railing used to be.

She reminds me of Ellery, the first friend I made after the virus hit. We watched each other's backs and survived in the shadows for more than four months until she was shot while keeping watch as I checked houses for food.

My first post-virus lesson on making friends was short. *Don't.*

Sweat trickles down my spine beneath my shirt as I leap off the watercraft's edge, my instincts screaming to get away from the people behind me and the ones in front of me at the same time.

You've survived worse, Briar. Pressure builds diamonds.

For five years, my humanity has been stripped away, piece by piece. If fate wants me to die on this beach, at least the last of it will be taken all at once. I'll be able to rest.

The cool, crisp water infuses me with new energy. I swim cautiously, keeping my head above the surface. The others are doing the same. No one wants to get within range of the arrows.

We move toward shore in a cluster until we get close enough to make a choice about where we want to exit the water. Most people are going for dead center between the warring groups, probably hoping to make a run for the jungle.

"I'm a hunter!" a man yells from the water. "I can help you!"

My feet find sandy footing and I slow down, looking in every direction. Amira moves with me. We watch as the first person walks up to the beach, quickly going from waist-deep in the water to mid-thigh, to calf-high.

"I'm not your enemy!" he calls out, his hands in the air.

The guy with the spear runs toward him, his brows lowered in a determined expression. Others follow.

"Shit." Amira's voice rises with panic. "What do we do?"

The attackers are everywhere. They're even coming into the water after us now.

I shove my feet into the soggy sand in a bogged-down run, eager to have full control of my legs again. People are screaming. My stomach churns as hands reach for me and I barely evade them.

I grab Amira's arm, fear clawing up my throat. "Run."

2

If you're taken to the ground, don't panic. Prioritize protecting your head and finding enough space to get up as quickly as possible. Use leverage. The ground is not a good place to be.

Excerpt from a police training manual written by Ben Hollis

I was five years old when my father gave me my first self-defense lesson. He taught me where to kick to inflict the most pain and how to shove my thumbs into an attacker's eyes and push until they squish back.

And how to scream like a warrior. My voice, he always told me, is my greatest weapon. I use it now.

The raw, visceral sound that travels up my chest and out of my mouth takes the person grabbing me by surprise. I stomp on her foot and swiftly kick her knee back. She drops with a swear that's half grunt.

I crouch, taking in the chaos around me. A massive man with long, tightly woven braids is fighting someone, blood spraying through the air as the huge man lands a punch to the other guy's nose. A prisoner is crawling out from between them, frantically trying to clear the sand from his eyes.

The peaceful beach has become a battlefield. I don't even know who's on which side. The people waiting for us are all dressed similarly. Some have their faces painted with dark smudges.

"Come with us!" a woman cries, her expression as terrified as the prisoners', even though she has a spear in her hand. "We'll get you to safety!"

"Stop fighting me!" someone says, using a staff to block punches.

"Leave me the fuck alone and I will! I got sent here for murder and you're about to be next."

He swings at the staff wielder and hits him square in the jaw. A flying arrow lodges in his upper thigh and he howls with pain, dropping to his knees.

"Briar!"

I turn toward the voice and see Amira taking off toward the jungle. I follow, but I only make it a few steps before a powerful arm wraps around my chest and picks me up.

"I'm here to help you," a deep voice growls. "Don't fight me."

Yeah, right. The guy whose head is bleeding all over the sand a few feet away might have believed that, but I don't.

I squirm, kicking him as hard as I can with my feet in the air. He starts to walk, my panic rising. I won't be dragged into the jungle and violated. These people are savages, but that's nothing new to me. The only novelty is the tropical island location.

Wait, though. I remember another one of my father's lessons and I reach for my attacker's balls, my hand landing on his thigh. I feel my way there, then twist and squeeze until there's a painful burn in my fingers from the force.

"Fuck!"

He drops me and I scramble upright, running. If I can get to the jungle, I can hide. Evading capture kept me alive for more than three years after the virus until my luck ran out when Lochlan saw me at a market. I was there to trade for food; he was there to stomp on people who couldn't fight back.

"Listen to me! We won't hurt you!"

The blond woman from the second group is standing on top of a huge boulder, yelling. She's lean and muscular, her expression earnest. I don't know if she's crazy or arrogant for standing up there without any weapons. Maybe both.

"Get behind this rock and we'll protect you! You have my word!"

Words are worth as much as hundred-dollar bills in

New America. An arrow slices toward her, and she dodges to the side to avoid it, somehow not falling off the rock. Another follows it and she dodges again, glaring in the direction it was shot from.

The giant man I saw earlier extends a hand to me, blood and sweat swirling together on the deep-brown skin of his face. "Come. Please. We're here to help."

I back away. A bearded man barrels toward him, knocking him to the ground. I take the opportunity to run, moving around a woman wailing on the ground, her arm bent at an unnatural angle.

The jungle's dense foliage should allow me to blend in quickly. As I race toward it, I frantically look around for Amira. Maybe she already made it into the jungle. Together, our chances of surviving are better.

I see her and my heart plummets into my stomach. The dark-haired man who had been standing in front of his group is now carrying her over his shoulder like a sack of grain. She's punching him in the back, but it's not fazing him. He breaks into a run, calling out orders to the rest of the group.

They're leaving. And Amira's not the only person they're trying to take prisoner. Others are resisting as people work together to tie them up with what looks like wire.

Sweat rolls down my brow as I consider my options, the blazing sun a torch I can already feel burning my skin.

I don't owe Amira anything. I hardly know her. If I go

into the jungle, I can save myself. If I go after her with no weapons, we'll both get captured—or worse.

"No!" she screams, slapping and punching at her captor's lower back as she hangs upside down. "Briar!"

For a single second, I close my eyes. Shit. Why did I tell her my name? There's something so unbelievably difficult about hearing someone crying out for help from me specifically.

We're all linked together, Briar. From the tiniest little microorganism to the impossibly vast cosmos, life is connected. It's beautiful when you think about it.

My mother was a scientist, and her words to me when I was young flood back. I've thought of them many times in the five years since losing my entire family. She felt connected to nature. So I try to sense her there when I'm at my lowest, in the canopy of shade created by massive oak trees or the peaceful birdsong at sunrise.

I clench my fists, both inked with permanent warnings to the world that I refuse to be used. I'm proud of what the tattoos represent. My parents and sister would be too.

Amira is still alive right now, and we're connected. If I don't try to help another woman who also stood up against evil, risking her life to do so, there's no humanity left in me.

My feet sink into the sand as I set off in a run, going after her. There's a spear on the ground, and I bend and reach down to swipe it up. My father taught me how to use guns and knives, but I don't know anything about fighting with spears. It's pretty self-explanatory, though: Stick the pointy end into the bad guys.

I reel backward, the spear flying from my hand. Something powerful pulls on my midsection, the air in my lungs whooshing out in a rush. I'm lightheaded, fumbling my hands around my chest to figure out where I'm hit.

"Relax," a deep male voice says from behind me. "I won't hurt you. I'm here to protect you."

My fingers find a rope. I've been lassoed, like a fucking farm animal. My arms are locked at my sides, immobilizing me. I turn and lunge toward my attacker, planning to headbutt him. He reacts quickly, putting a palm out to absorb the impact. My head throbs from the force of the hit, and his hand doesn't even move.

"You're okay."

I scowl at him. He looks about my age, his wavy, shoulder-length brown hair and lean, muscular build making him look more like a surfer here to catch waves than a warrior capturing prisoners.

"I know this is a shit show, but the Dust Walkers will kill you. I'm saving you."

"I didn't ask to be saved," I snap. "Leave me alone."

His expression softens. "You can't survive alone here. If we don't take you with us, the Dust Walkers will chase you into the jungle and kill you."

"You're the one who just tied me up."

A smile plays on his lips. "I get it. But you'll be untied when you get back to our camp. I swear, this is for your own good."

"And I swear I'll kill you if you don't let me go."

It's an empty threat from a helpless woman, once again tied up and unable to defend myself. And my throat is so dry and sore I can hardly talk. When I try to lunge at my captor, a wave of dizziness makes my world spin. I fall to my knees instead.

"She's probably got heat exhaustion," a female voice calls. "Let's go!"

My captor bends down beside me. "My name's Pax. What's yours?"

"Eat shit."

He chuckles lightly and scoops me up with hands beneath my back and knees. My resistance is weak, my arms leaden.

"You can't keep up with us in your state. Try to relax. We're going to take care of you."

Nausea hits like a tidal wave, making me cringe and curl into myself. I'm drenched with sweat and on the edge of passing out. As much as I want to argue with him, it takes all my energy just to breathe.

"Good. Try to relax. The worst is behind you, I promise."

I don't believe him, but I'm too drained to fight anymore. I got minimal food and water in prison, and I'm still groggy from whatever the guards used to knock us out.

Fighting is all I have left, though. Every day, I silently consider all the ways I can make Lochlan pay for what he's done to me. It's been my driving force since the day his soldiers captured me at the market.

These people who are taking me back to their camp aren't my enemies. Lochlan is. I have to rest up, gather my strength, and come up with a new plan. I'll find a way to get home and look him in the eye one last time—as I'm ramming a dagger into his chest.

3

It's working. God help us all.

- Excerpt from the journal of Dr. Randall McClain

I wake with a jolt, the thick air carrying the earthy scent of decaying vegetation. Pain spikes through my head, but I shove it aside, writhing to escape my captor's hold.

He smiles at me, amused. "Easy, tiger. You're not in the best shape. Thought you might've passed out on me."

"Put me down."

"We're almost home."

"It's not my home, asshole. It's yours. I'm your prisoner."

I claw at his hands, desperate. There's a chance I can

escape one person. But a whole camp of them? That'll be much harder.

"Yeah, we're the worst. We save people's lives. Feed them and give them a place to stay. Monsters, aren't we?"

The tsunami of pain in my head is crushing me beneath its weight. It's debilitating. If I got free, I couldn't outrun him like this. I stop struggling, hoping he means it about feeding me. I'm weak with hunger and thirst.

"Do you have any water?" I ask.

"Yeah, I've got a canteen in my pack."

It's too bad my pride isn't ice cold and refreshing, because it's the only thing I've swallowed in a while.

"I'd...really appreciate some water."

"So you *can* play nice." He stops and sets me down, removing his lasso from around my body and arching his brows in a look of warning. "Don't. Run."

I dip my chin in agreement. It's all I can do to stand upright, and from the shakiness in my legs, I know I won't be able to do that for long.

I focus on slow, deep breathing as Pax unshoulders his military green backpack and takes a beat-up stainless canteen from it.

Must. Stay. Conscious. If I pass out, I won't know where to go when I escape my new prison.

"Drink as much as you want," he says as he unscrews the cap, removes it and passes the canteen to me. "We have a well in camp."

A well. A weight lifts from my shoulders as I tip the

canteen up to my mouth. I was worried about finding safe water to drink here, especially when I'm already in desperate need of it. Maybe I'll be able to find a way to take some with me when I go.

The water is a soothing balm on my aching throat. Though I know I should drink slowly to avoid getting sick, I can't help myself. I finish the entire canteen, out of breath when I pass it back to him.

"Thanks."

He nods, packs the canteen and reshoulders his bag.

"Hey, not sure if you caught it, but I'm Pax." He extends a hand to me, his playful tone telling me that he *knows* I got it and he wants to know my name.

I hesitate before answering. "I'm Briar. And who shakes hands anymore?"

People don't even get within twenty feet of others unless they know them well or have no choice. And then we're all wary. The closer you get to someone, the more opportunity you're giving them to rob you, stab you, or give you a virus that could kill you.

"Call me old-fashioned." He shrugs and drops his hand.

I don't object this time as he picks me up. My stomach is swirling, the water already threatening to come back up.

"How do you have a well?" I ask as he follows a narrow path through the jungle.

"It's part of our camp. You'll see. We've got a good setup. We take care of each other."

I hold in my retort. No one takes care of anyone

unless it benefits them. People used to do that, before the virus. But now it's kill or be killed. Or sometimes, kill and be killed anyway.

He turns slightly, avoiding a tree branch that's growing over the path at shoulder level.

The jungle is dense with trees stretching so high I can't see the sky. Their branches form a tight canopy, only slivers of light making it through. Vines encircle thick tree trunks and branches, brightly colored flowers the only contrast to the thousands of shades of green here.

A primal howl cuts through the exuberant cawing and singing of birds, making me snap my head upright and scan the thick jungle around us.

"That's a wolf." I pinch my brows together, listening as the keening howl repeats.

"Yep."

"That's..." I shake my head, confused. "Wolves don't live in jungles. The environment is too hot for them."

Pax's lips tilt up in a grin. "This place is full of surprises."

A wolf in a jungle isn't a surprise. It's a scientific impossibility. Unless...

"Someone brought the wolf here."

He shrugs. "Wasn't me."

My heart races with fear of what else might have been brought to this island. Whitman exiles people here for the crimes he considers the greatest offenses to his new world order. Speaking out against his government.

Refusal to register DNA in his database. Any form of resistance to his laws. Or in my case, using birth control because I refuse to be bred against my will like an animal.

Now you get to play a little game. The guard's words ring in my ears as I realize what sort of twisted, cruel game he must have been talking about.

I'm going to be hunted on this island. Whitman's troops have seeded it with predators, human and animal. They're probably watching it play out with buckets of popcorn in their laps, cameras hidden all over to feed it to them in real time.

We're approaching a tall rectangular archway. The wooden sign at the top of the arch has the words *Rising Tide* burned into it in neat black letters.

"This is your camp?"

"It's *our* camp." He says it like I had any say in coming here. "You're a Tider now."

I don't argue, because the more compliant I pretend to be, the better my chances of getting out of here.

Massive green leaves spread out on the ground grab my attention. They're close to three feet wide, some of them starting to brown at the edges. I lean forward, trying to get a better look.

"Is that...Alocasia?"

I must be wrong. There's no way the giant elephant ear leaves scattered here are Alocasia.

"What, the leaves? No clue. They grow like crazy and we use them to keep the ground from getting muddy in some places. Just don't pick them up or walk on them with bare feet, because—"

"The calcium oxalate crystals can cause skin irritation," I say softly, puzzled. "But this species is native to Asia and Australia. How far from the US are we?"

"Are you a human computer or something?"

I don't respond. I've given too much away already.

I'm mentally calculating. If there was something added to the water at the prison that knocked us all out, how long could we have been on the boat to get here without anyone dying of dehydration?

Six people *did* die, though.

Could they have hydrated us with IVs? I check my arms for bruises and don't find any. They could have put IVs in veins we can't see. I'm dehydrated, though, so that doesn't track.

People can survive around three days without water. Less in high humidity because of all the sweating. How did they get us as far as Asia or Australia so quickly?

I slump with defeat. It's not how they got us here I'm as concerned with, it's how I'll get back. On my own, it's going to be near impossible.

"I can walk now."

The water infused me with a little strength, and I want to be able to take everything in. Pax sets me down, my legs still shaky but better than before. He stays beside me, leading the way around a bend in the dense vegetation.

Long rows of what looks like housing stretch back,

the front doors of both rows facing the wide path we're walking on. There's a second story stacked on top of the first, ladders leading up to a walkway to access the doors. Hundreds of people could be housed here.

The units are small, but they look well built, the walls made of mortared concrete blocks. The roofs are metal sheets. Each unit has a real door with a handle. It's not what I was expecting. I thought there would be primitive shelters for the few people who haven't been picked off by Whitman's twisted game yet.

This seems too elaborate to be a game.

"How many people live here?"

Pax glances at me, then focuses ahead. "I don't know, depends on how many we were able to save back there."

"How many did you have before today?"

He shifts a shoulder in a half shrug. "That's not really my area."

"What is your area?"

A bald man with a shaggy salt-and-pepper beard approaches us from the other end of the path we're walking on. Pax waves at him, ignoring my question.

"Hey, Noah. This is our last new arrival, Briar."

"Commander." Noah nods at Pax, the title he uses catching me by surprise.

Noah has dark-rimmed glasses and is wearing thick, olive-colored pants, hiking boots and a white T-shirt. He does a quick head-to-toe once-over of me.

"Hi Briar, I'm the Rising Tide medic. Can I examine you to see if you need treatment?"

No way is he *examining* me. Been there, done that.

"I'm fine." I hold his gaze, trying to sound better than I feel.

"She's dehydrated," Pax says. "Other than that, I think she's fine. She fought like an absolute beast on the beach."

Noah nods, pulling a small pad of paper and a pencil from a pants pocket.

"Briar, what's your last name?"

I hesitate. I'm already at the bottom of the deepest hole Whitman throws people in. It was either a quick death—execution—or a slow death—this. There's no way I can make things worse for myself by telling them my name.

My *real* name. Every time someone called me Briar Murphy, I felt sick. I didn't want Lochlan's name any more than I wanted anything else about him. But here, I won't be forced to use it.

"Hollis. Briar Hollis."

Tears form in my eyes as I say the name my parents gave me. It makes me feel like they're close, at least in spirit.

"Briar...Hollis." Noah writes my name on his notepad, then looks up at Pax. "You want me to take her to the infirmary, Commander?"

"Nah, I'll do it."

A group of three women passes by us, all of them eyeing me curiously. They're all wearing the same green pants, hiking boots and white T-shirts as Noah. Must be standard issue.

"I'm not sick," I tell Pax as he resumes walking. "I don't need to go to the infirmary."

He catches my eye for a moment. "It's where everyone goes when they first get here. You need food, hydration and rest."

I can't argue with that. My feet keep getting heavier. I could easily curl up in the middle of this dirt path and go to sleep. The oppressive heat has already soaked my clothes through with sweat.

"What happens after the infirmary? Why are any of us really here?"

"When you get cleared from the infirmary, you'll be assigned a mentor. You'll get a work duty assignment, clothes, boots, some soap. Then you can get a shower."

He ignored my second question, but I'm too distracted by the mention of soap and a shower to call him on it.

"You have showers?"

His lips quirk with a grin. "Yeah, and we've got a couple of engineers in camp, so the water pressure's actually not bad."

The rows of housing end and he turns right, stopping at a door with an "Infirmary" sign. He opens the door, standing aside so I can enter first.

It's one massive room, the subtle, sweet scent of vanilla lingering in the air from the maple planks that line the walls. The ceiling is open, the wooden beams supporting the structure's roof visible.

There are three rows of ten beds, all made up with

bright-white sheets. Three men and two women who were on the boat with me are in beds, and there are two other men I don't recognize. Large rectangular windows along two walls of the room are propped open, allowing a slight breeze in.

I can't believe there are actual beds. They're calling out to me, begging me to curl up and rest. The ring of burning discomfort around my arms and midsection from the rope Pax lassoed me with is throbbing.

A pretty woman with her dark hair tied back walks over, her eyes on Pax and a palm on her slightly pregnant belly.

"Commander." She greets him with a coy smile.

"Hi, Lana. This is Briar, our last newcomer for today."

Lana pulls her gaze from him to me. "Let's get you a bed and something to eat, Briar."

I nod, numb. I'm not myself. Whether it's from whatever the guards knocked us out with, the heat, dehydration or just plain exhaustion, I don't know. My thoughts are muddled. A strange stab of jealousy toward Lana hits me right in the chest as she sneaks a peek at Pax while leading me to a bed.

I have to sleep. If I can't think clearly, I'm putting myself in danger.

Lana brings me a small wooden bowl of smoked fish and a cup of water. I drink the water and eat three bites of fish, then curl up on my side, facing the door to the infirmary.

I survived the beach. I can still see the faces of some

of the people who didn't, their eyes staring blankly at the sky as their blood soaked into the sand.

The sound of Amira screaming my name still echoes in my mind. I wish I could have saved her. Even though life is a series of losses and disappointments in the hellscape that is New America, it's been a long time since I had a friend.

4

What an exciting time to be alive. Without red tape, there are no limits to what we can accomplish.

- Excerpt from the journal of Dr. Randall McClain

A woman's primal scream cuts through the air, snapping me out of a deep sleep. I sit up in my infirmary bed and see a man and a woman each holding the arm of a very pregnant woman by the entrance.

"Breathe through it, Peyton," the woman says. "We're almost to a bed where you can lie down."

"Ohhhhhh.....it hurts," Peyton wails, panting frantically.

She looks and sounds like her baby could drop through her legs any second now, her rounded belly a bulky center of gravity.

The contraction subsides and she makes it to a bed, the woman who helped her there pulling a curtain made of bedsheets around the bed for privacy.

My headache has improved, but I'm sweaty, though I'm only covered by a lightweight sheet. Even with the windows open, the stagnant, heavy air turns up the dial on my disgusting smell. Blood and grime are caked beneath my short nails and my long dark hair is greasy, sand from the beach itching my scalp.

I glance around the room, finding two other people asleep and one sitting up in bed eating.

A loud gurgle of hunger sounds in my stomach. The rest of the smoked fish I left beside me in the bed is gone. It's been so long since I've had a real meal. That was one perk of living in Lochlan's household—I ate better than most people.

"Do something!" Peyton cries from behind the curtain. "I can't..." She lets out a piercing moan of agony.

"Hey, you're up." A woman with tightly coiled, shoulder-length blond curls approaches me. "Feeling better?"

I nod, wary. Though I appreciate the food, water and rest, I'm still suspicious about this camp. About the entire island, actually.

"I'm Marcelle," the blond says, stopping beside my bed and smiling brightly. "I'm your mentor, and this is my first time mentoring, so I'm excited."

The green canvas pants and white T-shirt don't match her lithe, slim figure. With bright-blue eyes and perfect skin, she belongs in a cosmetics ad campaign. Not that those exist anymore.

"Can I get some food and water?"

"I'll check on that after you shower. Are you ready to get out of here?"

I push the sheet aside to get up, and Marcelle scoffs. Her gaze is locked onto the ink on the back of my hands, her frown disgusted.

"Yeah, they're...prominent," I mutter. "Guess that's the point to Whitman, though. So people can see us nondoormats coming from a mile away."

"Nondoormats?" She gapes at me. "You think women who bring children into the world instead of killing them are *doormats*?"

Oh hell. I didn't see that coming. I thought she was disgusted I'd been branded, but she's...not. I should have been more guarded.

"No, that's not what I mean. I don't think we should be forced."

We. As in, *this could just as easily have happened to you.* This is the worst part of the new world Whitman has shaped—or actually, *old* world, since we've regressed in every possible way. I'll never understand how women buy into it. It's only been six years since we didn't have to register our DNA into a database for genetic testing to see if we're "optimal breeding candidates."

Shaking her head, she turns toward the door. "Unbelievable. Let's go."

I slide on my worn shoes, which someone must have taken off me while I was sleeping, and lace them up. As I walk, my hand instinctively twitches slightly, wanting to brush over the hilt of the knife I used to keep strapped at my waist. Lochlan took it away when he captured me, but I carried it for so long before then that I still remember the feeling of security it gave me.

Marcelle leads me in the opposite direction of the housing. We pass a group of people who are all wearing packs on their backs made from what looks like wide, woven reeds. One of them has a hat on that's made of green grass, the brim protecting her eyes from the sun. They all eye me as they pass, my attention snagged on their bracelets.

They're thick cuffs worn around the wrist, a large white number placed prominently on each one. Everyone in the group whose bracelets I can see has a "3" on theirs.

The buildings we pass are all plain and well kept, some made from concrete blocks and others built with wood. Marcelle stops at a door marked "Supplies" and raps on it twice.

A small square cutout in the door slides open, a man's face appearing in the opening. Instead of greeting him, Marcelle holds up her own cuff, which also bears a "3."

"I have one who just got here and needs supplies," she says.

The man slides the opening closed and we wait, the thunking sound of a dead bolt indicating he's unlocking the door.

"Come in."

He steps aside as we enter a building that's much

deeper than it is wide. It has wood-plank flooring and its windows are open, though no breeze seems to be coming in. The windows here are different than the infirmary ones; there are only two in the whole building and they have thick wooden covers with metal locks. They're held open with hooks that latch into eyelets in the wall.

Interesting.

"You look like a size medium," the man says, walking over to a wall with wooden shelves lined with stacks of the pants, T-shirts and boots I've seen everyone wearing.

He pulls a pair of boots off a shelf and then gets two each of the other items, adding underwear and socks. Then he grabs a gray wool blanket and a square-ish block of oatmeal-colored soap. Its sweet jasmine scent reminds me I get to shower soon.

"Welcome to Rising Tide," he says without enthusiasm as he holds out his arms to pass me everything.

"Thanks."

Most of the shelves in the space sit empty. There are around fifty large wooden barrels around the perimeter of the room, all of them marked with the word "grain." Around a dozen plastic barrels bear the label "sodium hydroxide."

Lye. It's an ingredient in soap. My mom taught my sister, Maven, and me about pH levels one summer by showing us how to make hot-process soap. It was messy but fun. I layered lavender in mine for the scent.

The man asks Marcelle for my name and writes it

down. Without another word, Marcelle leads me out of the building.

"I'm supposed to tell you the rules," she says in a level tone, not looking at me. "Everyone starts out in group one and works their way up. You're on probation for your first thirty days. Our days are scheduled in four-hour blocks. Your off blocks are ten p.m. to six a.m. Your work duty is in the kitchen, and you start at six a.m. You'll work six to ten, train ten to two, work two to six, train six to ten."

My eyes lock onto a scaly, bright-green lizard a few feet away from us. With its tail, it's more than three feet long. I keep half an eye on it as we pass it.

"Train for what?" I ask.

She side-eyes me, sneering. "Physical training. You'll learn how to throw a punch and I seriously suggest you practice on yourself."

I press my lips into a thin line. Unfortunately, mean girls are like cockroaches. Even an apocalypse can't keep them down.

Sixteen hours a day of work and physical training? I don't mind, because it's far better than being confined to a dark, mildewed cell.

The row of buildings ends, the jungle just twenty feet away. Marcelle stops next to a crooked wooden sign on a post made of a small tree trunk. The word "Spa" is burned onto it in black letters.

"Shower." She still refuses to look at me. "The toilets are here, too. You get two minutes of water a day for showering and if you lose your soap, too bad." She crosses her arms and sighs heavily. "Go. Feel free to drown yourself."

There's a raised wood-plank walkway, showers on one side and primitive toilets on the other. I step onto it and then look back at her.

"Towel?"

Her face lights up. "Of course. Would you like it warmed? Shall I fetch a silk robe for you, too?"

Ignoring her, I glance at the toilets. They're about eighteen inches off the ground, constructed of wooden planks built into squares. There are half-wall dividers between the toilets, but other than that, they're open air.

The showers are about the same. Wood-plank floors, with the ground beneath them angled so the water runs off toward the jungle. There are dividers between the dozen or so showers, each one about five feet tall, but no doors.

I deliberately look at anything but the person in one of them, making my way to the stall on the very end. It's nothing fancy, but I have water and soap, and that's enough. I'm beyond ready to wash the filth from my skin, hair and nails.

My dad used to take us camping, and we learned to adapt, sometimes only having a creek and a bar of soap to get clean. Maven and I would spend a long time in the water, splashing, talking and washing each other's hair.

I smile as I remember a weeklong trip in our home state of Washington, where we got to swim in a crystal clear spring. My parents said they wished we'd never had to go back to civilization, and I couldn't have agreed more.

The showers have an ingenious system of ropes and pulleys to deliver water. The water sits in a rectangular tub a couple of feet above my head, a rope hanging down beside it.

Stripping off my shoes and clothes, I leave them on the edge of the wood-pallet floor with my pile of supplies. When I stand beneath the tub and tug on the rope, the tub tilts, a steady stream of warm water pouring down from a makeshift bamboo faucet.

I let the water flow over my hair and body for about fifteen blissful seconds before I release the rope. I lather the soap between my hands quickly, gasping in silent happiness as I rub my hands over my face.

It wouldn't surprise me if Marcelle stomped over here and made me come running after her naked for taking too long, so I speed wash, scrubbing every inch of my skin with soap and my hands. Then I focus on my hair, creating a big handful of suds to massage into my hair and roots.

I rinse as quickly as I can, timing myself. I've only used about a minute of water and Marcelle's not yelling at me yet, so I repeat the process, quickly washing my body and hair a second time.

Part of me wants to close my eyes and turn my face up to the stream of water, relaxing. But I can't risk taking my eyes off the open front of the small shower stall.

I finish, clean for the first time in more than a month. I gather my hair up in my hands and wring the water out of it, the waves of it already pronounced in the humid jungle.

Since I don't have a towel, I use the wool blanket to dry off, which is better than nothing. Then I dress in the new clothes I was issued, sweating before I'm all the way dressed. I didn't get a bra, so I rinse out my old one and put it back on.

Still, I'm clean. I even managed to get the grime out from beneath my fingernails.

I pick up my things and walk back, a male voice calling out to me as I pass.

"Hey, new girl. What's your name? I'm Ky."

Instinctively, I look over. He's sitting on a toilet, grinning and completely unconcerned that I can see his penis hanging down between his legs.

I fling my gaze away from him and pick up my pace, my cheeks warm with embarrassment.

"That's okay, I'll catch you later!" he calls after me.

Marcelle doesn't say anything to me. She glares at nothing and turns, going back the way we came.

"Unfortunately, you're bunking with me since I'm your mentor while you're on probation. I'm in bunk twenty-eight. You aren't getting a key. If I'm not there, wait outside the door."

Great. I'd probably be better off sharing a room with the lizard I saw earlier.

We arrive at a shelter that seems to be where the Rising Tide members eat. Around twenty rustic wooden picnic tables are arranged on a floor made of large square concrete pavers, a metal roof covering the space, which is supported by thick pillars in each of its corners.

Raindrops have started falling, wind carrying them to mist my face and arms. Marcelle takes me through the door of a building connected to the dining area.

The smell of rotting fish hits me like a punch. It's a wet, heavy, rancid odor. There are about a dozen people in the big space. One stretch of stainless countertop is about six feet long, and there's another twenty-plus feet of makeshift countertop made from pieces of bamboo lashed together and supported on legs made of tree branches.

"What the fuck is this, Marcelle?" A man whose hairline has retreated a long way from his forehead glares at us over the rim of his glasses, which are held together in one corner with what looks like tape. "I don't need more people prepping food; I need more people bringing me food to prep."

She gives him a tight smile. "I'm just doing my job and delivering your new girl, Billy."

With that, she leaves. Billy squints at the bundle in my arms.

"Why the hell are you bringing a bunch of dirty laundry in here?" he barks.

I open my mouth, but I don't know what to say, so I just close it again without answering.

"This fuckin' place," he mutters. "Put your laundry outside and then I'll find you a job."

———

Later that day, I'm sitting at a table with Rona and Olin, also kitchen staffers with bracelets bearing the number one, eating my first meal of the day in silence.

We got the same meal we've been feeding others all day: a big spoonful of mushy boiled grains with about half a cup of seaweed and a quarter of a coconut. We serve people in carved wooden bowls through a large window opening in the kitchen building. People actually line up to get this underwhelming meal, their expressions impassive as they receive it.

I thought Olin just didn't like me because he wouldn't respond to anything I said for the first couple of hours I was here. He's young, maybe nineteen, with textured bright-red hair that refuses to be tamed and freckles all over. Rona, a wisp of a woman with a buzz cut and colorful tats up and down her arms, finally told me Olin is mute.

"It's not so bad, working in the kitchen," Rona says, making me glance up from staring at my empty bowl. "I worked in a restaurant before the virus, washing dishes. Eight hours a day, nothing but dishes. What were you doing when the virus hit?"

"College student," I say. "I was helping a professor with a research project on a little island off the coast of Washington."

Rona arches her brows. "Fancy."

"Not really. I'm just a science nerd. I worked as a waitress too, at a pizza place."

The friendly gleam returns to her eyes. "Fuck me. I'd

kill for a giant slice of New York-style pepperoni, with grease pooled all over it."

The corners of Olin's lips quirk in a smile of agreement.

Two speakers mounted on posts on either side of the dining area crackle to life.

"This is Commander Marsden." The female voice is crisp and authoritative. "Please join me in welcoming our newest addition, Baby One-Three-Six Tide. The baby is healthy. Peace, order and prosperity."

The handful of people in the dining area clap and cheer over the announcement.

It must be Peyton's baby. But why doesn't it have a regular name?

"What's with the one-three-six Tide thing?" I ask Rona quietly.

"It's how we name babies here." She stands up, her empty bowl in hand. "You guys ready to get back to work?"

"Actually, Briar's needed elsewhere."

All three of us turn toward the voice and find Pax approaching. Rona stiffens her spine.

"Yes, Commander." She reaches for my bowl and takes it, she and Olin escaping quickly.

Pax is shirtless, sweat trailing down the carved muscles of his chest. His abs are defined; the waistband of his pants hanging low to reveal that *V* shape that makes women do stupid things.

"Hey." He grins at me. "Let's go do a thing."

"A thing?"

"You'll like it. Come on."

5

You don't need a background in botany for this course. I hope to build your knowledge of plants and their role in Earth's ecosystems from the ground up this semester. The only requirements for this course are a willingness to learn and curiosity.

- Excerpt from the Introduction to Plant Biology course taught by Dr. Lucinda Hollis

"Harder." Pax spits in the dirt and gestures for me to come closer. "Hit me like you mean it, Briar."

I do mean it, but every punch I throw lands on him like a light slap. It's starting to really piss me off. I've sparred with men bigger and stronger than me since I was thirteen years old. My dad wanted Maven and me to be able to defend ourselves, so he and some of his friends in law enforcement showed us how to fight someone when you're outmatched.

Nothing is working. Pax's reflexes are unbelievably fast, and he seems to anticipate my every move. We've been sparring at the Rising Tide training grounds for more than an hour, and I'm wearing down.

"Pretend I'm coming at you with a spear." He crouches slightly, putting his arm up and making a fist.

It takes me right back to the beach. The smell of saltwater and the metallic tang of blood are still fresh in my mind.

I drilled this scenario with my dad many times, but he used a rubber knife to simulate a real one. The concept is the same, though. If you're unarmed, you're beaten unless you can evade, distract or disable.

I go with disable, scooping up a big handful of sandy soil and chucking it in his face as Pax advances on me.

"Shit." He stops, his hands flying to his face.

I back up a few steps, relaxing slightly. He chokes out a single note of laughter, rubbing his fingertips over his eyes.

"Nice move."

A group of about twenty people who left for a run earlier returns to camp, still in the same neat two lines they left in. I do a double take because the leader of the group announced it was a five-mile run, and they haven't been gone very long. It doesn't even feel like thirty minutes.

They're finishing at what looks like a six-minute mile pace, but surely they didn't run that pace the entire time?

They don't even look winded—some of them are smiling.

"Have you picked all of this up since the virus hit?" Pax asks me.

I turn my attention back to him. Black soil and sweat are streaked on his face, a glob of dirt stuck in his dimple.

"No. My dad taught me."

"Was he in the military?"

I nod. "Marines. Then he became a police officer, and he worked his way up to teaching at police academies."

"And were you planning to become a cop, too?"

"No."

Thanks to the setting sun, I've stopped sweating so heavily. Still, I'm drenched. I pick up the canteen I left at the edge of the sparring area, draining what's left in it.

"You need to fill up?" Pax asks me.

"Yeah."

The training area is a huge clearing, sparring areas delineated with medium-sized rocks. The clearing runs all the way to the beach. When we got here earlier, a group of people was swimming hard and fast in the ocean, fighting cresting waves and high winds.

Pax picks up his own canteen and we walk over to a well at the edge of the practice area. The group that was running is huddled around the woman who was leading their run.

"Bring!" she shouts into a megaphone.

"Peace!" everyone yells back in unison.

"Create!" Her shrill yell makes me flinch.

"Order!" They pump their fists in the air as they respond.

"Ensure!"

"Prosperity!" They shout it like a war chant.

"What's that about?" I ask Pax, remembering the same words from the commander's announcement of the baby.

"That's our mantra. Everything we do in Rising Tide is to create peace, order and prosperity."

"For Whitman?"

He pinches his brows together tightly. "For us. Here. This island is beautiful, but it's also dangerous. There are animals in the jungle that could eat you in three big bites. And the leader of the Dust Walkers, Marcus, he'd kill any of us on sight, no questions asked. The rules we have here are for our own protection and prosperity."

My mind flashes back to Amira, carried away by someone from the Dust Walkers camp.

"That's what they do to the people they take on the beach? They kill them?"

His expression turns grim. "Yeah, and they're not merciful about it. They're savages. We train to protect ourselves from them."

Maybe I am safer here than alone in the jungle. I'm about to ask Pax what else he knows about the Dust Walkers when my eyes catch on the group that just finished running. Three of the women are visibly pregnant, one of them close to full term.

"What the hell?" I blurt it with no forethought. "There's no way they just ran five miles that fast."

Pax's grin is proud. "They did. The Dust Walkers go after pregnant women first, so women here train up until they go into labor."

I'm silent the rest of the walk to the well. I know the virus changed the world forever, and that New America is a cold, unforgiving place, especially for women. It's wise to make sure pregnant women can take care of themselves. It's what I'd want in their situation.

There must be very little to do around here for entertainment, because of the eight women in the group that's dispersing, three of them are clearly pregnant. That's almost half.

"So what were you doing when the virus hit?" Pax asks.

I shift my focus back to him. "I was a college student. You?"

"You won't believe me if I tell you."

"Try me."

"I was a twenty-four-year-old accountant working for a firm in Boston."

A laugh bubbles out of me. "An accountant?"

"I mean, I wore the hell out of my suits, I'm not gonna be modest. I was living the life and then"—he snaps his fingers—"there went civilization."

"Did you get the virus?"

"Honestly, I don't know. Everyone around me was so sick, and I never got sick. I heard some people are immune to it."

The scientist in me comes out. "Some people's bodies can alter the structure of the receptors viruses use to infect cells. There are also genetic mutations in humans that can prevent a virus from infecting their cells."

He had been filling his canteen as he spoke, and the water is now spilling over the edge. He pulls it back.

"How do you know all that?"

I hesitate, then decide to be honest. "I was raised by a scientist. I was a bio major myself, but I was only a freshman when the virus came."

He lowers his brows. "Your dad was a cop and a scientist?"

"My mom was the scientist."

"Gotcha. And you were a freshman where?"

"University of Washington."

"Oh man. I love Washington State. Or I guess, the state formerly known as Washington."

This is the first conversation I've had in a very long time that feels like conversations did before the virus. My dad told me about common tells he used to determine if people were lying to him when he was a detective, and I haven't seen any of them from Pax.

I'm lucky he lassoed me on the beach. Otherwise, I would have met the same fate as Amira.

"You want to spar some more?" he asks me.

I scoff. "Haven't you kicked my ass hard enough yet?"

His laugh is hearty, reaching his golden-brown eyes. "I've been at this a long time. You just got here. Were you training eight hours a day before you got sent here?"

My smile fades, the memories of my life with Lochlan still painfully fresh. Even if I had been training eight hours a day, I lived in an inescapable fortress. If I hadn't been caught with the herbal tea I drank monthly to prevent pregnancy, I'd still be living in that hell.

"No." I clear my throat, eager to change the subject. "Hey, what are the numbers on the bracelets about?"

His eyes narrow slightly in a puzzled look. "Did Marcelle not explain that to you?"

The last thing I need is for my mentor to get in trouble and hate me even more, so I cover for her. "Well, she told me a little bit, but we had a lot going on."

He puts his hands in the front pockets of his pants, making them hang down just a little lower, and I get a peek at the top of the light-brown hair that trails down. My heartbeat kicks up its pace and I look away quickly.

"You start out on probation, and then you become a one. That's our entry level, when people are learning and training. Ones have to stay in camp unless they're with a three or a four. Twos get better job duties, but they also can't leave camp without a three or a four. Threes get a lot more autonomy. They're our hunters and fishermen and gatherers. They can be mentors. And fours are in leadership."

"So you're a four?"

A corner of his mouth quirks in a grin. "No, I'm one of the two commanders here. I'm Commander Thatcher when it's not just the two of us. Then there's Commander Marsden."

"She was the one who made the announcement about the baby earlier."

"Yep."

"I think I saw her on the beach. Does she have blond hair?"

He nods. "She's thirty-five, long blond hair and a scar on her neck. Virginia's a hard ass until you get to know her."

"She called the baby one-three-six Tide. What does that mean?"

Pax's shoulders lift and then drop slightly when he sighs. "Well...part of prosperity for us is the next generation, so the birth of a baby is a happy occasion."

I wait for him to answer my question, but he doesn't.

"The numbers." I press him. "Do you guys not give away the baby's name for privacy reasons? And does that mean it's the one hundred thirty-sixth baby born here?"

He worries his lip for a second before responding. "Yeah, that's what it means. All babies here have the last name Tide, because we're one community."

I'm about to ask him to elaborate when he cuts me off.

"Here's some friendly advice for you, Briar. Listen and learn. Those are the best things a one can do. I see great potential in you. I can honestly say I've never seen anyone—man or woman—come in here with the defense skills you already have. And there's so much we can do to help you grow and refine what you know. Keep your head down and work, and you'll settle in here quickly."

I nod, his unspoken advice leaving me unsettled: *Don't ask questions.*

He's been good to me so far, though, and since he's in

a position of power, I don't want to make him angry. I paste on the placid expression I perfected on Lochlan.

"Thanks. It seems pretty great here."

It's my first full day, and so far I haven't seen any opportunities to escape the island. It may take me a long time to get away, and I have to take care of myself in the meantime. I can't settle the score with Lochlan if I get eaten by a wild animal in a remote jungle.

"Better now that you're here." His gaze roves up and down my body. "Come show me more of what you've got, Briar Hollis."

6

One Week Later

When defending yourself, your goal is always to control the threat, not engage in a back-and-forth of blows. To neutralize the threat, target major muscle groups and large joints.

- Excerpt from a police training manual written by Ben Hollis

Something is shaking my shoulder. No. Some*one*. I jolt awake, my effort to scramble away cut short by a wall at my back. I groan, pain radiating throughout my body, not from hitting the wall, but from soreness.

The sun isn't all the way up yet, but I'm able to make out the muted gray outline of a man, his palms out in front of him. I squint, recognizing his untamed hair.

"Olin?"

He moves slowly, keeping his palms facing out where I can see them. With his right hand, he pats the top of his left wrist, where a watch would go.

I'm groggy, my thoughts a murky, slowly creeping fog. My body is begging me to lie down and go back to sleep.

What is he trying to tell me about a watch? No one wears them anymore, and there aren't—

"Oh shit." I sit up, scrub a hand over my face and throw off my wool blanket. "I'm going to be late."

I was dead asleep on the walkway outside of Marcelle's door. Her schedule is different from mine, and she doesn't finish training until two a.m. Since she won't give me a key to her room, my only option is to wait outside her door, and with the intensity of the training I've been doing, I can't stay awake.

The first couple of nights, I tried to. It's dangerous to sleep out in the open. But eventually, my body took the choice away from me. Now, I cover myself completely with my blanket at ten every night and hope the darkness hides me well enough. Some nights, I don't even wake up when Marcelle gets here.

And today, I slept through the camp-wide alarm that blares over the sound system at five thirty every morning.

"Okay." I stand, the stabbing pain in my stomach making me cringe. "No time for...anything."

The woman I sparred with yesterday was relentless. She must have punched me in the stomach a couple hundred times. It's only my pride that gets me to the end of my six-to-ten p.m. training block; I don't have the energy by then.

It would have been nice to clean my teeth with charcoal dust and saltwater and take a quick shower, but I don't have time. The bathroom lines are long at this time of day.

I shove my blanket up against the outer wall of the housing block and walk over to Olin.

"Thanks for waking me up."

He nods. I was late on my fourth day here, and my punishment was no food for the day. The next time I'm late, I get three days without food. The training is too rigorous for that.

Olin hesitates, then walks over and picks up my blanket, folding it neatly. He passes it to me.

"You think I should take it?"

He nods.

"Because if I don't, someone might steal it?"

Another nod.

Despite the headache that never fully goes away, and the pain I feel from my scalp to my toes from training, my lips quirk with a smile.

"Thanks, Olin."

We walk in silence to the kitchen, stopping at the well next to it to fill our canteens. I drink two canteens full before filling it a third time and putting the strap over my shoulder so it rests on my hip.

I shouldn't be drinking so much water, because I know I'm feeling the effects of sodium deficiency. Water makes it worse. But I'm also usually dehydrated here. It's an ugly irony.

"Briar and Rona, you're on meat prep, get going." Billy wastes no time putting us to work.

Meat prep is a double-edged sword. It's hard to peel and slice juicy, ripe papayas when your own stomach is knotted painfully with hunger and you aren't allowed to eat any of it. Meat prep is gross, but not tempting, so at least there's that.

The term "meat" is all-encompassing at Rising Tide. It includes fish and kills brought in by the hunting team. Hunting kills are field dressed and sometimes come to us in pieces, and I'm only able to identify some of the animals because of my knowledge of biology.

We get a lot of boars, birds and reptiles. Snakes are the easiest to identify. Some days we get a lot of fish, and other days, hardly any. I don't think too hard about what some of the meat is, but Rona seems to enjoy pointing out the things she knows will make me cringe.

"Mmm, rat." She holds it up and waggles her brows.

The carcass still has its tail attached, wiry hairs sprouting between the scaly rings. Eating rats is bad enough, but what's worse is that Rona won't discard the tail. Everything gets eaten here—even fish skin and eggs. And still, it's not enough.

I hated training at first, but it's become my favorite part of life at Rising Tide. When I'm running, rolling massive logs, swimming or sparring, it takes everything I've got just to get it done. I'm always exhausted, sore and hungry, but I can't think about that during training.

Instead, I pretend my dad is beside me. I imagine what he would tell me to do and how he'd encourage me.

You don't have to be the fastest or the strongest, Briar. If you want to be the best, it only takes one thing—never, ever quit.

He didn't talk a lot about what he did in his Special Operations Marine Corps unit, but he did say he survived things he shouldn't have many times.

Maven and I complained about him forcing us to read Jack London books in our early teen years, but when the virus came, I clung to those stories of survival and the human spirit. I still do.

"What we really need is some canned fish," I say as I chop unidentified meat into small pieces.

Rona snort laughs. "Canned fish? If I could make any food appear before me, it would be a giant, juicy burger and fries."

"I wouldn't turn that down."

She slices the tail from the rat carcass and deftly chops it. "Why canned fish? Aren't fresh fish healthier?"

"Yes, but we need the sodium canned fish have."

"I thought sodium was bad."

I scoop up the pile of chopped meat in front of me and dump it into the big stainless pot. "Too much is bad, but humans need some sodium to survive."

Billy makes it clear that if he catches the kitchen workers complaining about the food or our work, he'll have us reassigned to laundry. I've seen the hands of the people who do laundry—they're so raw from scrubbing that they bleed.

Telling Rona the diet here is nutrient deficient might be seen as complaining, so I don't say anything else. And really, there's no point mentioning it. I figured out a few days in that there's not enough food to feed everyone here.

It's a cruel paradox, being around food for eight hours a day, but preparing it for others. When Rona and I get a five-minute break to eat our first meal of the day, it's two bite-sized chunks of smoked meat and a small sliver of hard, unripe papaya. At least it quells the dull ache in my stomach.

My limbs are heavy as we return to work, fatigue blanketing every inch of me. I don't know how everyone else makes it look so easy to get by on maybe five hundred calories a day.

There are no walls in the food prep area we're working in behind the kitchen, and I get a quick glimpse of a training group racing past us on the dirt path that runs through camp. It's a group of fours, and I swear they're running at a four-minute mile pace.

Not only are the fours surviving on very little food and not enough of a single nutrient, they're *thriving*.

I finish my meal in about a minute, and instead of sitting with Rona, I take my bowl back into the kitchen and find Billy.

"What?" He glares at me, his brow furrowed with annoyance.

"I, uh..." I clear my throat and straighten my spine. "I was a botany major when the virus came. I've loved learning about plants and biology my whole life. I could help identify edible plants if...that would ever help."

I'm waiting for him to bark out how stupid I am. That's what he does to everyone. But I had to say something. I don't think it's a matter of ones getting shafted on meals. Everyone—even the fours—is too lean, muscles out of place on bodies with visible hip and collar bones. Pregnant women get double rations, but even that isn't enough for them.

Billy sighs, his expression drooping with resignation. "We've been burned before. Had people die from some of the plants. The commanders don't want to risk it. Get back to meat prep."

I consider pressing it. Telling him I know how to identify plants and test them to see if they're safe to eat. But it's not his decision, so I drop it.

When I return to the meat prep area, Rona is already there, dumping a bucket of water into the cooking pot we filled about a third of the way full of meat. We'll cook it in water to make a stew of sorts. The next kitchen shift will do the same with the pile of bones, organs and fish skin we left.

Beef was on the menu almost every night at Lochlan's. A chef prepared it with spices and cooked it to perfection. Freshly baked bread and vegetables were heaped into serving dishes, still steaming as they were delivered to the table. And the butter the kitchen staff churned by hand was always available to be slathered on bread or melted on vegetables. We had steak, pasta, grilled chicken salads, vegetable soup and more. Bacon, eggs and toast for breakfast. Then there were the desserts—the most decadent of desserts every night, with rich chocolate and the raspberry sauce Lochlan often requested.

It was a very comfortable prison, but it was still a prison. I'd rather be on this island, my greatest hope that I get a bowl of watery bone and fish skin soup for dinner.

My kitchen shift ends. I check out with Billy and jog to the training area, because I don't want to be the last to arrive. That person has to run laps around the training camp for the entire four hours of the session. In my state of exhaustion, soreness and hunger, I'm not sure I could do it.

For a week now, I've watched the person who arrives last struggle to get through that four-hour run. They usually throw up, and they can hardly walk when it's over. Some of them crawl away from the training area.

It leaves me wondering what happens if you can't complete the run. I'm not sure I want to know.

———

That night, I stagger to the showers at the end of my second training session. My feet ache from running in boots and my right hand throbs from all the punches I threw. Pax and his co-commander, Virginia Marsden, watched me spar and I didn't want to show any weakness.

I don't understand it. I don't care about impressing them. They can call me a one or a four; it makes no difference to me. It would be nice to be able to leave camp and scout the island, but I'm only focused on survival right now.

Something deep inside me is fueling me, though. Telling me to *fight*. To get up from the ground faster. Punch harder. Jump higher.

Since I can't get into Marcelle's room, I hide my soap inside a bush near the showers. I fish it out and unwrap the leaf I put around it to conceal it.

Showering makes me feel human again. The salt left behind from drying seawater was added to tonight's evening meal, and I already feel better from getting some sodium. My headache is finally gone.

"Shower stall nine, move your ass! Time's up!" a male voice calls.

Shit. That's me. I was air-drying a little bit since I didn't want to use my blanket to dry off. It gets surprisingly cold here at night, and sleeping outside with a wet blanket doesn't help.

A woman who does laundry duty was sent to the infirmary during training tonight because she has an infection in one of the open wounds on her hands. I think about her as I put on my clean clothes.

On the walk back to Marcelle's room, a woman's moan makes me pause. My hand goes to my hip, though there's still no dagger there. I look around from my spot in the shadowed edge of the path.

"Fuck, I'm gonna come." The man's voice is ragged; more like a feral snarl than a groan of desire.

I silently turn toward the row of housing I'm closest

to; a man has a woman pressed to the outer wall, his hips driving into her and his pants pooled at his ankles.

"Yes, yes, yes," she whines desperately.

Okay, so she's good with it. I resume walking, wondering where the hell they get the energy.

I stashed my blanket behind an empty crate outside the kitchen. After grabbing it, I drag myself the rest of the way to the walkway outside Marcelle's room.

I curl up beneath the blanket, not caring about the jagged splinter of wood my cheek rests on. Immediately, I feel myself falling asleep.

My gasp is unconscious, my eyes flying open as I'm dragged, someone pulling hard on my hair.

"Close the door!" someone whisper-hisses.

I'm surrounded in blackness, panic coursing through my veins as I frantically reach for the hands wrapped around my hair.

They let go. I jump to my feet, my fatigue forgotten.

"Who's there?" I demand.

Someone moves. The sound of a turning doorknob grabs my attention. A crack of dim night light is visible as the door opens.

Marcelle walks into the room, a small, primitive torch made from a tree branch in hand. The flickering flames highlight the harsh lines of her thin face, vitriol swirling in her eyes. The corners of her lips turn up in a cruel grin. She presses the door closed and turns the lock.

"Time to find out what we do to baby killers here."

A hard kick lands in my stomach, doubling me over.

My feet are swept out from under me, putting me in a prone position on the ground.

Instinct kicks in. I shield my head with my hands and scoot away, hitting a wall.

We're in Marcelle's tiny room. She passes the torch to someone else and descends on me, her hands wildly punching me everywhere. Spit lands on my cheek.

Someone else is kicking my legs. My arms are being forced from around my head and held to the ground.

I try to resist, but they're all so damn *strong*. I get a hand free and use it to claw at Marcelle's face, hooking a thumb inside her cheek and pulling on her face with every ounce of my strength.

She mutters a curse and bites me, drawing blood. It's warm, a droplet falling onto my cheek.

I'm beat. There are too many of them. But I won't give them the satisfaction of hearing me cry. I hold in every moan and plea, taking my mind somewhere else.

I'm with my sister. We're kids again, running through a clearing of wildflowers. Her smile is carefree, the sun glinting off her caramel ponytail as it swings through the air.

Mae is with me. I'm not going to die alone.

7

Life is not always a matter of holding good cards, but sometimes, playing a poor hand well.

- Jack London, The Strength of the Strong

"Hey, she's waking up."

My eyelids are weighted. I want to open them and see who's talking, but I can't.

"Briar, open your eyes."

I'm faintly aware that my head hurts. My legs do, too. But I'll worry about that later. I just don't have the energy.

"Briar." The deep voice turns stern. "Come on, we don't have IVs here. You have to drink and eat if you want to live. Wake up."

The musky scents of decaying vegetation and wet

soil fast-track my return to reality. I'm on the island. And the voice belongs to Pax.

It takes all my energy to force my eyes open, and I immediately squint against the light. Pax slowly transforms from a blurry outline to someone I recognize.

"Attagirl," he says. "I'm gonna help you into a sitting position so you can get some water down. It's going to hurt, but you have to do it."

He wraps an arm around my middle back, stabbing pains shooting through my core. I groan and try to resist the movement, but I'm too weak.

"You were beaten." He supports my back with one arm, his other hand picking up a canteen. "Can you hold this?"

I look at him blankly. I can't even lift my arm up, let alone hold anything.

"I need some help," he calls over his shoulder.

"On my way, Commander."

A woman comes to the other side of the bed, unscrewing the canteen's cap and holding it up to my lips. I go limp, unable to stay awake any longer.

"Briar, drink the fucking water." Pax's harsh tone brings me out of my haze. "You want to live? Drink the water and eat the food. Mari will pour it in your mouth if you need her to."

Listlessly, I part my lips. Mari gently tips the canteen to my mouth, lukewarm water flowing out of it. It feels good on my throat. The dribble that runs down my chin and neck grounds me.

Marcelle's room. A torch. And a threat about being a "baby killer."

How did I live through that? I didn't think there was a chance. I turn my mouth away from the canteen and look to the side, expecting Marcelle and her friends to be standing there.

I cry out in pain from the movement. Everything hurts. I've had broken ribs enough times to know what it feels like. One of my eyes is so swollen I can only partially see out of it.

"I need to know who did this to you," Pax says. "Was it Marcelle?"

Somewhere on the edges of my consciousness, I'm slightly offended. He thinks one woman could do this to me and I wouldn't fight back at all? People were holding me down. I didn't get in a single hit or kick. They planned to do this to me, and they executed their plan well.

"You can just nod. It's not a big mystery—you were found unconscious in her room and she has scratch marks on her face."

That bitch spat on me. She didn't even have the guts to fight me one on one. When I'm able to stay awake, I'm going to be more pissed off about it. For now, it's just not important.

When he sees I'm not going to respond, Pax sighs, aggravated. "We can talk about that later. For now, you need to eat this." He holds something in front of my mouth.

I waver, sleep lulling me like a siren song I can't resist.

"Fucking eat it!" he commands. "You're not dying, do you hear me? Whoever did this to you violated the rules and they'll pay for it. Open your mouth and eat three bites of food and then you can sleep."

My eyes focus on him. Why does he care so much whether I live or die? And more importantly, why don't I seem to care?

Three bites. Maybe I can do it.

He nudges my lips open and puts something sweet in my mouth. Sluggishly, I mash it with my teeth.

Banana. At least it's not a piece of hairy rat tail.

I was tough before I got here. Now I'm a victim, lying down and letting Marcelle try to kill me. What happened to me? I was asleep in the open, the easiest of targets.

"These two will be harder to chew, but they're important." Pax's arm is warm and strong on my back. "You have to chew these or you'll choke. It's fish. Okay?"

I think I nod. He pushes one into my mouth, the fishy, smoky taste making me frown.

"There you go." His voice encourages me. "One more bite, a little more water, and you can go back to sleep. I'll be right here guarding you."

I'm going to be late for work. Billy won't let me eat for three days. I want to tell Pax, but I can't get my mouth to make words. He puts another bite of fish in my mouth and I slowly work it with my teeth until I can swallow it.

The woman, Mari, tips the canteen to my mouth again and I take a long drink. She removes it.

"Can you do a little bit more?" she asks.

Not waiting for my answer, she returns the canteen spout to my lips. I take two lazy swallows before my head slumps to the side.

"Okay, back to sleep," Pax says. "That was good, Briar."

My pained cry as he helps me lie back is raspy. I have questions. It's not safe to sleep. I can't fight it, though. My body slides back into blissful unawareness.

———

"How much blood has he lost?"

"I don't know...a lot."

"Oh shit. What happened?"

I don't recognize the first two voices, but I think the third one is Pax's.

"Fucking jaguar got him," a woman says, her voice steely with anger.

"Get his clothes off," someone says.

"Here, let's get him into this bed." That's Pax.

I open my eyes, grimacing as I try to get into a sitting position. I hurt everywhere and don't have any strength.

So that's not happening without help. I turn my head to the side. Several people are crowded around a nearby bed with the injured man on it.

"Start compressions," someone commands.

"How long has he been down?" Pax asks.

"I don't know. I mean, the jag took him down...maybe forty minutes ago. It took us almost ten minutes to get him away from it."

"Ten minutes?" Pax practically roars.

A few seconds of grim silence pass.

"We were afraid of hurting him. I take full responsibility."

"Goddamn right you do. You do compressions on him yourself, Maxwell."

"Yes, sir."

"His legs are turning blue," a woman says flatly. "It's too late."

"I don't give a fuck," Pax snaps. "You do compressions for the next twenty minutes, Maxwell."

I've never seen Pax like this. The normally easygoing commander paces away from the bed and back again, hands on his hips.

"How the fuck did this happen? A hunting party of six fours should be bringing back a dead jaguar, not a dead team member."

"It wasn't an average jaguar, sir." The man says the words so softly I hardly hear them. "It was on us before we even heard it."

Pax scoffs. "You're not average soldiers. And you let a goddamn cat spend ten minutes tearing Carpenter's guts out."

I can only see Pax's back and the profile of a woman who hangs her head, wiping tears from her cheek.

"Get the fuck out of my sight." Pax's voice is low and menacing. "I'll discuss this with Commander Marsden and send for you. Wait in your rooms."

"Yes, sir."

"Yes, Commander."

Before Pax can turn back to me, I move my head and close my eyes. I don't want him to know I overheard that.

My heart pounds so hard I swear it must be visible through my chest as I pretend to sleep.

"Bree, send for Luke and Colvin," Pax says. "Tell them to relieve me here so I can go to a meeting."

"Yes, Commander."

I relax and try to slide back to sleep, listening to Maxwell counting softly as he does compressions on a dead man.

———

The next time I wake up, bright sunlight is streaming in through the open windows of the infirmary. A bald Black man is sitting where Pax was, his gaze shifting from the window to me as I start to sit up.

It's not easy, but I manage. The pain is only a fraction of what it was before. My ribs are a little sore, but not broken. I was sure I had at least one broken rib.

"How long have I been in here?" I croak, reaching for the canteen on the table beside the bed.

"Uh...you woke up yesterday. You slept for two days before that."

I drink as much water as my body will tolerate, shaking my head as I screw the cap back on.

"That's not possible."

He shrugs. "It's what I was told."

The swelling in my eye is gone. I'm not completely healed, but I'm myself again. There's no way I made so much progress so quickly. Maybe I just thought things were worse than they were because I was in a drug-induced stupor.

"You're up. How are you feeling?" a woman with short brown hair and a hawkish face asks.

"A lot better."

My eyes flicker over to the bed where the man Pax called Carpenter was. It's empty now, made up with fresh white sheets. Did that really happen? Or did I imagine it due to powerful narcotics in my system?

"You guys must have some next-level medicine here." I smile at the woman whose fingertips are pressed to my inner wrist so she can check my pulse.

"You just needed rest." She says it breezily, like I'm a little kid who had a scrape on my knee. "Are you having pain anywhere?"

"No, seriously. Did you give me capsaicin? Please tell me you guys didn't give me kratom. I mean, if you did, I get it, but that stuff's addictive. Or was it actual medicine? How did I heal so quickly?"

"Are you having pain anywhere?"

My gaze darts to her wrist, where her bracelet indicates she's a three. I suspect the higher a Rising

Tide's number is, the more they know about this weird-as-fuck island.

"I deserve to know what you guys gave me."

A wrinkle of annoyance appears between her brows. "We didn't give you anything but food and water. Now, I have other patients, so *do you have pain anywhere?*"

"No, I'm fine. How long have I been here?"

"This is your fourth day."

My shoulders sink. I should be grateful I'm so much better, but the scientist in me can't blindly swallow answers that don't make sense. If I wasn't hallucinating the severity of my pain and injuries, what's going on?

"What were my injuries when I arrived?"

Her smile is tight and not remotely happy. "Commander Thatcher will be coming by soon. Talk to him about it. I have other patients."

She walks away and I arch a brow at the man sitting beside my bed. He ignores me—no surprise since he's wearing a four bracelet.

I slowly sip water, making a mental list of all the questions I have for Pax. By the time he strolls into the infirmary, though, all I can think about is the hollowness in my stomach. I'm so hungry it hurts.

"What a difference a day makes," he quips, grinning as he looks at me.

He's wearing a belt made of a narrow rope; his abs look carved from stone and his face seems leaner than it was before.

"You ready to go back to Marcelle's room?"

My heart hammers with fear, the image of Marcelle's

hateful, torch-lit expression burned into my mind. I really thought I was going to die.

"Your face tells me everything I need to know," he says. "I already cut you loose from her. I'm your mentor now, and you're bunking with Rona. That work for you?"

I nod, relief washing through me. I don't have to sleep outside anymore. Now that I know Marcelle and her friends are out to get me, I won't be a sitting duck again.

He nods at the man beside my bed. "You can go, Colvin. Thanks."

"Yes, Commander."

Pax comes all the way over to my bed, making my stomach flutter unexpectedly. "More good news—you're off kitchen duty."

I groan. "Don't put me on laundry."

The dimple in his cheek surfaces when he smiles. "You're with me because I want you on the hunting and security team. We don't usually put ones there, but you're special. I've seen it in training and I saw it when Olin brought you in here after you were attacked. You've got the heart of a fighter."

My lips part with surprise. "Olin brought me here?"

"Yeah. Billy sent him to find you when you didn't show up for work. He kicked Marcelle's door down."

"Oh, wow."

"The building crew is gonna be way too busy to fix that door, so I put it in storage. You don't think Marcelle will mind not having a door anymore, do you?"

I'm not a cruel person, but I do think everyone

should get what they deserve. And the thought of Marcelle having to sleep unprotected, unable to leave anything in her room because it could get stolen while she's gone...it's very well deserved.

"I think she's tough enough to get through it," I say with a smile.

8

He was a killer, a thing that preyed, living on the things that lived, unaided, alone, by virtue of his own strength and prowess, surviving triumphantly in a hostile environment where only the strong survive.

—*Jack London, White Fang*

"Way too slow." Pax grabs the bottom of my boot as I'm about to land a roundhouse kick to his chest and shoves me away from him.

I crash to the ground, mud sloshing into my armpits and hair as I land on my back. *More* mud, because I was already covered in it.

Mud is a decent makeshift sunscreen during afternoon training sessions, when the sun is at peak incineration levels. Rain showers are a welcome break from the sun's punishing rays, but they never last long. The baseline weather here is a hellish inferno. If we had eggs—or concrete—we could definitely do the sizzling egg on pavement thing.

It's my second day training full-time with Pax. I actually miss working in the kitchen, but this is where I need to be. Sharpening my fighting skills and making powerful allies. I won't give Marcelle a second chance to kill me.

"Have you heard of Moringa?" I ask as I get to my feet, wiping my hands on my already filthy T-shirt.

"Nope."

"It's native to...I think it's India, but you can find it other places. It thrives in tropical environments. It's a good source of protein, fiber, several vitamins and folic acid, which pregnant women need."

He creases his brow in thought. "I'm trying to figure out if you're cute when you're muddy or cute when you talk about plants and get all excited. Or is it both?"

I brush off his compliment, hoping his good mood will help me get what I want.

"I can identify edible plants. I know you guys have had some bad experiences eating plants in the past, but I can test them to make sure they're safe. I'll test them on myself."

He shakes his head. "I'd kinda prefer you stay alive, actually."

"I know what I'm doing. I can test plants without killing myself. This could be really good for the camp, especially the pregnant women."

"Yeah. Okay. We'll go out for a few hours tomorrow and see what we can find."

I just nod so I don't risk saying something that could make him change his mind. I didn't think it would be that easy. If I can find some plants to supplement the camp diet, it will add much-needed nutrition and calories. And plants replenish themselves much more quickly than fish and boar.

It's midmorning, and the training area is full of people at work. There are ones and twos doing muddy pushups and threes returning from swimming in the ocean. A group of three fours approaches me and Pax, all of them drenched with sweat after a run.

Two of them are women, one of whom is pregnant. Her bowling-ball-sized belly looks out of place on her tiny frame. Pregnant women who aren't getting enough food shouldn't be burning the calories these women do, but I know better than to say that.

"You want us to get started with the kids, Commander?" the man asks.

"Yeah, go ahead. You know what to do. We'll be there soon."

The other woman is tall, her long black hair tied back at the nape of her neck. She's giving me a cool, assessing gaze.

"You're a one, aren't you?" she asks.

I hold out my wrist with the bracelet. "What gave me away?"

Pax laughs softly beside me. "Cool your shit, Yelena. Briar's cool."

"I'm sure." Her voice is laced with sarcasm.

The man nudges Yelena's arm. "Let's go."

She glares at me for a couple more seconds before the three of them leave. I blow out a sigh.

"The women here just love me. It's these, isn't it?" I hold up my wrists so the X tattoos face him.

"Not for Yelena. It's jealousy."

I roll my eyes. "Right. Because I'm a one and I belong in the kitchen."

"No." Pax's eyes are locked onto me, swirling with intensity. "That's not why."

My body warms, an invisible connection between us tugging at me. I don't want to get involved with anyone, because it would sidetrack me from what's most important. But when I'm around Pax, my body doesn't seem to care about the plans my mind has.

I avoid his gaze. "She's welcome to switch places with me and find out what it feels like to have mud in places you never thought mud would be."

His lips turn up in a smile. "No one's switching places with you."

He glances over each shoulder like he's making sure no one can overhear him. My stomach knots because even though I feel a pull of attraction, I won't give into it, and I don't want to have to shoot down one of the two most powerful people in this camp.

"There's something you need to know. Did Marcelle tell you about the circle?"

"No."

He presses his lips together tightly, his expression

grim. "Yeah, I figured. We're about peace, order and prosperity here—you already know that. And part of prosperity is creating a new generation of Rising Tiders."

My attention snags on his use of the word "creating." Most people don't consider their children creations. But he's not hitting on me, and that's a win. So I listen and don't interrupt him.

"Some of the women here..." He stops, seeming to consider. "I don't know how to put it. They love having babies. They think it's their most important role here."

I put my palms up. "I have no problem with that. If it's their choice, it's their business."

"We agree with that. The X tats are...all-encompassing, I guess. They don't explain each woman's individual circumstances."

I narrow my eyes, not liking where he's going with this. "I don't owe anyone explanations."

"I agree." He steps closer to me. "Look, my point is...I think you probably got jumped by a group of women who judged you based on that ink. And if you give me their names, they'll be disciplined for it."

I shrug and look away. "I didn't get a good look at any of them."

"Bullshit," he mumbles before clearing his throat. "Anyway, probation lasts thirty days here. Then you're a full-fledged one. And once that happens, any other one can ask you to step into the circle with them."

I cross my arms. "What does that mean?"

"We have a circle over by the beach. An actual circle, where two people fight. There are rules: no weapons, no one else can enter the circle under any circumstances, and only one person walks out of the circle."

I just stare at him for a couple long, dumbfounded seconds as I digest his words. "You mean...fight to the death?"

"Yeah. I've been in the circle a few times myself. And if you don't tell me who attacked you, I'm pretty sure you'll end up there on your thirty-first day here."

His statement hangs in the air between us. It makes sense, then, why Marcelle didn't kill me. She's not allowed to beat me to death in her room, but in front of everyone else, it's fine.

This place is *fucked*.

"That's good to know." I put my fists in front of me in a defensive stance. "Are you ready to go again?"

He exhales heavily, running a hand through his hair. "Briar, you're not hearing me."

"I hear you fine."

"You don't know how ruthless Tiders are."

I throw my arms in the air and laugh, though I'm more angry than amused. "Add it to the list of things I don't know around here. Why are there wolves? Why can fours run five miles in twenty minutes, and then do it again right after, like they just took a little stroll in the park? How did I recover from that beating in three days?"

He closes the last of the distance between us, so close I can feel the heat of his body. I tip my chin up so I can meet his gaze.

"This island is special," he says in a low tone. "In time, you'll see how."

"You answered exactly zero of my questions."

"Yeah, well...there's a reason for that. I'm trying to help you here. If you want to live long enough to really experience what's special about the island, you need to train every waking hour. You're less than three weeks away from getting called to the circle."

I'm failing. My plan was to lie low. Keep quiet, not make any waves, and bide my time. Learn what I can without anyone realizing I'm doing it. Stay focused on my goal of finding a way off this island. Instead, I'm showing Pax every single one of my cards.

"Okay, I understand." I try to look apologetic. "You're right. Let's train some more."

He nods. "No more roundhouse kicks. You finish those two business days after you start them. Fight dirtier."

"Okay."

I told him what I was thinking just now, and that was a mistake. I'm being smarter about the training, though. He knows I'm good at defending myself because doing so is instinctive. I can't let people land punches on me when I know how to evade them.

He thinks my offensive skills are weaker. They aren't. I'm deliberately holding back during training because I don't want anyone here to know how strong a fighter I really am.

That's one card I won't play unless I have no choice.

———

An hour later, Pax is leading me through the jungle, the trail we're on wide enough to accommodate three people walking side by side. It's a different trail than the one we took from the beach to the Rising Tide camp.

The jungle is alive with monkeys chattering and birds singing, the steady hum of insects a constant in the background. A bright-green snake slithers up a nearby branch and I lean over, trying to get a closer look at it to identify the species.

"Stay in the middle of the trail." Pax is carrying a spear, his demeanor serious and alert. "And don't touch anything. You can die just from touching some of the stuff here."

"Are there dart frogs? I've always wanted to see a blue poison dart frog."

He squints skeptically. "This isn't a zoo. Shit will kill you before you even know it's happening."

I stop myself from saying I know how to be careful. I still have suspicions about the purpose of this island. Are people being trained for death matches in the jungle? And other than wolves, what else was brought here? The usual rules about predators and prey don't apply if humans are intervening and adding species that don't belong here.

After another five minutes of walking in silence, the trail opens up. My eyes widen as I take in my surroundings. Blue Arrow Island just got a whole lot weirder.

It looks like a modern private school campus, the sprawling brick building rising up two stories. A man is tending to the landscaping that surrounds the building, which is meticulously cared for, free of weeds and full of brightly colored tropical blooms. A wide, rectangular sandstone slab is set into the landscaping, the words "Peace," "Order," and "Prosperity" each engraved on its own line.

I follow Pax up the concrete stairs. A man in the same olive pants, white T-shirt and boots worn by everyone at the Rising Tide camp nods at him.

"Commander."

"Hey, Ray. This is Briar."

Ray nods politely at me, his gaze jumping to the bracelet that identifies me as a one.

"I'm mentoring her," Pax explains.

He keeps walking. The inside of the building is just as muggy as everywhere else is here, the air stagnant. There are no windows on the front of the building, but there are a few on the second story of the wall opposite the entrance, bright light shining through them onto the white marble flooring.

The lobby area is large and open, nothing adorning the walls. There are double doors ahead of us and a door on each of the side walls.

We go to the double doors. Pax opens them and nods to another guard on the other side.

After walking through the doorway, I find myself in a huge courtyard, at least fifty young children in different areas around it. Why didn't I realize sooner that there are pregnant women in camp, but no children?

"I just need to have a quick conversation," Pax says,

gesturing toward a wooden bench beneath the shaded overhang of the building.

I sit, keeping my expression impassive as I take in my surroundings. The children range from barely able to walk to maybe eight years old. All of them wear miniature versions of the uniform Pax and I have on. Their skin color ranges from very light to very dark, as does their hair. They all have the same close-cropped style, maybe an eighth of an inch of hair on their scalps.

An alarm blares inside my head. This place isn't right. None of the children are laughing or playing. Even the youngest of them is standing in line, watching and listening.

I babysat before the virus came. I've never seen such compliant children.

The man we saw at the training area is leading a group of older kids in a drill. They all run about eight feet before leaping into the air, my lips parting when I see more than twelve feet of air between some of them and the ground. After hanging in the air for longer than they should be able to, they drop back down one after the other, all of them landing in a predatory crouch.

Yelena is leading a younger group in a drill with short wooden staffs, all the kids moving in perfect unison. They can twist and pass the staff from one hand to the other easily, without even looking at it.

They look like they're playing dress-up as soldiers, but it's disgustingly real. I suddenly long for the blissful ignorance of meat prep with Rona. This is what the pregnant women at Rising Tide are creating—soldiers for the Whitman regime.

The youngest of the kids here, who should be toddling along and babbling, are instead sprinting down lanes outlined with rock, other stone-faced kids watching them.

I control my breathing, trying to quell the tears pooling in my eyes. Of all the things I've seen on this island that are outside the laws of science, this is the most disturbing and egregious. It makes me feel sick.

"Hey, I'm all set." Pax looks down at me from beside the bench I'm sitting on. "You okay?"

I smile, knowing it's going to take some world-class deception to eventually get myself out of here. "Yeah, I'm good. I just got emotional seeing all the kids. I love kids."

His expression brightens. "Yeah? Me too."

Fucking liar. No one who loves kids stands by and lets them be treated this way. Someone did something to these children, and it robbed them of what it means to be human.

Whitman. It all goes back to Whitman. My rage for him and every member of his regime burns white hot as I follow Pax out of the little soldier compound.

They'll pay. Even if it takes my entire life to figure out how to make them pay for this and everything else they've done, I'll find a way.

9

In law enforcement, we all face danger, provocation and disrespect. How we respond in these situations is a reflection of our character. Emotion is a part of our job. Our duty is to always maintain emotional control in high-stress situations.

- Excerpt from a police training manual written by Ben Hollis

The next morning, I wake up more rested and clear-headed than I've been since I got here. Before, I was like a kite on a still day. I knew I wanted to get off this island, but it was a huge, intangible goal that was overshadowed by just trying to survive.

Seeing the emotionless child soldiers being drilled yesterday was the powerful gust of wind I needed to fly.

It all makes sense now. Whitman is using the people of Rising Tide to breed soldiers. Those kids are probably being psychologically programmed along with all the physical training. I don't know where their supernatural skills come from, but that's beside the point.

It's cruel to create children just so they can serve. No matter the cause. I can't worry only about myself now that I know the truth.

"Hey, kid." Billy passes me a wooden bowl of murky, watery broth.

My stomach roars in protest, but I smile at him and say, "Thanks, Billy. It looks good."

A corner of his mouth lifts in a smile. "It's an old family recipe."

I sit down by myself at a table. Pax told me to meet him here at eight this morning. I felt guilty snoozing my way through the camp alarms at five thirty and six o'clock, especially when Rona had to get up to come to work. The extra rest was nice, though.

I'm not sure what time it is, but I know it's not eight a.m. yet. I take my time with the warm broth, sipping it slowly. Some people at other tables are talking and laughing, while others stare forlornly into empty bowls. I wonder how many of them know what's happening to the children here.

"You're fucking dead!"

I snap to attention, setting my bowl down. Everyone in the dining shelter turns to look at the man who yelled. He's stalking toward us, his blond hair unkempt and his expression unhinged.

A woman stands up from her seat as he walks into

the shelter, putting a palm on his chest. "Hey, take it easy."

He pushes her arm aside. My skin prickles with awareness of approaching danger. His furious attention is locked onto someone, and people are starting to get up and scatter. I'm on my feet, about to move, when the man wraps his hand around the back of another man's neck. He yanks him from his seat, the other man yelping with alarm.

"You got her pregnant! You fucking asshole. You knew I wanted her."

Before I can even process what's happening, the wild-eyed man is shoving the other guy into one of the shelter's thick wooden support posts. His hold on his victim's neck lets him smash the man's face directly into the post, the squishing and crunching sounds with each hit sending my heart rate soaring.

"You! Fucking! Knew!" He slams the man's face into the post over and over again, blood running down the wooden surface.

"Adler, stop." A tall, muscular man wearing a four bracelet barks the order, putting his arms around the attacker's midsection to pull him away.

The body of the man he killed falls limply to the ground. His head is halfway gone, the force of the hits so powerful that it broke his skull into pieces.

"What the hell happened?"

Virginia Marsden races up to the two men. It's the first time I've gotten a close look at her. She's lean, like everyone here, the lines in her face making her look like she's in her early thirties. Her blond hair is secured in a neat bun at the nape of her neck.

The four, who's holding on to Adler, waits for him to speak, and when he doesn't, he locks eyes with Virginia.

"Rodriguez was sitting here eating when Adler pulled him up and did that to him." He gestures at the body on the ground.

A muscle in Virginia's jaw tics as she turns to Adler. "Well?"

Adler's expression has morphed from madness to contrition. He looks like a different man now, fear swimming in his eyes.

"I shouldn't have done it."

She shakes her head. "What a waste. You could have called him into the circle."

His shoulders slump. "I know. I just...my rage just took over. I couldn't control it."

She pulls a knife from its holster on her hip, then turns to look at those of us still gathered here. There are around three dozen people, all of us silent. Some are deliberately looking away, but others, like me, can't help but look at Virginia.

"Briar."

My stomach rolls as she says my name. How does she know who I am? And what could she possibly want from me?

"Y..." I clear my throat, keeping my chin up despite my worry. "Yes?"

"Which of our tenets did Adler violate with this attack?"

Peace, order and prosperity. I almost say peace, but I change my mind at the last second. She didn't want the dispute to be avoided; she wanted it to take place in the circle.

"Order, Commander."

I'll play the part of an eager Rising Tider while I have to. No more questioning anything. I could easily end up like Rodriguez if I'm not careful.

She nods, turning back to Adler.

"Robert Adler, for taking the life of another Rising Tider outside of the circle, I sentence you to death."

He shrinks back, another four joining the first one to hold him in place. He screams, the sound cut short when Virginia swiftly runs her knife across his throat.

I've seen a lot of violence and death since the virus came, but I still feel the same horror every time. We didn't unite to rebuild after most of the planet's population was wiped out without warning; instead, those of us who remain are killing each other.

It's disappointing, but not at all surprising.

———

Of all the ways I've seen people die since the virus came, I think beheadings are the worst. It's horrible watching someone's head get lopped off their shoulders. A head without a body is a shocking sight, as is a body without a head.

But seeing that guy Rodriguez go from eating breakfast to no longer having a face in less than a minute was a violent wake-up call for me. If I'm going to get through this, I have to be smart. Careful.

"Watch it." Pax grabs my elbow and pulls me back a couple of steps.

"What did I do?"

"You were about to step on a scorpion."

I look back, finding a dark-brown scorpion that blends in perfectly with the forest floor. It has a venomous stinger, and though I have my pants tucked into my boots Rising Tide style, I wouldn't have wanted to risk a sting.

Pax is taking me on a long trek through the island's jungle to search for edible plants. I've already put three samples in the woven reed basket he's carrying on his back.

We're taking one of the paths Rising Tide's hunters use. It's washed out in places and it requires walking single file.

It feels like we've been heading away from camp for around three hours. My clothes are soaked completely through with sweat—not the best look for a woman in a white T-shirt.

I'm curious how big this island is. Based on the scarcity of game, I assumed it was fairly small. Now, I suspect it's just been so heavily hunted that there isn't much left.

The dull thunk of raindrops on the canopy far above us signals the start of an afternoon rain shower. They're usually fast, furious and short. Only a few stray drops make it to us; the rest are stopped by the dense tree ceiling.

Pax turns and calls to me over his shoulder. "This kind of ruins my surprise, but hopefully you'll still like it."

The thick jungle opens up, revealing the source of the dull roar I've heard in the background for the past fifteen minutes or so. A towering waterfall, about four stories tall, gushes into a crystal clear spring at its base. Even as the rainfall intensifies, I stare at the waterfall with awe.

It's spectacular. The first beautiful thing I've seen in this tropical hell. My throat tightens as I think of my mom. This is one of those moments that sustains me in a world without her. Everything is connected, like she said, and the part of her that loved nature will always be with me.

I open my arms and look up to the sky, the waterfall's spray and the rain washing over me. This island is like a rose, and all I've seen until now are the ugly, prickly thorns. The waterfall is the velvet-soft, bright pink flower I get to inhale the sweet scent of now.

The children I saw yesterday should be playing here, splashing and swimming and laughing. I wonder if they even could if they were brought here. I need to believe it's at least possible.

The rainfall lightens. At the edge of the spring, a trailing vine with a yellow flower grows, and I bend to examine it.

A splashing sound makes me look up. Pax is knee-deep in the spring, wearing nothing but a grin.

"Come on in. It feels amazing."

By his loaded tone, I know he's not just talking about the water. My quick glance at his naked body makes a needy ache bloom between my thighs. I want to strip my clothes off and go to him, my breasts heavy, sensitive and desperate for his touch.

I close my eyes. Where is this coming from? I don't find it sexy that he brought me here and got naked when I wasn't expecting anything like this. Even if I wanted to have sex with him—which I don't—I can't risk getting pregnant.

Having babies is natural. It would make him so happy.

The thoughts popped into my head unbidden, making me gasp and grasp my forehead. How did that happen? Did Pax put those thoughts in my head?

I know it's impossible, but my gaze goes to him anyway. His eyes are molten, hunger written all over his face as he palms his erection and strokes himself.

"Don't fight it, Briar. You want this, too."

The ache between my thighs intensifies. I do want it, but I also don't. My mind is fighting itself.

It would be nice to just feel good for a few minutes. To not worry about anything else.

No, those aren't my thoughts. My heart races over the invasion of my body and my mind. How can I maintain control? And how the hell is this possible? Is it Pax inside my head, or is it the island itself?

He's moving closer. Dread creeps down my spine. What am I going to do? I don't have access to the herbal tea I took on the mainland to prevent pregnancy.

"Don't tease me." His tone isn't playful anymore.

Anger lashes out inside me in a powerful wave that brings me fully back to myself. How fucking dare he accuse me of teasing him?

"Just a quick one. Five minutes, tops."

The unfamiliar male voice makes me turn.

"Fuck." Pax runs to exit the spring.

"Don't move."

The command came from a short, muscular Black woman. She's wearing dark pants, hiking boots and a gray T-shirt, weapons holstered at her waist and a long pole in her hand. The pole seems to be made of metal, the top foot of it crackling with an electrical charge.

Not only am I not moving, I'm not even breathing. But Pax sprints out of the water, going for his pile of clothes with a knife on top.

An arrow lands on the T-shirt on top with a twanging sound, pinning his clothes to the ground.

"Next one goes in your head."

The deep voice belongs to a man who walks past the woman, standing a few feet to the side in front of her. He's holding a bow, an arrow knocked.

My lips part, fury and fear coursing through me in equal measure. He's the leader of the Dust Walkers—the one who stood at the front of their group that day on the beach. The one who dragged Amira off to her death.

He's massive—well over six feet tall, his shoulders broad and his arms carved with muscles from shoulder to forearm. His dark hair is short, but still long enough that it has some wave, a few stray pieces falling over his forehead. His deep evergreen eyes are locked onto Pax, daring him to move.

"Stay behind me," he orders.

I flick my gaze to the three other people standing behind him, two men and a woman, all of them holding the same long, electrified sticks as the other woman.

"You've got balls, Marcus," Pax says, his tone hostile.

"Did we interrupt you with your thirtieth baby mama?" Marcus asks cooly.

The woman shoots me a look of disgust. It's not the time to think about it, but *damn*. Apparently a lot of those kids I saw yesterday were fathered by Pax.

"Why don't you call off your dogs and fight me like a real man, Marcus?" Pax says.

Marcus sneers at him. "You know why." A muscle in his jaw tics. "Look, we don't want trouble."

"You are trouble," Pax seethes.

"Nova's gonna tie you up. Then we're taking your friend with us until we get a half mile away. She can come back and untie you."

Pax scoffs. "Or. I kill every one of you and then jerk off on your corpse."

"You're not in a great position to negotiate, with no weapons and your dick out."

Marcus is pure steel. He doesn't flinch or show an ounce of indecision.

My pulse races nervously as I study the electrified spears. They're stun sticks of some kind, but if they're used against people who are in the water—like the water just a few feet away—the water will conduct the current directly into our hearts and kill us.

"Fuck you," Pax says. "Go ahead and kill me. Virginia will rain fire on you until every one of your people is dead."

Marcus narrows his eyes. "I don't want to kill you, Pax. I just want to go back the way we came."

"Go ahead."

"You know I can't turn my back on you. Nova's going to tie you up."

The woman near him reaches for a lightweight rope at her waist.

"No fucking way," Pax snaps.

I'm helpless, trapped in the middle of them. But there are no options to run through. All I can do is sit here and wait, my life out of my hands. I despise that feeling.

"Pax, don't!" Marcus's deep shout makes the hair on the back of my neck stand up.

I turn my attention to Pax, who's standing perfectly still, his eyes closed.

"Watch yourselves!" Marcus yells over his shoulder, alarmed. "Back to back!"

He pulls a short sword from his holster belt, the five of them forming a tight circle with their backs inside of it, all of them crouching with weapons ready.

Something streaks out of the jungle so fast I can't tell what it is, trees nearby quaking with the force of the wind. What the hell could shoot out of there so quickly it's a blur?

I run to stand behind Pax, my chest tight with terror.

"Fuck!" One of the men cries.

An anaconda as thick as my thigh is coiled tightly around his body. It happened in a second, which should be impossible.

The bulge of his eyes is unnatural; the snake is already applying a lethal amount of pressure. His lips part and his head slumps to the side. The snake must have bitten him.

"Finn!" Marcus's nostrils flare as he swings the sword back, sinking it into the snake's body.

The others use their stun sticks, trying in vain to get the anaconda to relent. Electrical sparks fly off the ends of the sticks. Marcus draws his arm back and hacks at the snake again, sweat flying from his brow.

"We have to go," Pax murmurs to me.

He swipes up his pile of things and darts into the jungle. I follow, my skin prickling in anticipation of an arrow lodging in my skull or my back.

Finally, I'm deep enough into the jungle that I risk a glance over my shoulder. No one is behind me. I keep running as fast as my legs will allow, Pax so far ahead of me I can't even see him.

The green shades of vegetation around me blur into one shade from the tears in my eyes. I don't want to go back to Rising Tide, but I don't know if I can survive this place alone.

It's a pick-your-poison situation. I choose the twisted-up mindfuck that is Rising Tide.

10

Though they lack nervous systems, plants have sophisticated survival mechanisms that have evolved over millions of years. Olive trees can roll their leaves in to minimize their exposure to the sun when facing drought conditions. They can also quickly close the stomate (pores) on their leaves during dry periods, limiting water loss to help them survive.

- Excerpt from a lecture given by Dr. Lucinda Hollis in her Plant Evolution course

My left foot sinks into the mud, sending me sliding so hard I nearly fall, my arms flailing at my sides for balance. I can't fall. Can't twist an ankle. Can't lose my way.

I've been running on the path back to Rising Tide for more than an hour. I don't know if I'm being followed.

My legs still feel strong, but the adrenaline is wearing off. And then there's the rain.

A few minutes into my run back, I started feeling droplets breaking through the canopy. The cool sprinkles on my sweating face felt good. But soon, it became a torrent. I can't make out much in front of me, because the rain is falling so hard and it's gotten darker.

There's also wind, which alarms me more than the heavy rainfall. This jungle is dense and I'm so deep in it that wind shouldn't be able to get through.

I can't think about the tropical storm raging outside this jungle, though. All my focus has to stay on getting out of here. Making it back to Rising Tide.

It's the devil I know.

I need time to think about the robotic soldier children, the thoughts I'm having that aren't my own, and the Dust Walkers. I don't have that luxury now, though.

You've got more in the tank than you think.

My dad used to say that when Maven and I started dragging on training runs. I try to remember the sound of his voice saying those words as I run. He's not here, but he's still with me. I want to make him proud, and that means I can't quit.

I slide in the mud again, and this time I land on my hands and knees. I push myself up carefully and keep moving.

Water gushes down the sides of the trail, the rain getting heavier. Hair that has escaped my ponytail is plastered to my face, a section of it in my eyes. I shove it aside with a frustrated groan.

I'm running, my head down so I can keep my eyes on the mud path. For a guy who's supposed to be fearless, Pax left me in the dust without a second thought.

That's a thought for later. Run, Briar.

More than two hours in, the path is so flooded I'm splashing through water. The front of one of my boots catches on something and I'm thrown. My head hits something hard, my teeth rattling from the impact.

Pain blossoms inside my head. I can't get a full breath. Instinctively, I reach behind my head to see what I hit. A tree.

I curl up, turning my face toward the ground to get a break from the rain. With every shallow breath, I get a nose full of earthy soil and decaying leaves.

I'm not dying here. Not in this jungle, not on this island. Every day since the virus has been hard in one way or another. And so damn lonely.

My parents begged me to stay on the small island where my summer botany internship was being hosted when the virus hit, to minimize my chances of getting it. Then the electrical grid and cell towers went down.

It took me more than a month to get to their house, and when I did, it had been ransacked by looters. The virus killed almost everyone, and I know my parents and sister are most likely included in the death toll.

But not knowing for sure, or how, or when, or if they were together—those are the things that haunt me. I didn't just lose my family but also the only people in the world I could trust.

Friends who were part of the research project turned on me, and on each other. If not for the small revolver my father insisted I keep with me at all times, I never would have made it back to the mainland.

I have to be close to Rising Tide. Bracing my hand against the tree, I turn and get to my knees, a wave of anger hitting me out of nowhere.

This island might be sentient. The scientist in me can't believe I'm even having the thought. But there are no scientific explanations for thoughts that aren't my own popping into my head, or children who can jump twelve feet into the air.

Somehow, this island may be inside me. Inside everyone here. It may have an agenda, and if it does, it's not good for any of us. But it can't have me. I'm not rolling over and letting this place mindfuck me.

I don't have my family, but I have everything my parents taught me. I have a bond with my sister that can't be undone by anyone—or anything.

Biting off a groan, I rise to my feet. My head aches and I can hardly see through the thick sheets of rain. The inches of water pooled at my feet shouldn't have been able to accumulate in a matter of two hours, but on this island, there are no rules.

I put my head down and keep going. As long as I'm not running into trees, I'm still on the path. And as long as I keep moving, I'll get there.

A gust of wind slams into my chest as I leave the jungle, sweeping my feet out from under me.

"Briar!"

Pax reaches down to help me up, his hair blowing in every direction and water trails running down his bare chest.

"Take shelter in your room!" He's yelling, and it's still hard to hear him over the howling wind and pouring rain. "There's a hurricane coming!"

I nod and head toward the room I share with Rona, my boots sloshing through standing water that almost reaches my ankles.

Hardly anyone is out at camp. I pass a few fours running with backpacks full of supplies, but no one else. A rectangular section of metal roofing just misses slamming into me as it blows past.

I need to get into the room soon. Staying out in this is too dangerous.

Clutching onto the handrail, I climb the stairs to our second-level room. A hunger pain punches me in the gut. Billy, Olin and Rona would normally be working in the kitchen now, but they're probably all holed up in their rooms like everyone else.

The housing is built from mortared concrete blocks, so it should be a safe place to ride out a hurricane. And hopefully, a dry one. I really want to get out of my soaking wet clothes and boots.

My room key is still safely stashed inside my bra. I get

it out, stumbling from the force of the wind. It's hard to see, but I manage to get the key into the keyhole.

I swing the door open, my eyes scanning the dark room for Rona.

She's not here.

I huff in aggravation. Of course she's not here. Not getting electrocuted or shot with an arrow back at the waterfall are the only things that have gone right today.

I step inside, taking shelter while I think about it. She could be sheltering in someone else's room. I don't think she'd be looking for me, because she knew I was with Pax.

As much as I want to close the door behind me and strip off my soaking wet clothes, I can't do it. I lock the door back up and head toward the stairs, cupping a hand over my eyes so I can see through the downpour.

It's getting heavier. I hold on to the railing as I go down the stairs, knowing time is critical. Soon this hurricane will be uprooting trees and killing anyone who dares get in its way.

Several pieces of debris fly past; only luck helps me avoid them. I can hardly see anything.

Putting my head down, I splash through the water at a jog.

When I reach the kitchen, I find the main door unlocked. I step into the deserted room. The wooden window covers have been latched closed, the strong winds making them rattle.

"Rona?"

Running a hand over my hair, I sluice water to the floor.

"Is anyone here?" I call.

The kitchen is neat and clean, everything in its place. It looks like they had time to plan an evacuation. I go to the door that leads out to the meat prep area, a gust of wind taking hold of it as soon as I open it.

It takes all my strength to close it. Then I lean my back against it, wind from one of the shelter's three open sides pelting my face. I don't see Rona, and I don't know where else to look.

I can't just blindly search the camp. I have to go to the room and hope Rona is safe somewhere else.

The meat prep table is situated against the wall, and I glance over it out of habit. The table is enclosed on its ends with little wooden walls, so the meat on it isn't gutting pummeled by the wind.

I guess they didn't have time to finish cleaning the meat before evacuating. I'm so hungry I consider grabbing a piece of raw meat.

When I reach toward the table, my heart falls into my stomach. There's a big toe lying there, the nail yellowed.

A human big toe. I recoil, gasping in horror. When I scan the entire table, I see three smaller toes, all severed from a foot. The "meat" on the table is unmistakably a human leg. A thin one.

My stomach pitches with a wave of nausea. I know the people here are starving, but this is beyond indecency. It's gruesome and so fucking...cold. Humans are supposed to be better than this.

I shake my head, and the sight of another foot beneath the table catches my eye. This foot has a dark boot on it. I bend, terrified of what I'm going to find.

Rona is sitting under the table, her back to the wall and her knees pulled to her chest with her arms wrapped around them. Her eyes are empty, like her mind is somewhere her body isn't.

"Rona?" I get to my knees, rain pelting the side of my face like a hundred tiny needles.

She just stares at me blankly. I've seen people like this before, sometimes after witnessing something traumatic. And unfortunately, I don't have enough time to just wait for her to be ready to talk.

"Rona, we have to go. There's a hurricane. It's going to get worse." I make sure she can see my hand as I slowly extend it to her. "Take my hand and we'll go together."

"Briar." She says my name like it's been a long time since we saw each other.

"Yes, it's me. We need to go back to our room now. Right now."

She sighs heavily, her shoulders sinking. "This isn't a life."

Shit. This is a really bad time for an existential crisis. "Listen to me, this is important. We have to get back to our room. Now, Rona. And then we can talk. I know it's hard here, but you're strong."

Her eyes remain vacant. "I'm not. I..." She closes her eyes.

"Yes, you are strong," I yell, hoping to get through to

her. "You're strong and you matter. Please, come with me."

"Just go." She lets her head fall back against the wall. "I'm not worth it."

"Yes, you—"

She narrows her eyes. "I ate some of it! Do you know what they do to people who steal extra food here? They exile them to the jungle. It's all there was left and Billy told me not to think about what it is while I prep it, and I..." Tears flood her eyes.

This fucking place. The apocalypse wasn't bad enough for Whitman, apparently. He pounced on it, making people into something they shouldn't be. Forcing them to make choices they shouldn't have to make.

"Rona, you're starving. We're all starving. You have to build a box in your mind and put this in there."

Her lower lip quivers. "I can't do it anymore, Briar. Just go. Leave me."

A gust of wind knocks me to the side. I catch myself and land on my hand. I'm running out of time.

"I don't want to die!" I yell at her. "I'm not ready! And I'm not leaving you, so you can either come with me or we'll both die here. It's your choice."

She grimaces. "No! Leave! I don't want your help."

"I'm not leaving you."

A piece of wood flies through the air and I quickly cover my head with my arms to avoid being hit. It makes contact with my arm and I cry out.

"Fuck! Fine!" Rona storms out from under the meat table.

Blood trickles down my arm as we run out of the shelter, holding on to each other for support.

We run, our arms locked together. The water comes up past our ankles, and it's sloshing around like an angry ocean of waves.

"Hurry!" I call out.

We make it to the stairs, both of us grabbing on to the railing with both hands and forcing our way up one step at a time, the wind battering us.

I didn't make it this far to only make it this far.

Rona's hands cling to the back of my shirt as I fight my way to the door and get the key out. I block the wind with my body, getting it in quickly and opening the door.

The door whips open and slams against the wall. Rona and I both grab it and push, but it's not enough. It barely moves.

I wedge myself between the back of the door and the wall, using my whole body to push on the door. Rona does the same, both of us straining from the effort.

Finally, it closes. I hold it shut while Rona flips the horizontal metal security bar into place and latches it.

Suddenly, it's quiet. Water pours off of us, pooling on the wooden floorboards.

I drop into a sitting position. I can't move anymore. I can't even think. So I just sit, waiting for my heart to slow to its regular pace for the first time in several hours.

11

Awareness is the most important part of defense. Trust your instincts and always pay attention to your surroundings. When interviewed after use of force incidents, a majority of officers stated that they sensed something was wrong before the incident began.

- Excerpt from a police training manual written by Ben Hollis

Twenty-four hours later, the rain hasn't let up. It's a roaring sheet of nonstop hammering against the metal roof. The roof held through the worst of the wind, which came while we were both sleeping.

It was a battle for a few hours, the storm howling in its dogged effort to pull off the sheeting above us, and the roof rattling at times, but never giving in.

Rona and I are both dressed in our dry second set of

clothing, our clothes from yesterday hanging by the door on makeshift rope clotheslines. They're still dripping, everything so soaked it will take days to dry.

"So...how are you feeling?" I ask Rona.

I can't see her in the pitch black of the windowless room, but I think she's awake. For around twelve hours, I slept through much of the storm, but I don't know how much she slept. We've just been lying on our sleeping pallets for hours, only speaking occasionally about the storm.

It takes her about thirty seconds to respond. "I don't know. I'm okay."

After all this time alone in the darkness with my thoughts, I'm feeling restless. I get to my feet and stretch my arms, reaching my fingertips toward the ceiling.

We usually work and sleep different shifts, so I don't usually get to talk to Rona, especially now that I don't work in the kitchen anymore. I test the waters.

"Weird things have been happening to me since I got here. Did you go through anything like that?"

She hums a note of amusement. "Yeah."

I hesitate, then say, "But we aren't supposed to talk about it, right? People here run faster than they should be able to and can pick up things they shouldn't be strong enough to pick up. I shouldn't have been able to run as fast as I did yesterday, and—"

"It's the island."

I twist my body at the waist, first to the left and then to the right. "What does that mean, though? That the island is magic?"

"I guess so."

"Does it bother you? Not knowing for sure?"

There's a shuffling sound as she gets into a sitting position. "Nope. I'm just trying to stay alive. Not get beaten to death in the circle or starve to death."

There's a tinge of bitterness in her voice. I should just drop it, but I don't have any other allies here. I'm not just in the dark in this room right now, but in every respect of this place. Whatever is responsible for the changes in people here—even if it is magic—it seems to be cumulative.

The fours can run the fastest and jump the highest. They're the ones chanting "peace, order, prosperity" the loudest.

I'm worried that the slower I am at finding answers and trying to get off this island, the less I'm going to want to. I don't want to become a loyal soldier and breeder for Whitman. I won't.

"Has there always been a food shortage here?"

"I don't know. I've been here for like...six months? I guess it's been worse lately, but it's all about how much fish and game the hunters can get."

I take a deep breath before continuing. I have to trust someone, and so far, Rona is the closest thing I have to a friend here, other than Olin.

"Do you know what they do to the kids here?"

"The kids are raised together because it's more efficient. We can't have women sitting around with babies on their tits all day. It's hard enough to survive here even with all the women contributing."

I don't understand it. Rona sounds like everyone else here. Indoctrinated. And technically, we're all prisoners. But the Rising Tiders seem almost *grateful* to their captors. I don't care what anyone says—I'll never think this place is anything but fucked.

"But...what's everyone training *for*?" I ask. "I saw the kids in their camp and they're a bunch of mini soldiers. It was creepy and sad. None of them were smiling or laughing. They were training like we do."

Rona's sigh is weary. "We don't smile or laugh, either. Just wait. I've seen people brought back from the jungle in pieces after the Dust Walkers got ahold of them. Or the jaguars."

"Do you ever think about trying to get out of here?"

She snorts derisively. "Out of here? Like out of this camp?"

"Off the island."

"And go where?"

"Back to the mainland."

She laughs scornfully. "Back to being beaten and raped every day? No, I don't think about it."

I should have realized Rona—or actually, everyone—sees life here through a lens of what their lives were like before. I hated every minute of my life locked away in Lochlan's gated estate, but I was safe. Well, safe from everyone but him. I was well fed. I could take showers and read books.

Most people don't have such comfortable everyday lives in the post-virus world. And though I dreamed of escaping his home and returning to scraping by in the shadows, not everyone wants that kind of life.

"I'm sorry that happened to you," I say.

"It happened to everyone. Women and men. I got sent here for grabbing a guard's gun and shooting him in the leg with it, and you know what? It's the best thing that's happened to me since the virus came. Rape isn't allowed, and now I can fight and defend myself."

I nod, even though she can't see me. "That makes total sense."

We sit in silence for a minute before she says, "Do you know why Olin doesn't talk?"

"No."

"Because he can't. He's been here for like two years and he's still a one. Probably always will be, because he wouldn't stop asking questions about this place. Pax cut his tongue out for it. The only thing saving you from that is that you're pretty and Pax wants to fuck you. That won't keep you safe forever."

A horrified chill runs through me. Poor Olin.

"Don't bring up conversations like this with me again," Rona says. "And if you want to live, don't bring them up with anyone else, either."

I respond automatically, my mind still stuck on the image of Pax cutting off Olin's tongue. I didn't want to think he was capable of something like that, but that was naive of me. I know better. Those in power don't use it to make things better for everyone. They use it to make things better for themselves.

"I understand. Thank you for looking out for me."

She doesn't respond. I sit down and let my head rest against the concrete wall, feeling more alone than ever as I listen to rainfall beating on the roof.

———

The next day, a four knocks on our door and tells us everyone is meeting up in the dining shelter.

It's still raining when I step onto the walkway, but the wind has died down. Beside me, Rona sighs heavily.

"Kitchen's got to be trashed."

The camp is still flooded, the buildings across from ours standing in a few inches of water. A tree fell onto one of the buildings, its roof mostly gone. Branches, boards, clothes, and other debris are scattered in the water over the dirt path, drifting lazily.

We follow the line of people from the housing block to the shelter, everyone quiet as we wade through ankle-deep water.

The concrete housing blocks are intact, but pretty much everything else is destroyed. The kitchen is missing most of its roof and one wall. The meat prep area is gone, as are the body parts that were on the table.

A few of the picnic-style tables from the dining area are in the kitchen now, one of them upside down and others scattered in pieces. It looks like Mother Nature reached a mighty hand down from the sky and twisted everything into a mangled heap.

More than a hundred people huddle into the shelter. Pax and Virginia stand on tall wooden boxes that are usually used for jumping over during training, Pax putting his hands out to quiet the talking.

"Our camp sustained a lot of damage from the hurricane," Virginia says. "Does anyone know of anyone who's missing?"

I scan the crowd, finding Olin and Billy. When my eyes land on Marcelle, she scowls back at me. I guess we're both disappointed to see that the other survived, then.

There are murmurs, but no one mentions any missing people.

"Good," Virginia continues. "We weren't expecting this storm, and there's a lot of cleanup to do. We're starting now. Pax will post a list with work assignments here in the dining area. We know there's flooding in the main-level housing, so upper-level people, you'll be getting some temporary roommates."

Our room is already tight, but at least it's just temporary.

"I see this as an opportunity," Virginia says. "You know what I'm always saying about training for field conditions. We have to be prepared for anything. Food will be very limited while we rebuild. As always, we prioritize the children and the pregnant women. The two of us get the same rations all of you do. I know it's tough, but so are we."

There's a low rumble of voices that seems to be split between frustration and agreement.

Pax takes over.

"We're not like anyone else," he says, surveying the

faces in the crowd. "We're Rising Tiders. We're stronger. We're more resilient. We can endure what others can't, and that's why we'll outlast all of them."

There's another rumble, this one almost all agreement.

"Now let's kick some ass, Rising Tide!" Pax raises a fist in the air. "Peace. Unity. Prosperity!"

The crowd responds with energy. "Peace, unity, prosperity!"

Their enthusiasm continues to blow my mind. I suppose there's unity here, but peace is questionable. And prosperity? Not so much.

I go along, though, my conversation with Rona still replaying in my head.

12

The proper function of man is to live, not to exist. I shall not waste my days in trying to prolong them. I shall use my time.

– Jack London

There's a desert plant called flower of stone that can survive the harshest of conditions. Known as a resurrection plant, **Selaginella lepidophylla** folds in on itself during dry periods, looking like a brown ball of dead leaves. It can remain like that for years without water, and then when it gets hydrated again, it opens up, turns green and thrives.

My time on the island so far has been like the flower of stone's dormancy. I've been conserving resources and waiting for better conditions to arrive.

And now they have. The hurricane created chaos, and

that's exactly what I needed. I hope to use the upheaval and uncertainty to gather information and start making a plan.

I thought about Rona's advice to keep my head down and go along. I can't, though. I suspect staying on this island means slowly giving up control of my mind. If my choices are to stay in Rising Tide and become a soldier-breeding four or die trying to escape, that's an easy decision.

Pax went to the children's camp with Virginia, and he left me a list of tasks to work on while he's gone. It's rare for me to be unsupervised, and I plan to make the most of it.

Before I tackle the list, I take the balled-up T-shirt I filled with greens to Billy in the kitchen.

What's left of it, anyway. The destroyed contents of the cooking area have already been removed, and a crew is working on tearing down what's left of the walls. They're rebuilding the kitchen as a log structure, thick tree trunks already being hauled into camp and stripped of their bark.

"Hey, Billy."

Standing at the end of a picnic table that was dragged out of the jungle, he nods to me. A massive cast-iron stew pot sits on the table in front of him. He's slicing up something that looks like a root to add to it.

"I found this right outside the training perimeter." I open the shirt and dump the wilted greens onto the table. "I tasted it myself this morning and I'm not sick."

He furrows his brow, skeptical. "How much of it did you eat?"

"About half a cup. It could still make me sick. But—"

"Get it out of here," he says briskly. "I know you mean well, but I can't risk it."

There's not even enough food for the pregnant women. The fish and game sheltered during the storm, and they haven't returned. Not that there's much left anyway. The dull ache in my stomach has been there for days and there's a hollowness in everyone's cheeks.

At least I tried.

"Okay." I pile the leaves back onto the shirt.

"You doin' okay?" he asks.

"Yeah, I'm okay. You?"

He lifts a shoulder in a shrug. "We're hanging in there."

Rona, Olin, and two other kitchen workers are peeling unripe coconuts and papayas on upside-down barrels nearby. I try to make eye contact with Rona so I can wave at her, but she keeps her gaze down.

Olin smiles at me, my heart clenching as I think about what Rona told me. I smile back, wishing I could get some time alone with him.

I have to work on the list Pax gave me, though. After dumping the leaves at the perimeter of camp for fear of getting caught eating them, I return the shirt to my room and go to what's left of the storage building.

It's just a pile of rubble now, a random, waterlogged boot lying on top of the mangled boards that used to be the building's walls. There's a folded paper stuck between two boards on what's left of the building's front left corner, where Pax told me I'd find it.

I pick up the wet paper and take it to the single-room office Pax and Virginia share. Once I'm alone, I carefully unfold the paper and scan the words on it.

It's a preprinted inventory list. There's an empty line next to each of the items, and there are two long rows of items. My heart pounds nervously as I read through it as quickly as possible.

The first things on the list are all foods: oats, beans, rice, barley, lard, salt, pepper, curry powder, honey, protein powder, and pasta. There's a zero written by the oats and a line drawn down all the other items to indicate they're also zeros.

Then there are medical supplies: amoxycillin, doxycycline, aspirin, morphine, ivermectin, iodine, alcohol, and various-sized bandages. There's a three by the ivermectin, but zeros everywhere else.

Other things on the list include different sizes of shirts, pants, underwear, bras, socks, blankets, and boots. There are numbers by all of those things, but not many.

I hold my breath as I quickly try to take in everything. There's too much to remember. But almost everything else has a zero by it anyway.

So there must have been a time when this camp was well supplied, but it isn't anymore. I fold the paper up the way it was before and set it on the desk on the right side of the room, where Pax told me to leave it.

His desk is otherwise mostly empty. There's a

sharpened pencil and a pile of papers. I flip through them, but it looks like it's just a handwritten list of people in the camp, with notes scrawled next to some of the names.

Eleven names on the list have lines drawn through them. Two of them are Robert Adler and Mateo Rodriguez. Another name also rings a bell. Jonathan Carpenter. The one who was attacked and killed by the jaguar.

The names crossed off must be people who have died since the list was made.

I turn toward the door, glancing at Virginia's desk. Only a blank pad of paper and a pencil sit on top, a small black safe sitting off to the side beneath the desk. Whatever's in that safe, I imagine it will answer some of my questions about this place. Getting caught touching it is probably a death sentence, though.

It's a risk I have to take. I rush over to the safe and pull on the handle, finding it locked.

My heart sinks. Of course it's locked.

I quickly leave the office, my pulse still racing. I'm disappointed about the safe, but I did discover a few other things that could be helpful.

My next task is to help a bunch of threes carry debris from the storm to the camp's dump about a mile away. I won't be able to do much digging for information, but I plan to keep my ears open for anything I might need to know.

———

The Rising Tide "spa" was gutted by the storm. Only the primitive toilets remain; the showers and the water delivery system will need to be completely rebuilt.

That leaves us with nature's bathtub—the ocean. Pax and I are walking toward the beach that evening to clean up, bars of soap in hand. Both of us are grimy and sweaty from a long day of sweating in the tropical heat.

"How long have you been here?" I ask him.

He shoots me a quick glance. "You mean on the island? Three years."

My bare feet squish through the mud; I can't take another minute of wet socks and boots, so I left them back in my room to dry. Or rather, get less wet. In this humidity, nothing truly dries.

"That's a long time."

He shrugs and grins. "It's a different life here. I know it's an adjustment, but..." He stops walking and turns to face me, crossing his arms as we both wait for the loud tittering of monkeys nearby to pass.

"That's one pissed-off primate," he cracks.

"Yeah, what was that?"

"Probably a mating thing." His eyes crinkle with a sheepish smile. "Nothing gets any animal going like mating does. Which is, uh...not the reason I stopped and makes me feel awkward even saying this."

I can't help liking him, despite everything. I don't trust him, but there's an underlying charm to Pax that's hard to resist.

His expression turns serious. "I got called into the circle. Tomorrow night."

The death-match circle? A pang of worry gnaws at my stomach. It's only because of Pax that I'm not still working in the kitchen, and now that I know what's included in the mystery meat stew, I can't go back there.

"By who? Can you say no?"

"A guy named Anders. A four. And I wouldn't say no even if I could." He drops his arms to his sides and clears his throat. "Look, I can't stop thinking about the way I treated you at the waterfall. I accused you of teasing me, and that—"

I wave a hand, dismissing his concern. "Forget it. It's fine."

He draws his brows down in an earnest look. "No, it's not. I like you, Briar. I really like you."

Heat floods me all at once. My nipples tighten and my core aches. I want to throw myself at Pax, literally. Just hurl my body at his chest and climb him.

Fuck him. Do it right here against a tree. It's what you both want.

My lips part with surprise. I'm having thoughts that aren't my own again, and why do I suddenly feel like an animal in heat?

"Something's wrong with me," I murmur.

Pax takes my palm and gently lays it on his chest over his heart. "There's nothing wrong with you, I promise. I feel it too. Only it's stronger in me because I've been here longer. I wanted to let you adjust and not come on too strong, but..." He puts his hands on my hips, squeezing lightly. "I've been with other women here, but it's never been like this."

You want him. Put your hand on his cock and show him how much you want him.

I close my eyes, pushing back against the thoughts. It's not really what I want.

His skin is so warm beneath my hand, though. I could run my fingers over his hard, muscled chest. And then lower. I could make his eyes wide and his cock hard. I could hold power over this powerful man—with just my body.

"Briar."

I open my eyes, and Pax tilts my chin up so our eyes are locked together.

"I don't want to go into the circle without knowing what it's like to kiss you. Just one kiss."

A kiss. Wetness pools between my thighs as I imagine sinking into him for a long, sensual kiss. His tongue sliding over mine. His mouth claiming mine.

It would feel so good. It's okay to let go, just for a little bit, and feel good.

He slides his hand up from my chin to my lower lip, slowly grazing the pad of his thumb over it.

"You're so beautiful," he whispers.

It feels good. Fuck him. Give in, give in, give in.

The words in my head play in time with the drumbeat that is my heart. I could let go of my control, for just a minute. Do what feels good instead of always fighting.

He slides his hand over my cheek and around to the back of my neck, cupping it as he lowers his mouth to mine. I melt against his chest, parting my lips.

Groaning, he moves his hand from my hip around to my ass, squeezing. His tongue brushes over mine, our bodies instinctively pressing together.

More. More. More. Give him more.

I pull away, the madness of having another voice in my head making my eyes wide with alarm.

"What's happening to me?"

A smile tilts the corners of his lips. "We're all animals here. Mating is instinctive."

I pinch my brows together, at war with myself. My body and part of my mind are ready to lie down in the mud for a primal, filthy fuck. But the rest of my mind— the part that's still me—is telling me to run.

As I shake my head, he puts a finger over my lips. "I got my kiss. That's enough." Arousal swims in his dark-brown eyes. "For now."

He drops his hands away, continuing to lead the way on the narrow jungle path. I just stand there for a few seconds, dazed. How can someone or something else be inside my head?

Maybe I'm losing my mind. Maybe this is what happened to the other women here who have babies and don't care that they don't get to be mothers to them.

I exhale hard, steeling myself and following Pax.

At least there will be other people in the ocean swimming and bathing. I don't trust myself alone with Pax. Nothing has ever made me feel more helpless than this loss of control over my own mind and body.

I have to get off this island. Soon.

13

It's a mistake to study a plant in isolation. A plant's relationships with pollinators, seed dispersers, root symbionts and even its enemy herbivores are all keys to a plant's true biological identity.

- Excerpt from a lecture given by Dr. Lucinda Hollis in her Introduction to Plant Biology course

The mood in camp the next day is charged with excitement. As some of us work in groups to remove debris and others carry in freshly felled logs for new buildings, every conversation I overhear is about the same thing: Pax and Anders.

They're all morbid versions of the watercooler talks people used to have before big sporting events. Who's gonna win? Who has the edge? How long will it last?

People are betting their meager belongings and work assignments on the outcome of the match. I keep my head down, focused only on learning to weave the reed baskets used to move produce and small game into camp.

"Pull it tighter." Keila, the three teaching me how to make the baskets, works circles around me, her fingers deftly working the wet reeds into sturdy baskets with arm loops for carrying.

The baskets were all blown away in the storm, and the sooner we get several done, the sooner we can get enough coconuts and papaya to feed everyone—hopefully. I haven't eaten since before the storm, though I don't feel as weak as I should from it.

"That's nice craftsmanship," a sweet female voice says from behind me. "For a dog."

My skin prickles with awareness as Marcelle sits down on the ground beside me, two of her friends sitting down on her other side.

"Pax's pet may be mangy and smelly, but she sure is a loyal little puppy, following him everywhere he goes. I bet you sit at his feet while he's taking a shit."

"Are you here to work?" Keila asks.

In answer, Marcelle reaches for the pile of supplies nearby, picking up some reeds.

"Do you suck him off while he's taking a shit?" Marcelle sneers at me.

I don't need to make waves. The clock is ticking on finding a way out of here before my mind completely turns on me. Arguing with Marcelle won't help me reach that goal, and it could make it harder for me.

She's a three, and I'm a one. There's a stupid amount of respect for the hierarchy here.

"I just really think baby killers are the most evil people there are," she says, her hands weaving reeds. "Wouldn't you guys rather take out a baby killer than literally anyone else?"

"I would," one of her friends immediately says.

I shouldn't say anything. But the beating is still so fresh in my mind. The terror I felt when they were holding me down and I thought I was going to die. And the worst part is, in a world where men use and abuse women without a care, it was other women who did that to me.

"Did you know it's my sixteenth day here?" I infuse enthusiasm into the question and smile at Marcelle.

"A better question is, do I give a shit?" She gives me a withering glare.

"Oh." I feign disappointment. "Sorry. I thought you'd care because on day thirty-one, I can call people into the circle."

Her jaw drops and her eyes dance with amusement. "I hope you do, bitch. I really do."

I give her a confident, full-faced grin. "Oh, you can count on it. Because I think the most evil people out there are women who try to kill other women without even knowing why they're doing it, especially when they're too chickenshit to try it without a bunch of their friends holding their victim down."

Keila chokes on a laugh beside me. Marcelle's face reddens with anger, her lips pressed into a thin line.

"I'm going to enjoy killing you," she says in a low voice. "It won't be fast. I'm going to make it as slow and painful as I possibly can."

"We'll see." I breeze over the words. "I've known people like you before, who talk big. But they're almost always all dick and no balls."

This time, it's not just Keira who snickers, but also one of Marcelle's friends. Marcelle shoots her a death glare and then gets up and walks away, her reeds still in hand.

Keira nudges me with her elbow. I look up and she gives me a nod of approval, whispering, "Good job."

I shouldn't have said anything. But there aren't many pleasures here on Blue Arrow Island, and I enjoyed that. A lot.

The circle is made up of rocks, each of them a little larger than a coconut, stacked side by side to form a circle that's about thirty feet in diameter.

That evening, as I walk into the clearing near the beach where the circle is, it's the outer ring around the rocks that grabs my attention.

It's dusk, so everything is cast in shadow. At first, I thought the larger ring was made from driftwood. But my breath catches in my throat when I see what it really is.

It's made of human bones. Hundreds of them. I make out femurs, skulls, partial rib cages and shoulder blades, all packed into a tight outer ring.

A bonfire roars in the center of the circle, its dancing flames casting flickering light over the human remains. These must be the bodies of everyone who has died here. I'm shocked by how many there are.

If the point of this place is to build an army, soldiers killing each other seems counterproductive.

Spectators are still coming in to line the circle, some of them carrying tall, primitive wooden torches. Pax's friend Luke stands on one side of me, another four I don't know on my other side.

I can see Olin, but it wouldn't be wise to talk to him in public. I've been hoping to get a minute alone with him since Rona told me what happened to him. But I have to be careful, because I don't want to get him in trouble.

"He's got this," Luke says confidently. "Don't worry."

Do I seem worried? It would make things harder for me if Pax isn't the one who walks away tonight, but I don't feel fretful over it. Mostly, I'm morbidly fascinated by this pointless ritual.

Some species of animals, like kangaroos, fight to the death over mates. But it's their innate biological drive to perpetuate their genes that makes them do that.

This is different. It almost seems like entertainment, the expressions of the onlookers lit with anticipation. Many people used mud to make war symbols on their faces, chests and arms, most of them just looking like lines. All the men are shirtless.

Everyone turns and I do, too. Virginia is approaching from the beach, a torch in hand. Pax is behind her, dark streaks painted across his cheeks and chest. Anders is next, the lines drawn on his face looking like dried blood.

The crowd around the circle parts as Virginia approaches the circle. She stands aside just outside the ring, Pax and Anders both stepping over the piled bones and rocks to enter.

Pax gazes at the spectators, his eyes stopping when they land on me. He holds me in a stare for a few seconds, my heart racing and my core aching.

How does he do that? A thrill passes through me at the thought of what he's about to do.

I close my eyes and look away, sending my mind somewhere else.

The types of plant tissue are dermal, vascular, ground, and meristematic. A plant cell structure has ten parts.

"Rising Tide, give your full attention to the circle." Virginia has backed away from the edge of the circle, now standing on top of a wooden box someone brought. "Anders has called Commander Thatcher into the circle. The rules must be followed. No one else may enter the circle, no weapons may enter the circle, and neither person may leave the circle until confirming the other is dead."

She's naturally authoritative, her tone commanding and her expression unflinching. The crowd is silent, everyone's full attention on Virginia.

"Anders, do you have anything to say before we begin?" she asks crisply.

He's average height, his lean body taut with muscle and his dark hair shaved. Tattoos and scars cover his chest and arms, one of the scars a jagged pink line running from the top of his nose down to his jaw.

"I'm here to say what most of us are thinking." Anders's voice booms, waves crashing and birds calling in the background. "This place needs new leadership."

There's a collective gasp. Pax stands about ten feet away from Anders, looking unfazed. He's using one hand to massage the other, working his thumb over his palm and knuckles.

"We're all starving!" Anders continues. "And they don't even care! We spend too much time training and not enough hunting and gathering. It's gonna catch up to all of us real fucking soon. There won't even be enough for the kids." His expression darkens and his voice rises. "I'm not selfish! I'm not just looking out for myself. I want better for every single one of you!" He points at the onlookers. "We're *people*. We have needs and wants. We deserve more than this!"

Virginia cuts in before he can continue. "Anders, we've heard you. Commander Thatcher, do you have anything to say?"

Pax lifts his shoulders in a half shrug, steel in his voice. "Anyone who thinks they can do better than me and Commander Marsden can meet me right here when I'm done with Anders. That's it."

Anders sneers and spits at the ground, advancing on Pax. "You arrogant prick."

He draws his arm back in a swing aimed at Pax's jaw. Pax deftly dodges it and lands a hard hook to Anders's stomach. Anders grunts and doubles over.

Pax is trying to look casual and Anders takes him by surprise, staying bent as he rams his shoulder into Pax's midsection, knocking Pax to his back.

Anders is straddling his stomach, raining blows on his face. Pax seems too stunned to do anything. A murmur runs through the crowd as everyone watches, transfixed.

Pax shoves his attacker off, springing up. Blood pours from his nose. His upper lip is also bleeding and swollen. He crouches in a defensive stance, taking Anders more seriously now.

"You'd be a fucking two if Virginia wasn't in love with you!" Anders yells, eliciting a shocked gasp from the crowd.

I don't dare turn to look at Virginia.

Pax lets out a deep, feral yell and he charges, landing a jab to Anders's left eye. Anders is fast on his feet, though. He dances around like a boxer, dodging blows and trying to land a few of his own.

Anders spits out a mouthful of blood and I see a flash of white in there. One of his teeth.

Pax uses his longer arms to his advantage, staying just far enough to be out of Anders's reach as he lands a mighty blow to his nose. Anders stumbles back, dazed.

"Come on, take him out," Luke mutters.

Pax charges. He sweeps his leg behind Anders's, knocking him to the ground. Then he kicks Anders in the side, his opponent howling and trying to curl up.

Unrelenting, Pax kicks him again and again. Anders cries out as he flips onto his stomach, trying to use his knees to get up.

Pax backs up and runs at him, jumping about seven feet in the air before he lands on Anders, his elbow aimed at Anders's back. It lands so hard that I hear the crunch of his back breaking.

It's over. Pax rolls Anders onto his stomach, Anders coughing up blood that pours from either side of his mouth.

He needs to quickly snap his neck and end the suffering. My heart hammers as seconds pass, Pax just standing there. I look around at the faces of the spectators, not seeing a hint of sympathy for the man dying in front of us.

Some people have a feral glint of satisfaction in their eyes. Others look almost impassive. I force myself not to let my horror show.

Where's the humanity? Whether they're afraid to admit it or not, Anders was right—we are all starving. And still, we train for eight hours a day. And to what end?

For Whitman. A maniacal tyrant who doesn't care if any of us live or die.

Tears pool in my eyes as Anders starts to choke on his own blood.

Pax dives on him, and just when I think he's finally

going to end this quickly, he instead buries his face in Anders's neck.

People in the crowd cheer and throw fists in the air. I furrow my brow, confused. Then my disgust is magnified as I realize what he's doing. Pax is biting Anders. Fucking biting him, like a vampire in a horror movie.

I want nothing more than to look away as blood spurts from Anders's carotid artery. Pax bounces to his feet and throws both fists in the air, spitting a hunk of Anders's bloody flesh to the ground.

My stomach twists with sickness. That mouth was on mine earlier. It makes me want to walk into the ocean and let the waves overtake me.

Pax's predatory gaze lands on me, the blood around his mouth making him look like a wild animal feasting on his prey. Which isn't actually that far off.

An invisible magnet pulls me toward him. I fight it. The slick heat between my legs is begging me to give in and go to him.

Fuck him, fuck him, fuck him. You want it more than anything. You want him deep inside you and nothing else matters.

He looks down at Anders, still dying a slow, painful death. Bending down, Pax grabs his ankle and quickly drags him over to the fire, rolling him into the flames.

Instinctively, I back up, averting my eyes from the inside of the circle. I have to get out of here. As soon as the first person leaves, I'm going to. I make it to the back of the crowd, where I stand right behind a couple of men. They should hide me from him.

The smell of burning flesh fills the air. As seconds turn into minutes, my pulse pounds, instinct telling me to run.

Run where, though? Back to my room? I'm not even safe there.

The men in front of me cheer. Someone hoots appreciatively, others quickly following.

I peek around the man in front of me and see Yelena, the four who was training the robot kid soldiers. She's topless, her nipples peaked as she slides her pants and underwear down. Her boots are already off.

Pax's pants are pooled at his ankles, his hand wrapped around his erection. His eyes aren't his own; they have an animalistic gleam.

I can't believe this is happening. As Anders's body burns, Pax picks Yelena up, the corded muscles of his arms standing out. Heat in her eyes as she reaches down to line his cock up. Then he slides her onto it, groaning as he works her up and down his length.

She throws her head back, moaning. On the other side of the circle, two women and another man are undressing, another woman already naked and on her knees.

Pax puts Yelena down, taking her waist to spin her around. She gets to her hands and knees and he drops to his knees, too. Then he thrusts himself back inside her, his hands locked on her waist.

Others are coming into the circle now, too. I only see threes and fours. Some of them don't even get their clothes all the way off before they start rutting.

Yelena straightens and leans back, taking Pax's bloody mouth in a passionate kiss. He returns it, still pounding himself into her.

I swallow hard, my mind spinning. I have to get out of here. I'm about to say screw it and start running when Olin catches my eye. He tips his chin slightly.

When he reaches me, he gestures for me to walk in front of him, heading toward the entrance to the circle. A few other people are starting to leave.

He's offering me cover. Letting me walk out unseen. I slip in front of him, forcing myself not to move too quickly. We need to look like people casually leaving now that the murder is over and the orgy is starting.

I hardly breathe in the two minutes it takes us to get out to the beach, the moaning and grunting getting louder now.

My heart rate slows. Olin is a steady presence beside me. There's so much I want to say to him, but I can't risk it with other people around.

"Thank you," I say softly when we walk back into camp.

He nods and goes the other direction. I walk to my room as fast as I can, sagging against the back of the door once it's closed and locked.

I get it now. Why the choices are this or execution. They're the same, really. It's either a quick death or a slow one. This beautiful, evil, tropical hell somehow makes people lose their free will.

It's the death of who you really are. And for the first

time since I got here, I'm not sure I have a chance of escaping it.

14

Plants are too commonly underestimated by science. They are not the passive nonstarters many think them to be. In fact, plants speak their own highly evolved language, a complex dialogue with their microbial partners, herbivore enemies and neighboring plants. This multispecies communication and coordination is a scientific wonder.

– Excerpt from a lecture given by Dr. Lucinda Hollis in her Introduction to Plant Biology course

My food bowl has a lump of algae and two thick, curled-up grubs in it. The sudden stab I feel in my stomach isn't hunger, but protest.

I consider passing it back to Billy, but only for a split second. Instead, I smile, though it's admittedly pretty weak.

"Thanks, Billy."

"Just pretend it's one of them fancy places from before the virus. They charged people hundreds of bucks for meals like this."

My smile widens. "True. You'll add this to my tab?"

"You know it."

Without tables to sit at, I walk around slowly instead. Before I have time to give it too much thought, I pop one of the grubs into my mouth, chewing it quickly. The gush of its foul-tasting guts in my mouth makes me cringe.

My time with Lochlan made me harder in some ways, and softer in others. Before the virus, I had to eat things I didn't want to. Once Whitman took over, he had crews raiding homes and taking everything. There was a lot of nonperishable food left, and very few people, but he hoarded it all.

I scavenged through trash for food sometimes. Ate bugs. And I wasn't as bothered by it as I am by the slippery, briny algae I swallow with my eyes closed.

When I was twelve, my dad took our family on a weeklong camping trip in northern Minnesota. He had weapons but told us he'd only use them in an emergency. We foraged for food, my mom showing us how to figure out what plants are safe to eat. We ate grasshoppers, grubs, even worms.

The meals served by Lochlan's chef were always lavish. Having more food on the table than the two of us could possibly eat was expected. I ate robotically, my skin crawling over being just a few feet from the man I hated with my entire being.

But I still ate. Tender steaks, fresh vegetables, fluffy dinner rolls, fruit tarts. I got used to that kind of food—came to expect it, even. And I hate myself a little for it.

Other people starved and dug through garbage, while I ate like royalty. Lochlan probably has a new wife locked up and guarded in his home, eating those meals and enduring her life.

I should've fought harder to escape. I tried sneaking out and bribing guards, and the punishment every time was severe. I would have taken the worst of beatings over Lochlan's sexual punishments, but it was never an option.

I hate it here, but it's still a better life than that was. For me, anyway. But not for the Rising Tide children. How many lives will they take one day, in the name of a power-hungry maniac who wants to rule every inch of the planet?

"Good morning."

I jump at the sound of Pax's voice beside me, the memory of his rabid expression and blood-smeared face in the circle making my spine straighten.

"Sorry." I force myself to smile. "I was off in my own world."

He grins, his face clean and freshly shaven. "I've got plans for us today, and they involve getting you wet."

An awkward laugh bubbles out of my mouth, my stomach dropping to the ground.

Fuck him, fuck him, fuck him. Stop fighting it. Do it now. Get on your knees for him.

No, I roar the word in my own head, pushing away the unwanted thoughts. They're getting stronger every day.

His smile slides into a smirk. "From the look on your face, I'm thinking I may have an adorably nervous virgin on my hands. The things I'm going to teach you..." His gaze roves up and down my body. "But I was talking about sparring on a log over a spring to work on balance. Everyone falls into the water a few dozen times when they start."

My jaw unclenches with relief. Now I only have to worry about making myself slip and fall a few times during training today. It's something I've practiced often, but I have to keep holding back so I don't get promoted to two.

He runs a hand over his face and looks away, chuckling. "It's hard for me to focus on anything else when you blush like that."

I groan inwardly. I just escaped this line of conversation and I don't want to go back to it.

"Did you eat already?" I ask. "I'm ready to get started if you are."

"Yeah, I ate my grilled crickets and algae earlier."

He nods at a group of fours walking past in a line, a thick tree trunk resting on their right shoulders.

They don't even look winded, and that trunk should be too heavy for them to carry. I lie awake at night worrying about getting called into the circle by a four. In less than two weeks, I'll probably end up there with Marcelle, and that's bad enough.

I'm hoping raw rage will get me through that. But the fours are another level entirely. There are two men and two pregnant women shouldering that tree trunk. They're starving, their arms and legs too thin, but they look well rested and strong.

Way too strong. I don't let myself think too much about Whitman having an army of fours and robot kids at his disposal. Regular people would be defenseless against them.

"Commander Marsden wants us to stop by the office before we start training," Pax says. "Is your canteen filled?"

I pat the stainless jug resting against my hip. "Yeah, I'm good."

Cleanup crews worked almost around the clock for two days, and storm cleanup is done. Rebuilding is underway, slowed by the muddiness of camp. Everyone's boots are caked in it, and it's common to slip and fall. None of us has had truly clean clothes since before the storm. Laundry isn't a priority. Pax takes me to the ocean a couple of times a day to cool down and rinse off, and we go in fully clothed to get the worst of the mud off our clothes.

The heat here is thick and oppressive, but it's dryness I crave the most. My inner thighs are so chafed they're close to bleeding. If I could choose between a real meal and a night of sleep in a dry bed with dry clothes on, I'd have to think hard about it.

We pass Rona, who's standing with some twos, and I nod in greeting. Her expression hardens and she looks away. I wonder what that's about.

"So was last night kind of overwhelming for you?" Pax asks me.

I want to laugh, because that's not the word I'd use to describe it. But I have to play it smart, so I nod.

"When I worked in an office and swiped left and right on women, I never would have believed I'd be doing something like that a few years later. The circle is important here, though. When the weaker Tider has been eliminated, we come together to celebrate being stronger."

Eliminated. Celebrate. I see how Pax rose to a leadership position here. He's great at putting a polished spin on things like murder and public group sex.

"There you are."

I'm saved from responding by Virginia, who's walking toward us, her lips set in a tense, thin line.

"I wasn't hiding or anything," Pax quips. "We were on our way to the office."

"This couldn't wait. It's about Briar."

A knot quickly forms in my stomach. Does she know I tried to look in the safe?

"What about her?" Pax asks, a note of defensiveness in his voice.

"I'm told she isn't happy here." Virginia crosses her arms and locks eyes with me, her gaze unnerving.

I smile weakly. "I mean, is anyone here super happy? I'm doing my best to fit in."

Virginia flicks a look at Pax. "Did you take her to see the children?"

He looks away, guilt etched on his face. "I had to do something there, and since she's shadowing me—"

"A decision you made without consulting me." Anger flashes in her eyes. "That's not how we do things here and you're well aware. She's telling other ones we treat the children unfairly."

Fuck. Rona. This explains the look on her face when I passed her. I'm going to have to talk my way out of this.

"I didn't say that exactly."

"I know what you said." She sneers, barely contained rage making her shake slightly. "You want to escape the island and you don't approve of how we do things here."

Alarm hits me hard and fast. Why did I think I could trust Rona? Why did I think I could trust *anyone*?

"Look, it's a big adjustment." I turn to Pax. "You know I'm working hard to find my place here."

"Don't look at him." Virginia points at me. "He's thinking with his dick, as usual."

"Virginia." Pax's pissed-off tone is also scolding. "This isn't the time or place."

She takes a deep breath and pinches the bridge of her nose, seeming to be trying to get ahold of herself.

"I apologize, Commander Thatcher." She gives me a withering glare. "You're going into isolation."

Pax scoffs. "Come on, that's excessive."

She puts up a palm. "It's not up for discussion."

"She was just asking questions! Lots of ones do that."

"You didn't take the report, I did. This was more than

asking questions. She's going into isolation. She's being called into the circle on her thirty-first day here, and if she survives it—"

"That's not fair and you know it," Pax says bitterly. "She's already at a disadvantage against Marcelle. Now you want to make her go without food or training for two weeks? It's a death sentence."

"This is the Rising Tide way. No one said it was easy."

A muscle in Pax's jaw tics. "Don't do this."

"It's already done. We're taking her there now."

He shakes his head, his voice low and menacing. "This isn't about her and you know it."

"Commander Thatcher, my decision is final."

My heart races as they stare at each other for a few long seconds, the tension palpable. Pax's glare is murderous. Finally, he breaks the stare-off, shrugging.

"Fine. Guess I'm going too, since she's shadowing me."

Virginia rolls her eyes. "Get your shit together, Commander. That's not an option."

"How is she supposed to train?"

"That's her problem."

They're going to put me in a cell. I can't be locked up again. The few weeks I spent in a cell were terrifying. I was helpless, trapped alone with only my fears and regrets.

"Can I leave instead?" I blurt, my heart pounding so hard I'm a little dizzy.

"Leave the camp?" Pax shakes his head, aggravated.

"No. I told you, you'll be dead within a day. You can't survive this place alone."

I'm not doing so great here either, but I don't say that.

"You can't leave," Virginia echoes. "You know too much."

Panic cracks my chest open, flooding me with anxiety. They won't let me go. I'll be kept prisoner here until I'm a mindless breeding and fighting machine.

That, or Marcelle will take me out in the circle, and the Rising Tiders will have an orgy next to my dead body. Both options are horrific.

"Let's go." Virginia grabs my upper arm to lead me away, and I pull out of her grasp.

She narrows her eyes at me, looking ready to pounce.

"I'm going. Don't touch me."

It was a reflex; being touched is almost always bad, and my subconscious knows it.

Pax and Virginia stand on either side of me, both tense, but for different reasons.

I have to stay calm. This is a big setback, but I'm still alive. What I do and say from here may determine whether I stay that way.

We're near the center of the camp when we stop by a worn raft. At least, I always assumed it was a raft. The side-by-side pieces of bamboo are lashed together with a thin rope made of woven vines that are brown and brittle-looking with age.

Virginia bends and picks up one end of it, flipping it

up and over, and I realize it's a hinged door. I inhale sharply when I realize where she's sending me.

It's a deep hole in the ground. It's about eight feet in diameter and fifteen feet deep, lined with smooth metal.

"No," I whisper, fighting the burn in my eyes. "Don't put me in there."

I give Pax an imploring look as Virginia goes over to a building to take a long ladder, also made of lashed-together bamboo, from an outer wall. He moves in front of me and meets my eyes, putting his hands on my shoulders.

"I'll check on you a lot. I promise. I'll make sure you're okay."

"Commander." Virginia snaps. "Help me with this."

She has no trouble with the ladder's weight, but she needs help maneuvering the long ladder into the hole. Pax sighs and takes one end.

I'm going to die in a dark hole in the ground. Alone. Starving. I'd rather throw myself from a cliff and be done with it.

"Don't do this," I beg. "Please don't do this."

I loathe the emotional crack in my voice, but I can't help it. I'm desperate. I'll be completely defenseless down there, a broken-down mess when I'm let out just in time to fight Marcelle.

Kill her. Kill Virginia. She's jealous of you. You aren't weak, so push her in the hole and let her die in there.

I close my eyes, a distressed cry coming from my throat. I'm losing my mind, having thoughts that aren't really mine, and that hole will be the final nail in my coffin.

"You can do this, Briar." Pax's stern voice brings me back to reality. "Be strong."

My dad used to say that to me. He said it's most important to be strong when you're feeling your weakest. That's now.

"Go," Virginia says, impatient.

Shaking, I refuse to look at either of them as I position the ladder so it won't tip, pushing the bottom of it to the opposite side of the hole from the top. The rickety ladder groans as I put my weight on it.

I think I might lose control of my bladder. Falling into such a deep hole could kill me or leave me too injured to get back out. My urge to attack Virginia is getting stronger.

Don't be weak. Kill her. You know how to strike a fatal hit she won't even see coming. It's her or you.

"No." I grit my teeth and fight the pull.

"Briar." Pax sighs, exasperated.

"I'm going," I grind out.

This isn't the time to lash out. I have to be smart. As hard as it will be to willingly put myself in a deep hole in the ground, where I'll be completely helpless, I have to. There are no other choices, with Virginia and Pax both just a few feet away.

I won't give Virginia the satisfaction of seeing how scared I really am. I won't beg.

Silently, I climb down the ladder, clinging to the rungs.

It's dark, the smells of stagnant water and dead vegetation getting stronger as I descend. When I reach the bottom, I step from the ladder into a few inches of standing water.

As soon as I release my hold on the ladder, it's pulled out of my reach, my lifeline gone.

Leaning my back against the smooth wall, I cross my arms and look down, using all my will to press my lips together as hard as I can. My heart hammers against my rib cage, frenzied.

I'm Ben Hollis's daughter. I might die down here, but no matter what they do to me, I won't break.

15

Water leaks from the bamboo door to my earthen prison, a stream hitting my hair and rolling down my shoulder. It's raining. I can feel the same rain the Rising Tiders can, which connects me to the real world.

I'm not completely alone. I hate that I have to keep reassuring myself of that. It's ironic that I like to keep people at arm's length, but I also fear being alone. Physically alone, that is. Inside, I've been alone for a long time, because it's better that way. Safer.

"Roses. I haven't done roses yet." I return to one of

the mental exercises I've been doing for the three days I've been stuck down here. "Kingdom: plantae. Phylum: magnoliophyte. Class: magnoliopsida. Order: rosales."

Light from above silences me. I look up hopefully.

"Hey, are you okay?"

It's Pax. The first day I spent down here, I was a ball of fury who wanted to tell both him and Virginia to go fuck themselves. But sitting alone in darkness for so long has mellowed me considerably.

"I'm okay." I stand, droplets of water dripping from my clothes. "Can I get some water?"

"I'm sending the buckets down. I'm sorry it took me so long to get back."

At least he's here. He comes once or twice a day, bringing me a bucket of water to drink and a bucket to pee in.

I'm exhausted. I only sleep for short stretches down here. The water at the bottom of the hole has finally receded into the ground, so I'm not sitting in water anymore. I'm still soaking wet, though, the humidity not allowing any part of me to get completely dry.

Marcelle occupies my thoughts. I run through how I can attack her in the circle. If my mind stays intact, I can beat her. That's a big *if*, though. The longer I'm down here, the more thoughts of killing Virginia and fucking Pax flood my head. I don't want power, and I don't want to be on this island, but I've started fantasizing about killing her and taking over as Pax's co-commander.

I'm losing control of my mind. It's getting worse, and as someone who believes in science, I have to follow the evidence. I'm eventually going to lose the battle I'm having with myself. What started as an occasional urge or thought has now become a powerful mental refrain that's getting harder and harder to fight.

I'd rather be dead than lead this camp on its twisted mission. And dead or alive, I'm beaten. Whitman and Lochlan will have won. That's the hardest pill to swallow —knowing I'll never get to make them answer to my blade for what they've done.

The buckets arrive and I untie them from the rope Pax used to lower them. Then I tie on the two buckets I already had, one of which is empty and one which is a third full of pee.

It's a really ungraceful situation, trying to pee in a bucket when you're in a muddy hole and it's dark. I can smell myself, and I'd give just about anything for a toothbrush and some toothpaste.

"You hanging in there?" Pax asks.

Like I have a choice. I could be breaking down mentally and he'd walk away and go about his day. Seeing who Pax really is when I need his help makes me loathe whatever power is making me want to screw him in every possible position.

"Doing fantastic," I deadpan, looking up at him. "Some guys opened the cover and pissed all over me last night; that was fun."

He shakes his head. "That shouldn't happen. I'll look into it."

"It's been three days. I need to get out of here if I'm

going to have a chance in the circle. Can't you please let me out of here?"

I despise this woman who's begging a man for help. It's against everything I am. But this place is a different kind of hell, and I'd say anything to get out. I'm losing myself, and the process may be over by the time I'm allowed to climb up the ladder. I don't want my final days of my mind still being partly mine to be spent in a dank, dark prison.

If it comes to ending my life to avoid becoming a robot soldier breeder, I want to let nature do it. I've spent a lot of time thinking about it down here. I'll eat some poisonous berries and curl up beneath a tree or free-fall from a tall cliff and let my last sensation be the wind caressing my face as I plunge to a quick end.

"I can't." Pax's grimace is apologetic.

I scream inside, wanting to tell him he's an impotent little bitch who isn't a co-commander at all. He's under Virginia's thumb. She makes the decisions and somehow makes him feel like he has power when he actually has none.

Silent tears slide down my cheeks. I sit down and pull my knees to my chest, resting my forehead on my knees and wrapping my arms around my legs.

Where was I? I was classifying the rose, and I stopped on...family. I scoff inwardly, longing for even ten seconds with my own family. Just to look at them one more time. To draw strength from my dad's hand on my shoulder or my mom's contagious laugh.

It's just me, though. I'm alone. The hole darkens as

Pax flips the door closed, confirming my solitude with a light thud.

So, roses. Family: rosaceae. Genus: Rosa. Species: various.

———

A few hours later, I can feel my racing pulse in my temples as I listen to the commotion above me. People started yelling about five minutes ago, but I can't make out what they're saying.

The voices are frenzied, sounding rushed. If there's another hurricane coming and they leave me down here, I won't survive. Even with the extra endurance this fucked-up island gives me, I won't be able to tread water for days.

I don't want to drown. My instincts are screaming at me to claw my way out of this hole. If the walls were dirt, I'd already have dug enough footholds to get out. The smooth metal walls taunt me, reminding me I can't outthink monsters who imprison people for questioning them.

"The boat's coming!"

My spine straightens as I make out a woman's words. She has to mean a fresh batch of prisoners for Rising Tide and the Dust Walkers to fight over.

Panic claws its way up my throat. If Pax dies on the beach, I'm dead, too. I'll die of thirst, which is a horrible way to go.

I force myself to breathe deeply, quelling the terror

that's threatening to take hold of me. Throwing up, which I'm close to doing, would dehydrate me at a time I can't afford to be depleted.

Do something, Briar. Don't just sit here. Do something.

"Let me out!" I yell, standing up. "I can help you!"

This might be my only chance to get out of here before Marcelle calls me into the circle. I cup my hands around my mouth to amplify my voice.

"I can fight! Let me out, and I'll fight with you!"

I listen for the span of a few frenzied heartbeats. Nothing. The voices have gone quiet.

Putting my palms on the metal lining my prison, I groan. I want to pound my fists against the wall and rage, but my dad's training won't allow me to. A hand injury will only make things worse.

"You cocksucking, piece-of-shit island! Just give me a fucking chance!"

A crack of light enters the hole. I tilt my chin up and the brightness grows. The man standing there looking down at me isn't Pax this time.

It's Olin. My jaw drops, tears springing to my eyes.

Then he walks away.

"No! No, please! Come back!" I cry out in frustration. "Help me, Olin! Please!"

Something appears at the top of the hole, but it's not Olin. I squint, dropping to my knees when I realize what it is.

The ladder. He's lowering the ladder into the hole for me. I want to sob with gratitude, but there's no time for that. He must be using the opportunity of everyone leaving camp for the boat to free me.

I spring back up and reach toward the ladder, relief flooding my entire body when I wrap my hands around the sides of it to guide it to the ground.

It's barely secured in the mud when I scramble onto it, the mud on my boots making my foot slip on the second rung. I force myself to slow down, keeping both hands and both feet on the unsteady ladder.

When I reach the top and feel the ground beneath my feet, Olin is smiling at me, the chaos of his coarse, bright-red hair a beautiful sight. I can tell from the flare of his eyes that I look and smell like a neglected farm animal, but I don't care. I throw my arms around him in a hug.

"I owe you my life, Olin." It's hard to get the words past the lump of emotion in my throat. "Thank you just isn't enough."

He pulls back, his brown eyes brimming with seriousness when I meet them. Bending, he picks up a reed-woven bag from the ground and passes it to me. Then he reaches into his pocket and passes me something that looks like a folded-up leaf.

When I unfold it, I see that he's used something to scratch words onto the leaf's surface.

RUN FAR. HIDE. THEY WILL COME FOR YOU.

I flick my gaze up to him. "You mean Virginia and Pax?"

He nods and rushes to get the ladder from the hole and hang it back up on the building wall. As soon as it's secure, he closes the cover to my underground cell.

Then he returns and picks up the last things on the ground, two spears. He passes me one and keeps one for himself, pointing at the jungle as he backs away.

He wants me to go.

"You're going to the beach? To fight for the people on the boat?"

He nods, his lips set in a solemn line. When he points to the jungle again, it's more emphatic, his brows lowered.

"Come with me. If they catch you, you'll be in huge trouble."

He shakes his head, points at the jungle again, spins away and breaks into a run. I only watch him for a second before I shoulder the pack and turn in the opposite direction, heading straight into the jungle.

16

Effective knife handling starts with proper grip techniques. In this week's classes, you'll learn forward grip, reverse grip, and transitional holds to maximize control and prevent disarmament.

- Excerpt from a police training manual written by Ben Hollis

A branch catches on my cheek, adding another burning scratch. The droplets of sweat falling from my chin to my chest are tinged red, my shirt a disgusting swirl of blood, mud and piss.

This was the smarter move, though. Instead of taking one of the paths out of camp, I went right into the dense, untraveled jungle. The thick vegetation slows me down and the shrill chattering of monkeys makes it hard to hear anything, but the paths would have been a death sentence.

If they come after me, they'll divide up their fours and send them each down one of the three established routes out of camp. With their speed and the possibility that they'll be coming after me soon, I couldn't risk it.

With luck, no one will realize I'm gone until tomorrow. I'm going to put as much distance between me and them as I can before then.

My feet are throbbing, and it's not from running. I dread the moment I have time to take off the soaking wet socks and shoes I've had on for days now. The skin on my feet feels like it's splitting open with every step I take, and I know I have some kind of infection. It could be bad, and I have no way of treating it, and no way of even letting my feet get dry.

This feels like the beginning of the end. Or maybe the dark hole I just got out of was the true beginning. I'm completely alone out here, the howl of wolves closer than it's ever been. Oh, and I'm also starving, bleeding and exhausted. The odds are against me.

I have a chance now, though. It's time to grit my teeth and bear the pain.

Pressure builds diamonds, Dad always said. And this race I'm running for my life is the highest pressure I've ever faced.

A low growl sounds to my left, and I glance over. A lion—a fucking *lion*—has its gaze trained on me. She's not huge, but she could easily take me if she wanted to.

Trees and brush stand between us, so she can't

pounce. I leap over a log on the ground and turn my face toward the lion again. She's following, her head lowered.

I've been on the move for a few hours, and the drop in temperature tells me it's getting close to sunset. I don't want to be in this jungle after dark.

Though the lion may take care of me before that. The laugh that pours out of me is high-pitched and frenzied. I wish my sister could see me right now. What would she say?

She'd probably tell me to move my ass and ask why I smell like a filthy gas station urinal.

The piss scent is not doing me any favors. It's attracting predators like the lion.

I slow to a stop, turning to check on the animal that's stalking me. She can't reach me because the jungle is so dense. Still, I don't like that she's this close to me.

Locking my eyes onto hers, I raise my arms in the air and yell out a quick, single note. I point the spear toward her and fake a lunge.

She steps back. I take a few steps toward her, holding the spear at waist level with both hands.

When she turns to leave, my shoulders sink with relief. My feet plead with me to take off my wet socks and shoes, but I force myself to ignore the pain.

I need water. I look in the bag Olin gave me, tears pooling in my eyes as I sift through its contents.

A full canteen. A blanket. A dry shirt, pants, socks, and underwear. A bar of soap. And three precious mangoes. These things are worth more to me than all the money in the world right now.

I blink, my tears falling and burning the cuts on my face from stray branches. I'm not alone out here. Olin might not be with me physically, but he's my friend. He risked his life to give me this chance, and I'm going to repay him by surviving. If he ever needs help, I want to be there to give it.

As much as I want to find a way out of this jungle and stop for the night to rest, I can't. I have to keep going.

I drink about half the water in the canteen and tear into one of the mangoes with my teeth, devouring it. The sugar in the fruit gives me an instant lift.

As soon as I find a safe hiding place far from Rising Tide, I'll dry my feet and let them heal. For now, I need them to keep me moving, despite the pain.

———

Warm air whispers against my cheek. I try to ignore it, but a rhythmic, gentle huffing makes my eyes snap open.

My throat is like sandpaper. I swallow against the ache, easing myself back a few inches so I can see what the huge black thing is that's practically on top of me.

Yellow eyes lock onto mine. I blink, making out a snout and pointy ears.

Shit. It's a wolf. But I've never seen a wolf like this one. It's solid black, with bright-yellow eyes, and it's huge—I'd guess two hundred and fifty pounds.

If I stand up, this creature's back would be at the level of my waist. It could tear a hole in me, I'd die from, in a matter of minutes, if not seconds. Fortunately, it's just sniffing me, seeming more curious than anything.

My piss-covered clothes are like a flashing beacon. My plan was to get rid of them before I stopped. I remember curling up on my side on the flat surface of a rock, hidden by trees, but I didn't mean to fall asleep. That was when the sky was just starting to shift from black to gray in preparation for the sunrise.

From the sun's position in the sky, I can tell it's late morning. I must have slept for around six hours. That means I need to move fast.

Slowly, I shift into a sitting position, my back and hip aching. The throbbing pain in my feet makes me wince. I can't use precious time looking at them now.

The wolf, a male, backs up a step as I move. He cocks his head to the side, watching as I get on one knee and then stand, holding in a cry. I take a few deep breaths, adjusting to bearing weight on my sore feet.

I made it all the way to the edge of the island. I could hear the roar of the ocean nearby when I stopped. Directions have never been my strong suit, but I think I'm close to the volcano. It's rockier here. Before stopping, I passed through several clearings and a stream.

There was a small waterfall not too far back, and that's where I'm heading first. I ease off the grouping of rocks, because jumping isn't an option with my feet in such bad shape.

After peeing and finishing the last sip of water in the

canteen, I get my supplies. I'm about ten yards away from the rocks when I realize the wolf is following me.

When I look at him, he stops. He doesn't seem to want to get too close, and he's not acting aggressively, so I ignore him.

It's nice to be out of the jungle. At its heart, it's a cacophony of trills, screeches and roars. I'd have trouble hearing the Rising Tiders approaching over all that noise. I'm planning to explore this part of the island today and find a hiding place. If it's secluded enough, I'll rest and dry my feet out there.

The waterfall is small, maybe twelve feet of water rushing into a small pool at its base. It's a perfect bathing spot. I gingerly remove my boots and socks, my swollen feet screaming at me with every motion.

My feet are white and wrinkled, patches of raw redness between my toes, weeping clear fluid. I fight tears from the burning sensation of standing on a rock in my bare feet.

Quickly, I strip off my clothes and get out my bar of soap and blanket. I don't have time to think about pain or hunger. Every second matters.

I lather the soap into suds and wash my grimy hair first. It feels like heaven, massaging my scalp and scrubbing out all the grossness. The waterfall is the closest I've had to a real shower in a long time.

As I wash away the filth from my body, I get a renewed sense of hope. Everything felt hopeless when I was in my underground cell, but it wasn't. I can't give up, no matter what.

Washing my feet is agonizing, but I swallow the pain and get it done as fast as I can. Using the blanket, I pat them dry, then sit in the sun for a few minutes.

Thanks to the humidity, I'm already sweating. But I no longer smell like anything but the jasmine-scented soap, which is a welcome change.

The wolf is watching me from about twenty feet away, sitting patiently like he has nowhere else to be. From the looks of him, he has no trouble finding prey to keep him full. Hopefully that means he won't turn on me if he's hungry.

Once my feet are dry, I dress in the clean clothes Olin packed, the dry socks worth more to me than a pot of gold. It hurts to slide my feet into the new boots, but they're dry, which I desperately need.

I fill my canteen and then use my hands to dig a hole deep enough to bury my dirty clothes and boots, not wanting to leave any signs I was here. My hands and arms are blackened with dirt by the time I've finished, so I wash them in the pool, pack my bag, and set back out.

If I wasn't worried about the Rising Tiders hunting me down, this would be peaceful. It's so muggy I could cut the air with a knife, but the backdrop of crashing waves is nice. Much better than the Rising Tide camp, where I'd be listening to soldiers chanting about peace, order, and prosperity while running ten-plus miles an hour to prepare themselves to kill innocent people for a greedy dictator.

The rocky terrain slows me down some, every step making my feet cry out. Though I want to walk all the way to the beach, I stay close enough to the jungle that I can take cover if I need to.

The sun's position tells me it's close to afternoon. I wander past a marshy field, careful not to get my feet wet. My heart leaps with excitement when I see a papaya tree, a cluster of ripening fruits just out of my reach.

With a stick, I'm able to knock several still-green fruits to the ground. I bite into one immediately, my stomach rumbling its approval.

I don't even care that it's not ripe. It's food, and I desperately need it. It's hard to stop myself from devouring a dozen of them, but I don't want to get sick from eating too much. My stomach isn't used to food, so I need to go slow.

I'm loading more papayas into my bag for later when a bolt of awareness zings down my spine. I freeze and listen.

Nothing. But something is telling me to run. It's like the urges I felt to kill Virginia and screw Pax; it's just there, taking over all my other senses, and it's strong.

Bag in one hand and spear in the other, I race for the edge of the jungle. I'm almost there when I hear a man's voice.

"Clear that section."

My pulse pounds, terror racing through my veins. I hold my breath. If I run too fast, I could tip someone off that I'm here. Instead, I creep in the opposite direction of the voice, my gaze on the ground so I can watch where I step.

I figured they'd look for me. Olin said they would.

But I didn't think Pax and Virginia would send people so far. Not when the Tiders are starving and rebuilding their camp.

I'm dead if they catch me. There's no way Virginia will just throw me back in that hole.

My best option is to take cover. If they're combing the jungle in sections, they'll find me if I'm not hidden.

There's a big rock formation about a hundred feet away. Every step I take toward it, I worry I'm going to get a spear in my back.

Finally, I reach the massive rocks, which have moss and small vegetation growing in their cracks. At its tallest point, the formation is about twenty feet tall, only a few cracks of sunlight breaking through the canopy of trees to illuminate it.

The sense of alarm hits me again, this time like a punch in the stomach.

Go.

I run my hand over the rocks, my stomach dropping with panic. There's no hiding place here.

Racing to the other side, I find a thick wall of vines, bright-orange blooms giving off a heavy, sweet scent.

Maybe I can hide behind them. It's the best option I have right now. I slide behind the curtain of twining green branches and leaves at one side, being gentle so I don't destroy my cover.

I keep walking, my palm out in search of solid rock. But after a few seconds, a damp, earthy smell fills my nostrils and I realize I'm entering a cave.

The path turns into a decline, cooler air washing over

my skin. I breathe a sigh of relief as I continue down, small rocks crunching beneath my boots.

Trickling water sounds from deeper inside the cave. It's completely dark in here, but somehow I can sense the space around me and I know I'm not about to walk into anything.

I descend about a hundred feet and then the ground levels out again. A single crack of light filters into the space, allowing me to see dim outlines.

Squinting, I creep closer to a flat rock at about my waist level. My breath catches in my throat when I see what's on it. There's a sheathed knife, the craftsmanship on the leather case like nothing I've seen on this island. Beside the knife, there's a big bowl turned upside down and...I run my fingers over the surface of the other item, which is so dark it blends into the rock. It's a flint for starting fires.

I swipe the knife and turn, looking over one shoulder and then the other. My heart hammers, fear gripping me by the throat. Is someone about to lunge at me? I wouldn't even see them coming.

Close your eyes. Use your other senses.

I release a slow breath and look down, shuttering my eyelids. It's not as scary as I thought it would be. There's the faint trickle of water. The musty smell of bat dung floats through the air and welcome cool air takes the sting from the scratches on my face.

I don't know how I'm aware of this, but somehow, I know that if there was someone else in here with me, I'd be able to feel them moving. The cave is still, and with every second that passes, my heartbeat slows.

Unsnapping the knife sheath, I pull the weapon from its case. When I've moved the bowl and flint to the ground, I sit on the smooth, cold rock and put the knife beside me.

Just knowing I have a weapon makes me breathe easier. I reach down and untie my boots, pressing my lips into a thin line. It's going to hurt, but I have to do it.

Gingerly, I slide each boot off, then make quick work of the socks. Tiny needles stab my feet. They're dry, though. And I should be safe here.

Unless the cave's occupant returns. I wrap my hand around the knife's hilt, the solid feel of it grounding me. I need to stay awake and alert, but now that the adrenaline has worn off, fatigue is calling out to me.

I can't give in. I can rest here, but I can't sleep.

17

Training during this course will progress from static drills to dynamic scenario work. Safety protocols will be strictly enforced throughout all practice sessions.

- Excerpt from a police training manual written by Ben Hollis

Lochlan is climbing over me. He reeks of sweat and alcohol and his large belly crushes the air from my lungs. I turn my head to the side, steeling myself to endure what's about to happen.

I gasp in a breath as I wake up, startled. The knife in my hand is poised to strike, and it takes me a second to remember where I am.

The cave. I must have fallen asleep. Since it's always dark in here, I can't get a sense of how long I slept. I'm groggy and thirsty, my throat uncomfortably dry.

For the first time since getting to the island, I didn't wake up drenched in sweat. This cave is going to make a nice shelter for me as I heal and figure out my next move.

I'll have to venture out to find food, but I'm hoping to get my water from in here. I ease my feet back into my socks and shoes, the pain not better or worse, and stand up.

I'm lightheaded, probably from lack of food. I'll eat a papaya after I get some water.

Keeping the knife in my right hand, I tiptoe deeper into the cave, toward the murmur of water.

I don't have to go far. In the darkness, I can clearly hear the trickle, but can't see it. I use my hands to search, my palm landing on a smooth rock wall with water gently flowing down. I bend to inspect the ground with my fingers, hoping to find a pool of cool water.

Instead, it's rolling along the edge of the cave floor. I follow the path for about fifty feet, where the water seems to seep into another wall.

Damn. No drinkable water source in here. That means I have to go out. I've got enough problems with my feet; I can't let myself get dehydrated, too.

I leave everything but the knife, spear and canteen in the cave. As the path takes me upward, pinpricks of light filter into the cave through tiny holes in the curtain of vines. I can smell the sweet, heavy scent of the tropical flowers even from twenty feet away.

Careful to ease out at the same end I entered through and not disturb the cave's covering, I blink against bright light when I emerge. The tree cover above is too thick for me to tell what time of day it is.

I consider waiting for the cover of night, but I'm just too thirsty. The small waterfall I bathed in yesterday isn't too far, and I know exactly how to get back there.

A snake as thick as my forearm slithers across the ground in front of me as I walk, unconcerned with my presence. It's black and red with an arrow-shaped head —probably venomous. I'm not tangling with venomous snakes, even though my mouth waters at the thought of grilled meat.

I'll have other chances at small game. I say another silent thank you to the universe for sending me this knife. In the light, I can see that it's very well made and sharp.

This weapon will give me a chance against anything I encounter. I can't help wondering who left it in the cave, and when.

It's mine now. I can live without everything I left in the cave if I have to, but the knife, spear and canteen will come with me everywhere.

When I exit the jungle, the sun's position tells me it's around late morning. I must've slept through the night.

Sweat is already running down my spine and gathering under my arms. I'd love to take my clothes off and sit in the cool water for a while, but I can't.

Kneeling beside the pool of crystal clear water, I bend and splash my face. It's a mess of scrapes, but none of them seem very deep.

Then I fill my canteen, drink it all, and fill it again.

This time, I drink half of it and then dunk it below the water's surface to get it full.

After screwing on the cap, I put the strap over my head so the canteen rests on my hip, pick up my knife and spear, and start back toward the cave.

I feel better. The rest helped. My head is clear enough now that I can think through my options and decide what to do after I let my feet heal.

"Any last words, Briar?"

My feet freeze, the voice setting off alarm bells in my head.

It's too late for that, though. When I turn around, Virginia is standing around ten feet away, her expression a cross between furious and smug. She's gripping a long metal spear, the corded muscles on her lean arms glistening with sweat.

"Just leave me alone." It's an effort to keep my voice level, a knot of panic tightening in my stomach. "You said I know too much, but there's no one to tell. I just want to be alone."

"I can't allow that."

She takes a step forward and I match it with a step back. The corners of her lips turn up slightly like she's enjoying my fear.

This bitch. She's got a major God complex, not unlike Soren Whitman.

"How do you live with yourself?" My voice drips with the contempt I feel for her. "You're a woman making other women into breeding machines for Whitman."

She scoffs. "And who are you? Just an arrogant loner

no one will miss when I leave your body for the animals to tear apart."

I'm my father's daughter. He was a smart, measured man, but he was also a proud one. And he taught me to never let an opponent see my fear.

Master it, he'd say. *Swallow your fear whole and use it.*

I walk closer to Virginia, my fingers aching from my tight grip on the knife. "You're nothing but a bully. And I've never been afraid of bullies."

That hits. A shadow crosses her face and she storms toward me, snarling.

I track her movements, evading her spear as she tries to put it in my stomach, and then my chest.

Instinct makes me toss my own spear aside. The knife is a better weapon for me, and I can use it with either hand if needed.

"You're not special." Virginia tries to circle me and I back away, crouching. "I've seen a thousand women like you, and I'll see a thousand more after you."

Kill her. Do it now. Strike her down.

I ignore the unbidden urges, remembering my training. Dad would tell me to play on her emotions. Make her sloppy.

"Will Pax want all thousand of them instead of you, too?"

A dark cloud of rage passes over her face. She reaches for my shirt with her free hand and I move back.

"Where the hell did you get that knife?"

I smile. "Prefer your opponents weak and unarmed, Virginia?"

She lunges at me and I evade, but she turns at the last second and changes course, sinking the tip of her spear into my thigh.

Pain blossoms in my left leg as I bring my right foot up, landing a hard kick to her chest to get her away from me.

She flies back ten feet and lands on her back. I shouldn't have been able to kick her that hard. Whatever is making the Tiders so strong and fast, it's in me, too. And right now, I need it.

Blood rolls down my thigh, Virginia's spear still in her hand. It hurts like hell, but I have to channel all my concentration on this fight. I can't outrun her. And even if I manage to escape somehow, she'll come after me again.

She's on her feet again, coming at me. "Maybe I'll just keep poking holes in you until you bleed out. I've got all day."

"I bet you do. You don't care that your people are starving. I've heard you make sure you get enough food, so fuck them, right?"

"Who said that?" Rage pours off her.

I use the lapse in her focus, racing at her and making it look like I'm going to try to stab my knife into her stomach. At the last possible second, I lower myself to the ground and swipe my blade over the side of one of her calves. Her spear makes a whooshing sound as it barely misses my head.

Leaping back to my feet in an instant, I can feel my strength surging. I'm not just stronger, though. Every reflex is sharper. My mind has tunneled down to a singular focus: killing Virginia.

Destroy her. Make her pay. She deserves to die painfully.

I stay in a crouching position, anticipating her next move. She rushes at me as fast and hard as she can, which I didn't see coming.

Shit. We're both on the ground, and she knocked my knife from my hand. I start to scramble up, but she shoves me back down and climbs on top of me, punching me in the face.

She hits me again, and again, and again. Terror and pain race through every nerve ending.

All she has to do is grab my knife and I'm dead. I raise a forearm to block her next punch, planting my feet in the ground.

She's strong, but wiry. I'm able to drive my hips up and force her off me.

I can't see. One eye is swollen almost shut and the other one has blood in it.

Run.

That knife is the difference between life and death for me. I can't run.

Furiously, I swipe my fingers over the eye with blood in it, trying to clear it. Virginia could be standing over me right now, knife poised to plunge into my back.

I'm not ready. I want to keep fighting. A cry of anguish rips from my throat as I crawl, my hands scrabbling for my weapon.

Please, please, please. Not here. Not like this. Not all alone. Not her.

I silently beg my family for help. I don't want to go out like this, and if I could just have a shred of my mom's clever problem-solving, my father's steel will, or my sister's fierce bravery, maybe it would be enough.

Help me. I need you.

The ground trembles beneath me. Vibrations shudder into my body, the rumble growing quickly.

Is it an earthquake? I grab the bottom of my shirt and frantically wipe my eye with it, blinking hard and begging the universe to let me see.

When I look up, I have partial vision back. There's a crack of sight through my swollen eye and everything is a little blurry through the other one.

There's movement off to the side, the ground still thundering beneath me.

It's Virginia. She's coming at me with the knife, a murderous gleam of victory shining in her eyes.

I scramble backward, my feet and hands unable to match the pace of her lunge. Instinct makes me curl into a ball so I can take the blow in my back.

Wind whooshes over me, every second feeling like a minute as I wait for the burn of the blow that will be fatal no matter where it lands.

But it doesn't come. I look up, breath trapped in my throat, and my jaw hits the ground.

Thick green vines are winding themselves around Virginia's body, the coils tight, perfect circles. They're at her chest, and she's scowling as she hacks away at them with the knife.

What the hell is happening?

Run.

The same unwelcome intruder in my consciousness that tells me I want to fuck Pax and murder Virginia is now trying to save me. I'd love to run, but I have to get that knife.

I get to my feet and stagger toward her, my pants soaked with blood from my leg wound.

This is madness. I'm too weak to use the knife on her now, but I *have to get it*. I need it and I also need her not to have it.

I can see well enough. I can do this.

When I get close, Virginia scowls and swings the knife at me. The vines are still twining around her, new ones taking over when she cuts one down. They're trailing out of the jungle, more slithering out like snakes.

It's not possible. They can't grow that quickly. They can't attack people. But I'm seeing it with my own eyes. Those vines saved my life.

She slices through another one, one arm raised in the air with the knife and the other one swallowed up by a coiling shoot.

I drop to one knee. I'm about to lose consciousness. I've lost too much blood. But I have to make sure Virginia dies, too.

For Olin. For the soldier kids who deserved so much better.

There's a hum as something slices through the air. As my hands drop to the ground, Virginia's scream pierces the air.

I glance up. The knife is gone. Her palm is gushing blood, an arrow lodged in it.

Someone's running, their footsteps sounding behind me. I want to be strong enough to see who it is, but I can hardly stay awake.

I fought hard. I tried.

"Briar, get up." The voice is clipped, worried. "We have to go *now*. You have to help me."

"The...knife."

"I got it." She yells the next part. "Get up! We have to go or we're both dead!"

An arm wraps around my waist, the woman groaning as she strains to get me upright.

Both of us. Dead. I don't want to be responsible for killing someone else. I put one foot in front of the other.

"Arm around my neck," she snaps. "Right now."

I do it, leaning against her. A curtain of smooth black hair fills the crack of vision I have left.

She picks up her pace and I do my best to match her steps, my feet dragging.

"Come on. You can do this, Briar."

I turn my face, catching part of her profile. "Amira?"

"Yeah. I've got you. Just move your feet for me, okay? You have to move your feet."

She's alive. How? I want to ask her, but it's all I can do to breathe and keep from passing out.

"I'm dying," I mumble. "Leave...me."

"No. Just move your feet. That's all I need you to do. We don't have that far to go."

I want to tell her the Tiders will find us. And then they'll kill her, too.

I breathe deeply, my feet aching but landing solidly on the ground now. Everything hurts, but I'm alive. I was so sure I was about to die—surer than I've ever been—and somehow, I'm still breathing.

A wave of nausea hits. I swallow it, forcing myself to keep moving.

We exit the jungle and Amira stops next to a cluster of overgrown bushes. She eases me into a sitting position on the ground, then bends so we're at eye level.

"Listen to me, Briar. This is really important. I'm going to get help, but you can't come any farther with me now."

I groan in a weak protest.

"If you follow me, you'll get sick. Remember how we were unconscious on the boat when they brought us here? They implanted something in us. It makes you faster and stronger. My camp has a device that makes anyone with that implant in them sicker and sicker as they get closer, and if they keep coming, they'll die. I need you to hide in these bushes and be quiet until I get back."

I just look at her, too stunned to even nod. There's something implanted in me?

She pulls a stainless water bottle from a pack on her back and pushes it into my hands.

"Get in there and drink water and *stay awake*." She looks at the pool of blood on the ground beneath my leg. "Fuck. Get in there now and I'll cover this up. Stay awake,

Briar, do you hear me? Do not go to sleep. I'll be back as soon as I can."

I crawl into the bushes, prickly branches scraping my already raw cheeks and arms. When I curl up, there's something hard poking into my back.

I don't care, though. This is as good a place to die as any. At least Virginia won't have the satisfaction of seeing the last of my life drain out of me.

PART TWO

18

We train differently than recreational shooters. When you're in a high-stress situation, your body enters fight-or-flight mode. Fine motor skills slip and your heart rate spikes. You may even experience auditory exclusion and not even hear your own gunshots.

- Excerpt from a transcript of a police academy course taught by Ben Hollis

"Briar, can you hear me?"

Droplets of water splash onto my face. I gasp and try to sit up, but everything hurts—even breathing. Best not to move, then.

"I'm here." A hand slides around mine. "It's Amira. You have to hold on."

Hold on. To what? There's nothing but pain and exhaustion, and I can't take any more.

"Nova, get me a bridge." The first voice that spoke to me is back, and it belongs to a female.

"Don't, Nova." A man's deep voice. "She's beyond saving, and she's not coming to our camp."

There's a scoff, and the first woman's voice returns. "Who put you in charge of medical decisions, Marcus?"

"You make medical decisions for our people, but she's a Tider. We don't save those assholes."

"That's not fair," Amira says. "How is it her fault they grabbed her instead of you guys?"

"This is my call," Marcus's tone is decisive. "We're not bringing a Tider into our camp."

"Nova, the bridge, please," the first woman says.

"I said no, Ellison," Marcus's voice is low and ominous.

After a few seconds, he speaks again. "Nova, don't give her that fucking bridge. Don't you—damn it!"

I feel a tiny prick in my arm. I think I just got a shot.

"She's lost a lot of blood. I don't know if this will be enough to get her back, but I have to try."

"Thank you, Ellison," Amira says.

"You can treat her here, but she's not coming into our camp."

I manage to open my eyes, and Marcus's face is the first one that comes into focus. His brows are drawn down and he's holding a bow, an arrow nocked. He's looking in every direction, prepared to shoot if he needs to.

Whatever was in that shot is powerful. Pure energy is

flowing through my body. I glance at the spot where I felt the poke and then at the woman kneeling next to me.

She has long, light-brown hair with a few silver pieces woven in. Her brown eyes are crinkled at the corners in an expression that's both worrying and reassuring at the same time.

"Briar, I'm Ellison. I gave you a bridge, which is a shot we use to get people from the field into our camp after serious injuries. You've lost a lot of blood. Do you know where you are?"

I glance around, half expecting to see Virginia running at us with a spear. "Blue Arrow Island."

"That's right."

"We're not doing this," Marcus says hotly. "It's too risky."

Ellison ignores him, her gaze still focused on me. "We don't have much time. When you were brought here on the boat, you were injected with a very small device. The device contains a compound called blue aromium. A flower that grows on this island is the base of that compound, and the flower is bright blue. That's why this is called Blue Arrow Island. Soren Whitman has a team of scientists who created it."

My heart races as I look at Amira. I hardly know her, but she saved my life when she didn't have to, so I trust her.

"It's true," she says softly.

Marcus speaks in a low tone, still checking in every direction and ready to fire an arrow if needed. "They've got a bunch of fours out here looking for her, you guys. We can't stay here."

Concern floods Ellison's eyes. "You have a decision to make, Briar, and you have to make it quickly. Your injuries are serious, and the aromium will help you heal faster. We can leave you here, or you can come back to our camp, where I can treat you and you'll be safe from Virginia. But I'll have to deactivate your implant before we go there. Our camp is protected against aromium and you'd die if you tried to come in with the implant activated."

Marcus hums his disapproval, shaking his head. They all look at me for a long second, waiting. Amira, Marcus, Ellison and Nova. I recognize Nova from the waterfall. A sheen of sweat shines on her dark, defined muscles.

"I can't go back there," I murmur.

"What were those vines that wrapped around Virginia?" Amira asks. "Are they alive?"

Marcus's scowl turns even darker. "We can't do this right now. If those Tiders find us, we're dead."

I shoot him a wary look as I sit up, cringing from the aches all over my body. "You're the ones who kill them."

Nova speaks for the first time. "We need your decision."

Her voice is deep and warm, like dark honey. It's soothing and authoritative at the same time.

"Come with us," Amira urges. "They lied to you. You can't survive out here alone."

I survey my leg and my shoulders sink. Virginia

buried her spear in my thigh, leaving a gaping hole. My pants are covered in blood.

There's no way I can clean and treat this wound myself. I don't think I could even walk right now. It didn't seem like things could get any worse than they were in the bottom of that hole, but this...yeah, it's worse.

"How far is it?" I ask. "I don't know if I can walk."

"Make your choice." Marcus's bark is laced with anger.

There is no choice. Virginia isn't putting me back in that hole if she catches me. She's going to kill me. She almost did—it was only those thick vines shooting out of the jungle that stopped her.

"I'll go with you." I put a palm on the ground, leaning on it when a wave of dizziness hits.

Marcus exhales heavily through his nose, scowling at me. He takes a black device from a holster strapped around his shoulder and chest. It's not much bigger than a deck of cards.

He shoots a glare at Nova. "When shit goes south, remember I tried to stop this."

"Deactivating aromium is never a bad thing," she says smoothly.

"Not that." His eyes lock onto hers. "Bringing her into our camp."

He looks at me, disgust and frustration swirling in his moss-green eyes. "Get on your left side."

Ellison glares at him. "She'll get dirt in her wound. Pick her up."

Marcus passes the device to her, inclining his chin at Nova. "Get her right side."

Marcus and Nova put their arms around me and lift. I'm as limp as a rag doll, too weak to help at all. My leg wound hurts like hell, but I press my lips together, refusing to let it show.

"This will just take a second," Ellison says. "It won't hurt, but you're going to feel weaker once the aromium is inactive."

She puts the device over my right hip and after a couple of seconds, I hear a beep.

"Done," she says.

Weaker? My life force pours out of me in an invisible flood. My head throbs and my leg feels like it's on actual fire. What hurt before hurts a hundred times more now. I can barely keep my eyes open.

I droop, letting out a pained moan, and Marcus puts his free arm behind my knees to scoop me up.

"This is a mistake." His voice is clipped.

My head is cradled against his broad, hard shoulder. Even though he's helping me, I want to argue with him. To not be reliant on someone who would rather leave me here to die.

But I'm powerless. I give up the fight to stay awake and let myself sink into unconsciousness.

———

"You don't have to watch her, you know. She's hardly a threat in her condition."

"You don't know that."

I recognize the voices. Ellison and Marcus. My eyelids are heavy, but I force them open.

I'm in a dimly lit room. Lying on a bed. There are machines behind me and cabinets along the walls, medical supplies lined neatly on the countertops. It feels like a hospital room.

Ellison is standing at the foot of the bed, a clipboard in hand, and Marcus is sitting on a chair along the wall, his elbows on his knees and something in his hands I can't make out in the darkness of the room.

"She's awake." Marcus straightens his spine.

His shoulders and thighs are so wide that he doesn't look comfortable in the metal chair.

"Hey, Briar." Ellison walks over to my bedside, smiling softly. "How are you feeling?"

I swallow against the dryness in my throat, trying to sit up. "Where are we?"

It comes out as a croak.

"At our camp."

I furrow my brow, confused. "It's not hot."

Her smile widens. "Not here, but most of the camp is. Do you want some water?"

I nod. "Thanks."

She goes over to the counter to pour water from a pitcher. Marcus stands and comes over to the bed, his scowl milder than before but still in place.

"Where did you get this?" He holds up the knife I found in the cave.

My lips part with surprise. I'm fully awake now. "That's mine. Give it back."

"No, it's not." A muscle in his clean-shaven jaw tics. "Tell me where you got it."

Ellison comes over with a cup of water. The cup is carved from wood, the swirling grains and smooth surface making it look like a work of art.

"Not now, Marcus," she says, passing me the cup. "She needs to rest."

"Give me my knife." I mean for my voice to be strong and sure, but it comes out wobbly and emotional.

When I picked up that knife, I felt safer for the first time since I set foot in this tropical hell. It's a real weapon. The only thing I have to protect myself.

"Did you see someone?" Marcus demands, his voice rising with anger. "Did someone give this to you?"

I slide myself into a sitting position, the pain in my leg much better than it was before. "I don't owe you anything. You took something from me, and I want it back."

He lifts a shoulder in a shrug. "You left it on the ground. Amira picked it up and brought it back. And it's very fucking important that you tell me where you got this."

"Why?"

His expression clouds with wariness. I use the silence to drink my water, trying to look unbothered.

But the truth is I'm in a vulnerable position. I'm defenseless, and once again, at the mercy of a man. And this man doesn't want me here.

"Can I see Amira?" I ask Ellison.

She says, "Sure," at the same time Marcus says, "No."

Ellison arches her brows. "Why not?"

His gaze remains focused on me as he answers. "Not until after she's been questioned."

My pulse thrums with worry, the pounding reaching my ears. "Am I a prisoner?"

"No," Ellison says.

"You're not a prisoner, but the safety of our people comes first and I don't know a damn thing about you," Marcus says. "You'll be under guard until you've been questioned."

"We're not them, Marcus," Ellison murmurs.

He turns to look at her. "I let you guys bring her here. But now we're doing this my way."

"She's on painkillers and she still needs rest."

He nods. "She can rest as long as she needs to. But when she's ready, I'm questioning her."

"I want my knife back." Fatigue is tugging at my eyelids, so I lie down again.

He ignores me, sitting back down with the knife still in his hands. Clearly, he thinks someone gave me that knife, and I doubt I'll be able to convince him otherwise.

But I'm not even going to try until I'm off this medication and able to think straight.

19

This place is a true natural wonder. The colors are more vibrant than words can describe. It's remote, isolated and virtually untouched by man. For my purposes, it's perfect.

- Excerpt from the journal of Dr. Randall McClain

It takes another three days for me to be able to stay on my feet for more than a few minutes at a time. I've been walking around my small room, drinking a lot of water, eating all the food Ellison brings me, and sleeping a lot.

I'm more confused than ever because not only do the Dust Walkers have medicine and electricity, but the food here is incredible. I get three meals a day. Breakfast is usually oatmeal with fruit and nuts and a piece of buttered toast. One morning, I even got scrambled eggs. I've had spicy fish and vegetable stew, grain porridge, and fresh fruit for lunch, and grilled meat and fish with vegetables, grains, and bread on the side for dinner.

How do they have so much food when the people on the other side of the island are starving? How do they have eggs, oatmeal, and butter that tastes freshly churned?

More than once, I've questioned Ellison about whether we really are on the island. For all I know, they could have knocked me out and taken me somewhere else. The pieces just don't fit together.

"Ready?" Ellison comes into my room, smiling warmly.

This morning, she took me to a bathroom a few doors down from my room, where I took a cool shower. They have composting toilets, so I don't think there's a sewage system, but they seem to have plumbing. There was tile on the shower floor and real soap and shampoo in the shower. I even got to shave my legs with a razor. I brushed my teeth with an actual toothbrush and toothpaste for a solid ten minutes.

I'm dressed in the clean clothes Ellison left for me. The lightweight gray pants and light blue T-shirt are much more comfortable than my Rising Tide clothes were. She also left me a clean bra, underwear and socks, and a pair of lightweight hiking boots in my size.

This is the cleanest and most comfortable I've been in a long time. Marcus seems like a real dick, but Ellison has been nothing but great to me. I'm still not sure about this place, but I'm hoping to see Amira soon and find out what she knows.

But first, I have to get through questioning by Marcus. Ellison leads me from my room, a man following us. The hallway we're walking down has a concrete floor, and there are simple light fixtures on the walls illuminating our path. The cool air reminds me of being inside a cave.

We reach the door at the end of the hallway and Ellison turns, sighing heavily.

"I'm sorry, but you have to be blindfolded until we get to where we're going."

My eyes bulge with alarm. "Blindfolded?"

She purses her lips, her expression apologetic. "I promise I'll be with you the entire time you're blindfolded. This is just for the walk to get there."

My heart pumps faster as the man behind us moves closer, a black cloth in his hands.

"This is Vance," Ellison says. "Vance, this is Briar."

Vance has shaggy strawberry-blond hair and a beard. His build is average and he's about six feet tall. Based on the blank look he's giving me, he'd rather be elsewhere.

Vance nods at me. "You ready?"

"I don't want to be blindfolded." I give Ellison a pleading look. "Can't I just close my eyes?"

She takes my hand. "I won't let go until the blindfold comes off. I promise."

I still don't like it, but I nod anyway. Ellison patiently fed me when I was too weak to feed myself. She's cleaned and checked my leg wound every day and made sure I have enough medication to keep the pain at bay. I trust that she doesn't want to hurt me.

Vance puts the blindfold around my eyes, tying it securely behind my head. Ellison squeezes my hand and I hear the door in front of us being opened.

"It's not very far," she says. "We'll be there in less than five minutes."

A sense of dread coils in my belly as I walk beside Ellison. My breathing is shallow and I have to force myself to swallow, my mouth like sandpaper. I'm at the mercy of the Dust Walkers. It's terrifying to be completely in the dark, not knowing whether someone is coming at me with a weapon.

"You're okay," Ellison says in a soothing voice. "We're walking through a room, there's nothing to be afraid of."

Then why am I blindfolded? There's something here they don't want me to see. And on this island, where the laws of science don't always apply, that's a terrible feeling.

"We're about to go through another door," Ellison says.

She waits, and there's a buzzing sound that makes me jump.

"That's the sound of the door being unlocked for us," she murmurs.

I hear her turn the handle and push it open, and then she leads me through. Vance follows, and the door closes behind him.

We're walking down another hallway. I'm not sure how I know but it feels like a hallway. It's completely quiet, not a sound in the space other than the hum of a light fixture.

"How close are we?" I clutch Ellison's hand, my own getting sweaty.

"Very close. Hang in there."

About ten seconds later, she stops and pounds on a door. It sounds like solid metal. This place feels like a secure military base.

"Come in," a deep voice calls from inside.

Ellison opens the door and leads me through the doorway. I hear the door close, and then the blindfold is pulled away from my eyes.

"You okay?" she asks me with a smile.

I nod, releasing her hand.

We're in a room much like the one I recovered in. It has concrete walls and no windows. There are two light fixtures in the ceiling, but the room still isn't brightly lit.

Filing cabinets line one wall of the room. There's a desk against another wall, a chair pushed into it. The space is dominated by a long wooden conference table that could easily seat twenty.

Across from me, on one long side of the table, Marcus and Nova are sitting. My knife is sitting on the table in front of Marcus, in its leather sheath. There's a pitcher of water and several wooden cups off to the side.

Marcus gestures at the chairs in front of me. "Sit."

I look at Ellison, wary. She gives me a reassuring smile.

"I won't be staying. I'll see you soon, though."

I nod and slide into a metal chair, taking a deep breath. As soon as the door closes behind Ellison, I fight the urge to jump up and run after her.

"So you're feeling better," Marcus says.

It's a statement, not a question.

He's offensively attractive. I'm not sure I've ever seen a more perfect combination of masculine features. It's off-putting. An asshole like him doesn't deserve to look that good.

Today he's wearing a plain gray T-shirt, his biceps and chest straining against the fabric. His dark hair is perfectly tousled, a few pieces hanging over his forehead.

His chiseled jaw and high cheekbones would be classically handsome, but his serious scowl and the small scar on one side of his neck balance him out in a rugged way.

At around six-four, he once again doesn't really fit in the chair he's sitting in. He has an imposing presence, but I won't let my intimidation show.

"Did you have a question?" I ask sharply.

The corners of Nova's lips quirk in a smile. She's also striking, her dark skin flawless and her hair stubble short. There are precise lines cut into it down to her scalp, the pattern swirling around her ears. She's wearing a simple silver hoop in her septum and her dark lashes are long and thick.

"Tell us about your life before the virus," Nova says.

I don't know what that has to do with anything. It feels like she wants to get a baseline of how I behave when I'm telling the truth. Part of me wants to lie, but I don't. Too many lies get hard to keep track of.

"I was a college student."

"And how did you survive the virus?"

"I was an intern for a research project on an island off the coast of Washington state. We were isolated and when we heard about the virus, we were able to shelter in place."

"What were you studying?"

"The effects of ocean acidification on shellfish." I shift in my seat, looking between the two of them. "What does this have to do with anything?"

"What was the crime that got you sent here?" Marcus asks.

His expression is stony. This guy is a brick wall, physically and emotionally.

I hold up my hands, palms facing me, and let the ink answer for me.

"Can I get a verbal answer?"

I narrow my eyes. "I drank wild ginger tea so I wouldn't get pregnant. And I got caught."

He studies me for a few silent seconds. "That's it? I've never heard of anyone getting sent here for that."

"Guess I'm special."

No fucking way am I telling him about Lochlan. I'm going to say as little as possible.

"What was your job assignment at Rising Tide?" Nova asks.

"Kitchen."

Marcus's nostrils flare slightly; it's so subtle that I almost miss it.

"What kinds of food did you prepare?" Nova rests her elbows on the table, steepling her fingers.

It's such a stretch to call what we served at Rising

Tide food. "At first, there was fruit. Some smoked fish. But after the hurricane..." I shake my head. "Bugs? Algae?"

Something holds me back from mentioning that the Tiders are eating their own people.

"Tell us everything you saw and experienced in the camp," Nova says.

I shake my head. "Look, I've been cooperative. I appreciate what you guys have done for me, but I have questions, too."

"You'll have an opportunity to ask questions."

"Yeah, which you guys may or may not answer." I cross my arms. "You want answers from me, you give me some answers first."

Marcus's expression remains impassive. "What do you want to know?"

"Where are we? Are we still on the island?"

"Yes, you're at our camp."

"How do you have electricity and plumbing?"

He considers before answering. "The camp was built with them."

I glare at him. "You know what I mean. Were you guys brought here on a boat as prisoners, too? How do you know about aromium?"

He rubs his jaw, his mossy-green eyes intent on me as he picks up the knife. "Where did you get this?"

The information he wants from me is the only power I have. I'm not giving it up for nothing.

"If I can have it back—and keep it—I'll tell you."

He lowers his brows. "No one here is allowed to have weapons except our security team."

I shrug and sit back in my seat. "Put me on your security team."

There's a shadow of a smirk on his face. "Not a chance."

I focus my gaze on Nova, hoping she'll be more reasonable. "I got here at the same time as Amira. I've been at Rising Tide the entire time until I escaped and Virginia tried to kill me. What is it that you guys suspect me of?"

Nova's expression gives nothing away. "People who have nothing to hide hide nothing. So where did you get the knife?"

I decide to try diplomacy.

"Put yourselves in my shoes. I don't trust anyone on this island. Every day since I got here, I've been fighting just to stay alive."

"You wouldn't be alive without our help," Nova reminds me.

I glance away. That's a fair point. "I'm willing to trade my information for your information. I think that's fair, don't you?"

Marcus exhales through his nose. "Tell us where you got the knife, and if I think you're being honest, I'll answer one of your questions."

I laugh, genuinely amused. "Um, no? You only have one question for me and I have about a thousand for you."

He shakes his head. "What makes you think I only have one question for you?"

"Why do you guys have so much food when Rising Tide is starving?"

His gaze sharpens on me as he holds the knife up. "An answer for an answer."

My heart races as I keep my eyes locked on his. "You first."

He looks up at the ceiling, the muscle tic in his jaw giving away his anger. "I've got better things to do than play games with you. Do you want to stay in our camp?"

The past few days have been the only time I felt reasonably safe on this island. I have lots of questions, but my instincts are telling me this is the best place to be right now.

I nod.

"If you want to stay here, there are rules," Marcus says. "And you'll have a guard for as long as I think you need one."

I'm trying to keep my temper locked down, but I slip.

"Rule number one—you're in control." Bitterness seeps from my voice. "And I have to do everything you say. Does that about cover it?"

It's been years since I got to go where I wanted. Do what I wanted. Fuck who I wanted. Be who I wanted. And I've had it with men asserting their control over me.

Marcus clears his throat. "You have to earn your place here. When Ellison clears you, you'll get a job. You have to respect everyone in this camp, and I have the same expectation from all of them. No one gets special treatment here. And don't lie to me. Those are the rules." He waits a couple of seconds. "Do you still want to stay?"

I look down at the flowing grain of wood on the table, which shifts from amber to dark brown and then back again. Though I don't have a choice, I'm pretending like I do.

"What are the work assignments?"

He turns to Nova, who responds by counting them off on her fingers.

"Sewing, security, construction, the farm, the garden, fishing, laundry, childcare, cooking...those are the main ones. You get to choose, and you can rotate quarterly if you want to."

"Can I have my knife back? Please?"

Marcus's brows shoot into his hairline. He bites out an unamused laugh. "Again, it's not yours. And no."

I sigh heavily. "I have so many questions."

"Yeah, same." He glares at me.

"Why do they inject people with that stuff? Aromium?"

Marcus stares at me like a stubborn ass. Finally, Nova answers. "It enhances the senses and physical abilities. You get faster, stronger, need less sleep and food. Over time, you develop sharper hearing and vision. And it heightens emotions."

I breathe out, leaning my head on my hand. "So that's what was happening to me."

Marcus cuts his glower in her direction.

"We tell everyone that when they get here," she says, turning her focus back on me. "It happens to everyone.

But it's different depending on your DNA. Everyone gets more volatile, violent and sexually aggressive, because that's what it's designed to do, but some people tolerate it better than others."

A knot of anger tightens in my chest. Whitman is playing games with people's lives. That's nothing new, but changing who we are? It's a brutal abuse of power.

"She just gave you an honest answer," Marcus says. "So tell us where you got the knife."

I hesitate. They did save my life. And they have taken care of me. I'll give him a partial answer.

"I found it."

Something shifts in his eyes. "When?"

"Recently."

He leans forward in his seat. "Where?"

I shake my head. "Not yet. You can try another question, though."

Sighing heavily, he runs a hand through his hair. It lands in the same perfect disarray. "Did anyone at Rising Tide say anything about their supply levels?"

That one, I'll answer. "There are no supplies. I saw the supply room. The shelves were empty. There were a bunch of barrels and I didn't see if anything was inside them. But there's no food. Almost no medicine. And people are getting upset about it."

A glint of satisfaction passes over Marcus's expression, so quick I almost miss it. Why is he pleased about the Tiders suffering? Not all of them are like Virginia.

There's a knock at the door.

"Come in," Marcus says.

Ellison opens the door and comes inside. She puts a hand on my shoulder.

"I don't want her to overdo it. Can you pick it back up another time?"

It's a small gesture, her touching my shoulder. But it makes tears well in my eyes. It's been so long since anyone cared about me. Olin does. He risked a lot to help me. But this small gesture from Ellison—openly supporting me in front of her own people—isn't small to me.

Marcus nods, dropping his brows with disappointment.

"I thought Amira could show her around camp," Ellison says. "And Vance will be with them, of course."

"That's fine," Marcus says.

I stand and turn, relieved to be leaving this room.

"Briar?" Marcus says.

It's the first time I've heard him say my name, and it sends a warm wave of awareness prickling over my skin. The tug in my gut, drawing me toward him, tells me the aromium isn't all the way out of my system. That's the only explanation for feeling a pull toward such a moody prick.

I glance at him over my shoulder.

"We can't risk you taking information back to Virginia. If you try to leave, we'll shoot to kill. I want to make sure you know that."

He says it nonchalantly, like he's talking about what he's having for dinner. Just another power-hungry man reminding a woman she's under his thumb.

"Aw. So you're an honorable asshole."

I don't wait for him to respond. It must kill him inside because I know men like him. They always want to have the last word.

Marcus is just a more polished version of Virginia. He wields control and leads by intimidating. The lesser of two evils is still evil.

20

We lost four of our thirty test subjects to the initial injection. We must move forward, though. All progress comes with a price.

- Excerpt from the journal of Dr. Randall McClain

We're underground.

The concrete floor of the long, wide hallway we're in has a gradual incline. The air is slowly getting thicker and warmer. That's why it was cooler and there weren't any windows.

"Feeling okay?" Ellison asks, glancing at me over her shoulder.

"Yeah, I'm good."

"If you need to rest at any point in the next few days, speak up."

I wonder if Virginia made it back to Rising Tide. Probably, she's a cockroach. More than once since I got here, I've had nightmares about her killing me. Slowly. Quickly. With a knife. With her hands.

I was moments from death that day in the jungle, and vines saved my life. Plants. They shot out of the jungle in a spectacle that looked like killer computer-generated special effects in a pre-virus movie. But it was real. It was like when that massive snake came flying out of the jungle like a missile by the waterfall that day. It might have even been airborne—it was moving so fast it was just a blur.

Impossible. But I saw it with my own eyes both times. Of all the weird shit I've experienced on this island, the vines were the weirdest.

Plants attacking a person? Everything I know about science says it's not possible. And yet, those vines wrapped around Virginia and kept her from reaching me.

After a long walk, we reach a metal door that requires a code to be opened. There's a slanted covering on the keypad that keeps me from seeing what Ellison keys in.

The door slides into the thick rock wall, sunlight illuminating a triangular opening about thirty feet ahead. I use a hand to shield my eyes from the brightness as we move forward.

Amira is waiting for us when we reach the end of the walkway, her smile taking the edge off my worry.

"You look so much better than you did the last time I saw you," she says, taking one of my hands and squeezing it.

"Thanks to Ellison." I give her a grateful look.

"I'm here for anything you need, Briar," Ellison says. "I have other patients, so this is where I leave you."

She goes back the way we came, Vance staying about fifteen feet from me and Amira. She's wearing the same thick canvas pants and white T-shirt the Tiders wear, and so is Vance. Amira also has a quiver of arrows strapped to her back, though she doesn't have a bow. Her shirt is soaked through with sweat, and her hair, pulled back in a ponytail, is sweaty at her temples.

"I'll show you everything I know, but I'm still learning myself," she says.

We start walking. I'm torn between looking around the camp and focusing on Amira, so I can ask her questions.

"If there's an order over the camp speaker to take shelter at the base, this is where you come." She gestures at the tunnel entrance I just came out of. "If they say shelter in place, you take cover in the nearest building."

"I saw Marcus grab you on the beach," I say. "I thought they killed you. The Rising Tide people told me they kill everyone."

She pushes her lips together in a thin line. "No. They brought us all to a shelter in the jungle and gave us water. Then Nova explained aromium to us and they gave us a choice to let them turn it off so we could come here, or leave it on and we could be on our own."

"And you wanted it off?"

She nods. "I don't want anyone controlling me. From what they said, people can start losing their minds. Killing each other. Did you see anything like that?"

I look over my shoulder, ensuring Vance is out of hearing range. "Yes. That, and the women all want to have babies they don't even get to raise. They keep the kids in a separate place where they're training them to be super soldiers."

Amira's lips pull down in a frown. "For Whitman."

She stops walking and squares her shoulders. "See that perimeter wall? It goes around the entire camp."

The wall is far away from us, but I can still see it. It's made of massive logs that stretch more than twenty feet into the air. On top of the logs are long metal spikes that come to a point, jutting out in every direction like a porcupine's quills.

"Damn," I say softly. "Guess nothing's getting in here."

Amira hums skeptically. "You'd think so, but I've seen the security team fighting off animals trying to break the wall down or get over it."

I give her an incredulous look. "What animals could do that?"

She speaks in a low tone so only I can hear her. "Ones with aromium implants."

A gust of harsh reality blasts into me like a powerful wind. The wolf that came to me before was much bigger than it should have been. There's also the jaguar that tore that Tider apart in the jungle. I don't have a clear picture of what Whitman is doing here—yet—but I have a fuzzy one that gets bleaker every time it becomes more focused.

"When they first brought us here, we were kept in a

large cell on the outskirts of camp," Amira says. She points toward a metal sign on a stake that says "Garden" as we walk past it. "That's the camp garden. It's huge and it has lots of vegetables and herbs. I think around twenty people work there."

She's trying to give me a tour while we exchange information, so I follow up on what she said before. "How long were you in the cell? Did they treat you okay?"

"More than okay. There were guards there around the clock and they fed us well." She shakes her head and looks away, then back at me again. "I guess I felt like everyone we came here on the boat with was on the same side as us, but some of them really are cold-blooded murderers and rapists. One guy attacked a woman in the night and they called Marcus. After some of us corroborated her story"—she takes a deep breath—"he shot the guy in the head right in front of us. He said respecting the other people here is a rule we were all told about and that guy had violated it."

That's sobering. Amira points to another metal sign on a stake that says, "Farm" and has an arrow. She follows the path.

"We were questioned individually. I was in the cell for two days, and then I got a room assignment and a guard."

"Not anymore, though?"

We're approaching the camp's exterior wall, which has inset double metal doors, both of them wide open.

She shakes her head. "I had a guard for about ten days. Before the virus, I was an archer. I've been shooting my entire life; my mom was an Olympic archer and she made me into one, too."

My jaw drops with surprise. "Seriously?"

"It's how I stayed alive after the virus. When I told Marcus and Nova, they put me on the security team. That's why I was in the jungle the day I found you—my partner and I were doing our daily perimeter check."

We just walked through the open double doors, and I see that the Dust Walkers' farm has its own security wall. It looks like the other wall, but the spikes on top of this one are made of sharpened wood.

The wind carries the scents of sunbaked earth, musky animals and sweet hay, along with the unmistakable acrid tang of manure. The ground is covered with a mixture of jagged wood chunks, the earthy scent fresh. Wood waste here must be put through a chipper.

"This place is huge," I murmur.

"Yeah." She gestures to the left. "Cows over there. Chickens ahead. Boars...somewhere. I don't know, this is as far as I came when I got a tour."

"The people in Rising Tide are starving," I say softly.

We share a look, her surprise genuine.

"They don't have anything like this?"

I shake my head. "They have nothing. We were eating algae and grubs."

She pinches her brows together, looking pained. "And there are kids?"

"They're kept separate, so I don't know if they were eating more than everyone else."

"Hey, keep it moving," Vance calls from behind us. "I've got other things to do."

"Is he an asshole?" I ask Amira softly, not moving my lips.

"I don't know. Haven't heard anything about him."

We go back the way we came, Vance staying closer to us now. Sweat rolls down my spine, not a cloud in the sky to impede the scorching orb that is the sun. The heat here is oppressive all day, every day.

"Want your hair up?" Amira offers.

"That would be great."

She reaches into her pocket and pulls out a small strip of fabric, then says, "Turn around."

I feel her gathering my hair into a bunch at the crown of my head and then braiding it into a thick rope.

"Give me your hand," she says.

I do, and she has me hold the braid she wound into a bun in place while she uses both hands to secure it with the strip of fabric.

A light breeze washes over the back of my neck, and even though the temperature is in the triple digits, it feels amazing.

"That's so much better, thank you."

We resume our tour, stopping at one of several wells around camp. She loans me her canteen and we both get drinks. When I'm drinking, a man and a woman walk past, both waving to Amira.

Unlike Rising Tide, there are trees in this camp that provide much-needed relief from the sun. In the shade of one, a woman is sitting on a stump, her face animated as she reads a book to several children.

A book. I haven't seen one of those in too long. It looks homemade, the neat letters of the story handwritten and pictures drawn and colored with pencils.

"I didn't order flies in my stew!" The woman imitates a deep, outraged voice, her face contorted dramatically.

One of the girls laughs and a boy covers his mouth with his hand, his eyes giving away his grin. Their happy expressions give me a light, warm feeling that brings tears to my eyes.

"You didn't see much of that back in the mainland, either?" Amira asks.

That's an understatement. I was pretty much a prisoner at Lochlan's compound. I never saw children. About once a month, I was allowed out to shop under heavy guard.

We go to a big concrete building with lots of windows next. A beautifully painted sign hangs over the door. It's made of wood and has the words "The Grub Hub" in neat, blocky black letters. Colorful tropical flowers and vines swirl around the words and over the rest of the sign.

Inside, there are large fans mounted in the corners and along the walls of the large space. All of them are running, making the space considerably cooler than the outside. Round tables, some metal and some wood, are scattered around the space, each one surrounded by about eight chairs.

When I see a painting hanging on one wall, I walk over to it, drawn in. It's big, maybe twenty inches by thirty inches, and it's magnificent. It's a soft watercolor painting of a simple cabin in the woods, the northern lights swirling together in shades of green and purple in the background.

My clothes are soaked through with sweat in several spots, but I can almost feel the flakes of falling snow in this painting. More snow is piled in banks around the cabin and it's accumulating at the base of the windows in uneven rows.

The room opens upward into the angles of the roof itself, two big ceiling fans hanging down slightly and spinning. The rest of the walls have more paintings, some showing more skill than others, but all making this place feel comfortable. Some of the art looks like it was done by children, the colors bright and the lines bold. One, a painting of a blue dog with a tongue that rolls out like a carpet, makes me smile.

"We eat here, but it's also where people come to hang out when—"

Amira is cut off by the wail of an alarm through a speaker in the room, making her spine straighten. A deep voice follows the alarm.

"This is a shelter-in-place notification. Animal at the wall, shelter in place."

I think it was Marcus's voice. Vance's hand goes to the holster at his waist, where he has a sheathed knife.

"You girls stay away from the door," he says, walking over to it.

I exchange an amused look with Amira, both over being called "girls" and Vance seemingly thinking an animal will be able to turn a doorknob.

Vance opens the door, looks from side to side, then closes it and moves a heavy metal bar into place, securing the door against anyone who might try to come in.

"I wish I had my bow," Amira says.

"I've got this," Vance says. "I worked in security before the virus."

I hold back about a dozen dry comments. It's best to stay quiet around people I don't trust.

To pass the time, I walk around the room and look at every painting. Some are realistic and others are abstract. One is a portrait of a woman with a lined face, her eyes telling a story of hardship and wisdom. Whoever made it is a talented artist.

There's a savory scent coming from the area behind a door with a "Kitchen" sign on it. A big metal sheet covers the serving area, which has a smooth wooden counter.

I sit down, fatigue catching up with me. Amira is telling me about archery, but I can hardly keep my eyes open.

Marcus's voice returns over the speaker. "The shelter-in-place order is lifted. The threat was eliminated."

Eliminated. It's a sanitized way of saying some animal that belongs here more than any of us do was just killed. That's reality, though, both here and back in the continental New America.

Kill or be killed.

21

Three Weeks Later

I hope by semester's end, you'll never look at a field of grass or an ancient oak tree the same way again.

- Excerpt from a lecture given by Dr. Lucinda Hollis in her Introduction to Plant Biology course

"Mornin', Briar." Felix touches the wide brim of his hat as I walk into the garden.

"Morning."

I turn and raise my palm in a cursory wave at Vance, who will return for me later.

It rained for a few hours last night, and the air in the garden this morning is lush and heavy. I breathe deeply, the rich, loamy scents of wet earth and vegetation infusing me with a sense of calm.

I've been working in the garden for more than two

weeks. Every day, I wake up excited about coming to my personal idea of paradise. I spend eight hours a day surrounded by plants—what could be better?

Felix is in charge, and the workers here say he runs the garden with a potting-soil fist, because he's easygoing. He's quiet, preferring to be wrist-deep in dirt. For a week now, Vance has been allowed to leave me under Felix's supervision for the workday.

I haven't wandered outside the garden because I don't want to lose that freedom. Vance watches me too closely for my comfort. Even when we're alone together in my small room at night to sleep, his eyes are always on me.

In my short time working here, I've learned a lot. I've ached to share this experience with my mom, who would have been blown away by it. The vegetables and fruits have been genetically modified in ways I never thought possible.

The garden is made up of raised beds built from lumber, laid out in rows that seem endless. Some of them stretch more than two hundred feet. There are lots of island critters that would get into the beds if they weren't raised. Protective screens arc around many of the beds, keeping birds and other flying pests away.

I'm starting my day harvesting sweet potatoes, and then I'll move on to lettuce and spinach. There are several varieties of lettuce in the garden: Batavian, Jericho, romaine, Boston Bibb, and buttercrunch. Like everything here, it's been bred to be extremely heat tolerant, require less water to grow, and regrow very quickly.

The lettuce I'm cutting away would normally take at least two weeks to regrow. But this lettuce will be fully regenerated within forty-eight hours.

This is the kind of breakthrough that could have helped many hungry people, both before and after the virus. This hardy garden is a scientific marvel, but I can't forget the others on this island who are starving while I'm surrounded by food all day, every day.

"Hey, how's it going?"

My garden coworker, Ray, kneels beside me. I murmur a quick hello and don't look at him. This isn't the first time he's left the work he's supposed to be doing to come talk to me. He's wiry and muscular, and he looks like he's in his thirties, his short hair and beard both the shade of rust.

"You think this place is kinda bullshit?" he asks in a low tone.

"The island?" I scoff. "That's one word for it."

"No, this camp. Marcus calls all the shots. He's just like fuckin' Whitman."

I bristle, worried someone will overhear this conversation and think I share his opinion. Whatever thoughts I have about Marcus, I'm not stupid enough to say them out loud. Especially not to someone I don't even know.

"This camp's a lot better than the one I was at before." I use my T-shirt to mop sweat from the back of my neck. "They're starving there and they work or train sixteen hours a day."

Ray sighs deeply, considering. "So it's like this place, then? One leader who makes the rules?"

"Two. And no, it's not like this place. I didn't feel safe at Rising Tide."

He looks over both shoulders before continuing. "I want to get the fuck off this island. I have a wife back home. It doesn't matter how nice this camp is, I'm not spending the rest of my life here."

"I get that. I don't want to either."

His eyes light with hope. "Which camp do we have a better shot of getting out of here with? Does anyone at the other camp want to try?"

I shake my head, alarmed by his use of the word *we*. "I didn't hear anyone talk about it. They train and work and that's it. Rising Tide is not a pleasant place. They're starving. And they fight each other to the death."

"No shit?"

"Anyone can challenge anyone to a fight in a circle. One person lives, the other dies. No one is safe."

"So someone could even challenge the leaders?"

I bark out a note of laughter. "Yeah, someone did while I was there. He's dead."

Felix is approaching, and even though I'm working and not doing anything wrong, I don't want him to think I want Ray here.

"I have to work," I say sharply. "You should do the same."

"Pfft. I've fuckin' had it with shoveling piles of cow shit. I'm finding a way out of here."

He leaves. I hope he doesn't come back. Even though I still want to get off this island, I plan to be smart about it. I'm okay biding my time. Whitman is building something here—a force of enhanced people—and whatever he plans to do with them, it'll strengthen his hold on New America. I won't stand by and let it happen, even if it takes time to make a feasible plan.

It takes me a couple of hours to harvest and clean more than one hundred sweet potatoes. Even though I'm wearing the wide-brimmed hat everyone who works in the garden wears, my face is flushed and my skin is warm when I walk to the covered shelter we use for water breaks.

My canteen here is about twice the size of the one I had at Rising Tide. The room I was assigned to is in the underground area. It's slightly bigger than the one I shared with Rona, but this one has a foam mattress, a light fixture, and a shelf. I have nothing to put on the shelf, but sometimes I look at it and imagine what framed photos of my family would look like there, if they were alive today.

Dad would have even more gray in his hair. Mom would have more "silver streaks" because she refused to use the word *gray* for her hair. Thinking of what Maven would look like hurts the most. Would she have a partner beside her in a photo? Someone who saw her and loved her the way she deserved? She never got a chance for that, like our parents did.

After my water break, I grab the handle of the steel wagon I loaded full of potatoes and pull it down the mulch-covered walkway toward the garden's entrance.

I deliver produce to the kitchen every day, a job no one else in the garden wants to do. I don't mind it at all.

As I walk, I pass people doing their jobs. A guy who barely looks eighteen years old carries two heavy pails, sweat dripping from his chin. Two women pass with a cart that looks like a wheelbarrow with a swinging lid, one of them nodding at me.

I'm almost to the kitchen when I spot Marcus and Nova. It's too late to pretend I didn't see them; my eyes went straight to Marcus's. When the butterflies in my stomach wake up and flutter at the sight of him, I get a flare of annoyance.

After nearly a month here, the aromium should be completely out of my system. But I still feel a powerful pull toward Marcus every time I see him. It's similar to the way aromium made me want Pax, but it's also different. With Pax, there was a frenzied need to fuck him as quickly as possible. I felt like an alcoholic—if I could just get the fix my body wanted so badly, the madness would subside.

With Marcus, though, it's not just sexual. He and Nova questioned me two more times, and we exchanged some information about both camps, but I still refused to tell him anything more about the knife I found.

I'm not proud of it, but I secretly like how much he wants something from me. His gaze locks onto me anytime we're in range of each other. That isn't often, which makes it that much more delicious.

He intimidates me, though I'd never admit it. It's not just his imposing physical presence, but also his intensity. There's nothing light about him. Whatever his mood, his expression is always the same—a partial scowl. The scowl deepens when he's angry or frustrated, but it never disappears. Even when I see him with other men on the security team, including Niran, the one he spends a lot of time with, he never laughs or cracks a smile.

While I'm gaping at him, a wheel of my cart rolls into a hole in the ground. I walk into it and bang my knee as the cart tips slightly and a few potatoes fall out.

I wish I had my hair down so I could hide my flushed face behind it, but it's secured in its usual inferno-survival bun on top of my head.

"You okay?" Marcus stops and bends to help me pick up the potatoes.

"I'm fine."

My knee hurts, but it's nothing major. I just want to pick up the potatoes and get away from him. Even in the apocalypse, I'm still a woman, and I don't like how much I enjoy his closeness.

Rationally, I know I need to keep my head down and avoid him. But when we both reach for a potato at the same time and his fingers brush mine, my heart thrums in a chaotic rhythm and any sense I had vanishes.

I pull my hand away like his is a scorching hot stove,

grabbing the final potato from the ground and then standing.

He looks at my injured knee, frowning even though he can't see it beneath my pants.

"Let me," he says, coming around the take the handle of my cart.

"No, you don't have—"

He ignores my protest and I step back. The cart is lopsided, one of the front wheels half buried in a hole. The potatoes are heavy, making the cords of muscle on his arms stand out as he pulls the cart back to get the wheel free.

"Thanks." I force myself not to look at him, because I don't want him to see the stars in my eyes.

It's ridiculous, feeling such a powerful pull to a man who wanted to leave me to die in the jungle. He's not a good guy, and I need to remind myself of that more often.

"I'll have someone fill that hole," Nova says.

Oh, that's right—other people exist. I had forgotten. My gaze flicks to her and I murmur my thanks.

Marcus starts moving the cart, and I furrow my brow and say, "I can get it from here."

"Going to the kitchen?" he asks, still holding on to the cart's handle.

I narrow my eyes, aggravated. "Yes, but *I've got it.*"

"You need that knee looked at?"

He pulls the cart with one hand, like it weighs nothing. It takes everything I've got when it's full of heavy produce to move it—both legs, both arms and the occasional break to swear and catch my breath.

"No." I fire the word at him like a weapon. "I'm capable."

"I know that."

"Don't patronize me."

I look to Nova, hoping for some female support, but she's examining something nonexistent on her arm.

When Marcus turns, the familiar stitching on the leather sheath of the knife secured at his waist catches my eye. It makes me want to hiss like a pissed-off cat.

"That's my knife."

He just shakes his head, Nova jogging ahead of us to open the door to the kitchen. I despise that a man who would so openly taunt me gives me butterflies. My type is kind. Happy. Generous.

Marcus is none of those. I fall into step beside him.

"Tell me where you found it," he says.

"You're carrying it just to get to me."

He arches a brow. "I'm carrying it because it belongs to someone who means a lot to me and I want to keep it safe."

Everything stops, including my breathing. *Someone who means a lot to him.* The knife belongs to a woman. That's why he's so worked up about it. She's not here anymore, and he wants to find her.

I feel an intense jealousy for someone I don't even know. Could it be residual aromium? I've never experienced this, and I don't like it.

I step aside, letting him push the cart into the

kitchen. When I follow him, the kitchen workers are all looking at him, frozen.

"Vadim." Marcus nods at the head chef.

His gaze shifts to mine for a brief second, and then he leaves. My pulse is still erratic, which makes me want to cap my other knee. I can't afford this weakness.

"Getting the boss to make your deliveries?" Vadim cracks, smiling widely.

The mood in the room relaxes now that Marcus is gone, and everyone returns to work.

Vadim is the man I first met on the beach the day I got here—the one who tried to save me by taking me with him. He's even bigger than Marcus at six-six, his shoulders wide and his legs like tree trunks.

But Vadim would rather have a whisk in his hand than a spear. He has dark skin and warm caramel eyes, and he's usually smiling. The apron he wears looks child-sized on him. He always wears a bandanna around his long braids, and today it's a red one.

"The cart got stuck outside the door," I say defensively.

A woman named Meg helps me unload sweet potatoes into a pile on a counter. Vadim walks over to us, wiping his hands on a towel.

"Those will do nicely," he murmurs.

"What are you doing with them?" I ask.

"They'll go into a stew that's a lot like chili." Vadim's eyes sparkle with enthusiasm. "Vegetarian, but loaded with smoky spices, ripe tomatoes, peppers and onions and sweet potatoes. It's thick and hearty."

"Sounds delicious."

Tomatoes shouldn't thrive here, but thanks to the modifications made, the vines are heavy with deep-red, softball-sized fruits pretty much every day. They're a staple on the menu.

Once the potatoes are all unloaded, I close my eyes and take a deep breath in and out, enjoying the smell of baking bread. The ovens are wood-fired, and they're outside the kitchen, but the scent carries.

"Are we getting bread with lunch?" I ask Vadim.

"Indeed. Bread, fish and papaya with a honey glaze."

"Can't wait." I give him a quick grin. "I'll be back with lettuce and spinach."

"Don't let your cart get stuck again," he says with a deep, rich laugh.

He thinks I did it on purpose, which is so much worse. I'm not a woman who wants to be rescued by a man. Especially not Marcus. He's attractive—I'm not oblivious to that. But if he didn't want something from me, I'd just be another woman here, who didn't even warrant a second glance.

It's obvious his heart—tiny and shriveled as it must be—is spoken for. Someone in this camp has to know who that knife belongs to, and I'm going to find out.

22

Your primary weapon is your mind. Fear is normal, but panic is deadly. Stay calm, think tactically and remember your training.

- Excerpt from a police training manual written by Ben Hollis

"More popcorn?" A woman carrying a huge bowl full of hot, buttery popcorn stops in front of me and Amira, her metal scoop poised.

I put a hand over my stomach. "No, thanks. I'm so full. It was delicious."

"Same," Amira says.

She nods and moves on to the next group.

This is the first time I've made it to the Dust Walkers' Friday evening social gathering. Before, I was still healing and felt too exhausted. After a dinner of beef, fish, vegetables, and rice in the Hub, a couple of kegs filled with tropical fruit juice were brought out.

It's a sweet, refreshing change from water. And the popcorn, which was made in huge cast-iron pots over fires outside and tossed with fresh-churned butter and salt, was heavenly. It was served in little baskets woven from leaves.

I'm too full to eat another bite, and Olin is probably starving with the rest of the Rising Tide camp. Some of the people there—like Pax and Rona—are morally gray, to put it lightly, but they don't deserve to starve to death. I don't wish that on anyone there but Virginia.

"So you were forced into marriage?" Amira asks in a low voice, returning to our conversation.

"Yeah. Lochlan's generals all have their pick of women. Or girls." I scoff. "And if they get tired of her, she disappears and they marry a new one."

"Disgusting." She stares at the flames of a nearby fire. There are campfires scattered all over the open space outside the Hub to help deter mosquitoes, and we're sitting on a log bench by ourselves. "And I suppose he forced you into...you know, too."

Anger wells inside me at the memories. "When he was home. Which, fortunately, wasn't a lot. It seemed like Whitman was aggressively invading territories and training new soldiers."

"What happened when you got caught?"

I shrug. "He never officially caught me with the tea. I was careful about never keeping any at the house. He just suspected after two plus years of me not getting pregnant, so he had me examined by one of Whitman's doctors, who said there was no medical reason I wasn't getting pregnant. That was enough. He had some of his men take me to the prison in Carson City."

"Bastard," she mutters.

"Yeah." I wrap my arms around my knees and glance at her. "What about you?"

Sadness flickers over her face.

"You don't have to tell me," I say, wishing I hadn't asked.

"No, I don't mind. I was in a relationship with someone. It hurts to say his name, so I don't. We met a few months after the virus. It was always consensual sex, we just...didn't want to bring a kid into this fucked-up world. We didn't always have enough food for us, and the thought of having a child we couldn't feed..." She clears her throat. "And one time when we were buying the contraceptive at a market, some of Whitman's soldiers came out to arrest us. He—my partner—shoved one of them off me and grabbed his gun. He told me to run. One of the other soldiers shot him."

Her devastation is written all over her face. I put an arm around her.

"I'm so sorry."

She sags slightly. "They treated me like an animal. Not just after I was captured, but before, too."

"Whitman's vision of a perfect society is fucked," I say bitterly.

"It's just crazy. Everything was so chaotic after the

virus that a billionaire was able to overthrow our entire government. I still can't believe it."

I hum in agreement. "Sometimes I wake up and don't immediately remember. There are a couple seconds of blissful unawareness. Then the boulder of reality falls on top of me."

She sits up straight, giving me a serious look. "Is there anything we can do?"

I glance over one shoulder and then the other, making sure no one else can hear me.

"I think there's a lot we can do from right here," I say in a hushed tone. "It was Whitman's guys who brought us here, so we know this is some sort of training ground for him. The aromium, the kid soldiers, even the genetically modified crops—it's all a big chess move for him. He plans to use the technology and the soldiers in the future."

She nods, the corners of her lips tilting up in a smile. "So we sabotage it."

"Right. I think what we need to do is gather as much information as we can about everyone and everything here."

I'm surprised when a hearty laugh bubbles out of her.

"I'm trying to make it look like we're talking about hairstyles or something so no one suspects we're plotting destruction and shit," she says.

I smile. "Good idea."

My gaze wanders to another fire, where Marcus is sitting on a log with Nova, Ellison and Niran.

Nova has her arm around Ellison, the two of them laughing. Marcus's eyes lock onto mine, his broody scowl dialed down. Niran is talking to Marcus and it looks like he's also whittling something out of wood with a knife.

"Is it just me, or is he always intense?" I murmur.

Amira follows my gaze to Marcus. "Always. When it gets closer to sunset, Jun will get out his ukulele and play and people will dance, but not Marcus."

"Never?"

She shakes her head and looks around. "I don't see her out here, but have you met Zara?"

I lower my brows, considering. "I don't think so."

"She's tall and blond. She's on the security team. Anyway, I hear she's been trying to get with Marcus for literal *years*, and he won't bite."

"Hmm. Gay?"

"Nope. I've overheard him and Niran talking about women."

Marcus's eyes bore into me, his expression unreadable. Just in case he's a lip reader, I turn to face Amira.

"I think there is someone," I say softly. "Whoever owns the knife I had that day you found me in the jungle. He wants me to tell him where I found it, but I won't."

"Why not?"

"Because information is the only power I have. I'm not giving it away for free."

"Smart. You think the owner of the knife is a woman he's in love with?"

Irrational jealousy twists like a knife in my chest.

"He's desperate to know about the owner of it. He said it's someone important to him."

"Interesting. If it's true, she's been gone for years, because why would people tell me Zara's been chasing after him if he already has someone here?"

I nod. "That's a good point."

"I'll ask around, see if he was ever with a woman here."

The happy, gentle sounds of a ukulele being played fill the air. My eyes dart back to Marcus. Ellison has already gotten to her feet and is holding on to both of Nova's hands, encouraging her to get up.

"They're together?" I ask Amira.

"Who? Oh, Nova and Ellison. Yes, aren't they adorable? Ellison is the sweet, effervescent one, and Nova is the serious, dedicated one. She'd behead anyone who tried to hurt Ellison, no questions asked."

Nova slumps to the side, trying to fight getting up, but she quickly relents, putting her hand on Ellison's lower back as they walk over to an empty spot to dance.

"I love that," I murmur.

Both women beam at each other as they dance, Ellison leading. My gaze flicks back to Marcus, and when I find him already looking at me, my heart pounds unevenly. Niran isn't sitting next to him anymore.

Amira clears her throat. "Um. For a guy who's possibly in love with someone else, he looks at you kind of ... a lot."

My head whips to the side and I gape at her. "At me? I told you, it's because of the knife."

She pinches her brows together. "You think he thinks staring at you will make you tell him where you found it?"

"I think he thinks I'm a spy Virginia sent here. That's why he won't let me out of his sight, and that's why he thinks I did something to ... his knife-owning companion."

"His knife-owning companion." She fights a smile. "Okay."

"What?"

"Nothing."

"I promise you, he's very suspicious of me. Exhibit *A* is sitting right over there."

I tip my head in the direction where Vance is sitting with some other guys, a plate of meat in front of him. He picks a bone clean with his teeth and then tosses it into the fire, grease shining in his beard.

"How's it going with him?" Amira asks.

"Fine. We don't really talk. He just follows me and sleeps on the other side of my room every night."

Amira opens her mouth to say something, but the sound of a man yelling steals our attention. I look past the fire and see Ray, my garden coworker, shoving Niran's shoulder as he yells at him.

Marcus is on his feet in an instant, a blade in hand. It's not the knife I found, but a different one.

I stand up and walk closer, so I can hear what's going on without getting too close. Amira follows.

"... such a load of shit!" Ray cries. "*He* likes it here"— he stabs a finger in the air toward Marcus—"because he gets to be the big shot. But I don't want to live on this fucking island until the day I die! I have a wife back home. We need to be building a boat."

Nova walks up beside Marcus, her hand on a knife in a sheath at her waist. Niran, who's not as tall as Marcus but taller than Ray, stands with his hands on his hips, his expression impassive.

"We don't have the resources it would take for that," Marcus says levelly. "And we don't put our hands on people."

Ray takes a step toward Marcus. Nova has her blade at his throat before I can even take a full breath. Putting his palms in the air, Ray steps back.

"I'm not gonna hurt anybody."

Amira snorts softly because hurting Marcus, Nova, or Niran doesn't really seem like an option for Ray.

"I'm tired of all your *we* shit," Ray snarls at Marcus. "You don't speak for me! I want off this fucking island, and I know other people here do, too."

Marcus lowers his brows slightly. "Anyone who doesn't like it here can leave anytime. They just can't come back."

"Bullshit!" Sweat drips from his chin. "Why do you get to control everything? All the food and medicine? And whatever's in that bunker? No one but you can access it. Maybe what we need is a change in leadership."

The camp was already quiet, but now it's deathly silent. Everyone stares at Marcus and Ray, Nova's blade still drawn.

Marcus looks around, his expression neutral.

"Anyone with Ray? If ten people ask for an election for a new leader, we'll have one."

Ray's shoulders sink with relief and he looks around. "Come on, guys! If you want to build a boat and get back home, this is your chance!"

A man calls out from beside another fire. "You don't think we should, Marcus?"

Marcus shakes his head and crosses his arms. "We don't have the right tools, the know-how, or the manpower for it. And we'd have to leave the safety perimeter to source enough trees."

Some people nod. No one comes forward.

"Come on!" Ray bellows, walking away from Nova. "Speak up! This place is bullshit and he's a dictator!"

The camp is quiet. Ray's wild-eyed gaze lands on me.

"You. You said you want off this island. Tell him!"

My pulse hammers as everyone turns to look at me. The entire camp isn't out here, but there are at least a hundred people staring at me and thinking I'm Team Ray. What the fuck?

"That's not what I said." I approach Marcus, who's scowling at me. "He's twisting my words."

"It's okay to agree with him." Marcus's tone is cool and detached.

"I don't." I shoot a glare at Ray. "You never said anything to me about building a boat or getting a new leader. You wanted to know about Rising Tide and you said you're tired of shoveling shit and you want to find a way out of here."

His eyes narrow at me, his expression hard and

hateful. "You're just afraid of him like everyone else. But there's power in numbers."

I balk. "Do you have any idea what's in that jungle? In the Rising Tide camp?"

He shrugs. "Can't be worse than this place."

"I saw the body of a man who got *torn apart* by a jaguar. People kill each other for fun at Rising Tide. There's no food. They're eating algae and bugs. A snake —not a normal snake—killed someone from this camp. If you think this camp is the worst place on the island, you'll be in for a shock when you leave it."

"Is that what you want?" Marcus asks Ray, his tone brusque. "We'll give you supplies if you need them and you can go."

Ray considers, then shakes his head, his voice cold. "No."

"Then quit running your fucking mouth," Niran says, spitting on the ground.

Marcus shakes his head, his expression dark. "He can say whatever he wants." He focuses on Ray. "But the next time you put your hands on someone in this camp will be the last. Clear?"

"Yeah, whatever."

Ray walks away, hanging his head in dejection. After the way he threw me under the bus, I don't feel sorry for him.

I want to assure Marcus that I wasn't talking shit about his leadership, but when I turn, he's already walking away, Nova and Niran on his heels. Amira puts an arm around me.

"It'll blow over," she says.
I have a feeling it won't.

23

Sometimes what looks like disease is actually cooperation, and what seems destructive is actually beneficial. There are fungi that appear to attack plant and tree roots, but really, they are helping them absorb nutrients.

- Excerpt from a lecture given by Dr. Lucinda Hollis in her Plant Biology course

I leave my room the next morning and walk out of the tunnel, planning to go to the Hub for breakfast before I start my shift in the garden.

Vance puts his hand between my shoulder blades, steering me in a different direction. I move away from his touch and give him a questioning look.

"We're going this way." He doesn't even look at me as he says it.

"Can I get some water first?"

"Did I say we were getting water first?"

I narrow my eyes, his tone catching me off guard. "Where are we going?"

"The ring."

"I don't know what that is."

He huffs out a sigh. "You'll find out in about five minutes. Let's go."

Trepidation weighs down every step I take. I don't want to follow him, but what choice do I have? I know this has something to do with what Ray said about me last night.

Everything was going fine. I was keeping my head down and feeling more like myself every day. Not just more like myself than I have since I got to the island, but since before Lochlan.

Vance has a sheathed knife on his hip. It's just a few feet away, but with all the people around us, it might as well be a mile. He doesn't have a snap on it; if I could grab the hilt, I'd be able to pull it free quickly. My fingertips twitch with the urge to do it.

But then what? I can't make it on my own in the jungle. Especially not if Virginia is still looking for me. Whatever device this camp has that creates an invisible perimeter to ward off anything with active aromium, it's the only thing keeping Virginia from getting to me.

We reach the furthest buildings I've been to in the camp. I know one of them is the housing block for the security team, where Amira lives. Dread curdles in my stomach as Vance leads me past the buildings toward a huge fenced area with a well-worn dirt path around it. The fence, around six feet tall, is made of small tree trunks lashed together.

A small group of people rounds a corner, running on the path around the fence. Marcus is at the front of the group, and he's only wearing shorts, low-cut socks, and shoes.

It's all I can do to keep my mouth closed so my tongue doesn't roll out of it. His chest is as bronzed as the rest of him, slick with sweat and defined with muscle. I swallow as he gets closer, my pulse racing with awareness. He has defined abs and dark chest hair, a trail of it dipping beneath the waistband of his shorts.

And the scowl. I never thought scowls were sexy, but pair it with that dark, intense gaze of his, and *sexy* is putting it mildly.

He breaks off from the group and jogs over to us, sweat droplets flying from his hair when he runs his hand through it. When I scan the rest of the runners, I spot Amira in the back. She smiles and gives me a little wave, which settles my nerves a little.

"Hey." Marcus jerks his chin at Vance. "I've got her. Join the run."

"Oh." Vance arches his brows, surprised. "I haven't been running at all since I started guarding her."

Marcus's scowl deepens. "All the more reason to get your ass in there."

"Right."

Vance jogs after the group and Marcus turns his focus to me.

"Let's go." His tone is clipped.

"Wait!" I clear my throat as he gives me a questioning look. "Um, about last night, when Ray said—"

He cuts me off. "This isn't about that. I know what Ray's about."

My breath stills. "Are you..."

"Come into the ring and we'll talk."

He stalks off, leaving me a view of his broad, muscled back and his damn near perfect ass. Even his calves are defined with muscle.

I square my shoulders and follow. I need to relax. I'm a tightly wound ball of nerves. A few deep breaths help slow my heart rate a little.

The area inside the fence, which he called the ring, has a door built from small tree trunks. Marcus opens it and gestures for me to walk inside.

The space is wide open, the ground mostly covered in mulch. There's an area with a pile of tree trunks and stacks of different-sized rocks. Next to it is what looks like a pull-up bar, well constructed from smooth, sanded wood.

Marcus stands in the middle of the ring, facing me with his hands on his hips. I try to look casual as I walk out to meet him, but I can't help scanning the sky. This feels like a trap. Are arrows going to come flying over the wall at me?

"What's going on?" I ask when I reach him.

He puts a hand out. "Relax. Nothing bad's about to happen."

"I'm fine."

He pushes his brows together. "You look like you're about to puke or pass out."

Or pee my pants, but I don't admit it. "Just tell me why I'm here."

He exhales heavily, looking away and running a hand over his stubbled jaw before looking back at me. He's usually clean-shaven. Now that I'm close to him, I can see dark circles beneath his eyes.

"I just wanted to talk to you in a place no one can overhear." He crosses his arms and widens his stance, looking uncomfortable. "I keep things close to the vest for a lot of reasons. A big one is that I don't want to worry my people."

I nod slowly, more confused than ever about why he wanted me here.

"I'm asking you not to repeat anything from this conversation with anyone. You good with that?"

I open my mouth, then close it again. "I think so."

His brows shoot up. I relent, nodding.

"Okay, it'll stay between us."

My gaze falls on a bead of sweat rolling down his chest. It trails into a line on the side of his pecs. I force my eyes up to his. They're a mix of dark chocolate and caramel—possibly the only thing about him that's remotely sweet.

"I'm on the team that does the last perimeter check every night. Last night, we found one of our emergency supply stores emptied." Worry is etched into his expression.

"What kind of supplies?"

"Stuff we'd need if we had to evacuate this camp. Weapons, tools. Things Virginia didn't have access to."

"Fuck." The reality of it hits me. Virginia is already terrifyingly strong thanks to aromium.

"Yeah. We have caches buried in several places around the island. I don't know how she even knew to look for them."

"You're sure it was her?"

He shrugs a shoulder. "It's probably her. But there's a chance it's the person whose knife you found."

He's so damn tall, and big, and intense. I force myself to keep my eyes locked on his.

"Who is she?" I ask. "Give me something. Friend or foe? Do you think she could be working with Virginia?"

He furrows his brow. "*He's* definitely not working with her. And..." He rubs his jaw, looking like he's at war with himself about whether to continue. "Again, keep this between us. If our aromium shield ever goes down, we're fucked. Virginia checks it every day and she'll know immediately. The owner of that knife—if he's still alive—is the only one who can help."

I turn and look at the fence, needing to think and knowing I can't do it while looking at him. The knife didn't belong to a woman he's in love with, which is more of a relief than I want to think about at the moment. And despite his cool, *I've got it all handled* demeanor, leading this camp is more stressful than he wants anyone to know.

After a few seconds, I look back at him. "What would Virginia do if the shield went down?"

He shakes his head. "Honestly? She'd either boot us out of camp and take it over or kill us all and take the supplies. We're dead either way."

"They're starving," I murmur. "I get why she wants the supplies."

Marcus's expression darkens. "She doesn't just want to feed her people, Briar. She knows I'll feed anyone as long as I can turn off their aromium first."

That revelation sends me reeling. "Really?"

"It's a lot to take in, I know. You don't respond well to...my usual questioning, so—"

I laugh. "Does anyone respond well to it?"

He bristles. "Plenty of people do."

I roll my eyes. "You want to know where I found the knife so you can try to find the guy it belongs to."

"If he's still alive, yes."

"How long has it been since you saw him?"

A flicker of something passes over his expression, passing quickly. "About a year and a half."

My lips part with surprise. "He would have had to live in the jungle alone this entire time?"

He nods. "Yeah, it's a long shot. But it's all I've got. And if anyone could stay alive in that jungle, it's him."

I cross my arms, matching his stance. "I'll take you to the place I found it. But only if I get to come with you every time you search, and only if we can leave some food for Rising Tide."

"What the actual fuck?" He turns around and paces a

few steps, then returns to glare at me. "Tell me you think you're funny and that was a joke."

"Which part?"

He gapes at me like I just grew two new heads. "All of it! I try a softer approach and you respond like this? You said you wanted information for information and I held up my end of the bargain."

I shrug, trying to look resolved even though I'm shaking inside. "Now I want something else too."

He puts his hands on his hips, narrowing his eyes in a furious look. "Absolutely the fuck not. Tell me where it was."

"Your softer approach sucks."

I look away, hoping he thinks I'm unconcerned even though my heart is beating so hard I'm surprised my rib cage isn't audibly rattling. The location where I found the knife is my only leverage. I need information about this island, and going with him is how I can get it. Also, I can't leave Olin and the others at Rising Tide to starve while I eat three meals a day. It's not right.

The muscle in his jaw tics as he pinches the bridge of his nose, takes in several deep breaths and lets them out.

"It's not safe out there," he says, his tone measured.

"That's a risk I'm willing to take. Put a weapon in my hand and you'll find out I'm not as helpless as you think."

"I don't think you're helpless." He says it like I'm a five-year-old he's trying to placate.

Fuck this guy, and all men who underestimate me. The well of fury inside me, usually at a steady simmer, is threatening to boil over. I tip my chin up a notch, holding his intimidating gaze.

"Pick a woman from your security team. No weapons. If I pin her within ten minutes, I get to go with you." I hold out my hand to him. "Deal?"

Brows hiked up to his hairline, he stares at me for two long seconds before shaking my hand. His enormous hand dwarfs mine, his touch warming me all over.

"Okay, deal. One round only. No two out of three or three out of five."

I laugh, knowing he doesn't think I have a chance of winning. "One round."

"Tomorrow morning, first thing."

"Great. We can start searching right after. If Felix can spare me in the garden, I mean."

Something in the way he's looking at me makes the bottom of my stomach fall out.

"All this confidence because your dad taught you self-defense?" There's an edge of amusement in this voice.

I told him and Nova during questioning that I had "some" fighting skills, but I made sure to downplay my abilities, just like I did at Rising Tide.

"He was a really good teacher." I shrug.

We stand in silence, our gazes still locked. This close to him, the pull of residual aromium is stronger. I don't even care that he's sweaty. In fact, I might even *like it*. Marcus doesn't have the edges aromium gave Pax, but somehow, he seems even more powerful to me. He could command me with his expression, his voice, or his touch, and I don't know if I could—

The aromium is taking over again. I clear my throat, making myself stay focused.

"And the food is part of the deal? We can spare it, and they're starving."

"That's the idea. They've got a choice—food or aromium."

I glare at him, his oversimplification aggravating. "Virginia's not giving anyone that choice and you know it. She's choosing. And there are children."

His scowl returns. "You don't get it. Those kids could kill us in two seconds flat. And they would if Virginia told them to."

"It's just some food, Marcus. Not a lot. We can leave it in a place they'll find it so they can all have one good meal."

He shakes his head. "This is a hard line for me. No way."

My mouth comes up with a new deal before my head has time to think it through.

"Your two best female soldiers against me, one at a time. Five minutes each. If I take both of them down, you and I deliver food for Rising Tide. No one else has to know."

He scoffs, then bursts into laughter. It's the first time I've really heard him laugh, the amusement even reaching his eyes. It throws me off balance, because I like it and hate it at the same time. He's laughing *at me*. But damn, *that smile*.

"You're cocky as fuck. Our women are just as good as the men." He holds his hand out. "Deal. And props for trying."

Our second handshake sends the same thrill of awareness shooting through me as the first one did. How long will it take to be completely free of the aromium's influence?

I pull my hand away, the reality of what I just shook on settling over me. I have a feeling Marcus's people are very well trained, and I'm out of practice. There's a good chance he's right and I'll get my ass handed to me.

But I'm too stubborn not to try.

24

Humans have always been drawn to plants that produce psychoactive compounds, but that's not a coincidence. Opium poppies (used in morphine and codeine), cannabis (THC and CBD), coca plants (cocaine), coffee plants (caffeine) and tobacco plants (nicotine) are all well-known and ingrained in our daily lives. Every one of these plants evolved to produce these compounds specifically to affect the mammalian nervous system.

- Excerpt from the Introduction to Plant Biology course taught by Dr. Lucinda Hollis

I tug my hair free from its tight bun as I walk into the tunnel with Vance later that night, the air cooling quickly as we descend. My sweat-soaked hair trails down my back, the waves full from the thick, humid air.

After talking to Marcus earlier, I ate and worked in the garden all day, harvesting food and pulling weeds. My neck and shoulders ache, and once dinner was finished, I only hung out with Amira for about an hour in the Hub. I need a cool shower and my bed.

My room is midway down a long hallway, one of forty rooms in the underground area. There are twenty on each side of the main walkway, and most of them are occupied by two people. Then there's the security team housing block above ground, and another above-ground block for families.

Even though this is my room, it's currently programmed to only accept Vance's thumbprint on the keypad outside the door. He presses his thumb to the pad and the door slides open with a whooshing sound.

"I'm taking a shower." I grab my towel and clean clothes, feeling Vance's watchful gaze on me.

He follows me out of my room, as usual, silently shadowing me until I get to the bathroom door. That's where he waits for me every time I shower. I don't know if it's because of my fatigue, but I'm extra annoyed by his presence tonight.

If Marcus trusts me enough to tell me the things he did earlier, he should trust that I'm not going to run back to Virginia and tell her. It's something I plan to discuss with him when I take him to the cave's location.

Or maybe I should say *if*. I backed myself into a corner earlier, and I'm not sure I'll be able to beat two of Marcus's best fighters. I asked him to match me with women so I'm not physically outmatched. Some of the men on the security team—Marcus included—are far bigger and stronger than I am.

I know as well as anyone that women are underestimated, though. If I lose, I'll have nothing. Marcus and I have a shared enemy in Virginia, and if he's telling me the truth, I want to help him. If we can find a way to bring her down, it could change everything for the Tiders.

With all of us working together, we could find a way off this island. Warring factions are exactly what Whitman wants, because if we're fighting each other, none of us are focused on the real enemy—him. He's the one who shot us all up with his experimental serum and dumped us on this island.

There's a woman at a sink brushing her teeth, but other than that, the bathroom is empty. With only four shower stalls and six sinks, it gets crowded in here right before most people go to bed and first thing in the morning.

The shower stalls here are made of concrete, only the floors tiled. There's a small opening to get into the shower, and then as long as you stay right under the showerhead, no one can see you. I never take the initial spray of cool water on my hot, sweaty skin for granted. We only have five minutes to shower, but I always spend my first ten seconds or so letting water wash down my face and body.

My skin is bronzed from the sun now, though my torso is about ten shades lighter than the rest of me. Some of the women here go to what they call "the pool" on days off, which is a spring with a waterfall. They swim nude, taking turns guarding the perimeter. I'm too modest for that, but I've thought about going and keeping my underclothes on.

The ache in my neck when I crane it up makes me cringe. Soreness is the only downside of working in the garden. I'll have to push past this discomfort tomorrow.

I mentally run through my dad's lessons as I lather my hair. He used to tell me and Maven about something he learned when he was a Marine, called *you're already dead*. By reframing your thinking and accepting that you're already dead, you can eliminate your worries about living or dying and focus only on the task at hand. I've drawn on that many times since the virus.

Eyes, throat, solar plexus, groin. Be decisive. Strike first.

Movement in the doorway of the shower stall makes me clear the soap and water from my eyes with my hands and step out of the shower stream.

Vance is leaning into my shower stall, his predatory eyes locked onto my body. Adrenaline courses through me as I scream, "What the fuck are you doing?"

He looks smug as he says, "Sorry, thought I heard you yelling."

I draw my fist back, about to punch him, when he steps back, getting in one last head-to-toe sweep of my nakedness.

Fury and fear battle for control inside me. I'm fucking pissed at him, but I know I'm at his mercy. What can I do? If I complain, he'll say he thought he heard me screaming, which is bullshit.

I'm not starving and I'm not alone at the bottom of a hole in the ground, but am I safe here? Truly safe? Hell no. There's a strange man following me everywhere and sleeping in my room every night, because Marcus thinks I'm the one he needs to worry about.

A wave of contempt for him swells inside me. Marcus did this. He could have assigned a female soldier to guard me, but instead, I got a man who makes me feel violated and disgusting.

I don't even know if I'm angrier at Vance or Marcus. After turning the handle for the shower to stop the water, I grab the towel I left hanging on a hook and wrap it around myself.

Vance's leering expression is still fresh in my mind. I close my eyes, willing myself to stop shaking. If he thinks I'm afraid of him, I'll lose what little control I have.

Quickly, I dry myself and dress in the clean clothes I left just outside the shower stall, reaching out to grab them so I can stay hidden inside.

As soon as I walk out of the bathroom area doorway, Vance pushes off the wall, a smile still playing on his lips.

I narrow my eyes at him, my tone loaded with malice. "If you ever do anything like that again, I will kill you."

He laughs lightly. "Oh, will you? With what, your hands?"

"If I have no other weapon, then yes."

His expression shifts, turning serious. "It was an accident. I was coming to help you."

"You're disgusting. I don't need your help."

He turns away and starts walking. "Sure you don't, little girl. You think you know what this place is, but you ain't seen shit."

My blood boils with anger over being called *little girl*. Everything in me wants to rush him and make him pay. I can't risk the consequences, though. My survival is on the line.

It's all I can do to stay silent. Once he uses his fingerprint to get us back in my room, I go to my cot and wrap myself in my blanket. It's a worthless shield, but at least I'm completely covered.

He's lying on his back on a cot directly across from mine. I lie on my side, my eyes never leaving him.

First thing tomorrow, I'm changing the terms of my deal with Marcus. I want Vance out of my room and as far away from me as possible, more than I want anything else. And I want it, win or lose.

I need to sleep and don't want to at the same time. Taking on two of Marcus's security team members is going to be hard even if I am fully rested. But I'm afraid to even close my eyes while trapped in a room alone with Vance.

If only I had a weapon. Like the knife I found in the cave. Instead, Marcus has it, and he has access to any other weapons he wants, too. Makes me wish I was fighting him tomorrow. He'd be hard to beat, but it would feel damn good to punch him.

Pinching my arm beneath the covers, I fight to stay awake. After my long day working in the sun, I'm sapped. I don't trust Vance, but my eyelids are getting heavier by the second.

I'll just rest my eyes for a little bit while staying awake and alert.

———

My blanket is being pulled out from beneath me. I wake up with a gasp, trapped in the cocoon I created for myself.

Vance. I can't see him, but I know it's him tugging at my blanket. It only takes him a few seconds to strip it away and drop it to the floor.

My cot dips as he puts a knee on it. I react immediately, knowing I'm in for a harder fight if he gets all his weight on top of me. Moving into a sitting position, I brace a hand on the wall and kick him in the chest, using both feet.

With an "oof" sound, he staggers back a couple feet, muttering, "Bitch."

He's back on me before I can get away from my cot. One of his hands gropes my breast and I scream like a feral animal as I drive the butt of my hand into his nose.

"Hold still." His voice is low. "Or I'll say you tried to escape."

"Fuck you."

His hand wraps around my throat, the sound of fabric ripping making my stomach roll. It's the cotton pants I wore to sleep in.

Fight like hell, Briar.

I can hear my father's voice in my head, reminding me why he taught me everything he did. It wasn't because he relished seeing his daughters punch each other in training, but because we were so dear to him that he wanted us to be able to get ourselves out of the worst situations.

Kicking and kneeing Vance's groin, I manage to get him to take his hand off my throat. I suck in a deep breath and try to get off the cot, but he punches me in the face.

I'm dazed, but I move anyway, because I can't afford any hesitation. He's still standing over me, though, the metal bar at the side of my cot digging into the center of my back.

He tears my shirt open. I scream with everything in me, kicking and clawing at him. I have to get on my feet.

He hisses in pain after getting close enough for me to rake my nails down his cheek. Grabbing my shoulders, he slams my head to the cot. If it was a hard surface, that would have rung my bell, but instead, it gives me a chance to wrap my hands around his throat.

I squeeze, refusing to let go. My life depends on not letting go. Vance could kill me right here and have my body buried in the woods by morning without anyone ever knowing what happened.

When he tries to get his hands around my neck, I turn my face to the side and bite his hand as hard as I can, holding on like an attack dog.

"Fuck!" He rasps out the word, then backs up a few steps.

I spring out of bed, taking a slow, calming breath and silently moving away. It's pitch black in here, which works for and against me.

"You're dead, bitch."

I quietly creep over to the wall where I know the shelf's hanging, finding it with my hands and tearing it down. When I hear him coming at me, I swing the shelf at his head, making contact.

He gets ahold of my torn shirt and pulls me toward him. I hit his head with the shelf again, then again. It's a solid metal shelf—the weapon I didn't realize I had until I was desperate for it.

Vance retreats. Knowing he's going for his knife, I race to the door and try to open it, but it's locked.

Shit. I bang the shelf against the door over and over, screaming as I do.

"Help me! Someone! I need help!"

I'm pulled back by my hair, so hard my feet slide out from under me. My hands instinctively move to free myself, the shelf clattering to the ground.

"No!" I fall to the floor, screaming and thrashing.

This isn't happening. Never again. Part of me died every time I let Lochlan have me against my will, telling myself it was the only way to survive.

Now I know, though. If it's give in or die fighting, I'd rather die.

25

Base extract is a novel alkaloid compound previously unknown to science. The petal tissue on the flowers from Island 7 contains the highest concentration of active compound. Root extraction yields compound with unknown effects.

— Excerpt from the journal of Dr. Randall McClain

I'm clawing at Vance's face when light appears. The door to the room opens, a spotlight shining in on us.

"Move away from her."

It's Nova, her voice level and lethal as she points a handgun in our direction. Vance puts his hands in the air and moves off me, standing.

"She's the one who attacked me when I tried to stop her from escaping."

Tears of relief cloud my vision as I get to my knees, breathing hard.

"Briar, on the cot," she says. "Vance, don't move a muscle."

I back my way to my cot. She switches on the room's light, keeping the weapon trained on Vance, then presses a button on a radio that's mounted to her shoulder.

"This is Athena, I need command team one in underground housing block two right now."

There's a crackle over the radio and a male voice answers. "Copy that, Athena. Stand by."

My left eye is swollen, and I have aches and pains all over, but I'm not seriously injured. I pick up my blanket and wrap it around myself.

Vance's hand is dripping blood where I bit him, a small red pool by his feet.

"Nova, you have to listen to me," he says, sounding calm and rational. "I was restraining her because she was trying to escape. She's going to come up with a story."

"Sit your ass on the cot," Nova says.

"You *know* me."

"Did I fucking stutter? Not. Another. Word."

I scratched the shit out of his face. It's covered with jagged, bloody lines. Even now, I stare at him, keeping the blanket bundled tightly around me. I don't trust that he won't try something, even with a gun pointed at him.

A minute later, Marcus calls out to Nova as he approaches, his deep voice reigniting my fury. Standing in the doorway, she steps into the room and he enters behind her.

He's shirtless, wearing only shorts. He doesn't even have shoes on and his hair is a mess. He's also carrying a handgun, a rifle slung over his back with the strap resting across his chest.

Marcus looks from me to Vance, and then back to Vance again. Niran walks into the room next, wearing shorts, a T-shirt and flip-flops. He's carrying a gun, too.

"Niran, keep your weapon on Vance while I talk to Marcus," Nova says. "If he moves, shoot him in the head."

Vance balks. "Marcus, she thinks I'm the one who did something! What the hell is going on? She was trying to escape!"

Marcus doesn't respond. Once Niran has his gun pointed at Vance, Marcus leads Nova from the room.

"Niran, man, help me out here," Vance pleads. "You know I'm a good guy."

"Yeah, I know. Just be cool and wait while they talk."

The exchange makes my stomach turn. Just a guy asking another guy to have his back. Even in the apocalypse, some things never change.

Soon, Marcus walks back into the room. His expression is different now, a dark storm in his eyes. He's still holding the handgun.

"Vance," he says. "Come with me."

I'm shaking. Not just from what just happened, but from what's going to happen next. Do I even have a chance of them believing me? Should I even bother telling them the truth?

"Niran, you can wait outside," Nova says.

He nods and goes, pulling the door closed behind him. Once it's closed, Nova puts the safety on her gun, putting her back against the door.

"I won't come any closer," she says softly. "Would you rather change your clothes with me in here or out in the hall?"

"He looked at me in the shower," I blurt.

Her shoulders sink slightly. "I'm sorry. Do you want to change clothes, or would you rather keep the blanket?"

Hot tears spill onto my cheeks, and I swipe them away. I have to get ahold of myself. I can cry later, when I'm alone.

"I'll change." I slide off the cot, keeping the blanket secured. "Can you just turn around?"

Nova complies, and I walk over to the small dresser where I keep my clean clothes. The Dust Walkers often wear the same canvas pants and T-shirts the Tiders do. I dress in one of the familiar uniforms, feeling more comfortable than I would in casual clothes. Then I add socks and my boots, because I'm not sure I'll be staying here anymore.

My hair is wild from being wet when I went to bed. I brush my hands through the slightly damp strands.

"I'm dressed," I tell Nova.

She turns around and meets my eyes, then opens the

door. Marcus, Niran and Vance are standing there. Nova clicks off her gun's safety and walks into the hallway.

Marcus comes into the room, closing the door. I sit down on the edge of my cot, my heart hammering with worry.

"What happened?" he asks.

I sigh softly, my gaze on the floor. "I was showering tonight, and I was alone in the bathroom. He came in just to..." My throat tightens. "Just to look at me. He said he thought I yelled, but I didn't. I tried not to fall asleep, but I did. And I woke up to him"—I tuck my hair behind my ear, holding myself together—"pulling on my blanket, grabbing me. I fought back."

"Are those the clothes you were wearing?" He nods at the pile I left on the dresser.

"Yeah."

"Can I take a look?"

I shrug. "You can do anything you want."

I hear him walk over and pick something up.

"Christ," he mutters.

He turns to face me, still standing in front of the dresser. "Will you look at me?"

I raise my face and turn, locking my gaze on his.

"Did he sexually assault you?"

"He was trying. But no."

He winces. "Briar ... I'm so goddamn sorry. This is my fault."

I nod. "It is. He could've killed me and gotten away with it."

Shame clouds his expression and he looks away. "Ellison is on her way."

"I don't need her. I'm fine."

"I want her to at least look you over."

"No." It comes out more forcefully than I intended. "It's my body and I know what my injuries are. I said I'm fine."

He nods.

"So you believe me?" I ask, still not sure I trust it.

"Yeah. No one pounds on a door screaming for help when they're trying to escape. I'm very fucking disgusted with myself for trusting Vance."

"Locking a woman in a room with a man against her will seemed like a good idea?" My voice shakes with emotion and I clear my throat. "I did *nothing* to earn your suspicion. He was armed, Marcus. I fought him off with a fucking shelf."

He pinches his brows together and looks away. "I'm very sorry. This is on me."

"Either let me have a weapon, or I'm leaving."

He jerks his gaze back onto me. "Leaving?"

"I deserve to be able to protect myself. This place is a literal fucking prison, and in this camp, you're the warden. What gives you the right?"

"We'll talk about this more. But right now I have to go."

"Why?"

"To deal with Vance."

"What are you going to do?"

He puts his hands on his hips. "You can come see, if you've got the stomach for it."

My single note of laughter is bitter. "That won't be a problem."

He opens the door and I follow him into the hallway. Vance looks between us.

"Hey, I'm willing to let this go. It was a misunderstanding."

Marcus ignores him, looking at Nova instead. "Tell teams two and three to meet us at the oak tree. Bring shovels."

"No!" The color drains from Vance's face. "You can't. Marcus—"

"Shut the fuck up," Marcus says.

The door of another room opens nearby, someone peeking into the hallway.

"Close it and lock it," Nova orders.

The door is instantly closed. Niran and Nova each stand on one side of Vance, who's still yelling about me trying to escape. He refuses to move, so they pick him up.

We leave the tunnel, Marcus in the lead, Nova, Vance and Niran next and me last. Ellison comes up to me, a medical bag in hand. She's wearing a long white nightshirt, pants and work boots, her long hair braided.

"I'm not going with you," I say. "I'm going with them."

She looks me up and down. "You're okay?"

I nod, and she falls into step beside me.

The camp is engulfed in inky darkness, the only glow coming from a few lights mounted on tall posts. We walk past the Hub, an outdoor housing block, and two other buildings, and then we're walking on ground that's been cleared but doesn't have anything built on it. After about ten minutes, we reach a big, old oak tree.

There are about a dozen people here already, some of them holding bright flashlights like the one Nova had. This reminds me of the circle at Rising Tide, spectators gathering to watch something big go down.

"Don't do this!" Vance yells. "I didn't do anything wrong!"

When the people gathered see Marcus, they group up in a semi-circle around him. Some of them look like they got out of bed to come here.

Marcus gestures to the ground on his right side and says, "Start digging."

My chin drops and I look over at Ellison. She presses her lips together and takes my hand in hers.

Vance is frantic now, his eyes wide. "No! You guys know me! He's setting me up!"

"Anybody bring a stick?" Nova calls out.

Someone brings her one of the long metal poles I first saw when Pax and I encountered the group of Dust Walkers at the waterfall. At its tip, it has a bundle of wires that crackle and buzz with electricity.

Vance shuts up immediately, switching to crying softly instead.

Ellison and I look on, stoic as Marcus and five other men quickly dig. Marcus's bare feet are muddy, but he doesn't seem to notice. His muscles cord as he buries a shovel in the soil and hauls a shovelful of dirt into a pile.

Other people jump in to dig, too, and it takes them about twenty minutes to complete a hole that comes up to Marcus's shoulders. He digs a foothold into one side of the hole, steps into it and reaches up, two large men each taking a hand to help pull him out of the hole.

He's breathing hard, sweat pouring down his face as he looks at Vance and says, "Get in."

Vance weeps. He's on his knees, his forehead on the ground. "Please. Cast me out. Just don't do this."

Shaking his head, Marcus looks at Nova and Niran. They each grab an arm and drag him over to the hole, dumping him inside it.

I'm taken back to the hole Virginia put me in, my skin crawling as the sense of total helplessness returns. I have to take a few deep breaths and remind myself I'm not going in there. Vance brought this on himself.

Ellison squeezes my hand as Vance screams, begging someone to intervene. Marcus walks over to the edge and looks down at him. Then he lifts his chin and speaks to the group.

"Tonight, Nova and I found Vance guilty of disrespecting a camp member and lying. I have no doubt this is the right call. Justice here is swift and brutal because it has to be."

The faces I can see in the faint glow of the flashlights are all resigned. There are both men and women, some of them glancing over at me and Ellison.

"Nova?" Marcus says.

"I agree with this decision." She says it without hesitation.

Marcus looks down at Vance. "You get one more chance to be honest with me."

One more chance? Was this all just a game to scare him? I look over at Ellison, who stares straight ahead.

"Thank you," Vance sobs. "Marcus, thank you. I'll never let you down again. I was wrong. She made me mad and I was trying to get back at her. I'll never—"

Marcus switches the safety off on his gun, pointing it at Vance.

"No!" Vance cries. "You said I had a chance to be honest and I was!"

Marcus narrows his eyes, his face impassive as he says, "In this case, honesty earns you a bullet before we bury you."

The shot rings out and I jump. Ellison releases my hand and puts an arm around my shoulders.

"I'm okay," I whisper, both to her and to myself.

Marcus tucks the gun into the waistband of his shorts, turning around.

"This is what happens when power is abused here."

No one breathes. It's eerily silent until the trill of a monkey sounds in the jungle. Marcus looks at Nova and says, "Finish it."

Then his gaze locks onto me, the sorrow I saw in his expression back in my room replaced with stern authority.

"Let's go."

26

*I've been pinned down in some tight situations.
Outnumbered and outgunned. But pressure builds diamonds.
When the going gets tough, keep your head. Never give up. As
long as your heart's still beating, there's hope.*

*— Excerpt from an interview with Ben Hollis for a book
authored by Margie Gillis*

I'm practically jogging to keep up with Marcus as he storms through the darkened camp, the ring of the gunshot still playing over in my mind.

I expected it to happen—why else would they dig a grave? As I watched them shovel earth from the ground and heard Vance beg for his life, I went back and forth over whether I thought he deserved to die.

I'm still not sure, but I know I feel safer knowing he won't be waiting around any corners for me.

"Hey," I say from a few steps behind Marcus. "You said we'd talk."

He casts a quick glance at me, his brow furrowed. "You want to talk now?"

"I've had questions since I woke up on the boat that brought me here, so yeah. Now would be good."

My pulse pounds as he walks back to me. A storm still rages in his eyes, and I know this isn't the best time to talk, but I'm done following orders and not getting answers.

"What do you want to know?"

Where do I even begin? I could spend hours asking him all the questions I have.

"Were you elected to be the leader here?"

He grunts. "More like appointed."

"Who appointed you?"

"The guy who used to be in charge."

I'm about to ask him to elaborate when something gently drifts onto my cheek. When I touch my fingertip to it, there's a tiny crunch before it melts into water against my skin.

Weird. I write it off as a fluke, but then another cold flake kisses my arm.

"That's snow," I murmur, even though I know it's impossible.

"Fuck," Marcus mutters. He puts his hands on his hips and looks up at the sky. "Really?"

He starts walking again, but I keep my feet locked

into place on the ground. After about ten feet, he turns around. "What are you doing? Let's go."

I cross my arms over my chest and shake my head. "I'm not moving until I get some answers."

He blows out an exasperated breath and walks back to me. "It's the middle of the night. Can we do this tomorrow?"

"No, I'm not letting you put me off for another second. Is that snow?"

A pause. "I think so, yeah."

"How is it snowing on a blazing-hot tropical island? And don't tell me it's magic because my tolerance is worn down to nothing at this point. I want a full, honest answer."

I can barely make out his expression in the faint glow of a nearby light, but I see the corners of his lips quirk almost imperceptibly. "Aromium is being used to experiment on people and animals here. It's not the only experiment. There are also microclimate experiments. The control panel for those was broken, but Virginia must have an electrician in her camp. With the tools she got from the cache, they must've fixed it."

For a few seconds, I'm too stunned to speak. And not just because of what he just said, but also because it was a real answer instead of a brush-off.

"Microclimates." I shake my head. "That shouldn't be possible."

"It is."

My scientific mind is reeling, coming up with questions faster than I can process them.

"Won't snow kill the crops?"

"It shouldn't. It'll take time for her to ramp up to produce enough snow for that, and we'll have time to cover the crops. But even if it killed them" —he shrugs— "we'd just replant. Everything is engineered to grow quickly."

I fire the next question that comes to mind at him.

"How many people are buried back where...we just were?"

He considers for a second. "Around fifty. And before you ask, no, I didn't shoot all of them."

"Did someone else shoot them?"

He exhales heavily through his nose. "Most of them died of natural causes or from being attacked by animals or Tiders. My friend Finn is one of them."

Finn. The one who was killed by the snake that day by the waterfall.

"Let's keep walking," he says.

I follow, speed walking so I can keep talking to him.

"So you've talked to Virginia? She knows you'll trade food for turning off aromium?"

"Yeah, she knows."

"Is Rising Tide for making soldiers for Whitman?"

He doesn't respond right away, and I look over and up at the tight set of his jaw, a snowflake settling onto one of his dark eyelashes. He really is the most brutally beautiful, savage specimen of a man I've ever seen. Dark. Intense. Strong. Volatile. I still feel pulled toward him, even though I'm furious with him.

"It's entirely about the kids. The child of two people

with active aromium is born enhanced with it. It can't be modified or turned off, and it's more powerful than what the parents were injected with."

I remember the kids I saw when Pax brought me to their camp. They were little machines, not a smile or laugh in sight. People, but also...not. Somehow, Whitman managed to do something even more evil than his previous crimes against humanity.

"That's cruel," I say softly, emotion welling in my throat.

"There's no easy way to stop it," he says, his voice clipped. "But it has to be done."

This is why he's trying to starve them out. It's like his decision to execute Vance—not the only option, but a decisive, effective one, even if it's also cold.

We're at the security team housing block, and he uses his thumbprint to open the outer door. When he steps aside for me to enter, I lower my brows in a skeptical look.

"Okay, but...why are we going here? Why can't I go back to my room?"

His response is a scowl, but it's a tired one—much weaker than his usual. When he speaks, his voice is so low it's practically a whisper.

"Vance has friends. When word gets out about what happened, I want to know you're safe."

I nod slowly, considering. "Don't you think they'll be angrier at you than me?"

"They mess with me, they'll end up in a hole beside him."

My eyes widen as I process that. He shifts, looking agitated, and rubs his jaw.

"Look, I don't kill people for questioning me. But Vance's friends might try to make this into something it's not. I just want to keep the peace, and if you're with me, there'll be peace."

"With you?" I'm appalled by this plan. "In your room?"

"Just...come in and hear me out. Give me five minutes. Then you can leave if you want to."

"You mean ... leave camp?"

"No. I mean, you can go back to your room."

"I can't unlock the door because someone thought it was a good idea for Vance to be the only one who could lock and unlock it." I give him a pointed glare.

His sigh is weary. "Again, I'm sorry. If you want, I'll leave my room and stay somewhere else for the rest of the night while you stay there. It's secure."

A cluster of people are approaching the housing block. Security team members returning from Vance's burial, I think. I really don't feel like making eye contact with any of them right now. Some of them could be the friends of Vance's that Marcus mentioned.

"Five minutes." I step into the building.

The housing block is enormous, its walls and floors made of concrete. The ground level doesn't have any doors. Its open, thick metal posts supporting the building's weight. There are built-in metal ladders leading up to the second floor. I assume it's because of flooding.

Marcus gestures at a ladder and I climb it. He follows and then leads the way down a short hallway, the floors on this level made of wooden planks that fill the air with a sweet, fresh scent.

He uses his thumbprint to open the door, and my heart hammers hard as I walk into his quarters.

When he flips a switch beside the door, a light fixture on the wall casts dim light around us.

We're in a room with the same wooden floors that were in the hallway, the planks also covering the walls and ceiling. The room is about twelve feet by twelve feet, a wooden table with six chairs taking up most of the space.

Marcus walks over to the table, and before he gets to it, my gaze falls on the knife I found in the cave. He picks it up and brings it to me, holding on to the leather sheath and offering me the handle.

I just look at him, confused.

"Take it," he says.

As soon as my hand is wrapped around the weapon's smooth handle, I feel a little safer. But I'm still wary, because I don't know if he's going to let me keep it.

"I get why you want it. You know how to use it?"

I nod, my eyes unintentionally roving over his carved chest and arms. The waistband of his shorts hangs low enough that I can see the tip of a black tattoo. I want him to push his shorts down, put me on that table and fuck away every thought and emotion swimming around my head right now. No one could take the world away like he could, with his body and his intensity.

It's just the aromium, I remind myself. I'm not actually a feral island bitch in heat.

He leans his back against the wall, meeting my gaze. "You won't be sparring with anyone tomorrow. Or I guess in a few hours, I don't know what time it even is. And we won't be going to find the place you found the knife."

"Why not? I told you I'm not injured."

He pulls his brows together, his expression troubled. "You don't have to make deals with me. I shouldn't have kept the knife. It's yours."

Can I trust this sudden change of heart? Is this just him feeling guilty over what happened with Vance?

"But you said the guy who left this knife behind can help with the aromium shield that protects the camp."

He nods. "Yeah, he could help with a lot of things. If he's willing."

"He may not be?"

His shoulders drop with defeat. "I don't even know if he's alive. And if he is, he chose to leave. So would he help? I don't know."

"But if he is alive, and if we can find him, could he help us reach the people at Rising Tide and tell them about aromium? So they can decide if they want to keep it on for themselves?"

He nods. "Yeah, he could help with that."

"Would he want to?"

He considers. "He knows how dangerous aromium is, and he knows it's only going to get worse. But I don't know what his state of mind is. If he's even alive."

My mind wanders back to the children at Rising Tide. Not only has Whitman stolen their lives, but he's also making them into weapons capable of mass destruction. I only wanted vengeance against Lochlan when I got here, but I can't unsee what I've seen. This is bigger than anything that's happened since the virus changed the world and Whitman seized power, and it's only going to get worse unless someone stops it.

"I think we should try," I say.

"Okay. Let's get some sleep and talk about it tomorrow."

I look around the spartan space. "I'm assuming you don't sleep on the table?"

Amusement flickers on his face. "No, this is a meeting room. Bed's in here."

He opens a door on the other side of the room and I follow him through it. As soon as I walk into the space, the scents of salt, wind and sun-dried cotton send a tingle of awareness dancing down my spine. There's a bed with a pillow and white sheets, a lightweight blanket half bunched on the bed and half hanging to the floor.

Weapons hang from several metal hooks on the wood-planked wall, one hook holding what looks like a dark jacket. On the small dresser, there's a framed photo of a woman who looks like she's in her forties, her hair dark and her facial features similar to Marcus's, other than her expression. She's smiling warmly, which I'm not sure his facial muscles know how to do.

A woven basket sits in one corner, dirty clothes piled into it.

"You can sleep in here." He takes what looks like a radio from a shelf. "I'll take this so it doesn't keep you up."

"Where will you sleep?"

He tilts his head toward the doorway. "In the other room. This door locks from the inside."

"You'll have to sleep on the floor, though."

He shrugs. "No big deal. Get some rest."

"Hey." I sit down on the bed and unlace my boots. "How do I get in to see Ellison?"

"When you wake up, go find the guard at the tunnel entrance and tell them you need to see her. They'll radio her."

"Okay, and after that, I'll take you to the cave."

"Cave?"

"Where I found the knife."

He nods, looking down at his dirty bare feet. "I'm going to take a shower. Lock this door."

I can't help smiling at his brusque tone.

"What? Is that funny?"

"No, it's just...nothing." I slide my first boot off.

He leans his shoulder against the doorframe, his expression relaxing. "What?"

I give in, working on my second boot. "Have you always been so bossy?"

He scoffs, the corners of his lips easing dangerously close to a smile. "Actually, yeah. Used to be a quarterback."

I arch my brows with surprise. I can see that. He most definitely has the body of an athlete.

"Professional?"

"Not quite," he says with a smirk. "All-state in high school, and then I played all the way through college."

As much as I'd like to dig into every detail of just how broad his shoulders looked in those pads, fatigue tugs on my eyelids, my neck and back still sore from my day in the garden yesterday.

"Thanks for letting me have your bed," I say.

Nodding, he pushes off the doorway, closing it behind him. I pull off one sock, then the other. Still sitting on the edge of the bed, I try to process the events of the last couple of hours. Vance is dead. If Nova hadn't been patrolling the housing block as part of her watch, and if she or Marcus hadn't believed me, things would have turned out much worse for me.

This place is harsh. There are countless ways to die. But I'm still here. And while I don't wholeheartedly trust anyone yet, I know Amira is my friend. I know Olin is too. And I believe Marcus, Nova and Ellison are all decent people trying to make fair decisions.

I'm better off than I was at Rising Tide. And if I'm not fighting Virginia alone, my chances of defeating her are better.

Is death the only way to truly defeat her? Maybe she could do some soul-searching from the hole she kept me prisoner in.

"Briar," Marcus barks from outside the door.

"What?"

"Lock the damn door so I can go take a shower."

Lightness flutters in my stomach as I get up to walk over to the door. He really seems to be looking out for me, which is nice.

There are three different locks on the door—two dead bolts and a metal bar. Once I've secured all of them, there's no way anyone could get through the door without a bomb or a pretty killer axe.

So that's something. I'm finally completely alone and safe for the first time since I got to this island.

I lie down in my clothes, covering myself up to the waist with the blanket. *Maybe tomorrow will be boring*, I think as I drift off to sleep.

Somehow, though, I doubt it. Especially if I spend any amount of time around Marcus.

27

Test subject horses showed dramatic increase in aggression and agitation. We are moving too quickly on trials, but Mr. Whitman is insistent that we have a usable compound within the next sixty days. The team is operating on very little sleep.

— Excerpt from the journal of Dr. Randall McClain

Lazy swirls of drifting snowflakes float on a light breeze as I wait outside the tunnel for Ellison several hours later. On this steamy day, the flakes fizzle and disappear as soon as they hit the ground.

It's bright and sunny, the snow falling from a massive dark cloud that doesn't fit in with the rest of the clear, blue sky. I've added artificial microclimates to the growing list of things on this bizarre island I wish I could talk to my mom about.

"Briar." Ellison greets me with a bright smile. "It's good to see you. Let's go to my office."

She leads me down into the tunnel, keying in a code to open the door. I can't help thinking about the last time I took this path, with Vance beside me.

Ellison nods to two men who are walking in the opposite direction, waiting until they're out of earshot to say, "How are you feeling today?"

"I'm fine. I got a few good hours of sleep."

"Good."

It took me no time at all to fall asleep in Marcus's bed, and I didn't hate waking up surrounded by the scents of saltwater, leather, and soap on his bedsheets. He was already gone when I unlocked the door and left in search of a bathroom.

On the table, he left me a fresh bar of soap, a towel, toothpaste and a toothbrush, a piece of paper on top of the pile bearing a handwritten note.

Briar,

You're off work duty in the garden until further notice. Take the time you need. Find me if you need anything.

Marcus

Reading my name in his handwriting gave me butterflies. Ridiculous. I feel like a teenager with a crush, only I'm a grown-ass twenty-four-year-old woman who knows better.

Acting on feelings is a death sentence in the new world

order. Even though I rely on logic, intuition, and experience, I've had several near misses with an eternal nap. I have to stay sharp, which means no more closing my eyes and breathing in the smell of Marcus's pillow like a lunatic.

Ellison leads me down a hallway and through another secured door that requires a code for entry, and then into a room that takes me aback.

Shelves on the walls are lined with plants, artificial lights above casting them in wide arcs of brightness. Other shelves hold glass jars of medical supplies like gauze, pills, and dried, crushed plants.

There's a loveseat with a blanket folded neatly over one side, and colorful paintings crowd the walls. It's maximalist, with no rhyme or reason. An oil painting of a Black woman carrying a basket on her head hangs next to a watercolor of a portly pink pig with aviator goggles flying through the sky, his wings minuscule.

Tears prick my eyes and I clear my throat. This is the warmest, coziest room I've been in since before the virus. The last time I was in a place that gave me this feeling, it was my mom's office. She had a freestanding office behind our home with a big greenhouse attached to it. The vibe was plants, comfy furniture and bright colors, and I loved it.

"Please sit." Ellison gestures at the loveseat, sitting down in a wooden rocking chair.

I sit on the loveseat, breathing in the scent of eucalyptus. It's one of my favorite smells.

"This place is beautiful," I say.

"Thank you. Nova calls it my den of organized chaos."

I smile. "My mom had one of those, too."

"You said she was a scientist, right?"

"Yes. She was a professor at the University of Washington."

"You miss her." It's a statement, not a question.

I nod. "Especially since I got here. My mom would be blown away by"—I gesture around—"all of this. Aromium, genetically engineered crops that defy anything science has been able to do yet, controlled microclimates...all of it."

"How are you feeling today?" A crease appears between her brows.

"Right. You're wondering why I'm here." I smile sheepishly.

"Not at all. I hope you know you can drop in to see me anytime, even if it's just to talk. I've just been thinking of you and wanted to ask."

Today her brown hair is in a loose braid, a few strands loose around her face. She's wearing a lightweight, flowy blue dress and looks like she could be on a tropical vacation.

"I'm okay." I meet her warm gaze. "Vance didn't get very far with trying to assault me."

"I'm proud of the way you fought him. Not that I judge women who don't fight." She sighs softly. "I did a rotation in the emergency department when I was in school and domestic abuse was one of the hardest things

I saw. Abuse is far more nuanced than many people realize. It's not just physical."

"What did you do before the virus?"

"I was an oncology nurse practitioner."

"That seems like a tough job. Was it rewarding?"

The corners of her eyes crinkle as she smiles. "Oftentimes. Also heartbreaking. Stressful. It helped that I'm an incurable optimist."

I glance at a painting of a vase of flowers on her wall, taking a reassuring breath before looking back at her. "I need to ask you about aromium. How long will it take for it to be completely out of my system?"

Her brows drop down a notch. "What are you feeling that makes you think it's still affecting you?"

My cheeks warm with embarrassment. "Just...I don't know."

She sits back in her chair, hands folded in her lap. "Aromium has two different components. There's the physical side, which, as far as I've seen, affects every person the same way. You get stronger, faster, and need less sleep and food. These effects strengthen over time. Once the aromium is fully bound to your DNA, you hardly need any sleep or food at all. Just water. And I'm sure you saw how strong and fast the fours were."

I nod, remembering the pregnant women who ran mile after mile in the hundred-degree heat, sprinting it all.

"Then there's the other part of aromium, which was designed to amplify certain urges and emotions. That component proved...difficult." She presses her lips into a thin line.

"What urges and emotions?"

"Well, we didn't know which ones we'd get when we injected our first test group, but—"

My chin drops and my heart speeds up. "Wait. You were part of that?"

There's a pause before she responds. "Regretfully, I was."

"Is this Whitman's project to make super soldiers?"

Her smile is tinged with sadness. "Nearly everyone who was working on it didn't know that was the purpose, but yes."

"So you got out when you realized?"

She nods. "As soon as I could." She leans forward. "Anyway, the aromium amplifies the desires to protect and procreate at any cost. So anger, jealousy, attraction, spite—those are all heightened. Knowing that, how are you feeling differently than you did before aromium?"

I don't want to lie and say it's anger. She might think I'm a danger to others. I swallow my embarrassment and tell her the truth.

"It's, um...attraction."

Her smile is half-amused, half-sympathetic. "And that's the only thing?"

With a cringe, I nod.

"Well, I don't know if this will be good news or bad news, but aromium's effects end immediately upon deactivation. If you're feeling an attraction to someone, I think it's because you're genuinely attracted to them." A laugh bubbles out of her. "Oh, honey. Your expression. I promise it will all be okay. I went through the same thing when I fell for an annoyingly quiet introvert who cracks her knuckles individually every night in bed."

My lips quirk up. "Nova."

"She's grumpy, I'm sunshine. She looks before she leaps, and I guess that's probably good for me. Not to mention that I *can't* not smile when we're together. I've tried. Can't do it."

"I love that," I murmur.

"This place is hard. Having someone special really helps. Whether it's romantic or just a great friend."

This is definitely not good news for me. I was convinced I'm too rational to get butterflies when Marcus is close, and to fantasize about him on top of me, scowl and all.

"And you're positive?" I ask. "Because this person I'm...you know, feeling this way for, he's not my type."

"Could it be situational?"

I frown. "You mean like I'm only attracted to him because we're on this island?"

"*Or*," she says gently, "because he was swift and certain with justice to someone who wronged you?"

I laugh and bury my head in my hands. Awesome. Now she knows it's Marcus. I must be completely transparent.

"That's definitely not it. I'm actually pretty angry at him for treating me like a criminal and making me stay locked up with Vance every night. And I'm not celebrating what happened to Vance."

A few seconds of silence pass before she speaks again. "One reason I think Marcus is an effective leader here is that he doesn't celebrate it, either. I was opposed to his black-and-white approach to punishment here, but I've changed my mind."

"Why?"

She sighs softly, her expression troubled. "We tried confinement. Most of the time, people were bitter about it and that led to even worse offenses. It's easy to forget that many of the people sent here really are violent criminals. Some are good people who only stole to feed their dying families or used birth control. But some...some people here are predators and murderers. Marcus's system is the best way to keep the good people safe and deter the others."

A soft knock sounds on her office door. She gets up to answer it.

"Henry's waiting to have his stitches removed," a male voice says.

She nods. "I'll be right in."

I stand up from my seat, taking one more look around her office. "I'll let you get back to work."

She walks me back the way we came, her voice low so the people passing can't hear her.

"Marcus is worth getting to know. I think you'll find there's more to him than meets the eye." She glances at me, a smile tugging at the corners of her lips. "Though what meets the eye is quite nice, too."

Our eyes meet and I can't help smiling back. I sniff, pretending to be unbothered. "I hadn't really noticed."

Her grin widens. "You're lovely, Briar. I hope you'll come see me again soon."

The door to the underground area is opening. It's like a massive metal garage door, chains pulling it up for someone to enter.

It's Niran, a much smaller man limping in beside him.

Ellison leans over and whispers to me. "Everything said in my office is confidential."

"Good."

She smiles again and locks eyes with me. "Get to know him. Trust me."

"Man versus bees," Niran says as the two men approach. "I think the bees had the upper hand. Or ... wing, I guess?"

Her brows shoot up. "What happened, Seth?"

He groans. "Tripped over a log and they swarmed me. I even got stung on the nipple."

"You loved it," Niran quips. "Heard you begging 'em to sting the other one."

His lighthearted comments leave me with a warm feeling as I exit the tunnel, the snowfall thicker now.

I put my arms out, letting them catch a few flakes. When I was growing up in Washington, we'd get snow, but it never lasted. Mae and I always wanted to build snow castles, but we rarely got enough accumulation to even make snowballs.

"There you are!" Amira runs up to me, breathless. She

looks me over from head to toe, her expression concerned. "Are you okay?"

"Yes."

She bursts forward to hug me, holding me tightly. "I'm supposed to be sharpening knives, but I had to find you. You're sure you're okay?"

I nod and quickly recount last night's events, her expression unsurprised when I tell her about Marcus shooting Vance.

"My team wasn't called there last night," she murmurs. "But I heard about it first thing this morning."

"I just talked to Ellison and found out some things I want to tell you," I say softly. "Will you be at dinner at the usual time?"

"I should be. If I'm not, I'll find you later." She hugs me again before darting off.

I'm not resting all day, so I need to find Marcus. When my heart leaps at the prospect of seeing him, I groan inwardly. I don't want to be this drawn to a man—*any* man. But he's my best chance of finding the answers I need about this place, so I have to find a way to be around him without letting on how I'm feeling.

My boots slush through mud as I make my way to the ring, assuming that's where I'll find Marcus. I pass the kitchen entrance, where Vadim is standing next to a cart of produce, inhaling the scent of fresh basil. His expression is pure bliss.

He waves as I pass, a pang of jealousy hitting when I see another garden worker with him. She probably delivered the produce today. I liked my routine in the garden, but Vance ruined it. At least temporarily. I hope to be back there soon.

When I reach the ring, no one's outside it. I hesitate outside the closed door before opening it and walking inside.

There are around fifty people inside the ring at various stations. Some are practicing archery, others are using rocks like weights and lifting them, and others are doing pushups in the mud.

Through the swirling flakes, I see Marcus demonstrating archery form to a small group. I get the usual flutter in my stomach, but I ignore it, walking around the perimeter of the training area to reach him.

I watch as he nocks an arrow and takes aim at a target, talking to the people nearby as he does it. He goes quiet for a few seconds and then shoots the arrow, which lands dead center on the target.

A woman claps, but he silences her with a scowl. He glances in my direction, doing a double take when he sees me.

Passing the bow off to a woman, he talks to her for a few seconds before coming over to me.

"How long've you been there?" he asks.

"Since before you were applauded."

He shoots me a quick, halfhearted look of annoyance. "How you feeling?"

"Good."

"Did you find Ellison?"

Did I ever. I laugh inwardly over the absurd idea of telling him what we talked about.

Not a chance in hell. I just nod.

His eyes land on the sheathed knife at my waist. "You still interested in taking me to the place where you found that?"

My pulse pounds as his gaze locks onto mine. I'm stuck on the word *interested*. So stuck that I can't seem to get a single word out of my mouth. "Um, yeah. Sure."

He dips his chin toward the knife. "You said you've been trained. What weapons can you use?"

"Handguns, rifles, knives and ... probably staffs, but it's been a long time since I used one."

His brows arch up. "Any interest in being on the security team?"

"What would I be doing?"

"Training, defense of camp, security, perimeter checks."

The snowfall is so thick now that even though he's only a few feet away, I can hardly see him. I don't like the idea of training all the time, though it would be good for me. Getting to leave camp, though ... I don't think I can pass that up.

"Could I still do one day a week in the garden?"

"Yeah, sure."

I nod. "Okay."

"We test everyone to help us place them in the right group. You don't have to do that today, though."

What better day than today? I'm still sore from fighting Vance off. It's a reminder of how cutthroat this place is. I don't know when I'll see Marcelle and Virginia again, but I will. And when I do, I want to be as sharp as I can. Especially considering the edge aromium gives them.

"I'm ready."

"You don't—"

"You said that already. But I'm good. Let's do it."

With a nod, he leads me over to an area where two people are sparring, several others watching from nearby.

"Zara."

The blond perks up immediately when he says her name. "Yes?"

"You're gonna spar with Briar. Briar, you choose the weapons."

He leads me over to a small wooden wall, which has wooden practice staffs, spears and knives. I take a knife.

"You can pick whatever weapon you want," I tell Zara.

She ignores me and also grabs a practice knife. Marcus speaks into his radio and then tells the people in the sparring ring to finish up.

I size Zara up. She's lithe, but fit. A few inches taller than me. The snow could work to my advantage. Or not.

It's been a while since I sparred. Years. But as I take a few practice swings, my dad's lessons come back to me. One of his most important lessons was *never show your hand*, so of course the swings are terrible. I'm not even holding the practice knife the right way.

Zara is smirking by the time we're positioned across from each other, most everyone who was training in the ring now gathered around to watch us.

"This is over when I say it's over," Marcus says sternly. "You're sparring, so no one gets seriously injured. Got it?"

"Yes, boss," Zara says sweetly.

Kiss ass.

"Yeah, got it." I don't take my eyes off her.

"You've got this, Briar," Amira says from somewhere.

"Go," Marcus says.

Zara is crouching, light on her feet. I raise my right arm up like I'm going to strike with the practice knife, and she moves to block. I drop the knife as I drive the heel of my left hand into her solar plexus, the hit sending a jolt of pain from my wrist to my shoulder.

"Oof." There's a collective inhale as she drops to her knees, the knife falling to the ground.

Her palms hit the dirt next. She rasps in a breath, fighting for air. I walk over and put my hands over her shoulders.

"Do you want me to pin her?"

I make out Marcus fighting a smile through the thick blanket of falling snow. "No, you won."

"That wasn't a knife spar," a male voice calls out. "She cheated."

"She did not!" Amira cries. "Who said that?"

Marcus silences Amira with a look, then says, "Hobbs, there's nothing wrong with hand-to-hand combat even when you're holding a weapon."

"It was a cheap hit. That's not skill."

Marcus said Vance had friends here. It's not

surprising to hear someone's bitter toward me. I should just stay quiet and prove myself.

"You can go next," I say, doing the exact opposite of what I should do.

"Bring it, bitch."

I'm able to make out Hobbs, who is stocky and average height, because the people on either side of him move away. Before I can tell him to choose a weapon and join me, Marcus is hovering over him, his gaze murderous.

"Did I hear that right?" He yells directly in Hobbs's face. "I think you just said you want to fight me. I'm right here, man. Let's go."

Hobbs cranes his neck to meet Marcus's eyes. "You took her word over Vance's. She's one of them."

"Vance lied," Marcus says, his tone harsh. "And I brought Briar here because I trust her. Why don't you call her a bitch again? See how many teeth you have left after you do."

The ring is silent for a few long seconds, no one daring to speak.

"Sorry," Hobbs mutters, looking away.

"Didn't quite get that," Marcus says.

"I'm sorry."

Zara is back on her feet, still gasping dramatically.

"I think … something's … broken," she says.

I shake my head. "It was a solid hit to your solar plexus. I would have felt it if I'd broken anything. Give it five minutes, you'll just be sore by then."

"Briar." Marcus nods toward the door to the ring.

I follow him there, more than a few people glaring at me as I go. Not Amira, though. She's grinning at me like a proud sister. It reminds me so much of Mae that I have to clear a lump of emotion from my throat.

I meet her eyes and nod. Hopefully after this outing with Marcus, I'll have even more to tell her tonight.

28

Do you find a walk through the forest relaxing? If so, it may be because pine trees release compounds called terpenes, which have measurable calming effects on both humans and animals. If you're feeling stressed, a walk in the woods may help.

— Excerpt from a lecture given by Dr. Lucinda Hollis in her Plant Evolution course

"Did you think I doubted you?" Marcus asks as we walk out of camp about half an hour later.

We went into the Sub, which is what they call the underground area the tunnel leads to, and he got us each two handguns, a bow and arrow for himself and a stun stick for me.

He set the stick up to activate with my thumbprint

and told me it works like a super Taser. I feel safer with it in hand as we head into the jungle.

"We both know you doubted me." I give him a knowing look.

"I did underestimate you," he admits.

"You aren't the first."

He's leading the way back to the spot where Amira hid me in a bush, walking a worn dirt path. A line of sweat trails down his spine, rolling all the way past the waistband of his shorts.

"Do you just not like shirts?"

He grins at me over his shoulder. "It's more than a hundred degrees. I soak every shirt with sweat by nine a.m., so I save the laundry team some work and just don't wear one a lot of the time."

"God, those people must have to wash so much sweaty underwear." The thought of track marks added in with the sweat makes me cringe on their behalf.

"We have big tubs with hand cranks. A few of 'em are set up behind bikes, so right before sunrise some of the laundry people ride around camp and the pedaling turns the cranks for them."

"They scrub their hands bloody at Rising Tide. And hardly have any soap."

If he responds, I don't hear it. After another minute, he stops and I follow suit. He listens for a few seconds. A roar cuts through the chatter of birds, making me break out in goose bumps.

"Lion," he whispers. "But it's not close."

That's not much consolation. But he starts walking again, so I do, too.

"Where does the electricity come from?" I ask.

He hesitates for a second before answering. "We have solar and hydro sources."

"So if aromium is Whitman's experiment, did he have the camp built? The Dust Walker camp?" I immediately regret calling it that. "Sorry, I don't mean to offend you."

"We don't mind being called that. The Tiders mean it like we're Luddites because we're against aromium."

I hum with amusement. "That's kind of funny considering all the technology you guys have in your camp."

"Most of them don't know what we have. They just know what Virginia tells them."

"And Pax. You never mention Pax, but they're coleaders."

"In name only. Virginia's running that show."

He's right about that. It occurs to me that he knows a lot about Rising Tide. More than an outsider would.

"You didn't come here with the scientists' camp, did you? You were a Tider."

"Yep."

He pulls out a bandanna, wrapping it around his forehead and tying it behind his head. It's already brutally hot, only a few snowflakes making it through the thick jungle canopy.

"What did you do before the virus?" I ask him.

"Med student. First year."

"Really?"

He turns to glance over his shoulder at me. "Why does that surprise you?"

"I guess because when you said you were a former quarterback, I only thought of you as a football player."

He uses the machete in his hand to hack away at a vine near his head, making his shoulder muscles ripple. I shake my head, wondering what he's bad at. That body and intensity, and he was in medical school?

"Let me guess—you were going to become a gynecologist."

He barks out a laugh. "Nope. I hadn't decided between pediatrics and pediatric surgery."

Oh, my ovaries. The thought of him cradling a baby is just too much.

"You may have been a little scary to kids."

"Me?" He says it lightly.

"Just a little."

He stops and turns around, looking in every direction. His gaze freezes on something behind me. I whip myself around to see what it is, my heart racing with worry.

"It's him," I say softly.

"Him?"

"This wolf came to me when I was at the cave I'm taking you to. When the Tiders were chasing me. He could've eaten me, but he didn't."

Marcus grins, amused. "Flavius is a good boy. Aren't you?"

At the sound of the name, the wolf cocks his head at

him like he recognizes Marcus. I look from Marcus to the animal and then back again. "From the Latin word for yellow?"

He nods. "For his eyes. He's following to look out for us."

"You're sure?"

"Positive."

He turns and continues walking. I sigh heavily and follow, looking over my shoulder every few seconds to make sure Flavius is still a safe distance behind me.

But what really is a safe distance from a two-hundred-fifty-pound predator? If he launched himself at me, I'd have no hope of getting away. I rest my hand on the gun holstered at my waist.

"This is farther from camp than I realized," I say after a few minutes of silence. "How did you guys get me back to camp after you found me?"

"I carried you."

My lips part and my already high temperature rises another degree. He carried me, and I was too unconscious to even enjoy it.

"Well, that was nice of you," I say stiffly. "Thanks."

We stop for a water break, Flavius sitting and keeping his distance of about fifty feet behind us. It takes us almost another half hour to reach the bush I nearly bled to death in.

"You okay?" Marcus asks me.

I nod. "Just thinking about that day. Virginia tried to kill me just for leaving their camp. I don't understand why."

"She didn't want you telling us anything about their camp."

I knew I was about to die. I'd accepted it. But then that vine shot out of the jungle and saved me. I'll never forget the buzzing sound of it rapidly growing and wrapping around her.

"How did a plant save me?" I ask. "Why?"

Marcus's expression clouds. "We need to keep moving. I don't want to be out here any longer than we have to."

"It's this way. Not too far from here."

We walk side by side through a clearing, Flavius still trailing. The snow is lighter here, but it's still falling.

"Did you sleep okay on the floor last night?" I ask.

He shrugs. "Good enough."

"Well, you can have your bed back tonight."

He looks over at me, his mossy-green eyes drawing me in. "I'd rather you stay a few more nights in my room. If you don't mind."

He wants me in his room. In his bed. I don't dwell on the fact that he wants me to be in his bed *by myself*.

"I guess I made a few more enemies this morning." I spot the curtain of bright-orange flowers at the cave's entrance. "There."

He gives me a confused look. "Where?"

"Come on."

I lead the way to the flowers, then say, "Follow me."

Like I did the first time, I gently slide behind the dense jumble of vines, making sure not to disturb any of the flowers.

"Are you fucking serious?" Marcus murmurs as he follows. "I've searched this area so many times. I thought this was solid rock."

"Surprise," I deadpan.

He shakes his head. "And the smell of the flowers masks other scents. This is a good hiding spot."

Taking a flashlight from his pack, he illuminates the path in front of us. Our boots crunch on the tiny rocks beneath us, the cool air carrying a musty scent.

I keep my hand on the gun at my waist, checking in every direction. Small cracks of filtered light slowly disappear as we descend deeper into the earth.

"Here," I whisper. "I think. It's close to here."

Marcus shines his light around the space, walking about ten more feet before he says, "I found something."

"Hang on, don't touch it yet."

I walk over to where he's standing. The bowl and flint I found with the knife are still here.

"Those are exactly where they were when I was here before. The knife was right there."

He sighs softly and picks up the bowl, sniffing the inside. "There's no way to know how long this stuff has been here."

"I don't think it's been a long time."

He arches a brow at me. "What makes you say that?"

I take the light and illuminate lines on the cave wall about two feet from the ground. "This line tells us water has sat in this cave at this level before. In that recent hurricane, Rising Tide flooded badly. And I think this cave is at a lower elevation. So if these items were sitting here then, they would've been washed away. They were put here together by someone and they've stayed that way."

He exhales through his nose. I shine the flashlight at him so I can see his reaction. The corners of his lips are tugging up in a grin.

"I'm sorry I didn't trust you before. I was wrong."

I smile back at him. "Have you ever said those words before?"

Not only is he not scowling, he's almost *smirking.* "No, but I've never been wrong before, so..."

A high-pitched squeal sounds from deeper in the cave. I turn the flashlight that direction, now making out the sounds of scratching on rock and loud chittering.

"What is that?"

"Shit," Marcus murmurs.

He grabs my stun stick from my hand and quickly sets it on the ground, then gives me an apologetic look.

"This won't take long."

"What—"

He wraps his arms around me and sweeps my legs out from beneath me. I barely get out a squeak of protest before we're on the ground, his massive body covering mine.

"What the hell are you doing? Look, I like you, but this isn—"

A whooshing sound comes from the cave's belly, fast as a freight train speeding down tracks. It sounds like heavy fabric flapping together, clicking sounds added to the chittering, squealing and scratching.

Oh, fuck me. *Bats.*

The roar is deafening. It's a massive bat colony, all exiting the cave. Thousands of wings flutter around us, but Marcus has me completely covered. One of his arms is on the cave floor around my head, the side of his face resting against mine.

"It's okay," he says, his warm breath a caress over my cheek.

It takes a couple of minutes for me to be able to hear anything other than the whooshing and flapping of the bats. I can feel Marcus's heart beating steadily against my breast. He's supporting most of his weight on his knee and elbow, so he's covering me without crushing me.

There are only a few light squeals and flutters now. He starts to move, but I grab his waistband.

"Not yet. I'm afraid of bats."

He stays in place, a droplet of sweat falling from his sweatband onto my forehead.

"They won't hurt you," he says in a soothing tone.

"They carry rabies," I hiss. "And bacterial infections."

"They're not gonna bite you."

"I got bit by a bat as a kid."

"Shit, really?"

"Yeah. My family was camping. It was a fluke thing; there was only one. But we had to leave the camping trip and go to the hospital."

"Damn."

"It was hairy. And it hurt like hell when it bit me."

"I think they're gone now. But we can wait longer if you want."

I release his waistband, my cheeks warming. "Sorry about grabbing you."

"I grabbed you first."

"True. Maybe you should apologize."

He arches a brow, amused. "Twice in one day?"

"You don't need to apologize. I would've probably died of heart failure if you hadn't done that."

He hums a laugh.

"What's funny?"

"Of all the things you could be afraid of, I'm surprised it's bats."

"Everyone's scared of something."

He gets up and then offers his hand to help me to my feet. I brush dirt and rocks away from the back of my clothes, my heartbeat almost back to normal.

"Hello?" Marcus cups his hands around his mouth and yells into the cave. "Anyone in here?"

His voice echoes in the silence. There's no response.

"Let's head out," he says. "We can look around some more outside."

"Can I walk out ahead of you?"

"Sure."

He stays several feet behind me as I leave the cave, jogging. I don't want to spend any more time in a bat lair than I have to. Now that Marcus knows where I found the knife, hopefully I'll never have to go back in there again.

29

The chain of command is important, but you have a duty to consider who will benefit from orders you're given, and to speak up when you know something is wrong. Blind obedience and misplaced loyalty can lead good people down very bad paths.

- Excerpt from a police training manual written by Ben Hollis

A gust of wind blows loose strands of hair across my face when I emerge from the cave. When I look up at the sky, my gut churns with nervousness. It's not just the cloud the snow has been falling from that's gray now—it's the entire sky.

Marcus's brow furrows when he steps out of the cave. "We have to go back to camp. It's never good when it comes on this fast. Virginia's storm will gain momentum from the temperature drop."

I tuck errant sections of hair behind my ears. "What's the point of the microclimates?"

His expression is sober when he responds, a storm much like the one in the sky brewing in his eyes. "The ultimate goal is probably weaponizing climate. Heating or freezing people in certain areas to death."

My lips part with shock as the horror of it sets in. Whitman could kill large groups of people without sending in a single soldier. The implications are terrifying.

"But here, the microclimates were being used for training at Rising Tide. People were being taught to endure the worst weather conditions. To build shelters out of the materials around you."

I lock eyes with him, a bad feeling settling over me. "But now she's using it against your camp."

"*Our* camp."

"Ours."

"Virginia was sowing chaos any way she could, but she slowed way down in the past few months. I think the lack of food and supplies forced her to change gears and focus manpower on surviving." His lips purse in a thin, grim line. "But now she's desperate. She's going to throw everything she can at us."

I nod, wind rustling through the trees around us. "What if we give them some food? Do you think it would help?"

"No. It would take a lot of manpower to deliver it,

and I can't risk her killing those people." He glances around. "Flavius is gone. We need to get back as fast as we can."

"Let's go."

He casts a quick look at the tall volcano on the other side of the island. Then he takes off his pack and pulls out his radio, pressing a button on it.

"Ares to Athena."

He waits, and a response comes a couple seconds later. "Athena reads, Ares."

"Implement all storm protocols immediately."

"Copy that, Ares."

Nova's voice is cool and calm. Marcus packs his radio and shoulders his pack, giving me a quick look. "Ready?"

I nod and we start the trip back at a light jog.

"God of war, huh?" I say, keeping my gaze ahead.

"I didn't choose that call sign."

"Who did?"

There's a pause. "Finn."

"The two of you were close?"

"We were. I'll never forgive myself for what happened to him."

I flick a glance at him, confused. "It wasn't your fault. It wasn't anyone's fault."

His jaw is set in a tense line. "I should've turned my team back the moment I saw Pax."

"Why?"

Almost a full minute passes. I don't think he's going to respond, but he finally does. "Pax was controlling the snake."

On a surface level, it shocks me. But also ... I knew. A part of me knew and just didn't want to admit it. His expression changed right before the snake flew out of the jungle. It was too convenient that the snake showed up right at the moment Pax needed to flee.

"He ran ahead and left me that day. I was so afraid you guys were behind me, planning to kill me."

Marcus scoffs. "Pax is out for Pax. He's not as evil as Virginia, but he's a self-serving bastard."

Wind whips hair around my face and I brush it away from my eyes. The snow has turned into sleet. Wet, mushy blobs land on my arms as we approach the jungle entrance.

"I asked Ellison to give you a pregnancy test when you were unconscious after you first arrived," Marcus admits, scanning back and forth for any threats in the jungle.

"Me? Hell no."

"When I saw you with Pax that day, I assumed the two of you were together."

I'm jolted by the memory of kissing him. I genuinely thought I was losing my mind because of the way aromium made me feel around Pax. And he knew the entire time, but never told me.

"Absolutely not. He tried, but I'm smarter than that."

I think. Who knows? If I'd never been thrown into that hole by Virginia, maybe my aromium would've just gotten stronger, and eventually I wouldn't have been able to resist Pax's advances. The thought of being pregnant with his robot soldier baby makes my stomach turn with a sick sensation.

"So if we ran into him right now, he could get that monster snake to attack us?" I ask.

"Yeah. If there's a group of people, he can't target exactly which one he wants it to attack. But if someone was hurting him, the snake would go for that person."

"Why? How?"

He lowers his brows. "Aromium."

I slow slightly, unable to keep Marcus's pace. He matches me.

"I can't believe any scientist with a shred of ethics would create that nightmare," I seethe. "We have to destroy it. All of it."

"I'm trying. Not having much success so far, though."

"Tell me about the owner of—"

"Fuck!" Marcus stops and bends to grab his calf, where bright-red blood seeps from a fresh slash.

I don't even take time to think. I swipe his machete and jump in front of him, slicing the head off a massive praying mantis. At least, that's what it looks like, but it's the size of a full-grown golden retriever, Marcus's blood staining one of its razor-sharp forelegs. It's covered with a brown, leathery skin.

"What the fuck is that?" I yell.

"Genetically engineered mantis," he mutters. "They're mean fuckers."

I gape at him. "Who thought that was a good idea? They have compound eyes and they can see in 3D. And those legs are like razors."

He grimaces. "Let's talk about it later. We have to get back."

"Let's see your leg."

"It's fine."

This asshole. I'm in no mood for his heroics. I can't carry him back to camp.

"Move your hand!"

He does, and I groan when I see blood gushing from the four-inch gash in his calf. "Get out the first-aid stuff."

"Briar—"

I turn in a circle, my thumb poised over the activation pad on the stun stick. If any other mutant creatures are coming our way, I'm going to zap the shit out of them.

"Stop wasting time and get it," I snap. "You know it needs bandaged."

I hear him riffling around in his pack. I give him about fifteen seconds, and when I look back at him, he's wrapped the wound with an entire roll of gauze and he's getting to his knees to stand.

"Let's go," he says, his voice strained.

"No more running."

He scowls at me. "I missed the part where I put you in charge."

"Get over yourself. And radio Nova and tell her to have someone meet us to help get you back."

"I can't."

"Pretty sure you can."

He narrows his eyes at me, putting more weight on

his uninjured right leg. "We don't give that kind of information over the radio."

My instinct is to argue, but it makes sense, so I don't. Instead, I put my arm around his back and force him to put an arm around my shoulders.

"You said you liked me back in the cave, but this really isn't the time," he quips.

"Oh, you've got jokes? Right after a dog-sized mantis attacked you and I cut its head off?"

"I told you this jungle isn't safe."

I scoff, his back hard and warm beneath my palm. "You could've been a little more specific."

"What fun would that be?"

My note of laughter is humorless. "There's nothing fun about this place."

"I'm fine to make it back. We can jog."

"We're not jogging."

"Because I'm faster?"

My eyes widen as I look at him, nervous energy coursing through me. "I'll stab you in the other leg, and I'll enjoy it."

"Okay, okay. Keep your arm around me. We're almost there anyway."

The camp has a tall tower at its center, where someone keeps watch around the clock with binoculars. Whoever is there must've seen us, because Niran is racing out of the camp entrance as we approach.

"What happened?" he cries.

All traces of the carefree Niran I know are gone. His expression is panicked, his gaze locked onto Marcus.

"I'm fine. A mantis grazed my leg."

Niran looks at the back of his calf, his brow furrowed. "You're bleeding through the gauze. That's not a graze."

Marcus grunts with disapproval as Niran takes over for me, shouldering his weight. "I need a few stitches, but I'm fine. Briar can take me. Work on storm protocol."

I've been so concerned about Marcus that I forgot about the storm. When I look up, I see that the sky is now a darker gray than it was before, clouds moving quickly. The mushy sleet has gotten harder and is now more like hail.

"Nova's got the storm protocol," Niran says.

Marcus shakes him off with a growling sound. "There's a lot to do, get your ass moving! This is gonna be a bitch of a storm. The animals have to be moved and the crops have to be covered."

We just walked through the front gates, which the guards close and lock behind us. I breathe a little easier knowing we're protected by the tall, spike-covered fence.

"I'll take him," I tell Niran, giving him a sympathetic look.

He nods. "Thanks. He's a real asshole when he's in pain."

"Oh, you mean..." I look from Niran to Marcus and back to Niran again. "This isn't just his usual personality?"

Niran grins. "Well, that too."

He leaves, and Marcus limps the rest of the way to the Sub entrance, a guard opening the door for him.

"Why is this place called the Sub?" I ask him as we descend.

"Subterranean research center. Sub for short."

"Damn. And here I thought there was a dom somewhere in camp."

He arches a brow, a smile playing on his lips. "Who says there's not?"

Still hot. Even when he's bleeding and cranky.

When we make it to Ellison's office door, I knock on it and she opens it with a smile that slides away when she sees the gauze on Marcus's leg.

"Mantis nicked me," he says.

"Let's go to the exam room."

"Should I go find Nova to ask how I can help with the storm stuff?" I ask Marcus.

"No. Everyone has assigned jobs for it. You need to shelter in place in my room."

I lower my brows, not liking his answer. "But you said there's a lot to do, and I can't even get into the room. I can help."

"I'll radio for someone to let you in."

I back up a few steps, still facing him. "So I'm just going to find Nova, then."

"Do you ever listen to me?" He glares at me, exasperated.

"I listened when you yelled *fuck*. Hacked off that mantis's head. You're welcome, by the way."

Ellison fights a smile, putting a hand on his shoulder to try to lead him in the other direction.

"It's gonna get bad fast out there," Marcus warns. "When Nova puts out the shelter order, do it."

I give him a confused look. "Of course I will."

I turn around, letting myself break out in a full smile. I was wrong about nothing here being fun. Bantering with him is my entertainment.

"At least you listen to someone around here!" he calls after me.

I just wave, not turning back.

When I exit the tunnel, my light mood vanishes. The sky is a dark, ominous gray and the wind is stronger than before. People are running, some clutching children to their chests.

I don't even know where to find Nova. Instead, I run to a woman trying to carry two toddlers, taking one of them from her.

"Where are we going?" I ask her.

"The Sub! But I still have to find another one who got away from me." Her expression is pained, her cheeks tearstained.

"Give me both of them. I'll take them to the Sub and come back to help you."

"Thank you! The guard will know where you need to take them."

She passes them to me. One of the kids clings to me for dear life, shaking, while the other one cries into my shirt.

"It's okay, guys," I assure them. "You're safe."

I race toward the tunnel, protecting the garden the

furthest thing from my mind. Making sure everyone gets to a safe place is more important.

A gust of wind hits my back and I drop to my knees, one of the kids wailing.

"I've got you."

I turn to see Vadim behind me, his hands on my waist to help me stand. He takes one of the children.

"They're going to the Sub," I tell him, yelling over the howling wind.

He nods, putting a hand on my lower back. We take off for the tunnel entrance together.

30

Human test subject males showed increased aggression and emotional volatility. Increasing procreation urges is proving difficult. For our next round of test subjects, we will increase the compound's testosterone.

- Excerpt from the journal of Dr. Randall McClain

"Would you rather have no front teeth or a butthole that never stops itching?"

Marcus shakes his head, lips quirking as he rubs his jaw. "Really?"

I roll my shoulders, tired of sitting at the table in the front room of his quarters. "Just answer."

He exhales heavily. "I guess the itchy butthole."

"But not just a little itch, like a hardcore, driving you so mad you have to scratch it all the time kind."

We've been sheltering for a couple hours, the reports Marcus has gotten over his radio about the storm going from bad to worse. Apparently, high winds and small chunks of ice have made visibility near impossible. But everyone in the camp is accounted for, so all we can do now is wait it out. I've convinced him the time will seem to pass faster if we play Would You Rather.

"Which one would you pick?" he asks.

I smile. "I see what you did there. Like picking your butt because your butthole itches."

He rolls his eyes. "I didn't make that connection."

"I'd choose no front teeth. But I'm not vain."

He barks out a laugh. "I see. And I am?"

I shrug. "I don't know. Are you?"

His amused expression slides away. "I used to be, but not so much anymore. The only time I look in the mirror is to make sure I don't cut myself while I'm shaving."

"Bigger things to worry about?"

He nods, then says, "I thought of one. Would you rather have a beard you can never shave or be bald and you can never grow your hair back?"

"Hmm. I think I have to go with baldness."

He flicks his gaze to mine. "You have nice hair, but you could pull off bald. I'd probably take the beard."

I'm so used to scowling, order-giving Marcus that it's a strange feeling to just be hanging out with him. I figured he'd be going stir crazy, not smiling and giving me compliments.

"Do you guys have a massive stockpile of food and toiletries? Like enough to last you years?"

His expression closes off, and I realize how much that sounded like I'm prodding for the information a spy sent by Virginia would want.

"You don't have to answer."

"We do have a lot stockpiled, and we get deliveries. You may have already figured out the supplies are supposed to be for both camps, but I stopped sharing with them a long time ago."

I stand up and walk around, needing to stretch my legs. "And you're hoping she'll eventually trade people whose aromium you can deactivate for supplies?"

He lifts a shoulder in a shrug. "I'd be open to that. I don't think she would, though."

"Why not?"

He leans his elbows on the table, a crease forming between his brows. "The last thing I want is to make you sympathetic toward Virginia, but she's in a bad situation."

I narrow my eyes, skeptical. "She has options. She could at least negotiate for food."

"The reason she fights so hard for people on the beach when the boat comes is because she has to make this program succeed. There'll be a day when Whitman comes to get the kids, and he's going to expect a lot of them."

I nod, knowing how ruthless he is. Maybe she's just as much a prisoner here as the rest of us are.

"Virginia can't have children." Marcus holds my gaze across the table. "She's known that since before the virus. The only family she has left in the world is one niece, and Whitman's got her."

My chin drops with surprise. "You mean like as a hostage?"

He nods, his expression grim. "She's in his custody, that's all Virginia knows. And the results of the aromium program will determine what happens to her."

I put my hands on the back of the chair I was sitting in, seeing Virginia in a new light.

What if Whitman had one of my family members? I'd do whatever it took to get them back.

"Would you rather be responsible for the deaths of a lot of people you don't know, or the one family member you have left?" Marcus asks, our light game suddenly becoming all too real.

I look down at the table's surface, considering. "I don't know."

"Me either."

My pulse races as I raise my head to look at him. "Were you and Virginia...close?"

He knows a lot about her. Things most people at Rising Tide have no idea about. It's clear they *were* close, and I'm not sure how I feel about that.

"I knew her better than most. But we weren't romantically involved, if that's what you mean."

Warmth creeps up my neck, reaching my cheeks. "I heard she has a thing for Pax."

He grunts, looking disgusted. "Can't imagine why."

Static sounds over the radio. "Atlas to Command

One. We just heard a loud crashing sound outside the Sub. Want me to investigate?"

Marcus picks his radio up from the table, pushing a button on the side and talking into it. "Copy that, Atlas. This is Ares. Stay where you are. I've got it."

"Copy, Ares."

He stands, picking up his radio.

"If you're going out, I'm coming with you," I say.

He furrows his brow as he walks into the bedroom, where he stores his weapons. "I've only got storm gear for one."

"I don't need special gear."

He stops zipping the heavy raincoat he's putting on, giving me a look. "I'll just be getting soaked while I try to figure out what made the crashing sound."

"Better two sets of eyes than one."

His eyes stay locked on mine as he pushes the button on the radio. "Ares to Athena. What wind speeds do we have out there?"

An invisible thread tugs on me, beckoning me to move nearer to him. I keep my feet rooted in place, but all I want is to be closer to him. Close enough to see the flecks of brown and gold in his mossy eyes and smell the leather-and-saltwater scent that's so unmistakably him.

Nova responds a few seconds later. "Athena to Ares, fifty-three miles per hour."

"Copy, Athena. Thanks."

He shoves the radio in his pants pocket and gives me a pointed look. "There's got to be debris flying all over the place out there. Just stay dry in here and I'll be back soon."

"It's not safe to be out there alone."

He shrugs. "It's not safe to be out there at all. But I have to make sure our walls are still standing."

"I can help. You can either let me come, or I'll follow you."

He narrows his eyes, aggravated. "Are you ever going to listen to me? Just once?"

"I do listen to you ..." I look away. "Sometimes."

He huffs out a single-note laugh and I hear him unzipping the jacket. "Put this on."

"No, I'm not—"

"Yeah, you are. If you're coming, you're wearing the gear." He slides out of the jacket.

"I've been wet before," I argue.

His brows jump to his hairline and his eyes lock onto mine as he smirks. "I'd love to hear more about that later."

I bury my face in my hands, mortified. "You know what I meant."

"You don't need to be embarrassed about the effect I have on you."

I shake my head. "I should just let you get swept away. You deserve it."

"I'm twice your size. If anyone's going to get swept away, it's you."

I take the jacket from him and put it on, the sleeves hanging past my fingers and the jacket's waist hitting me mid-thigh. When he tries to pass me his rain boots, I shake my head.

"My feet will fall out of those, Sasquatch."

He unlaces his regular boots and puts on the knee-high rain ones. When he walks over to his weapon wall, a realization hits me.

"If you're still getting deliveries of supplies from Whitman, he doesn't know what's going on here. He thinks you're still supplying both camps."

He's quiet as he secures the belt of his holster around his waist, then glances at me. "Yep."

Excitement swirls in my stomach. Marcus has shifted the power dynamic, and I'm giddy over the prospect of being even a small part of that.

"Okay, this is ... I was in before, but now I'm a hundred and ten percent in. Making a fool of Whitman *and* blowing up his plans for robot soldiers? Let's fucking go."

His eyes land on my tattoos, his hands working on securing his shoulder holster. "You said when we questioned you that you're here because he did that to you."

He's asking me— without actually asking—to elaborate on the minimal explanation I gave for the ink when he and Nova were low-key interrogating me. But I don't even want to think about what Lochlan did to me, let alone recount it.

"He deserves to pay for a hundred reasons, and that's one of them. He's a festering sore on the asshole of humanity. He's ruined countless families and lives. And he bought all that control. He'd be nothing without his money."

"Couldn't agree more."

I look at the black *X* marks on my hands. "I took birth control so a man I was forced to marry couldn't get me pregnant. In what fucked-up hellscape is that a crime?"

His expression softens as he passes me a handgun. "Keep that dry if you can."

"How are you doing it? Does he still think there's research going on here?"

He nods. "Yeah. But I can't keep the charade up forever. It could all blow up at any moment. That's why I need to find McClain. He's the key."

It's the first time he's told me the name of the man who owned the knife before I found it.

"But what if he's dead?"

He drops his brows, looking grim. "Then I'll move on to Plan *B*, which is ... messier."

My heart pounds as I follow him out the door of his quarters, which he locks behind us. We're both silent as we descend the ladder, the roar of the wind and steady pounding of ice on the roof reminding me what we're about to walk out into.

Marcus stops in front of the exit door, giving me a serious look. "You have to listen to me out there, Briar."

"I will."

He arches a brow, skeptical.

"I will." There's a note of annoyance in my tone. "Let's go."

When he opens the door and walks outside, I follow.

He offers me his arm and I take it, because I can't see much through the sleet and ice whipping around in the powerful wind. It grabs ahold of my jacket and I tighten my hold on Marcus's arm, which is rock solid beneath my hand.

"Let's check the fence first!" he calls out.

The ice chunks are almost the size of golf balls, a few thudding against my head as we walk. Marcus leads the way to the Sub, and I can feel his relief when he finds the door to the tunnel securely closed and nothing damaged.

We're moving toward the wall when I stop, putting a hand over my eyes to shield them.

"I see something!"

He follows my gaze, then walks in the direction I'm pointing. When we get there, we find a lone piece of gray, weathered wood on the ground. He heads toward the center of camp, and soon we find another piece of wood that's smaller, but looks the same as the first.

My hair is blowing in every direction, making it hard to see. I lean in to Marcus, whose broad body shields me.

After a few more steps, he stops, turning his face toward me. "The tower came down."

Damn. I follow his line of sight to a pile of wood, which was the top of the tower, where a guard kept watch around the clock. Good thing no one was in it when it came down. It's a big loss, but at least it wasn't the fence.

Marcus leads me back to the Sub entrance, where we're more protected from the elements. He keys in a code to open the door and says, "Change of plans."

We're both dripping wet when we walk inside. I put my fingertips on my scalp to check a tender spot where an ice chunk hit me as he pushes the buttons to close the door.

I take off the heavy raincoat, Marcus grabbing his radio. He's about to speak into it when a voice comes out of it instead.

"Atlas to Command One. Code brown. Repeating, we are at code brown."

"Fuck." Marcus runs a hand through his hair, water droplets flying. He takes a second, hands on his hips, then says, "Okay."

He pushes the button on his radio. "Copy, Atlas. This is Ares. I need Command One armed and ready at the interior Sub entrance immediately."

My pulse races with worry as he meets my gaze. "We're running on partial power, which means one of our sources was damaged."

"Oh shit."

He nods. "Please listen to me, Briar. I like you. I want you here. I ..." He looks out into the storm. "Fuck, I'm bad at this. We have a system here, and even though I'm pretty sure you've got the skills to be on the first command team, you're not on it yet. I need—really, actually *need*—you to stay in here while we do our checks. We've drilled for this. I know—"

I nod, cutting him off. "Okay."

He frowns, looking unconvinced. "You sure?"

I put a hand up. "I get it. Emergency protocol, you

don't have time to be explaining everything to me. How can I help?"

He meets my gaze, something I can't identify swimming in his eyes. "Stella is in charge of command team two. Find her. If shit goes bad for my team, she'll take charge."

My heartbeat turns erratic as I look up at him, longing to reach out and touch him. "Don't say that."

"We have to plan for the worst. Virginia will do anything to breach this camp and take it over, and I'm dead if she succeeds. Take care of yourself, okay? I mean it. You're—" He looks away, seeming unable to find the word he's looking for.

I launch myself at him, wrapping my arms around his shoulders. He tenses for a moment, then returns my embrace, his massive arms encircling me at my back. Every nerve ending in my body fires as I press myself against him. I rest my cheek on his shoulder, which is as hard as a rock.

"It'll be okay," I say softly against his neck.

He tightens his hold on me, the security I feel in his arms calming the chaotic rhythm of my heart.

"Shit, sorry," someone mutters.

Marcus and I pull apart, our moment of connection severed by someone's arrival. His gaze stays locked onto me, the intensity of his earthy green eyes making my stomach drop to my feet. The corners of his lips quirk, hinting at a smile.

Nova clears her throat from behind me, trying again. "What's up, boss?"

"Walk straight until you get to the locked door," Marcus says softly to me. "Knock on it and find Stella. Tell her privately about the tower and the partial power."

I nod, my pulse still racing. "Okay. Good luck."

On my walk to the door, I do a deep-breathing exercise to calm my racing heart. I may not want to feel a constant urge to be closer to Marcus, but I do. I can admit it to myself. Being around him is unsettling, terrifying, and unwise. But it's also addicting. Breathtaking. Freeing.

Hugging him affected me more than I thought possible. It lit me up.

He's told me twice now that he likes me. I can't give in fully to this attraction, because his intensity could consume me. But I also can't shut down my feelings. Instead, I'm walking an intoxicating, thrilling line between the two.

I didn't realize how much I needed something just for me until I started getting to know the real Marcus. And somehow, I know he needs it just as much as I do.

31

Leadership at the aromium-enhanced camp has informed me that they've named their group Rising Tide. It gave me goose bumps of excitement. There have been hardships, but these people now see themselves as one cohesive unit with a clear mission. Just as nature's rising tides wash away all that came before, so will they, in favor of something better.

- Excerpt from the journal of Dr. Randall McClain

"I get nervous shooting apples on top of people's heads, but I've done it."

I gape at Amira. "Really?"

She shrugs. "When you get to a certain point, you know you can make the shot. I've won a lot of bets doing it."

We're sitting side by side on the concrete floor of a

huge room with a domed ceiling inside the Sub. There are about thirty people sheltering in here, some of them restless kids playing tag. It's been a couple hours, and I'm getting more nervous as time passes.

"Have you ever let anyone shoot an arrow at an apple on your head?" I ask.

"Sure. If I knew they could make the shot. It's pretty messy when an apple explodes in your hair, though."

I study my nails, cut short because they had to be for working in the garden. Before the virus, I had long, pretty nails. Even though I was a broke college student, I always found the money for manicures. My life now is completely disconnected from what it was then.

What if I had met Marcus back then? Things would have been very different if we'd met as a quarterback and an aspiring scientific researcher.

The apocalypse has taught me a lot about what's important. Trusting someone and feeling genuinely secure in their presence is a rarity to be cherished. My gut tells me I'm right to feel that way with Marcus, but I've been burned before.

"We'll see a lot more of each other with you on the security team," Amira says.

"You like your team members?"

She shrugs. "They're okay. I'm still pretty new."

I spent my first half hour in here talking to Stella. After I told her what Marcus wanted her to know and that I'm joining the security team, she quickly explained the structure here.

Command teams one and two handle camp security

and enforce camp rules. Security teams one through four only train and handle security. The camp perimeter is checked four times a day.

Amira and I are talking when the lights in the room suddenly go out, people murmuring in alarm. A couple seconds pass, and then there's a loud whooshing sound and spotlights mounted on the walls switch on, providing a little light.

"We're running on low power," Stella announces. "Everything's fine."

I see more than a few side-eyes in response.

"You think that aromium shield needs electricity to work?" Amira asks me in a tone only I can hear, barely moving her lips.

"Yeah."

She sighs heavily.

"You have plenty of arrows?" I ask her.

"Yeah, but not all of them with me." She leans in, her head right next to mine. "Should we come up with a rendezvous point in case shit ever hits the fan?"

Just the thought makes my stomach feel like a tumbling dryer, spinning endlessly. As far as life on Blue Arrow Island goes, we've got it great. But that's all dependent on the shield that keeps anyone or anything with aromium out.

"The beach? Where we were first dropped off?"

She nods. "Okay."

"I killed a dog-sized praying mantis."

I hear her sharp intake of breath. "Are you shitting me?"

"Nope. It was a walking nightmare."

Her groan is weary. "This fucking place."

My gaze wanders the room, landing on Stella. She's listening to something over the radio, her brows drawn together with worry. A few people near her stand up.

"Everyone, stay here," she says, her voice stern. "Ellison, Breck, come with me."

Breck is a tall, burly member of Command Team Two. Ellison's face is drawn with concern as she follows Stella.

"She's worried about Nova," Amira whispers.

She takes my hand, both of us holding on tight as we wait. Marcus is so strong and capable that I've never considered him dying. But I'm holding my breath, staring at the doorway when Nova walks through it a couple minutes later, blood splattered on her face and in her hair.

Marcus comes through next, a woman limp in his arms. He scans the room, his gaze landing on me. The agony I see in his expression makes me want to run to him, but I can't. Not now.

"Put Shan in the surgery room!" Ellison flies through the doorway next. "Des in an exam room. Niran, keep pressure on that wound."

Everyone who's been sheltering here is standing now, people putting their arms around each other as we all look on in shock. The woman in Marcus's arms leaves a trail of blood as he carries her through a doorway.

"What the hell happened?" Amira says softly.

"Virginia." My fury for her seeps through my tone.

She's on the wrong side of the battle for control of this island. Her niece's life isn't worth more than those of the people she's hurting and killing here. All so Whitman can build a supernatural army to help him murder more people and amass even more power.

Marcus said Whitman could find out what's really going on here at any moment. And if that happens, there'll be no stopping Virginia. If she has all the supplies she needs and no one keeping her in check, she'll be able to supply Whitman with countless pseudo-human soldiers.

"Everyone!" Stella calls out, her hands cupped around her mouth. "The storm has weakened. We're calling everyone else here so we can all be briefed by Marcus. Hopefully we can start that soon."

Marcus comes back into the Sub, his eyes finding mine immediately. He's hurting, and not from his swollen black eye or the cut on his bicep. Bone-deep ache is written in every line of his face.

"What's happening with you two?" Amira says, her voice so low I can hardly hear her. "I feel like I just walked in on an intimate moment, but you guys are just looking at each other."

I break Marcus's hold on me by looking away, not wanting to give my feelings away to the entire camp. "It's nothing."

"I'll take *total bullshit* for a thousand, Alex," she quips.

Within five minutes, the room is filled, well over a hundred fifty people packed into the space. Marcus crosses his arms over his chest and speaks to us.

"Command Team One encountered a group of Tiders while we were coming back to camp after assessing damage to our solar array. I'm deeply sorry to tell you Shan was killed and Des was wounded. Ellison is working on him now."

The room is eerily quiet, everyone's attention fixed on him.

"Our walls are all intact, but we lost the tower to the storm. For now, we're keeping everyone in the Sub who isn't essential to running the camp. We have to get the tower back up."

"What about the power?" someone asks.

Unease flickers over Marcus's face, passing quickly. "I don't know if we have what we need to fix it. And even if we do, we'd have to leave our shield perimeter to do it. There'll be Tiders waiting to ambush us."

"Unbelievable," someone mutters from the other side of the room.

Everyone turns, people craning their necks and standing on their tiptoes to see who spoke.

"This is why we should've been building a boat," Ray says, raising his voice with every word. "We can't survive here long term. We have to get the hell out of here."

There are a few nods of agreement. Marcus's jaw muscle tics, his tell for being pissed.

"Ray, if you want to build a boat, go ahead. You're not building it inside our walls, though. I'll give you a few tools and you can get started immediately."

Ray balks. "I can't do it by myself."

"Ask for volunteers."

"Are you gonna provide us security? Give us weapons so we can defend ourselves?"

Marcus shakes his head. "Our resources are for protecting the people who live in this camp."

"We don't have to choose!" Ray looks around, gauging who's with him. "We can have crews rebuilding here *and* building a boat."

Marcus shrugs. "Like I said, go ahead. But I'm not asking anyone to leave our security perimeter. You'll have to get volunteers."

"Who's with me?" Ray puts a hand in the air. "We can do this, guys. Don't you want to go home?"

No one raises their hand. After about fifteen seconds, Ray scoffs, narrowing his eyes at Marcus. "They're all afraid of you."

Marcus shakes his head and moves on. "I need all command and security team members in the lab for security assignments." He meets my gaze. "And also you, Briar."

Amira and I exchange a look. Neither of us knows where the lab is, and since everyone is busy, we wander instead of asking.

"Do you think there's a sign on the door?" she asks me as we walk down a hallway.

"Maybe we should go back to where we were and ask."

She puts a finger to her lips and creeps forward, her footsteps silent. I follow, both of us staying close to the wall. As we get closer, I hear the voices of a man and a woman talking.

"… walking into another shit show out there." It's Marcus, and I'm immediately stabbed with guilt for eavesdropping on his conversation.

"She's got the tools and some weapons, but at least we hid the ammo separately." That voice is Nova's.

"Yeah, we're fucked if she finds it."

"We have power banked," she says.

"It won't last long." Marcus's voice is tight and tense. "She's not getting this camp. I'll die before I give it to her. I should've turned my aromium back on before we went out to check the solar array. I could've protected Shan and Des."

Amira's eyes lock onto mine, wide with shock. My heart is racing so hard and fast, I'm worried Marcus and Amira will hear it.

"You can't." Nova hisses the words, catching me by surprise. "You're not risking yourself like that. We're not there yet."

"I can provide cover for the solar array repairs."

"No. It's too dangerous, and we don't even know if we have the parts to fix it."

Marcus exhales heavily. "We're running out of options."

"We need to find McClain. He's our best hope."

"Even if we do find him—which is a big fucking *if*—we don't have the flowers."

"If he's been out there on his own the whole time, maybe he knows where they are."

It's the most I've ever heard Nova say, and I can see why Marcus depends on her. She's giving him sound advice and sharing the load of stress so he's not carrying it alone.

"We need to get in there," he says.

Amira gestures for me to follow her and she quickly tiptoes back the way we came. I follow, and she turns around when we've gone about twenty feet.

"Be cool," she mouths, before talking out loud. "I like carbon fiber arrows with broadheads for hunting, preferably made from one-piece stainless steel." She starts walking. "You wouldn't believe how hard it is to make wooden arrows that fly straight."

"I didn't know that." I play along, pretending we're just happening upon this spot for the first time.

"Think we're close to the lab?" she asks as we round the corner we were hiding behind.

There's no one there. Niran opens a door nearby from the inside, frowning at us. "You two waiting for engraved invitations?"

"We didn't know where the lab was," I say. "Sorry."

"Ask someone next time."

Amira and I walk into the room, joining around forty people already there. Marcus's gaze finds mine and a ripple of something passes between us.

He clears his throat, scanning the faces in the room. "Let's get started. First things first, I know we usually do this differently, but Briar and Amira, are you willing to join Command Team One?"

Someone scoffs. "That's not fair."

It was Zara, who's probably still salty about our three-second sparring match.

"We need strength on both teams, and I vouch for both of them," Marcus says. "Amira's a crack shot with a bow, better than anyone else in this camp. And I've seen Briar in the field. She's swift and decisive with a knife. There's no time for infighting, guys. We have to stay united and take care of each other. We just lost a valued member of Command One, and Des is out of commission." He looks at me and Amira. "It's optional. You don't have to."

"I'm in," I say.

Amira nods. "Me too."

I glance at Zara, hoping I can heal things with a little humility. "I'll put in the work and take direction from those of you with more experience."

"Same," Amira says.

"Perfect." Marcus moves on. "Command Two, you're going to oversee the transfer of whatever the kitchen needs for cooking into the Sub and then get a crew together to start rebuilding the tower. Security One and Two, you'll assess damages to the farm and the garden and secure all livestock. Security Three and Four, patrol the perimeter."

He nods at the door and most of the people in the room clear out.

Once they're gone, we're down to eight people, including me and Amira.

"This fucking sucks, guys," Marcus says grimly when we're all alone. "Shan died a hero and we can't even give her the burial she deserves right now. But we have to put that aside."

"What's the situation with our electricity?" a man with blond wavy hair asks.

"We're at partial capacity."

"Yeah, but do we have enough for the shield?"

"We'll need to divert power from everything else. It's gonna get rough." He turns to Nova. "Do we have radios for our newcomers?"

Nova brings two radios over to me and Amira, cringing as she wipes the blood off one with her shirt. It must have been Shan's. I take that one.

"We use the names of Greek gods as our radio call signs," she says. "Never, ever use your real name, or anyone else's over the radio. Never say anything that gives away security information. If you aren't sure if something is safe to say, don't say it. We speak in code as much as possible."

"Amira has to be Artemis," the blond man says. "I know that used to be Kelsey's call sign, but I think she'd approve."

Marcus nods. "Artemis it is. And Briar, you're Aphrodite."

A smile tugs on Nova's lips. "We've never had an Aphrodite."

"So I'm Ares," Marcus says. "Nova's Athena, Niran is Atlas. And Briar, I don't think you've met Chance." The blond guy waves. "He's Helios. Wyatt is Hades." A dark-skinned man with a shaved head nods at us. "And Adele is Circe."

"The call signs—are they top secret?" Amira asks.

Marcus considers. "Not really. We have a Command

One channel that we communicate over and then there's a channel for all command and security team members. You'll get the hang of it."

"So what are we doing?" Niran asks, looking impatient. "Kicking some Rising Tide ass, I hope."

"You guys are going to patrol the edge of our shield area in shifts. Virginia is likely to try to make moves on us while we're vulnerable."

"If she even knows we're at partial power," Nova says.

Marcus nods. "They know our tower came down. They're starving and desperate. They had almost nothing when Briar was there, and it can only be getting worse."

"Why'd you say *you guys*?" Niran asks, his brow furrowed. "Where will you be?"

Marcus sighs heavily. "I have to go do something on my own."

"The hell you do," Nova says sharply. "You're not going out there alone."

Marcus shoots her a disapproving glare. "It's never been this unsafe out there."

"Out there?" Niran gapes at Marcus. "You think you're going outside the perimeter alone?"

Marcus looks away.

"I'll go with you," I offer.

"We'll all go," Nova says.

Marcus shakes his head. "Absolutely not."

"Call for a vote," Nova says breezily.

"Goddammit, Nova," Marcus barks. "We can't afford to lose the entire team."

Niran slams his fist on a table, making Amira jump. "Drop the martyr shit. Shan just died. Shit's really fucking real, and whatever needs doing, we do it together."

Marcus runs his hand over his jaw, which is covered in a shadow of dark stubble. "You guys might want to wait until you hear what I'm planning before you vote."

"I'm in." Niran grins. "Don't need to hear it."

"Me too," Wyatt says.

Marcus rolls his eyes, then turns serious. "I have good reason to believe McClain is alive on this island somewhere. I'm going to find him, and I'm turning on my aromium so I can work faster and not sleep."

32

Ever had a roommate who was always short on rent? This week we'll be talking about parasitic plants like mistletoe, that can tap into the vascular systems of other plants to steal water and nutrients. So give that freeloading roomie a mistletoe plant for the holidays and only you'll know the true meaning behind it.

- Excerpt from the Introduction to Plant Biology course taught by Dr. Lucinda Hollis

Marcus is met with stunned silence. After a few seconds, Niran laughs.

"I'm still in, brother. Go big or go home, right? And I guess going big is our only choice by default, because we sure as hell aren't going home."

Adele speaks up next, her shirt stained with blood

from the fight with the Tiders earlier. "Yeah, me too. Sometimes you have to fight fire with fire."

One by one, everyone in the room tells Marcus they're with him. I'm last, and I smile when his eyes land on mine..

"You know it's a yes from me."

He scrubs a hand down his face, looking tense. "This is dangerous shit, you guys."

"Hey, we'll have a better chance of killing those fuckers with our aromium on," Chance says.

"The aromium *is* what's dangerous," Marcus says. "The effects are ..." He furrows his brow. "You don't start back at zero when it's reactivated; you pick up right where you left off. So if you were ninety percent of the way to bonding, which makes it impossible to turn off the aromium, every day it's on brings you closer to that. And if you were feeling volatile when it was turned off, you'll be right back there. You'll only want to fuck and fight."

Niran scoffs. "Don't threaten me with a good time. We said we're in, so let's fucking do it."

Marcus looks up at the ceiling.

"What should we do if we find him?" Adele asks.

"Call me on the radio. We'll use the code word eagle for him. So radio the team that you've located the eagle and then stay with him. Do *not* radio location or coordinates." He pinches the bridge of his nose with his thumb and forefinger. "Fuck it, I might as well just tell you guys the rest. Aromium is made from a flower that grows on this island. The flowers are huge and shaped like bells. They're bright blue—very distinctive. McClain said he thinks he can make an aromium stabilizer with a component of the plant, probably the root. I've been low-key searching this entire island for it for a long-ass time. If you run across a plant with a flower that looks like that, dig up a bunch of them and bring them back to camp. Radio that you located...I don't even know, just call it a pot of gold. And for fuck's sake, don't forget the location."

I'm staring at him, open-mouthed, because that was *a lot*. It looks like everyone else, other than Nova, is doing the same. I can tell by his expression that even Niran didn't know about this flower.

"Oh ... I get it," Amira says. "That's why it's Blue Arrow Island. It's not actual arrows, it's blue aromium."

Marcus nods slowly. "The compound retains the blue color from the flower."

"How do you know all of this?" I ask him, unable to wait until we're alone.

He exhales through his nose, meeting my gaze. "Long story, but the short version is when I was a Tider, McClain found me in the woods and turned off my aromium. He told me everything he knew because the team of scientists fled the island bnd he was alone. If something had happened to him, no one would've been left to communicate with Whitman about the aromium project. He showed me how to do everything. Order supplies, send emails as him—"

"Email?!" Adele cries. "We have email here?"

"Not really," Marcus says. "It's only a connection with Whitman; there's no access to anything else."

I put a hand up. "Wait. If the other scientists left the island, why didn't Whitman do anything? Does he think his experiment is still rolling along as planned?"

Marcus pinches his brows together in a pained expression. "McClain knew that would happen if they made it back, so ... they didn't."

"What?" Amira whispers next to me.

"He sank their boat," Marcus says. "It was a submarine, and he was able to sabotage it from here. Look, you guys, we could spend all day in here on this stuff, but we need to be out there finding McClain. The life of every person in this camp depends on it."

Niran's usually playful expression is serious. "The shield can't stay up without the solar array, can it?"

Marcus hesitates. "I honestly don't know. We've never been in this position before. But I think we should assume we're on borrowed time." He scans the faces of everyone in the room. "I can't say this strongly enough—everything I've shared with you in here is for this team's ears only. Do not fucking repeat it. I don't want panic breaking out."

"We should divide into pairs to cover more ground," Nova says. "I'll take Amira, you take Briar?"

He nods. "Niran and Adele, you two pair up, and then Wyatt and Chance."

Chance holds a fist out to Wyatt. "Let's go cowboy the shit out of this."

Wyatt bumps his fist, his expression stoic.

Marcus exhales heavily. "Okay, let's all get changed and gear up. We'll meet up at the front entrance and take Stella with us so she can turn our aromium on when we're out of shield range."

I squeeze Amira's hand, exchanging a glance with her. "Good luck. Be careful."

"You too."

Marcus is silent on our walk to my former room in the Sub. Or maybe it's still my room, I don't know. He opens the door with his thumbprint and I gather the few clothes I have there.

We start the walk to his quarters then, and I search for the right thing to say the entire way there. I want to tell him it's going to be okay, but I can't, because it might not be. False reassurances annoy me, and I have a feeling he's the same.

Once we get to his rooms, I go into the bedroom and close the door, changing into a clean Rising Tide uniform of canvas pants and a T-shirt. Marcus changes into a clean pair of the same pants and a gray T-shirt, his arms and shoulders filling every inch of the worn soft fabric.

"Have you ever turned your aromium back on?" I ask him.

"No." His brow is lined with worry.

He passes me the shoulder and waist holsters he got for me from the Sub. We both sneak glances at each other as we get our holsters and weapons on. I've got a handgun in the shoulder holster and a machete and McClain's knife on my waist.

Marcus is strapped with two machetes and a

handgun. He also has a high-powered rifle attached to his pack. His pack is loaded with extra ammo, food, our canteens and other supplies.

"Where's my pack?" I ask.

"You don't need one."

"I can carry supplies."

He lowers his brows. "I want you traveling light. This is nothing for me."

I decide not to fight him on it. There's so much tension thickening the air in the room that I wouldn't believe we're the same two people who recently played Would You Rather in here and laughed about it.

We stand a couple of feet from each other, my chin tipped up so I can see his face. I can tell he wants to say something, but he's just brooding silently, scratching his jaw.

"What is it?" I finally ask.

He sighs softly. "I don't like who I am with the aromium on." He looks away. "I guess I don't want you to know that version of me."

Something inside me softens at his admission. I offer him a small, reassuring smile. "I know that's not really you, Marcus. And I know you're using the aromium for a good reason."

He shakes his head, agitated. "Fuck, this is hard." He runs a hand through his hair, then meets my eyes. "Aromium amplifies attraction. That's gonna be an issue."

I can't help it—my smile widens. This massive,

muscled, scowling man is wrecked over this conversation, of all things.

"What can we do about that, though?"

He huffs out a groan. "I was able to control it before. I never felt like I *had* to have any of the women at Rising Tide."

I shrug. "Maybe you'll feel that way about me, too."

He glares at me. "You're going to make me say it, aren't you?"

My heart takes flight because even though I shouldn't be letting this happen, it feels incredible. For a few moments, I'm not a prisoner in a tropical hellscape, racing against time to save myself and those around me. I'm just a woman, feeling light and giddy because a man I want feels the same way about me.

He grunts, clearly annoyed. "I think about you constantly. You're the most beautiful woman I've ever seen. Sometimes I forget to breathe when I'm looking at you. And it's not just that." He rubs his jaw, looking away. "You're also strong and smart and ... *fuck*. You're so blindly brave I want to tie you up sometimes to keep you out of trouble."

My hands tremble and my breath stutters at his admission. I knew he liked me, but I didn't know it was like *this*.

"I ... wouldn't mind being tied up by you."

That's all I can get out. I'm afraid to tell him I feel the same way because it's too dangerous. If we both give in, the spark of attraction between us will soon become an all-consuming inferno.

I'm a weapon. A sharply honed spear, my tip pointed directly at Whitman, Lochlan, and the regime they've forced on so many innocent people. But if I let myself completely fall for Marcus, I won't care about that anymore. I'll crave him instead of payback and destruction.

"I'm fucked either way." His note of laughter carries a bitter edge. "I can switch with Nova and take Amira, but I'll be thinking about you every fucking second. Worried about you. Or I can keep you with me and fight my urges."

There's nothing I want more than to hear more about his urges. But it's only going to make things worse for both of us. I look at the floor, and then up at him.

"I feel it too, but we have to focus on finding McClain. We can't just think of ourselves."

He nods. "I know. I just wanted you to know what you're getting into."

Closing the distance between us with a step, he brushes a curl away from my face and cups my cheek in his huge hand, the brush of his thumb over my cheekbone sending a spark of awareness dancing down my spine.

"You sure you want to do this?" he asks, his voice gruff.

I put my hand on his waist, nodding because I don't trust my voice. Even now, I'm not as close to him as I want to be. My body practically hums with the urge to climb him. Even on aromium, I've never wanted someone like this.

"If I get out of control, you know what you need to do." His voice is earnest, the pad of his thumb still stroking my cheekbone.

"I won't need to do that."

"But if you do need to, can you?"

My brows drop with worry. Could I kill him? If it came down to it, I don't know if I could. But there's only one acceptable answer to give him.

"Yes. To save my life or the lives of other Dust Walkers, I could."

Some of the concern slides away from his expression. "Good. And before we go out there ... this might be the only chance I get to do this."

He leans in, my pulse quickening as his warm breath caresses my lips. He slides his free arm around my waist, melding our bodies together as he kisses me, my lips parting eagerly for him.

His tongue brushes over mine, the kiss lighting my body up from the tips of my toes to my scalp. It's like I was dying of thirst and I'm drinking fresh, cold water. I wrap my arms around his back, moaning softly into his mouth.

It's not just a kiss—it's an awakening. His mouth plunders mine until I have to pull away, breathless. My eyes find his, the hunger and need I find there matching my own.

He rests his forehead against mine, speaking softly. "I know we're still getting to know each other, but ... this is who I really am. Remember that."

"I will."

He steps back, a smile tugging on his lips. "I haven't kissed anyone since before the virus. That was worth the wait."

My heart somersaults wildly. I love being the only one who gets to see this soft, sweet side of him. I just wish I could have more. Somehow, though, I know he'd be like a drug for me. No matter how much I had, it would never be enough.

I'd never be able to quit him, so no matter how much I want to, I can't give in to anything physical between us. There's too much at stake.

33

Human test subject males demonstrate different reactions to the newest test compound. Test subject seven choked test subject three over a minor disagreement involving the potatoes served at dinner. Without a larger test group, it's hard to discern whether it's the aromium or existing emotional volatility.

- Excerpt from the journal of Dr. Randall McClain

A rush of energy washes through my veins when Stella pushes the button on the handheld device to reactivate my aromium. I was thirsty; now I'm not. I felt a little lethargic; now I'm ready to run a marathon.

I take a deep breath in and out, letting myself adjust. There's definitely a sense that I might jump out of my skin.

"Okay?" Stella asks.

I nod and she moves on to Amira.

Marcus went first. He's walking off the transition, his back to me about thirty feet away.

"I don't feel any different," Amira says, looking relieved. "Probably because mine wasn't on for long."

Stella moves on to Niran, who howls softly when his aromium is reactivated.

"Holy fuck, that's more like a bump of coke than an actual bump of coke is. I think I might be able to fly now."

Adele glares at him. "I'm not jumping off a cliff to save your ass, so don't do anything stupid. *Extra* stupid, I mean, since you're ... you."

"You love me. We'll be boning by nightfall."

She laughs heartily. "Not a chance in hell. I'll fuck a tree before I fuck you."

"Okay, that's uncalled for. And frankly, unsanitary."

Marcus returns, his expression unreadable. Command Team One's members gather around him in a half circle.

"Team leaders are me, Nova, Niran and Wyatt." Marcus crosses his arms over his chest, his arm muscles an impressive display. "Team leaders make the final calls on everything. Stay low out there. Don't use guns unless you have to, but don't hesitate to use them when you need to. It's not just the Tiders who can kill us out here. Stay together at all times. Go back to camp if you're having trouble with the aromium."

"If someone finds the eagle or the pot of gold, do we all go back to camp?" Chance asks.

Marcus shakes his head. "We need both. Nova's meeting Stella here once a day for a briefing on things in camp. If shit goes south, Nova will call everyone but me and Briar back." He looks around at the people gathered. "Questions?"

No one has any. We all head out in separate directions, all of us searching a different quadrant of the island. The quadrant Marcus and I are going to is the farthest from camp; it includes the volcano on the other side of the island.

We aren't following a path, which is smart because Tiders are probably patrolling paths. Instead, we're cutting our way through dense jungle. There are muddy areas our boots sink into, and within a couple of hours, we're calf-deep in swamp water. I'm constantly swatting away bugs, sweat rolling down my face. Sunlight doesn't penetrate much of the thick canopy high over our heads, but the humidity is intense.

Marcus is silent as he leads the way, a machete in one hand and a bandanna in his other. He wipes his face every couple of minutes, the bandanna dripping sweat into the murky water at our feet.

It's good that this is physically exerting, because even with most of my focus spent just keeping up with him, I'm still fixated on his body.

Use him. Fuck him. Bring him to his knees.

With Pax, the aromium only enhanced the slight attraction I didn't even realize I felt for him. But with

Marcus, there's a constant throb to not just forget everything and have sex with him, but to use his desire for me to control him.

"Take a water break." Marcus stops walking and glances over his shoulder at me.

My canteen rests against my hip. I unscrew the cap and tip the canteen to my lips, the croaks and squawks of the jungle seeming louder now that we're stopped.

"How's the aromium feeling?" I ask.

"I'm fine."

"You didn't answer my question."

A couple seconds pass before he answers, gravel in his voice. "All I can think about is stripping you naked, dropping my pants, and holding on to your ass so hard I bruise it while I work your pussy up and down my dick until I fill you with my cum." He glances over his shoulder at me, a brow arched. "Does that answer your question?"

My pulse races, my core aching with desire for him to fulfill his fantasy. But I remind myself that he's been exposed to aromium for a lot longer than I have. I need to stay levelheaded and keep us focused on the important task at hand.

"Yes," I manage, screwing the cap back on my canteen. "Let's keep moving."

We make it back onto dry ground again, my soaked feet giving me flashbacks to what happened when I was trapped in Virginia's underground cell.

"I know this isn't ideal, but we have to dry our feet and boots," I say.

Marcus nods curtly, not looking at me. "Yeah, you're right."

It's dusk—within an hour, the sun will set and we'll be in the dark. Marcus's advanced aromium means he has good night vision, but I don't.

We packed extra socks, so even though the socks we're wearing now and our boots won't dry fully if we stop for the night, the boots will dry enough that we can wear them tomorrow.

"There's a good spot to stop for the night about a quarter of a mile from here," he says.

We continue walking in silence, my stomach swirling with excitement at the prospect of stopping soon.

Then I can ride him. He wants me. I can give him what he wants most and then he'll want more.

I push back at the thoughts aromium is putting in my head. I'm not having sex with any man on this island. It's too dangerous. One of us has to be alert and on watch at all times.

Give in. Let yourself feel good. Fuck him.

The sound of rushing water ahead is welcome. Hopefully it means I can get clean. I'm covered with sweat and mud, my shirt soaked through.

"Fucking pests," Marcus mutters as he smacks a bug on his arm.

Soon, we reach a clearing, where he finally turns around and makes eye contact with me.

"We can't have a tent or a fire, but we can dry out here and you can get some sleep. You want to wash up in the waterfall?"

"Yeah, I'd love to."

He leads me around a wall of rock and the waterfall comes into view. It's not tall, but it's wide, water gushing into a pool at its base. The pool is mostly surrounded by spiky vegetation and a plant with large yellow flowers, a grouping of boulders providing a place for me to get into the water.

Marcus's face is drawn tight with tension as he passes me a bar of soap and turns his back on the pool. "I'll keep watch. Let me know if you need anything."

What I need is for him to follow me into the pool and explore every inch of my body with his hands. My skin prickles with desire for him to touch me, the sensation somewhere between itchy and uncomfortable.

I strip my clothes off quickly, the whisper of muggy air on my bare skin making desire pool between my thighs. If Marcus would just turn around ... we could be living out his fantasy within ten seconds.

The thought of him inside me makes me breathless. It's been years since I did anything just because I wanted it. And I want him desperately. My nipples are peaked as I wade into the water, my gaze locked onto his back.

The faster I can finish this and get dressed, the better it will be for both of us. I bend my knees to submerge my head in the cool, crystal clear water, then lather the bar of soap until I have thick suds to wash my hair with.

Marcus's shoulders are stock-still, his body tense and his chin dipped. While I'm washing my body, I imagine sneaking up behind him and tugging on the back of his shirt, forcing him to turn around and look at me.

He wants you. He's greedy for your body. You can own him.

I force my mind away from the tempting thoughts, instead trying to remember the exact words to a paper I wrote for an English class. It was about Jack London.

By the time I've recalled what I think were the first couple of paragraphs, I'm clean and climbing out of the pool, wringing water from my long hair. I'm dripping as I approach Marcus and grab the pack he left behind him.

I sort through it, finding the set of dry clothes he packed for me. His heavy exhale steals my attention, and when I look up at him, his whole body is trembling.

"Are you okay?" I ask, worried.

"Just hurry up and get dressed." His voice is clipped.

My brow furrows as I struggle to get into the clean clothes while still wet. He seems to be suffering, and it's painful to watch.

"Are you in pain?" I ask him when I'm finally dressed.

"Not like you think of pain. I just have to adjust to the aromium."

I hesitate, unsure how to ask him what I need to. "Are you feeling any urges to hurt me? Or anything else like that?"

He hums a sardonic note of laughter. "Nope. I just want to fuck you until my body gives out."

Yes, yes, yes. Let him.

"Would ... a hug help?" I offer weakly.

"No." He says it harshly. "Don't touch me. I'll have you underneath me on the ground in two seconds if you do."

He's still shaking all over, and aromium is telling me that only I can make it better. Or is it aromium? I don't know.

"What about ... I don't know, dry humping? Maybe if you could—"

He puts a hand out to the side, cutting me off. "No. Stop talking. I'm not touching you with my aromium on. Keep watch while I clean up and then we'll eat and you can sleep."

I nod, cringing inwardly over my offer of *dry humping*. He takes the soap I offer and avoids looking at me as he walks closer to the water, pulling his sweat-soaked T-shirt off over his head.

The sight of his bronzed, muscled back and shoulders, plus aromium, is a combination that makes me start panting like an overworked dog. My lips part and the dry underwear I just put on becomes a little less dry. He kicks off his boots and pulls his wet socks off one at a time, and even *that's* sexy.

Then he unfastens his pants and I hear him unzipping them. I shouldn't be able to hear that from this far away, which means it's the aromium.

My heart pounds, my breasts heavy and my throat dry. It takes every ounce of my self-control to turn around right before he pushes his pants down.

The water ripples when he steps into the pool. That's the luckiest water in existence. It gets to touch him all over.

Remembering that we could be ambushed at any second, I scan the clearing and jungle. I refuse to die because I'm daydreaming about a man instead of paying attention to my surroundings.

Marcus is done within five minutes. I bite my fist as he gets dressed, fighting my urge to turn around.

"I'll hang up our wet clothes," I say, gathering his from the ground.

He only eats a couple bites of dried beef. I'm ravenous, so I eat more beef, a mango and some cashews. We haven't spoken much, because I don't trust what I might say.

"Sleep for a couple of hours," he says. "We'll get moving again after that."

I'm exhausted when I curl up on my side, my bare feet dry and my stomach no longer growling with hunger. Even though I still want to get closer to Marcus, my feelings are dulled by my fatigue.

If our urges for each other are only going to get stronger from here, I don't know how we're going to get through what could be weeks—or more—of searching.

I'm close to giving in to the pull of sleep when two yellow lights in the darkened jungle catch my attention. I lift my head up.

"What are those lights?" I ask.

"Flavius's eyes."

The wolf. I squint and see that he's sitting at the edge of the jungle, watching us. It doesn't make me nervous. Somehow, I know he's not here to hurt us, but to protect us if we need it.

34

Five Days Later

I've received a report of a new practice at the Rising Tide camp called "The Circle", in which any camp member can challenge another to a one-on-one fight to the death. It's a primal, but effective means of incentivizing hard work and cohesion.

- Excerpt from the journal of Dr. Randall McClain

It's been raining for hours. We got caught out in it while searching on the beach, so we were soaking wet by the time we found shelter beneath the overhang of a rock formation.

It's not a perfect setup; the wind is blasting sheets of

wind at us. But I'm too cold to look for someplace better. I'm huddled against Marcus's side, his arm around me.

"You okay?" he asks.

"Yeah."

It's been a fairly miserable five days of nearly nonstop searching. Two days ago, Marcus found a button on the ground, so we've been combing the radius around where he found it as methodically as we can. We haven't seen any sign of Rising Tide, and there's been minimal radio traffic from the other teams.

"That photo on the dresser in your room ... is that your mom?"

A few seconds pass and I'm not sure he's going to respond. "Yeah. Her name was Natalie. She was an emergency department nurse."

"Is that why you wanted to study medicine?"

"She was definitely an influence. She was a single mom from the time I was five, and there were times I had to hang out in the staff lounge for a few hours because she couldn't get a sitter."

It's hard for me to imagine Marcus as a little boy. He doesn't seem like he was ever silly or carefree.

"Can I ask what happened to your dad?"

I feel his scoff beneath my cheek. "He was a deadbeat who did us both a favor when he took off permanently."

"I'm sorry."

"Don't be. My mom taught me everything I needed to know about being a man. She worked sixty hours a week and never missed one of my football games."

I sit up straight so I can see his face. "Sounds like she was a great mom."

A hint of a smile quirks at the corners of his lips. "The best. She made me volunteer a few hours a week in the hospital day care from the time I was ten. I changed diapers, helped kids learn to read, and rocked sick kids to sleep. And as soon as I hit high school, every time I left to do something with friends, she'd ask me if I was ready to be a father. Of course I said no. Then she'd give me this look and tell me to remember that when I thought about having sex."

I can't help laughing.

His smile grows and he shakes his head. "I was a virgin until I was nineteen, thanks to Nat Wells."

"Wells? That's your last name?"

"Yeah."

"So who was the lucky woman when you were nineteen?"

"Her name was Nicki. We met in a freshman history class."

Jealousy toward someone I don't even know burns hot in my chest. I change the subject before he tells me anything more about it.

"Have you seen Flavius today?"

"Nope. But I don't think he's far."

The rain gets lighter and I stand up. "We might as well get back at it."

"Yeah." He's too tall to stand up fully beneath the rock overhang, so he steps outside of it.

I can't sleep more than a couple of hours a day.

Somehow, my body knows we're exposed and it won't fall into a deep sleep. As long as I get enough water and some food every day, I feel okay.

Marcus has adjusted to his aromium. He has an erection most of the time and he still looks at me like he's starving and I'm dinner, but he seems to be able to focus on the search, too.

It's late afternoon, the heat at its peak for the day. My feet are sore from constant wetness and walking, but all I can do is let them air out once a day and try to dry my socks and shoes.

"I have to use the facilities," I say, walking toward a grouping of trees nearby.

He busies himself checking supplies, staying in earshot but not watching. I'm crouching behind a massive tree when I see movement in the corner of my eye.

My heart drops to my stomach. It's a jaguar, slowly stalking in my direction. My mind freezes; I can't remember what to do when a jaguar is near. Should I run? Play dead?

It takes another step, dropping its head slightly. I stand and pull my pants back up, calling Marcus's name without screaming it as I zip and button my pants.

A jaguar mauled that Rising Tide guy to death, and he was surrounded by people with aromium. I apologize to the universe for my thoughts about our search conditions being tough.

My sore feet and sunburned scalp don't compare to getting my throat ripped out by a jaguar.

"Marcus," I say, a little louder this time.

Help me.

Something thick and coiled drops down from a tree branch above me. I jolt, thinking it's a snake, but it slithers through the air, not hitting the ground.

It's a vine, and it's not the only one. Vibrant green vines in a variety of thicknesses are all moving swiftly toward the jaguar. The one from the tree reaches the cat and crawls onto its back.

The animal turns and retreats, racing toward the jungle. As soon as it's gone, I breathe again and the vines slither back the way they came, gone as quickly as they arrived. The one from the tree lightly brushes my upper arm as it goes, the touch almost ... affectionate.

"Briar, you okay?" Marcus calls.

I jog back to him, his eyes widening when he sees my face. His hand goes to the gun on his hip.

"What happened?"

"Vines." I swallow hard, still not believing what just happened. "There was a jaguar, and I was afraid it was going to kill me."

His eyes bulge, his gaze darting behind me. "What the fuck? Why didn't you yell for me?"

I lower my brows. "I kind of did, but forget that. Vines came out from all over and they were going for the jaguar. They scared it off."

He runs a hand through his hair, scanning our surroundings. "You're sure it's gone?"

"Yeah, but more importantly—what the fuck was

that? It's the second time vines have protected me. How is that even possible?"

He shrugs. "People and animals aren't the only experiments on this island."

My pulse races as realization sets in. "Are you saying *plants* have been injected with aromium too?"

He nods. I haven't even processed my shock yet when his arm shoots out and he moves me behind him.

"Something just moved on the beach," he whispers.

Not the jaguar again. I groan inwardly. We've been lucky to not have confrontations with predators so far, but luck always runs out.

Marcus gestures for me to stay behind him as he creeps toward the beach, machete in hand. We didn't bring stun sticks because they're cumbersome, but right now I wish I had one.

I draw my handgun, leaving the safety on, scanning our surroundings as Marcus keeps his gaze ahead.

When he has a clear view of the beach, his shoulders drop with relief. "It's Flavius."

I lower my gun. When we step onto the fine ivory grains of beach sand, Flavius is sitting midway down the shore, looking at us.

As we get closer, he walks farther down the beach. Marcus follows, both of us constantly checking the area around us for any movement. Normally, I'd marvel at the pink-and-orange sunset over the ocean, but I can't afford the distraction.

"We're too exposed here," I murmur. "I don't like it."

"Let's move faster."

We don't have to worry about walking quietly out here; the wet sand makes for quiet footfalls. Flavius looks over his shoulder, making sure we're still following.

The melee on the beach the day I arrived here is still fresh in my mind. I'm imagining an arrow from a concealed archer hitting Marcus in the chest, my heart racing faster with every step we take.

"I don't like this," I repeat.

He glances back at me, nodding at the ground beside us. "Look."

I've been looking everywhere but down, and when I do, my jaw drops. There are footprints in the sand a few feet away, leading in the direction we're walking. Flavius's large paw prints are visible right beside the footprints.

Marcus is moving faster now, almost at a jog. I manage to keep up, but it's hard to scan our surroundings thoroughly at this pace.

"Fucking hell." Marcus skids to a stop.

I put my hand on his arm to help stop my own trajectory. When I follow his gaze, I find a very lean man with sun-weathered skin sitting on a flat rock that's part of a big rock formation at the shoreline. He's holding on to a fishing pole made from a stripped tree branch.

Flavius sits beside the rocks, his mission accomplished.

Marcus stalks over to the man, shaking his head as he studies him.

"Hello, Marcus."

"Dr. McClain."

My pulse pounds with nervousness, though I don't know why. This man is maybe five feet, ten inches, and he can't weigh more than a hundred and twenty-five pounds. He has no weapons and his expression is placid.

"You really fucked me," Marcus says, his tone harsh.

McClain pushes the nosepiece on his dark-rimmed glasses up higher on his nose, staring out at the watercolor sunset. "I didn't expect you to understand."

Marcus crosses his arms over his chest. "Here's a little something *you* need to understand. I'm fighting a losing battle. Virginia has more numbers than I do. She has the microclimate controls back online."

"You turned your aromium back on."

Marcus shifts, tension tightening his muscles. "Didn't have much choice. The Tiders are picking off my people. I need your help."

McClain meets Marcus's gaze. "I have to live with what I've done. All I can do now is not add anything else to the list."

Rubbing his jaw, Marcus laughs bitterly. "The fire you started is raging out of control, and there's a hose in reach. Not helping innocent people is a choice, and it's the wrong one."

"I can't, Marcus."

Marcus's expression darkens, a storm raging in his eyes. He's restraining himself, but I wonder if, after all the work it took to find McClain, his refusal to help will spark Marcus's temper into action.

"You have to. It's not too late to land on the right side of this."

McClain's face is lined with regret. He's shirtless, the lines of his ribs visible. It's hard to look at a person who seems to be straddling the lands of the living and the dead the way he is.

"I searched this island every day for nine months for the flower," he says, his voice flat and hopeless. "That's all I did, from sunrise to dusk. I combed every inch I could get to."

"Don't you know where it is from the first time you found it?"

McClain shakes his head. "A team of scientists came here to survey the island. Those flowers were dug up by a woman who filled her bags with them and was attacked by a lion on her way back to camp. We found the bags when we found her body."

Marcus's shoulders sink, a little more hope dying inside him. It pains me to see his resolve cracked by this man who gave up when things got hard.

"As long as we're alive, there's hope," I say, moving to stand beside Marcus. "We're not giving up."

Marcus nods. "Briar, meet the elusive Dr. Randall McClain. And we're not giving up. I brought rope in case we needed it. He's coming back with us, one way or another."

McClain smiles sadly. "I'm an empty vessel, Marcus. Tie my hands. Push me off a cliff. I no longer care what happens to me."

Marcus roots around in his pack. "That may be true, but you're going to witness the destruction you caused.

You're not watching peaceful sunsets while my people get hunted."

McClain braces his hand on a rock and climbs down, his arms and legs sticklike. "I knew you'd find me. I've been moving for days. You've got people hunting *me*."

"Couldn't happen to a more deserving guy," Marcus says stiffly as he pulls out a rope. "If I didn't need you, I'd shoot you in the head right now."

McClain sighs, looking defeated. "I won't work in the lab. I won't analyze or create anything. Even if you torture me. Finding the flowers was the only hope, but there are none."

Marcus shakes his head. "You're a piece of work. Are you going to walk, or do I need to carry you?"

"I'll walk."

McClain's gaze lands on the knife at my waist. "I've been looking for that."

Marcus ties the rope around McClain's midsection, then secures it around his own waist.

"You try anything, I'll knock you unconscious and carry you the rest of the way," he says.

"There's no fight left in me. I'm just existing until the day I die."

Marcus scoffs, disgusted. "How fucking zen, you selfish bastard."

When his eyes meet mine, I offer a sympathetic look. His tortured expression reaches inside me, making me even more curious about his history with McClain.

I know enough, though. McClain made aromium,

which means he worked for Whitman. Which makes him my enemy.

35

Construction has begun on a wall around our camp. The aromium shield is effective, but an enhanced jaguar became so crazed that it was undeterred by the shield. It died from the shield's effects about twenty yards outside our camp. A physical barrier between our team and the aromium-enhanced creatures has become a necessity.

- Excerpt from the journal of Dr. Randall McClain

We're the last team of two to make it back to camp. Nova's waiting for us at the cutoff area for the aromium shield, holding a torch that lights up the inky darkness of night. Her expression goes stony when she lays eyes on McClain.

Amira's with her, and she throws her arms around me in greeting as Nova deactivates Marcus's aromium.

"You guys did it," she murmurs in my ear.

"I can't believe it."

She pulls back, her hands on my shoulders. "We ran into a group of megamantises. Total horror show."

A smile pulls on Nova's lips as she runs the aromium device over my hip. "Our Artemis took five down with arrows."

Amira beams proudly. "Got two of 'em right in their freakishly large eyes."

The device beeps and energy seeps from my body. I stumble, unable to stay upright with the aromium off. Marcus is there. My back lands against his chest and he wraps an arm around my waist.

"Give it ten seconds," he says. "It'll get better."

"What should I do with Runaway Randall?" Nova asks, untying the rope around Marcus's waist.

"Put him in a cell. Bring him some food and water."

"I don't need food," McClain says.

Marcus gives him a murderous glare. "Nova's going to monitor your food and water intake. Try some hunger strike bullshit and I'll force-feed you."

"I won't hunger strike. I just don't eat very much."

Marcus's face is drawn with anger as Nova leads McClain, the rope still secured around his waist, toward camp. Amira walks on one side of me, Marcus on the other.

"I didn't notice when my aromium was turned back on, but I definitely noticed when it was turned off earlier," Amira says. "It was like getting hit with a tranq dart."

"Yeah, I could sleep for the next few weeks," I say.

"Want me to bring you guys some food?" Amira asks.

Marcus puts an arm around my shoulders, looking over my head at Amira. "Will you ask someone in the kitchen to leave some food outside the door of our room?"

"Sure." Her eyes shoot to mine, her knowing smile making my cheeks warm.

Our room?

The past five days in the jungle have brought Marcus and me closer. We had to rely on each other, and we got to know each other better. The thought of going to our separate quarters to sleep has been making me uneasy the whole walk back to camp.

I can't keep taking his bed while he sleeps on the floor, though. He didn't sleep the entire time we were out searching, and he has to be exhausted now that his aromium is off.

Amira says a quick goodbye and ducks off toward the kitchen, glancing back at me with a conspiratorial smile.

"She's subtle," Marcus says lightly.

"Is it done already?" I look up at the tower in the center of camp as we pass it.

"Looks like it. I think Stella might be after my job."

He keeps his arm around me, and we're almost to the housing block when we see Niran approaching.

"The team that lassoed the eagle!" he cries, grinning.

He embraces Marcus, clapping him on the back. When they part, I'm surprised when Niran hugs me, too, lifting my feet a few inches off the ground.

"You guys coming to the Hub?" he asks, setting me down. "A bunch of us are hanging out there."

Marcus shakes his head. "We're wiped, man. Just showers and sleep for us."

My stomach twists with excitement. We kept our hands off each other for five very long days, even though aromium made me feel like a bitch in heat. And now that I've seen Marcus's erection tenting his shorts, I know what I'm missing, making it extra tragic.

"See you kids tomorrow," Niran says, waving as he turns toward the Hub.

Marcus uses his thumbprint to open up the door to the housing block, letting me step inside first.

Fatigue tugs at my limbs as I climb up to the second floor. I can't wait to take a shower and finally dry my feet fully.

Marcus speaks into his radio. "Ares to Operator, do you read?"

"Loud and clear. Welcome back, Ares."

"Can you open up the keypad on my quarters for the next two minutes?"

There's a pause before an answer crackles over the radio. "Ares, I can't do that without more information."

A corner of Marcus's lips tilts up in a half smile. "Right. Peanut butter and cherry preserves on wheat."

"Copy, Ares."

Marcus puts his radio away and I ask, "What was that?"

"Code. We're cycling through everyone's favorite sandwich. That one's ... Breck's, I think. We'll set a new code tomorrow. But more importantly, put your thumb on the pad."

I pinch my brows together, pressing my thumb to the small black pad beside his door.

"Leave it until the light turns green," he says.

It takes around twenty seconds for the light to switch from red to green, and then I remove my thumb.

"You can get into our block and room with your thumbprint now."

I arch my brows, smiling. "Ours, huh?"

He opens the door, holding it for me. "Casa de us, baby."

My pulse races with happiness as I go inside, him following and closing the door behind us.

"I might need to do some redecorating," I say lightly, looking around the spartan space. "Just a few dozen doilies and some decorative plates on the walls, maybe some potpourri..."

He sweeps me into his arms before I realize it's happening, his lips meeting mine in a short, soft kiss. "You've got ten minutes to shower and get back here."

I bracket his head with my hands. "And if I go over?"

"I'll carry you back from the shower, naked and dripping. And I'll enjoy the hell out of it."

I think he means it. I brush the tips of my fingers through his hair, my gaze locked with his. My exhaustion is forgotten. Though we've been alone for most of the past five days, we haven't been *this* alone. Now it's just the two of us, no aromium influencing our thoughts.

It's no surprise I want him just as much as I did

before. Now it's a yearning I feel deep inside, though, instead of just a magnetic pull to get closer to him.

We both grab clean clothes and our shower supplies and silently head in separate directions for the showers. There's only one other woman in a stall on the women's side.

I close my eyes and soak in the feel of cool water washing away the sweat and dirt from my skin. Only for a few seconds, though. Then I get to work lathering myself with soap from head to toe. I have a lot of bug bites and little scrapes, my skin more bronzed than it's ever been.

My shower is finished in record time, my body and hair scrubbed clean and my legs and pits shaved. Sliding into soft, clean clothes feels heavenly. I don't know how this buttery blue sleep set of lightweight pants and a tank top made its way to this island, but I'm glad it did.

I brush my teeth last, then put all my supplies back in my tote and head for ... I smile huge just thinking about it. *Our room.*

Marcus is waiting when I get there, my breath hitching when I see him. He's only wearing black shorts, his wet hair pushed back from his forehead.

"Thinking about this is the only way I got through the past five days," he says, his gaze dark and hungry. "But I do understand if you need sleep instead."

I set my shower caddy down on the table and approach him, my heart thudding like a drumbeat.

"I need you more," I say simply, gently touching his stubbled jaw.

He closes his eyes for a few seconds, then takes my other hand and puts my palm on his warm, solid chest. "I swore I'd never be with a woman on this island. But I can't ..." He shakes his head. "I need you as much as I need to keep breathing, Briar."

I run my fingertips down his chest, all my hesitation forgotten, too. "Ellison has something that will keep me from getting pregnant. I saw it in her office."

He takes the hand that's on his cheek, kissing my fingertips. "I don't deserve you, but I'm a selfish, greedy bastard."

Need throbs between my thighs as I whisper, "Show me."

I inhale sharply as he wraps his hands around my waist, picking me up. I wrap my legs around him, resting my forehead against his as he carries me into the bedroom.

Still cupping my ass with one hand, he uses the other to secure every lock on the door. I run my fingertips through the waves of his hair, kissing his forehead, his nose, and his cheek.

He's gentle as he lowers me to the bed, bracing himself on a knee. Questions swim in his eyes and a crease appears between his brows. "If you change your mind, I'll stop."

I nod, tracing a fingertip down the curved, solid muscle of his arm. "Okay, but I won't."

He kisses my jawline, sending a shiver of awareness over my skin. Then his lips find mine, and I put a hand on his lower back, urging him closer as I open my mouth to him.

When our bodies meet, he groans, his kiss turning deeper and more passionate. I can't get enough of his warm, smooth skin. My hands rove over his back and shoulders, and finally I slide them down the waistband of his shorts and sink my fingertips into his ass.

"Fuck," he murmurs against my lips. "I think you're greedy, too."

"Also impatient."

He hums a smile, gently smoothing a lock of hair away from my face. Still holding some of his weight on his knees, he slides my shirt up and over my head, groaning long and loud when he sees I'm not wearing a bra.

Lowering his lips to my nipple, he flicks the tip of his tongue over it and then sucks it between his lips, making me gasp.

"I spent a solid four hours of every day on aromium fantasizing about these." His warm breath caresses my peaked nipple. "Had to force myself to walk away from you so many times when all I wanted was *this*."

He moves his attention to the other one, switching between them until I'm panting with desire.

"I want you," I say as I squeeze his ass and push his shorts down farther. "No more waiting."

He gets to his knees and then his feet, pushing the shorts to the floor. My eyes widen when I see just how thick and long his erection is. The pulse between my thighs becomes an ache as I watch him palm his cock, running his hand up and down its length.

His gaze on me is predatory as I slide my pants down, frantic to get them off and have him inside me. With his free hand, he grabs the waistband, his knuckles brushing over the curls of my sex as he tugs the pants off in one sweep, letting them fall to the floor.

He climbs back on the bed, his eyes holding mine captive.

"No more waiting for what?" His voice is gruff, his shoulders shaking slightly, like they did when his aromium was on and he was struggling to keep his hands off me.

"For you to be inside me."

He runs his calloused fingertips down my chest, between my breasts, over my stomach, to my ravenous pussy. I jolt and moan, my back arching slightly.

"Say my name." He runs his fist up and down his length again.

"Marcus," I whisper. "I want you. Please."

He leans over me, lining himself up at my entrance. His forearm rests above my head as he pushes himself inside me, my slickness making it easier. He groans and then goes still.

"Still yes?" he whispers in my ear.

"Yes." I push on his lower back, urging him to sink in farther.

When he does, I gasp and keep ahold of his back. "I'm okay. I like it. Just go slow."

He kisses my neck and pulls back out, gentle as he

slowly slides himself in again. "Goddamn, you feel amazing. I'm out of practice."

I hum with amusement. "You're perfect."

He continues, keeping the pace slow until I grind my hips against his, silently setting a faster pace. My nerves are like a fireworks display, the bliss growing brighter and stronger with every thrust of his hips.

I'm breathing hard, already feeling the build of an orgasm when he captures my wrists in one hand and pins them above my head, putting his other palm behind my thigh and pushing it until he's sinking even deeper into me.

"Fuck," he mutters, strain etched into his face. "So fucking good."

The combination of his control over my body and his arousal pushes me over the edge. I shamelessly roll my hips against his as I come, crying out his name.

He knows how to make it last, and he does, thrusting into me so hard the bed is hitting the wall. I'm starting to come down when he lets out a sound that's more roar than groan and then stills inside me, his arm muscles beautifully defined as the last of the wall between us crumbles away.

He stays inside me for several heartbeats, his breath returning to normal. I miss his closeness as soon as he kisses me and moves to the side, propping himself up on his elbow and draping his other arm over my stomach.

My eyelids are suddenly leaden, my blissed-out state making me sleepy.

"My toes actually curled," I say, smiling.

He grins down at me, affection in his mossy eyes. "I'll take the floor so you can get some good sleep."

"The fuck you will. You're staying right here."

The last thing I see before my eyes slide closed is his amused expression and a nod.

———

When I wake up, I'm alone in the bed. I put my hand on the side Marcus slept on, finding it still warm.

I'm groggy, which I think means I slept for a long time. I walk into the other room, finding a filled canteen and a note on the table.

Briar,

Meet me in the Hub. I have something to show you.

x Marcus

I smile, my body deliciously sore. I'm thirsty, so I drink all the water in the canteen before getting dressed in a clean Rising Tide uniform and going to the bathroom, where I brush my teeth and secure my long, wild hair in a thick bun at the nape of my neck.

We never ate last night. Whatever food was delivered is gone now. My stomach rumbles in protest when I head for the Sub instead of the kitchen.

When I try my thumbprint on the Sub's entrance

door, it opens. A woman walking out of the Sub nods at me as I walk in.

I can't keep the silly grin from my face as I descend into the Sub. I did a terrible job of resisting Marcus. Zero stars, honestly. But right now, I can't even remember why I wanted to resist him. Being near him makes me happier than I've ever been. And since we're dancing with death all the time here, if my ticket gets punched, I'd rather go having had incredible sex recently than being celibate.

My thumbprint also works on the entrance to the main Sub area, where I sheltered during the last storm. I find Marcus there, leaning against a counter as he talks to Niran, Adele, and Chance.

As soon as our eyes lock, he gives me a warm smile, the others turning to see what caught his attention.

"Hey," I say in greeting.

"Great job on the op," Adele says. "Marcus was just telling us about it."

"Yeah, I still can't believe we found him." I focus on Marcus. "How's he doing?"

He shrugs. "He's alive. Other than that, I haven't checked. I'm planning to keep him as isolated as possible to increase the chances he'll break."

Pushing away from the counter, he says, "Hey, we have to take care of something; we'll catch you guys later."

He puts an arm around me, pulling me close and kissing the top of my head. "How'd you sleep?"

"Amazing. What time is it?"

"Almost noon."

"I slept for more than twelve hours?"

"Yep. I slept for eleven."

He leads the way to a door I've never been through, opening it with his thumbprint. It takes us into a long hallway, where we walk to another door that he opens with his thumbprint.

He takes a flashlight that was clipped around his waist, switching it on. "We're still on low power, so no lights in here."

He shines the light on a computer. It's been a very long time since I saw one—pre-virus.

When he pushes a button, the computer hums to life, the screen taking time to load.

"I know McClain, and since he said he looked for the blue flowers, that means he'll make a stabilizer if we can find them. Since you know a lot about plants, I figured I should show you all the records we have about them. Maybe it'll spark something that will help you narrow down where we can find them."

I nod. "Of course."

The screen loads, my eyes quickly scanning the icons. One of them catches my eye.

"What's that?" I point at it.

"It's a database. People who survived the virus and people who didn't. It hasn't been updated in a couple of years, though."

I look up at him, my breath caught in my throat. "Can I look up my family? Maybe there's something about how they died or where they were found."

"Of course." He puts a hand on my shoulder as I click on the icon.

It's basic, the cursor on a blank search bar blinking at me. I type in my mom's name first.

A photo of her loads, bringing tears to my eyes. I run my fingertips over the screen, overjoyed to even be seeing a picture of her. It's been so long since I saw her smile.

Lucinda K. Hollis: DECEASED

That's the only information it has on her. In my heart, I knew she was gone, but it's still a stab in the gut to read the impersonal, all-caps declaration.

"She's beautiful," Marcus says, smoothing a hand over my hair. "You look like her."

I wipe a tear from my cheek. "Thank you."

I type in my dad's name next.

Benjamin R. Hollis: DECEASED

There's another stab. My dad isn't smiling in his photo. It's his all-business expression. That's not what I picture when I think of him. I remember him laughing as he tried to do the TikTok dances Mae taught him. His face always softened with affection when he looked at our mom, like she was the only woman in the world.

"I miss them."

He squeezes my shoulders as I type in my sister's name.

Maven J. Hollis: Northeast quadrant

My heart stops as I reread the words and look at the photo. Her hair falls just below her chin, shorter than I've ever seen it. Her face is leaner. This is an older, more reserved Mae than I knew. Her expression is close to a smile, but not quite.

"Is this real?" I choke on the words as I look up at Marcus. "Is my sister alive?"

"Hopefully. She was as of the update."

I cover my mouth with my hand, sobbing. I hadn't even hoped she made it. Even with all communications offline after the virus from a darkened power grid and disabled cell towers, I thought my family would find a way to contact me if they were alive.

Mae is alive, and I might as well be on another planet. I can't get to her. It hurts deeper than anything else could.

"We have to find that flower." I swipe the tears from my cheeks, resolved. "And then I have to find my sister."

PART THREE

36

You've heard of catfishing? Certain orchids are so perfectly able to mimic female wasps that they can fool male wasps into trying to mate with them. The males then, inadvertently, pollinate the flower. So if you see a wasp on Tinder, swipe left.

- Excerpt from the Introduction to Plant Biology course taught by Dr. Lucinda Hollis

Seven cells were carved into a hillside that faces the ocean when the Dust Walkers' camp was built. Three of them are large enough to hold many people; the other four were designed for just one each. The cells are all empty, except for one of the smaller ones.

I'm walking alone down the path that descends to the cells, the lapping of ocean waves providing a peaceful backdrop. It's the morning of the fourth day since we found McClain, and it's my third day in a row of bringing him breakfast.

Marcus protested me coming on the first day, but I reminded him that solitude isn't a punishment for a man who's been alone for more than a year and a half.

"Oatmeal and toast today," I announce, sliding the dish through the small opening at the bottom of the metal bars.

The reinforced steel cell seems like overkill for the slight man inside. I don't know if McClain is trying to starve himself to death or if he's ill, but he doesn't look well.

I sit down on the ground, setting my own bowl of oatmeal beside me. McClain keeps his gaze focused on the ocean's waves and doesn't make a move toward his breakfast.

"Have you ever heard of flamboyant flame trees?" I ask him.

He shakes his head in answer.

"They thrive in tropical climates. They're actually very cold-intolerant. And when they bloom, they're covered in beautiful orange-red flowers. But their blooming season is short— a few months at most." I pick up my bowl. "So what if the flower we're searching for has a limited blooming season and that's why we haven't been able to find it?"

He clears his throat. "It's a good theory. I was searching during the transition from dry season to wet season, though. That's the least likely time for tropical flowers to be dormant."

"But maybe you didn't search in the right place at the right time."

"It's possible."

I scoop a spoonful of lukewarm oatmeal into my mouth, breathing in the mix of saltwater and the light, sweet scent of plumeria.

"The people at Rising Tide are starving," I say.

"Marcus isn't withholding food to be cruel."

Interesting that the man Marcus detests is defensive of him.

"I know, and I understand why he's doing it. But food is precious here, and I think you should eat yours."

He doesn't respond, but a few seconds later, he picks up his bowl and takes a bite of the oatmeal.

After both of us eat our oatmeal in silence, he says, "We didn't study the effects of turning aromium off and on. If Marcus is doing it, he may reach a point where he can't turn it off."

I don't let my alarm show. Even though I know there are risks to turning our aromium on every day to search and off when we get back to camp, there are also risks to not turning it on.

We heard a group of Tiders in the jungle yesterday. We hid and stayed quiet until they'd passed. But we could encounter them at any point, and we're walking targets without aromium.

I stand, brushing the dirt from the back of my pants. "I hope that doesn't happen, but no one can convince him to stop doing it at this point."

McClain looks up at me through the thick lenses of

his glasses, his brow furrowed. "The long-term effects of aromium haven't been studied, either. We fast-tracked everything."

"The solar array was damaged in the last storm."

The worry lines in his brow deepen. "Is it repairable?"

I shrug. "We'd have to cross through unprotected territory to find out, and Virginia's just waiting for us to do it. She killed one of our team members last time and injured another one."

McClain's shoulders slump. "The shield will go down."

"We're searching for the flowers. It's all we can do."

He nods, his expression grim. "This is all my fault."

"Maybe you'll be able to do something to help."

He shakes his head. "It's too far gone. Even if I had the flowers and could make a stabilizer, Virginia wouldn't let her people take it."

"Let's hope that's a problem we get to work on a solution for." I hold my hand out. "Can I take your bowl?"

He takes the piece of toast from the bowl and passes it to me. I nod to him as I take it and walk back to the rock path that led me here.

The past few days have been a contradiction of sorts. Marcus brings me to the highest peak of happiness, both in and out of bed, when we're alone together. But we're also running on borrowed time as we search for the flowers every day, because our supply of electricity is dwindling by the day and because every day his aromium is activated so close to full bonding, the more likely it is that it won't go back off.

I'd be devastated if he was sentenced to a lifetime of aromium. When I start to think about it, I force the idea from my mind. We're not there yet.

When I get to the Sub's entrance, Amira, Nova, Chance, Wyatt and Adele are all gathered there, waiting for the rest of Command Team One to arrive.

A small tree nearby that had leaves yesterday morning is blackened and bare today, because yesterday afternoon Rising Tide members shot two dozen flaming arrows into our camp.

Thankfully, two of the security teams were drilling in the center of camp when it happened, and they were quick to get everyone sheltered and get the fires put out. One man was grazed by an arrow, but he wasn't seriously injured.

Just when I think my anger for Virginia has peaked, she decides firing flaming arrows into a camp of innocent people is a good idea. I should have finished her off when I had the chance. She was restrained by vines and I had a knife. I could have cut her throat and ended her, but I didn't. Something tells me that decision will come back to bite me hard later.

"Everyone ready?" Marcus asks.

He and Niran are approaching, and my stomach does a full somersault just from looking at him. All six feet, four inches of him are mine every night, and I still can't get enough. We fall asleep wrapped around each other in his small bed, waking up sweaty the next morning in the tropical heat, but also content. Maybe even more than content, but I don't want to tempt fate by even thinking words like *happy*.

"Hey, B." Marcus passes me a hair tie and my canteen, which he filled for me.

"Thanks."

Niran smirks. "You two are gonna put me in a sugar coma. I'd think you just stare into each other's eyes and recite poetry every night if my room wasn't on the other side of the wall your bed bangs into."

Marcus scoffs and rolls his eyes. "Put some lipstick on your hand and maybe it'll feel more like a girlfriend, asshole."

"It's like a battering ram! I thought you might actually bang that bed all the way through the wall the other night."

I clear my throat, my face warm. "Moving on. The flower we're looking for may only bloom at certain times every year, so just because you've looked somewhere already, that doesn't mean we shouldn't search it again."

"Stay alert," Marcus adds. "The Tiders are probably out looking for us. If you encounter them, radio as soon as it's safe."

Ellison insisted she be there when our aromium is turned on and off, so she joins Stella in walking us to the perimeter where it can be safely reactivated.

"How's everyone doing with being locked down?" I ask Ellison.

"There's worry, of course, but overall it's okay."

Only essential workers are allowed out of the Sub.

Everyone else remains sheltered in there because it's the safest place in camp to be if the shield goes down.

"If you have a chance, tell the laundry and kitchen workers how much we appreciate them. Clean clothes and good food make our work easier. I know they work hard."

She trades a glance with me, smiling. "They'll appreciate hearing that."

"This could be the day, guys," Amira says.

After looking over the files on the computer about the flower, I can't say I'm positive of anything about it. But my best guess is that if it's still here, it grows in well-drained soil rather than the swamp, and that it grows best in full sun. I only told Marcus about those theories because I don't want to limit the search areas of the other teams.

We reach the perimeter, and I stand beside Marcus as we wait for our turn.

"Please reconsider staying," I say in a low tone meant for only him.

He shakes his head, refusing to meet my eyes.

Last night, he had a hard time with his aromium deactivation. When he was walking it off, he vomited and almost passed out. I'm concerned about him turning it on and off again today. But he's about as flexible as a brick wall, so he refuses to stay at camp while the rest of us go out. We argued about it hard in our room last night, and I was so frustrated I tried to turn my back to him and go to sleep without us having sex.

It only took him about five minutes to change my mind.

"McClain still alive?" he asks me.

He doesn't like me visiting McClain every morning, but he isn't fighting me on it anymore.

"He is."

"Awesome," he deadpans.

Ellison finishes activating all six of the other team members' aromium, sending them on their way. Once they're out of earshot, she pinches her brows together and gives Marcus a serious glare.

"If you get sick when I turn it on, you're not going out there."

"I'll be fine."

"I hate to break it to you, but you're not invincible."

He gives her a placating smile. "Just push the button, El."

She does, and she watches him as he paces away, hands on his hips and gaze on the ground. I don't know which is harder for him—having the aromium turned on or having it turned off.

"Bring him back here if he's having problems," Ellison whispers to me. "I'm worried about him."

"I am, too. I'll do my best."

"Radio if you need help," Stella says. "I'll do whatever I can."

Ellison activates my aromium, and I feel like I just downed three cups of strong coffee. It's not a bad feeling at all. Truth be told, I feel stronger and less vulnerable with aromium on, and I like that.

"Good luck," Stella says.

"Thanks."

I catch up with Marcus, touching his forearm. He jerks his arm away.

"You want to get shoved up against a tree and fucked?" he asks briskly.

My heart pounds. "I mean ... yes? Is that the wrong answer?"

He flicks a look at me. "I won't want to stop if we start. Let's get moving."

I check our surroundings, patting my knife and my gun to reassure myself they're where they should be. Then I follow Marcus, distracted by the way his back muscles are outlined in the light army green T-shirt he has on today.

Shaking my head, I force myself to look away. We have to find this damn flower, and I could miss it if I'm busy ogling him.

Finding the flower is a distant hope, but it's the only chance we have. My only chance of seeing my sister again. I think of the photo of her as I walk past a thick, coiled snake.

It's either find that flower or die trying.

37

A knife is often best used as a deterrent or defensive tool. In this course, you'll learn defensive knife applications such as blocking, parrying, and finding escape opportunities.

- Excerpt from a police training manual written by Ben Hollis

The next afternoon, I'm too furious with Marcus to even look at him. Things were tense between us yesterday when we got back to camp right before sunset, having seen no sign of the flower once again. And it got worse when Ellison switched off his aromium.

He dropped to his hands and knees and immediately threw up the entire contents of his stomach. Once there was nothing left, his body dry heaved for more than fifteen minutes. We had to call for help and it took Niran, Wyatt, and Chance to carry him back to camp.

And did he heed that warning from his body to stop messing with aromium? Absolutely not. He crawled into bed and slept, then downed a canteen of water this morning and pronounced himself ready for another day of searching.

It wasn't just me, but also Ellison and Nova, who begged him to change his mind, but he was resolved. I'm terrified of what will happen when his aromium gets switched off tonight.

And again tomorrow. And the day after that, if he's still even able to walk. I've given up hope we'll find the flower, though I'm pretending otherwise because giving up goes against everything I believe.

It's time to discuss other options. We could try cornering Tiders one or two at a time and switching off their aromium, although that idea carries more risk than reward.

We need to spread the truth throughout the Rising Tide camp about aromium. If the ones, twos and threes know what it is, and that it can be turned off if they want to live peacefully and share the supplies, it could change everything.

Most of Virginia's power comes from keeping her people in the dark. If we can enlighten them, we'll weaken her.

That's what she's doing to us. She's trying to weaken us, one nonlethal blow at a time. The storm and its destruction of our camp, picking off our people one at a time, firing flaming arrows into our camp. She's chipping away at us, and I think we need to do the same thing to her.

"B."

I turn to look at Marcus, and when I do, I find his gaze locked onto something.

A jaguar. It's bigger than the one I saw a few days ago, and it's snarling as it stalks toward Marcus.

"Stay behind me," he commands.

My fury for him is immediately replaced with fear. His machete is drawn in his left hand, his handgun in his right.

Gunshots are our last resort. The sound will broadcast our location to the Tiders, but if it's pull the trigger or be killed ... we'll have to take our chances.

I'm caught off guard when, instead of waiting for the jaguar to strike, Marcus attacks it instead.

He drops his gun, wrapping both hands around the machete's hilt and swinging it at the jaguar's neck.

The cat snarls, a bright-red gash appearing on its neck. Marcus is so fast and strong that I'm left stunned. Its front feet stumbling, the jaguar changes gears and lunges toward me instead.

I hardly even see Marcus moving and then the animal's head is dropping to the ground, sheared off by his knife.

I gape at him, knowing how much strength that had to take.

"Let's move," he says, not even breathing hard. "The blood's gonna—"

The wail of a siren makes me jump. It's shrill,

resembling community-wide storm warning sirens before the virus.

"That means a boat of new prisoners has been spotted," Marcus says. "We have to go."

"Where? Back to camp?"

He shakes his head. "We'll go straight to the beach. Our aromium will help."

I turn around, but he calls out my name, stopping me.

He comes toward me and I turn. Tilting my chin up with his forefinger, he brings my gaze to his. "Don't do anything dangerous. We get who we can on beach days, but it's not worth getting yourself killed."

My pulse races because I know this is his way of telling me he cares about me. The day I arrived here was a free-for-all shit show. And the worst part is, none of the Tiders even realize what they're truly doing. They aren't saving the newcomers from the island's more dangerous faction—they *are* the more dangerous one.

"So you want me to listen to you and not get myself killed, but you won't listen to me?"

He groans and sighs heavily. "You don't understand."

I cross my arms over my chest. "Make me understand."

He hesitates, then gives me a pained look. "I've done horrible shit. If something bad happens to me, I deserve it."

"Really?" I arch a brow, skeptical and even angrier than I was before. "You think you're the only one who's done things just to survive?"

He looks off in the distance, a crease forming between his brows. "We don't have time for this. We have to go."

"You have to promise me no more aromium."

He scoffs. "I don't make promises I can't keep."

"Fuck you!" I shove his chest, but he doesn't move. "Why did you make me care about you just so I could watch you kill yourself?"

His expression softens. "I didn't do that. It's just that there's no other way."

"Bullshit." I'm seething, so furious I ignore the brush of something against my lower leg. "The rest of us can do it. Our aromium wasn't on as long as yours was. Send Stella in your place."

His eyes widen with alarm. "B ... you have to relax."

I look down and see vines coiling around his legs, another one sliding up my left leg in a soft caress.

"Oh shit."

They're up to Marcus's thighs now, encasing him like a mummy. He meets my eyes.

"It's your anger. They're responding to it. And since you're mad at me, they might squeeze me to death if you don't relax." He cringes as the vines encircle his waist.

I close my eyes, picturing a meadow. My parents are there. So is Marcus. My dad is giving him a warm look.

"Good," Marcus says. "Deep breaths. Good thoughts."

I imagine I'm taking my mom's hands, looking into her eyes. Telling her how much I love her. How much she taught me. How much I miss her but still feel her with me.

"Think about being okay," he says. "Try to send that message out with your mind."

I open my eyes, following his direction.

I'm okay. I'm safe. I'm not angry.

The vines slow, then pause. It's almost like they're waiting for me to tell them what to do.

I keep assuring them—in my mind—that I'm okay. They retreat, uncoiling from around Marcus. The one that climbed up my side brushes a small leaf across my cheek before sliding away.

Marcus exhales softly, locking his eyes on mine. "We need to go. Keep your emotions in check."

"Why are the vines only responding to me?"

"It's too much to explain right now. We have to go. You take the lead."

Aromium allows me to race through the jungle faster than I could move without it. I'm dodging obstacles before my mind fully registers them. Marcus is right behind me, reminding me when I need to change course.

It's not great timing for a new boatload of prisoners. But I suppose it's not great timing for the Tiders, either.

"Do you talk to people or just take them by force?" I call over my shoulder.

"Some people try talking, but I don't."

A smile tugs at my lips because that tracks. Marcus can be a bull in a china shop.

When the beach comes into view, I slow to a stop.

Finding a safe vantage point, we scan the area and find the Tiders gathered on their end of the beach. Not everyone from our camp is here. Most of the command and security people are, and several other adults who can hold their own in a fight.

The boat is almost here. I can make out people on the deck shielding their eyes from the sun to see the beach better. I know the terror they must be feeling, being forced to swim toward danger.

I creep closer to our group, calling out to them so they know it's us.

Relief flashes over Nova's face when she sees us. She's wearing a fitted, sleeveless black shirt and sand-colored canvas pants, the lines on her scalp freshly shaven. With her defined arm muscles and a stun stick in her hand, she looks like a warrior going into battle.

Ellison isn't here. That makes sense, since her skill set is so valuable to the camp.

"Lean into your aromium," Marcus says softly, his hardened gaze locked onto Virginia, who's just a small figure at the other end of the beach from this distance. "But control your emotions."

That's easier said than done with some of the people here. If I get a shot at Virginia or Marcelle, I'm taking it, mission be damned.

It's more complicated with Pax. He's complicit in Virginia's scheming to keep everyone at Rising Tide in the dark about aromium and he cut out Olin's tongue, which I can't forgive. But I don't think he's all bad.

The first boat passenger jumps into the water. Marcus stalks to the front of the group and I follow. Amira comes to my side, an arrow nocked and ready.

"Be careful," I say under my breath.

"You too."

Marcus is the first to move. He bursts toward the first couple of prisoners, a man and a woman. He scoops them both up with an arm around their waists and rushes them back to us.

Arrows fly from Tiders who are moving toward us, but Marcus is so fast he's out of range before they land.

Adele and Stella each take one of the prisoners from Marcus. I run toward the water, hearing boots kicking up wet sand behind me.

Pax is throwing someone over his shoulder when our eyes meet. Knife in hand, I head straight for him.

"Fight him off!" I yell to his captive. "I'll help you!"

The man thrashes, kicking his feet at Pax. But he can't get any momentum. I grab his shirt and pull, Pax growling as he tries to keep his hold.

"What the hell are you doing?" he bellows. "You've made a mistake switching sides."

When I grab the man's midsection and pull, he falls to the ground. Pax swipes his knife at me, narrowly missing when I jump back. The man gets to his feet and runs away.

"You lied about aromium," I snap at Pax. "You're just Virginia's toy."

His eyes narrow with anger. "We tell people when they're ready."

I balk. "You mean when it's irreversible? You disgust me."

I'm about to engage him in a fight when someone barrels into my shoulder, knocking me to the ground. I'm breathless, and I can't see because there's sand in my eyes.

"Shit!" I rub my eyes, not knowing what else to do, but it doesn't help.

I know what Marcus said about keeping my emotions in check, but it's hard when I'm this vulnerable.

"Get away from her." It's Amira, her voice deadly calm. "Briar, my foot is right by you. Grab it and get behind me."

I blink rapidly as I feel for her foot, the vision in my right eye clear. I find it and crawl behind her.

"My knife. It flew out of my hand."

"I see it. I can't get it right now, though."

"Hey, Olin," someone says from nearby. "Take him."

It's Pax. I gasp, my left eye watering in an effort to rid it of sand.

"Olin! Amira, we have to get Olin."

There's a pause. "I don't know who that is." She fires an arrow, immediately grabbing another one. "Who is he?"

I get to my feet. "He has a baby face and wild red hair. He's my friend."

I frantically scan my surroundings, and my half gaze locks onto Marcus and Pax, fistfighting about ten feet away.

Marcus is pure fury. He grabs Pax's shirt, hauls him into the air, and slams him down on his back. One knee on either side of Pax, he punches him so hard his head sinks down into the sand.

Pax lands a powerful blow to Marcus's side. Marcus doubles over and Pax rolls himself over, toppling Marcus to the ground.

"Olin!" Amira yells.

I blink, looking around. I can mostly see out of my left eye now, too. Amira passes me my knife and I murmur my thanks.

I find him. He's kneeling on the ground, putting pressure on the wound of a Tider who's already dead. His face is sunken and sickly, the leanness of his frame sending a wave of guilt through me.

I take off toward him, my heart racing with fear and excitement.

"Olin!" I reach him and bend down. "Come with us, please. Just trust me and come."

His eyes meet mine, confusion rippling over his expression. His hands are covered in blood.

"Olin, she's gone. I'm sorry. We have to go. You've been lied to."

Something whooshes past us and I feel a thud on the ground. Amira shot an arrow at someone who was running toward us.

Olin stands, looking at his bloody hands.

"Please," I implore him. "You can trust me. We have food. You'll be safe."

His nod is almost imperceptible, his expression dazed. My eyes flood with relieved tears as I take his arm and run away from the fight.

"Let's go!" Nova yells. "Back to camp!"

Marcus races up to me, blood splattered on his face and chest. His left eye is swollen almost shut and he has a fat lip.

"You okay?" he asks.

"I'm okay." Emotion clogs my throat, making it hard to talk. "This is my friend Olin. He saved my life."

Marcus locks eyes with Olin and says, "You're gonna be okay. The hard part's over." He glances over his shoulder. "Command Teams One and Two, in position!"

I turn and see about ten Tiders in a full sprint toward us. Panic for Olin flares in my chest.

"Take your friend to the aromium switch location," Marcus says levelly, drawing his gun. "We've got this."

I can't leave them. But I also can't leave Olin.

The other command team members turn back to join us, and I see that Adele has a wound in her side. She's bleeding, but still holding a stun stick in one hand and a knife in the other.

"Adele! I need you to get my friend to the aromium switch spot." The Tiders are almost here, so my words are spilling out in a rush. "You're injured. Take him, and I'll stay. Please."

Indecision flashes in her eyes.

"Go, Adele," Marcus barks. "Take him."

Olin gives me a final quick look as he and Adele take

off. I spin to face the Tiders, drawing the handgun from my waist.

One of them drops. Then another. Marcus and Nova are firing their guns at them.

We have limited ammunition, so bullets are precious commodities. But I'm certain the wild-eyed people racing toward us are all fours, permanently bonded to their aromium. It's definitely the right time to use bullets.

I don't even have time to turn off my gun's safety and aim it before all the rushing Tiders are on the ground, dark-red blood soaking into the sand around them. One of them looks familiar.

Her long, dark hair is partially covering her face, but I can still tell it's Yelena. She never liked me, but no one deserves to die like this, their mind and body chemically warped to fight for a cruel overlord's regime.

For around half a minute, no one says a word. We're battered from the fight, swollen bruises and gashes marking nearly everyone.

Marcus tucks his gun back into his holster. "Team One stays here to burn the bodies of the Tiders. Team Two, take the bodies of our people to camp and bury them."

"You sure it's safe to do it now?" Nova asks. "We usually wait."

He nods, his expression grim. "Virginia heard the gunshots. They won't fuck with us again today."

No one but me would recognize him as the man who draws light circles on my back with his fingertip as we're falling asleep at night. He has to be detached to do what he does and keep his sanity, but I can't help wondering what this is all costing him. The death and destruction. The impossible choices.

I admire what he does, but I don't envy it.

38

Root system of plant indicates adaptation to mineral-rich soil with high metal content. The flower structure does not give specific indications about a pollinator relationship.

- Excerpt from the journal of Dr. Randall McClain

There are vines everywhere. They twine and wrap through the air and around my legs. My waist. Ranging in shades from the lightest green to a dark pine, some sturdy and thick and others lithe and deft. There's one winding around my neck, poised to go into my open mouth. I can't close it, and I can't scream. I'm helpless; frozen as the vine slithers past my lips.

I wake up with a jolt, gasping. Sweat coats my brow even though I'm in an underground room, Olin asleep on the bed beside my chair.

At least he was asleep. I just woke him up.

He sits up, his brows lowered in a look of concern.

"Sorry," I say sheepishly, standing. "I had a bad dream."

His concern slides away. I reach for the pitcher of water on the table beside his bed and pour him a cup of water.

When I pass it to him, he drinks it. There's also a small bowl of rice and a cup of fruit juice on the table.

"Do you think you can eat a little?" I ask him. "And drink some juice? Ellison said you should have a little bit every couple of hours."

He nods, looking groggy.

"There's a pencil and paper here if you need to say anything." I pass him the cup of juice.

I survey him as he sips it. He's been wasting away at Rising Tide, his hair thinner and his cheeks hollow. It hurts to know I've been here, eating my fill every day, while he's been starving and suffering.

Sitting down on the end of his bed, I tell him what I've learned since I last saw him. His eyes widen when I mention McClain and genetic engineering, mirroring my own feelings when I found out.

"I wanted to be here when you woke up," I say softly. "But I have to get back to searching for the flowers. You're in good hands with Ellison. Please just rest and heal. Switching off the aromium makes you tired and weak. I'll come check on you when I get back."

He nods, leaning against the pillows at his back. The warmth in his gaze reminds me of my mom. I don't have a brother, but I think the tenderness I feel toward Olin is how I would feel for a brother if I did.

I kiss his forehead. "You're okay now. I'll see you later."

On the walk out of the Sub, I twist my neck to one side and then the other, trying to work out the stiffness from sleeping in a chair. I reach the Sub's exit, squinting against bright morning sunlight.

"What time is it?" I ask the guard stationed at the entrance.

He looks at his watch and says, "Almost seven a.m."

I can't believe I slept in that chair the entire night. Going on and off aromium like we have been isn't just getting harder for Marcus. I'm feeling it too.

I push the button on the side of my radio. "Aphrodite to Ares. I'm at the meeting point."

A few seconds later, his deep voice responds over the radio. "Copy, Aphrodite. I'm at the switch point."

That's the spot at the shield perimeter where we meet to activate our aromium in the morning and turn it off in the evening. My aggravation flares because Marcus has no business having his aromium on again.

I don't even bother with a shower. I change into clean clothes, wash my face, brush my teeth and braid my hair, winding the braid into a thick knot at my neck and securing it. I'm seething the whole time, playing out the conversation Marcus and I are going to have when I reach him.

He knows there's a pissed-off woman heading his way. He wouldn't leave without me, would he?

Even though I shouldn't, I grab my radio and press the button, barely containing my mood as I speak into it. "Aphrodite to Ares. I'm almost on my way. Your ass better be there."

"Copy, Aphrodite." Amusement laces his tone. "My ass will be here, along with the rest of me."

I strap on my weapons, grab a stun stick already set to respond to my thumbprint, drink some water and refill my canteen. By the time I set off, I'm about to boil over.

That won't work once my aromium is on. I can't have vines choking the life out of Marcus, no matter how angry I am.

Deep breathing it is. I reframe Marcus's decision in my mind. It's careless and self-destructive, but that's not how he sees it. He's stubborn to the point of defiance, and he's in charge here, so he's used to his word being the final one.

I'm calmer by the time I reach him. He's somehow glowering at me and arching an amused brow at the same time.

"Morning, sunshine."

Stella is waiting with him. She avoids eye contact with me as she quickly activates my aromium and power walks back toward camp.

Smart. She doesn't want to get caught in the middle of a dustup between me and Marcus.

I sigh, reminding myself to stay cool. "Morning, stubborn asshole. All set to go?"

His expression darkens. "Oh, I'm the asshole? I had to

search the fucking camp for you last night when you didn't come to bed."

"Did you *have* to though?" I exhale long and slow, making myself stay as calm as I can.

He stalks toward me, getting so close I can feel the heat of his body towering over me. "I was puking my guts out and looking everywhere for you, and you're flippant about it?"

My pulse pounds; not because I fear him, but because I want him. Aromium is clouding my judgment and emotions.

"You won't listen to me about the aromium." I hate the way my voice catches. "You don't trust me to search without you overseeing me."

He shakes his head, a storm raging in his eyes. "I trust you with my life. I just want to protect you."

"I want to protect you, too. But you won't let me."

He shakes his head and looks away. "I don't deserve your protection."

I close my eyes and take a few deep breaths. "I can't do this right now. Not with the aromium on. Unless you want to risk vines cutting off circulation from your dick until it falls off."

"I'd prefer to keep my dick attached."

"Then let's go."

"Next time you're too pissed to come home, can you at least send someone with a message?"

"I didn't do it on purpose. I fell asleep in the chair by Olin's bed."

The muscle in his jaw tics with annoyance. "Oh, I know. Took me more than an hour to find you there."

"What's with the tone?"

"Who is this guy to you?"

I roll my eyes, my jaw dropping. "Are you serious? He's my friend. He saved my life."

"Can you blame me for asking?"

"Yes. I can and I do. If you haven't noticed, I sleep in *your* bed every night. When you're not being an obstinate dickhead ... I like you."

He narrows his eyes. "It's a little deeper for me than that, and I don't share."

I'm horrified by the way my nipples harden, a tingling sensation farther down signaling I'm wet over not just his feelings for me, but also his possessiveness. I've never been one of those women.

"He's just a friend. You know how I feel about you. Do you honestly think I could have you and then want anyone else?"

He looks away. "I knew you were mad at me, and I ... wasn't feeling very reasonable."

We start walking, side by side. The jungle air is already thick with humidity, the caws and calls of the animals a familiar backdrop that no longer scares me like it did when I first got here.

"I'm staying out until the flowers are found," he says. "So I don't get sick from turning the aromium off every day."

I let that sink in for a few seconds. "I'll stay out with you. But what if yours bonds and it won't go off?"

He shrugs. "Then I have to hope McClain can make a stabilizer."

"Marcus." I put a hand on his arm and he stops, tension tightening his expression.

I pull my hand away. "It's likely we'll never find this flower."

"I know. But I'll regret it if I don't give this everything I've got."

Unease churns in my gut. He takes my hand and leads me to a rock formation that's about ten feet tall. There's a space just large enough for us to both stand in, and he backs me into it, cupping my face in his hands. His shoulders shudder and his hands shake, his gaze so dark and hungry it takes my breath away.

"I don't know if touching you will help or hurt, but I'm dying here."

He lowers his mouth to mine, the warmth of his mouth making me forget the sharp rocks poking against my back. I moan and wrap my arms around him, my worry disappearing as he kisses me harder.

I press my hands against his back, urging him closer. He nibbles my lower lip and I bite the tip of his tongue. We're groping at each other's clothes now, the aromium in my veins surging with something that feels ... right, somehow.

"I need you," I say, whimpering as he cups my ass and lifts me, allowing him to reach my neck with his lips.

His stubble brushes over the sensitive skin on my collarbone as he kisses my neck. I breathe in his leather-and-saltwater smell, desperate for more of him.

His hand goes to his waistband, where he fumbles with his button and zipper, pulling down his pants. He deftly handles mine next, and then his hands are on my bare ass. He lowers me onto his erection, both of us groaning with pleasure as he sinks into me.

"Fuck." The warmth of his breath sends a shiver over my skin. "I can't breathe without you."

My cry is strangled, because I know we have to be quiet. He's so deep inside me, his hands digging into my skin and my nails sinking into his back.

"Yes," I whisper in his ear. "Don't stop. I need you so much, Marcus."

My words spur him to move faster, the pain of his punishing thrusts sending me spiraling so high I quickly combust, tears leaking from the corners of my eyes as my orgasm blasts through my body like a bomb detonating. For a few seconds, I'm broken into a million pieces of floating bliss, and when they knit back together, I'm a more complete version of myself.

He cries out, holding my hips and grinding into me. I feel him coming, his whole body tensing and then going slack.

After setting me on my feet, he steps back. His lips are parted in an incredulous look.

"What the fuck?" he whispers.

I put a palm on his chest. "I feel it, too."

The pull of the aromium is quieter now. I don't even have the words to describe the state of satisfaction I'm in. It's like the aromium has been calling me toward something every second it's been active in my body, and I finally gave it what it wanted.

"I'm more ... myself." He runs a hand over his jaw, disbelief in his tone as he refastens his pants. "More than I have been since I first turned the aromium back on."

"Me too." I quickly fasten my own pants, not liking that his back is exposed to anyone who might come by. "We have to get moving."

He stops me with a hand around my wrist. "Hey ... you good?"

"More than good."

His lips tug up into a grin. "Wish we would've done that sooner."

I stretch up on my toes to kiss him. "We can always make up for missed opportunities."

———

Several hours later, we're searching as close to the Rising Tide camp as we're willing to get when a snowflake lands on my cheek, immediately followed by one on my arm. I look up.

"Oh shit."

This time, the dark cloud is inside the jungle instead of high in the sky. It's a floating haze in the trees above us, heavy snow descending from it.

"Marcus," I murmur, a sense of dread falling over me.

He stands beside me, his expression masked by thick sheets of enormous snowflakes.

"Virginia must be in a rage over losing those fours," he says near my ear. "They'll come on fast and hard."

"I can't see. How will I know if I'm fighting them or you?"

He's silent as he considers. Then he shakes his head. "I don't know what will happen if we split up. This cloud can follow our heat signatures, but I don't know what it will do if there's only one person to follow."

"No splitting up. We stay together."

My breath clouds in front of my face, thoughts of fighting a bunch of Tiders while I can't see making my worry spiral. One-on-one, I could hold my own. But a dozen of them against the two of us, when none of us can see? I'll be too worried about wounding Marcus by accident.

"I'm not doing so great with controlling my emotions," I murmur.

"Don't."

I huff my annoyance. "I'm trying, but it's h—"

He cuts me off. "No, I mean don't control them. Call out to the vines with your mind. If there's a way to help you, they'll find it."

"But what about you? I don't want them to hurt you."

The faint sound of a woman's sharp voice makes me reach for my knife. Virginia. A bullet is too quick and merciful for her.

"They'll respond to your feelings," Marcus says in my ear. "Don't send out anger. Send fear. Ask for protection. Do it right now. I can't see and I don't want to hurt you."

He presses a quick, firm kiss to my temple. It's the

first time I've heard worry in his voice. I wrap my arms around myself and close my eyes, the giant icy flakes on my skin and clothes making me cold even though I'm in a hot rainforest.

Help me. Protect me. Help me. Protect me.

I ignore the approaching voices, focusing only on sending the message out with my mind over and over.

The keening howl of a wolf sounds close by. A chill races through me and I feel a rumble in the ground beneath my feet.

"Watch yourself! They have guns!" a man yells.

I think it's Pax. More voices follow, but they're drowned out by a whooshing sound, vines arriving and whipping around my feet in a big circle.

Something zings past my head, missing it by just a few inches. I think it was a spear. I crouch, knife in my shaking hand, as the vines rapidly build a cocoon around me. It's like a small igloo, the snowfall stopping once I'm fully encased in darkness.

For a few minutes, I can't hear anything but the vines cutting through the air, more layers being added to my protective enclosure. Then it stops. Everything is muffled, but I think I hear the metallic clang of a knife hitting another one.

A man's deep, primal cry sounds, and somehow, I know it's Marcus. He sounds like hell itself, unleashed fury descending on anyone unfortunate enough to be within his reach.

There's snarling. The clacking of an animal's jaws.

And voices. Long minutes pass as I listen to the fighting, helpless.

The thwack of something hard against my shell of vines makes me jump.

"The fuck?" a muted voice says, hitting it again.

There's a squelching noise, followed by a thud that I think is the drop of a body.

There are so many voices out there. Marcus is all alone to defend himself. I want so badly to call the vines back so I can help him, but something stops me. It's a feeling deep inside me, soothing my fear and telling me to stay where I am.

You're safe now. We're here.

My eyes widen with disbelief. I've sent mental messages out to the vines a few times now, and they always show up. But now, somehow, they're communicating back.

39

None of the test subject plants have shown any measurable reaction to aromium. It may not work on them.

- Excerpt from the journal of Dr. Randall McClain

My nose is ice cold. I turn my face into the warmth of the blankets around me, sighing contentedly.

A kernel of worry tugs me out of my relaxed sleep. How can I be cold? The island is never cold.

My eyes fly open, darkness surrounding me. The blankets I'm snuggling into are warm, yes, but they're also moving up and down, like the rise and fall of a chest while breathing.

"Marcus," I whisper-hiss.

"I'm right here."

My panic recedes. His voice is calm, and he's very

close. But also, the cloying scent of pine is everywhere, and something sharp is poking into my leg.

It comes back to me all at once. After the fight with the Tiders, I willed my shelter away and the vines uncoiled and receded. Then we took shelter beneath a massive pine tree, cutting a few branches out to make room for us to burrow in since the snow allowed us no visibility.

"What's in here with us?" I ask.

"Wolves."

A sense of dread fills every cell in my body. The warm blankets are actually wolves—with massive teeth and predatory instincts.

"It's okay," he assures me. "I called them here. It's Flavius and his pack."

A frantic laugh bursts out of me. "You called them? Like on the phone? Do you have their contact info saved?"

"When my aromium's on, I have the same connection with wolves that you have with vines. They helped me fight off the Tiders."

I take a few seconds to process the news. "Okay."

"You were so cold. Grannie's at your back and Flavius is between us."

My brows drop. "Grannie?"

"Her fur's silvery gray like my grandma's hair was, so I call her Grannie."

I exhale a note of amusement. "Okay, well, we aren't ungulates, so hopefully Grannie won't decide to eat us."

"We aren't what?"

"Ungulates. Large, hoofed animals like deer and elk. Those are the most common prey for wolves."

"Goddamn, woman. Can I fuck you while you wear nothing but glasses and spout scientific facts?"

I smother my laugh in Flavius's fur. He lifts his head, probably wondering what the hell is going on. And honestly, same. I'm inside a pine tree in a rainforest while a blizzard rages outside, and a pack of wolves is keeping me warm.

I smooth a hand over Flavius's back and he drops his head back to the ground, huffing an exhale.

"Do you think the Tiders will come back?" I ask.

"No. They lost a few people. I got a good hit in on Pax, but with the aromium, he'll heal quickly."

They lost a few people means he killed them. I heard some of them go down. Marcus sounded like an angel of death, striking down anyone who dared come close to him.

"Really nice trick with the vines," he says.

"It seemed like ..." I hesitate, unsure how to describe what I felt. "Almost like they were communicating with me. But how? And why only me, and only wolves for you?"

He takes in a breath and lets it out before responding. "The bond gets stronger with time."

I wait for him to say more, but he doesn't.

"Marcus," I say, frustrated. "Why am I the only one who can communicate with plants, and you're the only one who can communicate with wolves?"

"There are different strains of aromium. McClain also

experimented with putting it in animals and plants, but every strain is different."

I shift, the tree branch in my leg scraping over my skin as I move. "You only tell me things when you have to. When I straight up demand to know. Why are you so secretive?"

He sniffs. "I'll tell you whatever you want to know, just ask. It's not my favorite subject, so that's why I don't bring it up."

"How many people on this island are connected to animals or plants?"

There's a pause before he answers. "I don't know for sure."

I make a low, grumbling sound of aggravation. "You know more than that. Keep talking."

"There's you and me. Pax has a connection with anacondas. Virginia can call ravens. They're giant fucking things, mean as hell."

"Why us and not other people? Or more people?"

"Because of the strain we were given. That's all I know."

My heart sinks, because I don't believe him when he says that's all he knows.

"The Tiders are eating people," I say.

His chin drops a notch. "What the fuck do you mean?"

"I worked in the kitchen there, and I did a job they call meat prep. They're eating everything they can scrounge, even rats. There were human body parts there one time. I didn't ... I was looking for someone, and I saw a human leg and ..." I grimace. "Several toes. On the table, with the other meat that was being prepped."

He's silent, the only sounds the rasp of his hand scraping over his stubbled jaw and the soft breathing of the wolves around us.

"Why didn't you tell me before?"

"I don't know. At first, I didn't trust you since I was under guard and you thought I was a spy. And then...I don't know, I just haven't thought much about it, I guess."

"Fuck." His sigh is aggravated. "This is something that's not common knowledge?"

"I don't think it is, but I don't know. I can ask Olin."

"Virginia's out of her fucking mind."

"Yes. Like you said, she's desperate."

He's quiet, but I can feel his tension. I clear my throat.

"I told you because that's the last thing I hadn't shared with you. Now you know everything I know."

He breezes past my attempt to clear the air. "What happens when people with one strain of aromium eat people with another strain?"

"Um. I don't know."

"I was just thinking out loud. McClain always told us to never hunt and eat animals with aromium."

Unease churns in my gut. I hadn't even considered that eating their own people was anything but horribly inhumane of the Tiders. What if they're unknowingly giving themselves even more supernatural abilities?

"What about the other strains of aromium? How are they different?"

"I don't know." He pushes up a branch of the tree, revealing more wolves and thick snowfall. "I think we can see well enough now."

We crawl out from beneath the tree and stand up, the wolves rising to their feet. The stretching and yawning of the dozen or so massive animals is at odds with the snarling and attacking I heard earlier.

Good thing they're on our side.

The snowfall is still heavy, but we can see well enough to know we're moving away from the Rising Tide camp. We often walk in silence so we don't draw attention to ourselves, but this time, the silence isn't comfortable. Marcus is troubled about the bombshell I dropped, understandably.

I constantly scan our surroundings as the snowfall gets lighter, knowing the Tiders could strike at any moment.

The image of my mom's face on that computer screen flashes through my mind, sending a pang of longing through my chest. She was an expert in her field; no one could help me navigate my newfound connection to plants like she could. Not just as an expert, but as my mom.

My dad would tell me to use the power I now have to protect myself and those who are too vulnerable to protect themselves. I'm glad I knew him well enough to know deep down how he would advise me if he were here.

Mae would first unleash every expletive she's ever heard and then make a crack about having vines fetch me drinks and wash my hair. But she'd also listen. That's what I miss most—our conversations. When the virus hit, she was doing a different summer research program than I was, hers in Quebec.

She has to be alive. And I have to find her. It means more to me than getting even with Lochlan, though I still definitely plan to do that.

But first, I have to help the innocent people on this island. Even with an invisible wedge between us, I know Marcus wants to stop Virginia as much as I do.

I never imagined so much would hinge on finding a flower. Bright blue and shaped like a bell. I imagine it in my dreams, waving in a light breeze. And when I wake up, I stare into the darkness and hope that somehow, it's here and we just haven't found it yet.

40

An experiment on Island Five shows great promise. The team there has worked tirelessly to create controllable microclimates. With this technology, we hope to affect mitigations in ecosystems being decimated by global warming.

- Excerpt from the journal of Dr. Randall McClain

I'm starting to wonder if that damn flower was ever on this island. It's been another three days of endless searching, on top of ... I don't even know how many days we've traipsed through this bug-infested jungle.

We walk and we walk and we walk, only stopping when it's dark so we can bathe and eat and I can get some sleep. That's also when we have perfunctory sex.

There's no emotional connection between us; we just rut like animals. He pulls my hair and I bite his shoulder. I straddle his lap and he bends me over boulders. We just fuck, both of us chasing the high that keeps getting higher.

The aromium practically sings through our veins when we have sex. The orgasms are transcendental. And even though Marcus wraps his arms around me when I sleep, it's not the same. Even his tender caresses feel like absent habits instead of true connection.

We don't bother rinsing out our clothes anymore. We're covered in sweat all the time, and I don't know why we even bother washing ourselves. The urge to fuck each other into oblivion will be there whether we're clean or filthy.

Maybe the filth is even better. We're just creatures out here, no different from the other animals whose only cares are surviving and mating.

We're stopped for a water break, searching the jungle on the far west side of the island, when I voice the worry that's been bothering me since yesterday.

"What if that scientist got the flowers from somewhere else and they were in her bag for a while?"

Marcus nods. "I've wondered that, too."

"What if giving up is underrated?" I crack.

He bends to refill his canteen in the softly meandering stream we're stopped at, a smile pulling on his lips when he stands and turns to face me.

"Ready to move?"

I sigh heavily. "Yeah."

"Time messes with your mind here. There's no Netflix. No great restaurants. No concerts. We've got nothing but time, each other, and a set of problems we never could've imagined before the virus."

It's the most he's said to me at one time since we crawled out from beneath the pine tree. I lock eyes with him, connecting, if just for a second.

"My mom named me after briars because they're thorny and hardy and they protect themselves fiercely. Some of them are even beautiful when they flower, like wild roses. She said when she first held me, she hoped I'd be all of those things."

"You are. And you're more beautiful than any rose."

My stomach flips, his words making me surprisingly emotional. I deflect his compliment with humor.

"So you think I'm thorny?"

"Minus the *T*. You drained me dry last night."

I look away, my cheeks warming as I grin.

"Don't get me wrong, I loved it," he says. "And yeah, you're thorny. But in a good way. You're tough and resilient. You don't take shit."

"And yet." I lower my brows in a mock aggravated look. "You keep testing me."

His gaze is so warm and affectionate that I can't make myself look away. I'm trapped, unaware of anyone or anything that may be lurking around us.

"You're not intimidated by me," he says. "I love that about you."

Slow down, heart. He didn't say he loves me.

I sigh dramatically. "Well, now that you said I'm resilient, I guess I have to search some more. And not bitch about it."

"Bitch if you want to."

I'm about to respond when a crackle sounds from our radios. "Circe to Ares, emergency. Get to camp. Don't respond."

It's Adele, and she spoke so softly into the radio that I could barely hear her. Marcus's brows are drawn together with worry.

"Fuck." He puts his hands on top of his head. "It sounds like Rising Tide got in. The shield must be down. She doesn't want us to respond because she doesn't want them to hear my voice on the radio."

I'm too dazed to speak for a few seconds. Tears well in my eyes as I imagine the savages at Rising Tide attacking Ellison, Olin, Amira, Vadim, and the kids. All the innocent people who work so hard to keep the camp going and take care of each other.

"I can get there faster than you can," he says. "I hate to leave you alone, but—"

"Go," I practically yell the word at him. "I'll be behind you and I'll go as fast as I can."

He gives me a warning look. "Don't come into camp just to get yourself killed. Be smart."

"You too. Don't race in there alone. We need to figure things out first."

He turns to go, looking over his shoulder at me. A dozen different emotions swim in his eyes.

"Be safe!" I call out.

He races off, my head swimming as I watch him go.

The Tiders will take everything. They'll want the camp, which is far nicer than what they have. They could kill everyone. Dread pools in my stomach as I check my holsters and weapons, packing my canteen into my bag.

What will Virginia do to McClain?

A vine curls over my shoulder, several tiny bright-green leaves sprouting from its end. I close my eyes and take a deep breath to relax. Then I take off running, wishing again that I'd killed Virginia when I had the chance.

———

I've gotten crazy fast from the aromium. It takes me around thirty minutes of running at top speed to reach the switch point, where I'm shocked to find Marcus.

His hands are folded on top of his head and he's pacing like a caged lion.

"The shield's still up," he says.

I stop short. "Are you sure?"

He nods. I keep walking, wanting to see for myself. I make it about ten feet before sharp pains in my head and my stomach send me to my knees. It's white hot, like my insides are on fire. I grit my teeth to keep from screaming, managing to crawl back to Marcus.

"What now?" I ask him, breathing hard.

He takes out his radio and pushes the button. "This is Ares. Someone get to the switch point."

"Wait." I get to my knees, still unable to stand. "The Tiders aren't in there?"

He shakes his head, moving his hands to his hips. "They can't be with the shield up. There's some other emergency."

"What if we're the only ones who can help and you just outed us?"

"I know, but I can't stay here and wait." He scrubs his hands down his face. "You should hide."

The effects of the aromium shield are still there. I can't stand, and I just want to throw up and lie down. Testing the shield was a dumb move on my part.

I crawl to a bunch of bushes, waiting for the sickness to pass. A few minutes later, I hear someone running, their boots pounding on the ground.

"There's a revolt." It's Adele, her voice frenzied. "He opened all the cells and let all the prisoners out."

"Who?"

"Ray. It was Ray."

I cover my mouth with my hand. That means not only is McClain free, but so are all the people we got from the most recent boat of prisoners. Marcus makes them stay in cells while they're questioned so they can try to root out who might cause problems.

I get to my feet, stumbling as I make my way over to them.

Adele's eyes widen as she looks me over from head to toe. I know I resemble a rodent that just crawled out from beneath a pile of hot garbage.

"I tested the shield," I say. "I'm fine. Did he kill anyone?"

"Stark, from Security Team Two. And ... I don't know, maybe more. I was with Chance when things went bad. I hid. Ray freed the prisoners and convinced a bunch of them to join his rebellion. He told everyone they could either help build the boat or be executed."

Marcus's expression darkens. "He's fucking dead. Where's Nova?"

Adele furiously swipes tears from her eyes. "Tied up. He tied up all the command team members they were able to find. Even Chance, and he lost part of his left arm yesterday."

Marcus balks. "What?"

"Jaguar. Wyatt thinks he killed it, but he's not sure. He was just trying to get him back here before he bled to death."

"Oh God." I look away, feeling sick again.

"He's alive. Ellison had to take part of his arm, but one of the prisoners dragged him out of bed and he's tied up by the tower with the others."

Marcus puts a hand on her shoulder. "You did great, Adele. Do you know who else from Command besides you is in hiding?"

"Um..." She tucks her hair behind her ear, her hand shaking. "Niran's not there. I don't know where he is. I didn't see Wyatt with the others, or Stella."

"Good. Did they get to the weapons?"

She shakes her head. "We told them only you can

access them. That's why they shot Stark, because they didn't believe him."

Marcus nods. "Okay. I need you to get the switching device so we can get our aromium off. And then you know where to go—don't say it, just get there. We'll be there soon."

"Okay."

"Be careful," he says as he takes his handgun from its holster and passes it to her. "Wait until it's safe for you to get it."

She nods, her eyes steely with resolve. Then she takes off at a run, her blond ponytail swinging behind her.

Marcus meets my gaze, running a hand through his hair. "We've drilled for this. There's a meeting point. So we should have six, including us."

"What's the plan?"

"We'll go over it when we get there." He takes my hand, his expression somber. "I need you to be my voice of reason. That's usually Nova in these situations."

"I will."

A crease appears between his brows. "If something happens to me, help Nova. And if something happens to her, too..." He exhales heavily. "I know this is a lot to put on you, but I need you to take charge if that happens. Promise me."

My lips part, shock coursing through me. "Marcus, I'm not—"

"It needs to be you." His tone is forceful when he cuts in. "You're smart and strong. You'll do the right things, even when it's hard."

I shake my head. "What about Niran?"

"I love him like a brother and trust him completely, but it needs to be you. There's no time to waste. Promise me."

I swallow, only taking a second to doubt myself before I say, "Okay. I promise."

He releases my hand and draws the knife from the sheath at his waist. "Let's go take our camp back."

41

Plant pathogens can share genetic material with each other, even across different species. This sets plants apart from animals because they can quickly acquire new virulence traits or resistance to treatments. This makes them potentially dangerous and unpredictable.

- Excerpt from a lecture given by Dr. Lucinda Hollis in her Plant Evolution course

Niran's shoulders drop with relief when he sees Marcus.

"Thank fuck," Niran says, coming over to put a hand on Marcus's shoulder. He glances at me and says, "Hey, Briar."

"Hey."

We just walked down the steep wooden stairs of a small underground bunker about a quarter mile from the shield perimeter. Its entrance door lies flush on the ground, a top layer of dirt, greenery and moss making it impossible to see if you don't know it's there.

I glance around the cool, dark space. It's about ten feet by ten feet, two tall candles on small metal disks providing the only light. The walls are lined with shelves of supplies. Large metal canisters have labels like "Medical Supplies," "Oats," and "Rice." Glass jars with fruits and vegetables are neatly arranged on one wall. Guns and knives take up another entire wall.

"Adele's getting the switching device," Marcus says, surveying the shadowed faces around us. "Tell me everything you guys know."

Stella, Wyatt and Niran all recount the takeover. Wyatt doesn't know much because he was training at the ring when Nova gave the order to everyone in camp to "hunker down", which, for Command officers, apparently means evacuate to this bunker if you're able.

Niran was at the Sub when someone radioed there was fighting near the kitchen.

"By the time I got there, it was a shit show," he says. "Stark was dead on the ground and Ray had taken Blythe hostage. The prisoners he released were jumping the command and security people, trying to disarm them and tie them up."

"They disarmed Nova?" Marcus's tone is incredulous.

"Yeah, because Ray had a knife to Blythe's throat."

"Fuck." Marcus looks away. "I should've done something about him. This is my fault."

"It's not," I say. "Focus on now."

"He'll pay," Niran assures Marcus in a level tone.

Stella picks up a piece of paper from the wooden table. "I wrote down everything I could as soon as I got here, while it was all fresh. We had twelve people in holding cells, including McClain. I know seven of them joined Ray and are working against us. And then from our people, I know Darien, Juno and Jax also joined."

"Darien?" Niran shakes his head. "I've always liked him."

Stella ignores him and continues. "So eleven people, including Ray. Only Nova was carrying a gun, so that's the only one they have. And I counted four hunting knives. No stun sticks, they're all locked up."

Marcus nods. I see why he considers Stella such an asset. The information she gathered is crucial to what we'll do next.

"I should go back up, Adele," Niran says. "And do recon."

"Yeah," Marcus agrees. "I gave her my gun. Come back within an hour if you can. We need to move as quickly as possible."

Niran puts on a holster and is choosing his weapons when there's a creaking noise, sunlight illuminating the space. Someone opened the door.

Marcus's arm shoots out and he moves me behind him, drawing his knife. I lower my brows over being treated like a damsel in distress, my gun already in hand.

"It's me." Adele is breathing hard as she descends the stairs. "I got it."

Small pieces of her light-blond hair stick out at her temples, just as sweat-soaked as her skin.

"Good work," Niran says. "I was just about to come offer you a hand."

"Didn't need it." She passes Marcus the device.

He turns off his aromium, then grabs a nearby bucket with one hand and passes me the device with his other. By the time I get my aromium off, he's bent over the bucket, throwing up.

I hardly feel the usual drain of energy from switching it off, adrenaline making up the difference.

"The fuck, man?" Niran says as he watches Marcus. "Are you okay?"

"This happens every time he switches his aromium off," I say tightly.

Wyatt, who hardly ever speaks, says, "That seems like a problem."

"It does, doesn't it?" I agree.

"Can I fucking puke in peace?" Marcus gripes.

I turn to Adele and ask, "How's your wound?"

She presses her lips into a thin line. "It hurts, but the stitches are holding. I'm fine."

Marcus secures two handguns in his holster. He told me to be his voice of reason, and I wish I could do it in private, but it has to be now, in front of the others.

"Every gun we bring into camp is a gun that could end up in their hands," I say.

He nods and meets my gaze. "They'll only get these if I'm dead."

Though his aromium is off, his eyes have the lethal gleam I'm only used to seeing when it's on.

"Niran, you're with Adele," he says. "You guys enter camp by the holding cells. Wyatt and Stella, circle around and come in by the command housing block. You know where the ladders are. Briar and I will come in by the garden. Stay out of sight, watch your backs and pick them off."

"Lethal force?" Wyatt asks.

"Yeah. They made the wrong choice, and I'm not giving them a chance to do it again."

I study his icy expression, which takes me back to the night he shot Vance.

He said I'm more beautiful than a rose. That he can't breathe without me. He holds me so close when I sleep that I can hear his steady heartbeat against my back. But he also decides whether people here live or die. He has to be hard and decisive; cold even.

I know both sides of him, but I wonder if he realizes that the hard decisions he makes aren't who he is. He carries so much on his shoulders, and he bears that weight alone.

Five minutes later, I'm climbing the stairs out of the bunker, the air thickening with every step. Monkeys nearby are whooping and chattering, oblivious to us.

We break apart, each pair taking a separate path. Marcus and I scan our surroundings as we slowly creep forward, watching our footfalls to stay quiet.

"Are you still sick?" I ask in a low tone.

"I'm good."

"Tell me the truth."

There's a pause and then he says, "Yeah. I might stop to puke, but I'm okay."

Within a minute, he needs to stop. He throws up twice and then wipes the back of his hand over his mouth before nodding and moving on.

"Think we lost McClain?" I ask softly.

"Yeah," he mutters. "That bastard's probably long gone, laughing it up."

"You think so? He seems pretty haunted by what he's done."

"He should be."

When I look at the ground to see where I'm stepping, I notice a deep emerald vine sliding along next to me. I lower my brows and stop walking.

The vine stops too. I bend down and examine it. Tiny dark purple thorns are scattered around it, and there's the occasional small bundle of leaves with purple vascular bundles that resemble veins.

I take two steps. The vine slithers to catch up, then stops again.

I don't even have my aromium on, and I'm not feeling a surge of emotions like I usually am when I call out to the vines. But Flavius followed Marcus before he turned his aromium back on.

"So I have a friend," I say in a low tone, glancing at Marcus.

He brings his index finger to his lips, signaling for quiet. I stop, listening intently.

There are voices in the distance. I ready my gun, forgetting about the vine by my feet.

We keep moving, watching every step we take. After a couple minutes, the voices have faded. Staying silent, Marcus leads the way to another bunker, the trapdoor to this one also covered with leaves and vegetation. He hooks his fingertips into a small crevice in the door and opens it.

This bunker is much smaller. It's only about two feet deep and about six feet on each side. It's stuffed full of weapons, empty plastic water jugs, some canned food in glass jars, and a metal ladder.

Marcus lifts the ladder out of the ground, his arm muscles cording from its weight.

"This unfolds and extends to twelve feet," he says. "We've never needed to use it, but it should get us over the wall."

I close the bunker door, making sure vegetation covers the small inlaid handle. It's only about a half-mile walk to the wall from there, and my pulse races as we get closer.

Marcus is quiet, unfolding the ladder and easing it against the wall. The sharp, pointed spears on top of the wall are going to be an issue.

"Are you sure about this?" I whisper.

He reaches into the pack on his back, taking out a rope. "I'll go first and secure this to the spikes. I'm going to use it to rappel down the other side. Then I'll throw it up to you when you need it."

It's a good plan—in theory. But getting over the long spikes isn't going to be easy.

Marcus climbs up the ladder, carefully taking in the view of camp over the wall before going all the way.

And then, not surprisingly, he makes getting over the spikes look easy. His legs are so long that he finds footholds in the openings without hitting the sharpened ends of the spears.

He quickly secures the rope, wraps it around his waist, and disappears over the wall.

After a deep breath, I put my hands on the ladder and climb it, not looking down. This is how I can get to Amira, Olin and the others I care about. I have to make it work.

Marcus throws me the rope. I miss it on the first try, but get it on the second.

Navigating the spikes is harder for me. They're far enough apart that I can't lie on them like a bed of nails, but too tall and close together for me to get around like Marcus did.

All I can do is squeeze my way between them, taking an indirect path. A short spike catches on my pants and tears a small hole in the fabric on my left thigh.

A couple minutes later, I make it to the other side and lock eyes with Marcus. He nods at me, hands on his waist.

It's been years since I rappelled. I was just a kid, and I only did light rock wall scaling with my dad bracing my rope the entire time. But I have to get down there.

"Get to the halfway point and I'll catch you," Marcus whispers.

I turn my back to him and push off, air flowing over my face. Then I crash into the wall with an "oof" sound, the breath knocked out of my lungs.

I drop, and Marcus catches me, a smile tugging at his lips.

"You okay?" he asks.

I groan and rub my left knee. "Never better."

My soreness is forgotten as he unties the rope from my waist and we rush through the garden. Tall rows of corn conceal us for a while, and we bend down when we reach the tomatoes, the fresh smell of the plants reminding me of when I worked here every day.

"Where the hell is he?"

An enraged male voice sounds from the center of camp, near the tower. We slowly creep toward it, the hairs on the back of my neck standing up when the voice returns.

"I'll cut her head off, Nova! You've got ten seconds to call Marcus on the radio or she's dead."

Marcus's eyes widen and he looks at me, sticking his gun into the back waistband of his pants.

"Nova won't talk. I'm going."

Before I can respond, he's running away, leaving me gaping after him. My heart drops to my stomach. I can't believe he just did that. He's going to get himself killed.

After checking in every direction, I move from the cover of the Hub's building to crouch behind a small stage near the center of camp. This is where performances, often by the camp's young kids, are hosted. It gives me a clear view of Ray, who has a knife to the neck of a dark-haired woman. She's crying, her eyes squeezed tightly shut.

"I want everything!" Ray yells. "You open every door in this camp for me! I want every weapon and all the supplies."

"Fine." It's Marcus, my gaze flying to him. "Let Blythe go, and you and I can handle this."

Nova, Amira, and the other captured command team members are tied to the thick support posts of the water tower. It looks like they ran out of rope, because Breck's wrists are bloody from what looks like wire that's wrapped tightly around them.

Not everyone is here. I only see three others who look like they're with Ray, all men holding knives. Around a dozen people are lying face down on the ground, their hands on the backs of their heads.

I take a deep breath, clearing my mind. Marcus is walking toward Ray, his hands out in front of him. One of the men working with Ray is chewing a fingernail, the other hand slack at his side with the knife in it.

I've shot guns many times, but never with stakes this high. Ray's head is turned so he has a clear view of Marcus, and I've got a good shot at the back of his head.

I move onto the stage, widen my stance, and take aim. I'm about to fire when Ray moves, Blythe's head now in the spot I was going to shoot.

My heart hammers so hard I can feel it everywhere. This isn't the time for shaky hands and second-guessing.

I imagine my dad standing next to me, telling me to be strong and do what needs doing.

Ray turns again, his head back where it was before. I squeeze the trigger.

The knife in Ray's hand drops, Blythe screaming. As soon as I have a clear shot, I put a bullet in Ray's chest.

Exhaling slowly, I turn the gun to the man who was chewing his nail. I fire once at his head and once at his chest.

When I try to aim at the next man, he's already falling, an arrow in the side of his head. It was probably Wyatt; he took a bow and arrows from the bunker.

Marcus tackled the last guy, and now they're on the ground fighting. I run toward them, someone yelling.

I go to Nova first, working on the knots around her wrists.

"We have a total of six people," I murmur in her ear.

"They're holding everyone prisoner in the Sub," she says. "One of them has my gun."

The knots are tied tight. I keep working on them, Wyatt and Stella running up to untie others.

"You're a crack shot," Wyatt says to me. "Nice job."

"Thanks."

I haven't even processed the gunshots yet. There's relief that I made them, but later I'll lie awake thinking about all the ways it could've gone bad.

It takes forever, but I finally get Nova's binds untied. When I'm finished, I turn to find Marcus approaching. He meets my gaze and nods his approval.

Niran yells at us from nearby. "The Sub door just opened!"

Marcus passes Nova one of his guns. I offer Amira, who just got untied, a knife, but she shakes her head.

"I'm useless without a bow," she says.

Marcus takes off at a run for the Sub, and everyone follows. People start flooding out of the Sub, most of them our own people trying to get to safety.

"There's been a big misunderstanding." Darien, one of our people who Adele said joined Ray, is approaching Marcus with his palms out in a calming gesture.

Marcus punches him in the face so hard he drops to the dirt, unconscious.

"Briar!" A man's frantic voice slices through the air. "Behind you!"

Instinct sends me flying to the ground. When I look up, Marcus has a knife buried in the chest of Jax, one of our other people who joined Ray. Jax was about to bury a hunting knife in my back.

I'm breathing hard as I get to my feet, meeting the gaze of the man whose warning saved my life.

Olin.

42

I could describe Agentic State Theory to someone who doesn't understand it. But all my previous understanding came from textbooks and professors. The reality is significantly more disturbing.

- Excerpt from the journal of Dr. Randall McClain

"You can talk?" I stare at Olin, stunned.

He nods, an apology in his brown eyes. "I can, yes."

"But ..." I shake my head, confused.

"When you're ready, I'll explain."

Marcus looks at his wrist, pretending to check a watch that's not there. "Now's good. You're obviously hiding something."

Olin holds his gaze. "I'd rather just talk to Briar."

"No."

I frown at Marcus. "Why is it up to you?"

"You're not the only one he deceived." He looks from me to Olin. "Give me five minutes and we can talk somewhere private."

He assigns tasks to everyone on the command teams, like head counts of our people and the insurgents, damage assessments and securing the places we entered the camp on ladders.

"A couple days ago, we lost all electronic controls except red level," Nova tells him. "There's no power in the kitchen and no one's room door lock works."

Marcus nods, his brow furrowed. Nova turns to me.

"Briar, thank you for what you did for all of us." Her words are thick with emotion. "You saved a lot of lives today."

I'm taken aback because Nova has always been quiet and stoic around me. Finally, I manage to say, "You would've done the same."

"Nova." Marcus inclines his head toward the Sub entrance.

She follows, and Olin joins us. The Sub entrance door is already open, probably because the lock doesn't work and there's no point in closing it.

Olin and I walk beside Marcus and Nova. I take his hand and squeeze it.

"Thank you. That was the second time you saved my life."

His lips curve up a fraction, but he doesn't answer. In the few days he's been here, his skin has taken on a better color and his cheeks are a little less sunken. His hair is still a wild riot of curls.

I'm still in shock that he can speak. There were so many times at Rising Tide he made me believe he couldn't. He made everyone believe it.

Marcus takes us into a room that used to be someone's office, gesturing for Olin to sit behind the desk, which has nothing on it. He carries another chair into the room so he, Nova and I can all sit down across from Olin.

There's a tense silence in the room, everyone seeming to wait for someone else to speak.

"So," Marcus finally says. "Why the mute act?"

Olin sighs softly, looking like he's considering his answer.

"Rona said Pax cut your tongue out," I say.

Something like amusement gleams in Olin's eyes. "I started that rumor. It worked out well."

I pinch my brows together, confused. "How do you start a rumor when you don't want anyone to know you can talk?"

"I told someone Pax threatened to cut out my tongue. So when I stopped talking, the rumor spread that he'd done it. He never corrected anyone, I think because he thought it made him look like a badass."

"He's such a fucking idiot," Marcus mutters.

"Why?" Nova asks Olin.

He folds his hands in front of him on the desk. "I was sent here three years ago by the ILF—the Idaho

Liberation Front. My assignment was to gather intelligence on Whitman's secret island."

My mouth drops open. Olin gives me an apologetic look.

"I couldn't tell anyone. I'm the fourth person the ILF tried to send, and the first one to make it. One person was killed in jail and the other two—we don't know for sure, but they probably died on the boat or the beach trying to get here."

"What's the Idaho Liberation Front?" I ask.

He shifts his shoulders in a shrug. "I guess we're the rebellion. One of them anyway. When I left to come here, we were the largest. Our goal is to eliminate Whitman's regime and restore democracy to the United States."

I sit back in my chair, a lump of emotion welling in my throat. There are people fighting back. They're organized. Maybe we can join them somehow.

"How many people are in the group?" Marcus asks.

"I don't know. And that's deliberate. We operate in small cells and very few people know everything."

"How does your silence factor into all this?" Nova asks, sounding skeptical.

"I was only eighteen when I got here. Very green and eager to prove myself to the ILF. I asked too many questions. Raised some suspicions. So I decided to play a role. I became the clueless kitchen guy who couldn't even talk. I was practically invisible."

He's not wrong. Everyone at Rising Tide overlooked and dismissed Olin when I was there.

"So why tell us all this?" Marcus asks, crossing his large arms over his chest.

"My work at Rising Tide is done," Olin says simply. "I'm only still here because I wanted to find out about the Dust Walkers." He gestures to us. "I can't go back and tell the ILF there's a rival faction at the base where experiments are conducted, but I don't know anything about it. Briar asking me to come here was the in I needed." He focuses on me, frowning. "I'm sorry. I guess I lied, but I hope you understand why."

"It's okay. I'm just ... thrilled to know people are working against Whitman. I'd join the ILF if I could."

Marcus flicks a quick glare at me.

"Olin, you said you can't go back without information about us for the ILF. So now that you have it, how do you get back?"

"I can request evacuation when I'm ready."

My pulse flies into overdrive. Evacuation. Maybe I can leave this island with him—and get to Mae.

"How does that work?" Nova asks.

A corner of Olin's mouth quirks up. "I've said as much as I'm willing to."

My excitement screeches to a halt. Why is he being cagey all of a sudden?

Marcus clears his throat. "So what will your report about us to your group look like? What have you figured out?"

"This was a base of some kind. Probably where people with aromium were monitored."

After a few seconds of silence, I look at Marcus. He's giving Olin an expectant look.

"That's it?" Marcus says.

A flash of annoyance passes over Olin's expression. "It's enough."

"Enough for what?"

Marcus's casual question isn't really casual at all. Olin thought he was holding all the cards, but Marcus is showing him he's wrong.

"Enough to file my report," Olin says dismissively. "Don't get the wrong idea—I'm not your enemy. I didn't have to tell you what I did. And I didn't have to save Briar, but I did."

I swallow my urge to speak. Marcus has questioned people many times, and I've never done it. He knows what he's doing.

"We appreciate what you've done," Marcus says. "But there's so much you don't know."

"Like?" Olin arches his brows.

"Like how to fight aromium. How to end it."

Olin's expression is a cross between smug and sympathetic. "If you guys knew how to do that, you would've done it by now. Rising Tide is a major thorn in your side."

"Ask Briar," Marcus says.

I give him a puzzled look as Olin says, "Ask her what?"

"Ask her if there's a lot you don't know. Information that would change everything for the ILF if it wants to destroy the experiments on this island. She won't lie to you."

Olin's gaze turns to me.

"He's right," I say. "There's a lot you don't know."

Olin sits back in his seat, looking troubled. "What then? I tell you how I'm going to get evacuated when I'm ready, and you tell me more about aromium?"

Marcus shakes his head and stands. "You can leave anytime you want; we won't stop you."

"Then what do you want from me?"

"Work with us," Marcus says. "Earn our trust. From what you're saying, it sounds like we all want the same thing."

"Your shield's going down, isn't it?" Olin asks.

"It's not down yet."

"What happens when it goes down?"

"We switch everyone's aromium back on and defend our camp."

Olin's brows shoot up. "You can turn it back on?"

"Take some time to think about it," Marcus says. "You're welcome here if you're willing to earn your place, respect everyone in our camp, and not lie to me. Again, I mean. We'll clean the slate."

Olin's shoulders slump. "I don't need time. I'll stay."

"For now, everything that was said in this room stays in this room," Marcus says.

He walks over to the door and opens it, meeting my eyes.

I'm still dazed as I leave the room and walk back out of the tunnel beside him. I thought Olin being able to talk was a shock, but finding out about the group he's part of hit me much harder.

"Any sign of McClain?" Marcus asks Niran, who's standing near the tunnel exit when we walk out.

"He's gone. So are two of the prisoners Ray freed."

All that work we did to find McClain, and he's gone. Now, even if we find the flower, we don't have him to make the stabilizer. This island is the definition of one step forward, two steps back.

McClain said things are "too far gone." Maybe they are. Maybe trying to get Olin's group to rescue everyone in our camp is our new best option.

That option makes my chest tight with aggravation. Virginia would still be free to receive boatloads of prisoners to make her robot soldiers. There would be no consequences for everything she's done.

When Niran and Marcus are finished talking, Niran walks away and Marcus turns to me. His mossy eyes are tortured, his face lined with worry.

"What's wrong?" I ask softly.

I think he's going to answer, but instead he looks away. "I need to go take care of some things. See you tonight?"

My heart sinks. He's shutting me out, and I don't know why. I've done everything I can to show him I deserve his trust.

"Yeah." The word is barely a whisper.

He walks away without another word.

43

*It's a sad day in our camp. An enhanced black bear attacked
Dr. Kristen Lynn yesterday and she died from her injuries.
This is the second attack by a bear since we arrived. We are
sending out a team to euthanize all black bears on the island.*

- Excerpt from the journal of Dr. Randall McClain

When I wake up the next morning, Marcus is already
gone.

Our room is pitch black, but even in the darkness, I
know he isn't here because I can't feel him. His bed is so
small that we can't even fit in it unless he's on his back
and I'm on my side. I always put my back to the wall and
snuggle into his warm, solid body to fall asleep at night,
my head tucked beneath his chin and my cheek on his
chest.

He was quiet when he came in late last night. We didn't exchange any words when he got into bed, both of us moving to get situated into our sleeping positions. Once his arm was around my back, his hand resting on my hip, he kissed the top of my head.

And that was it. Even though I was only wearing a tank top and underwear, he had no interest in anything sexual. I knew something was off with him, but now I'm even more certain.

I slide out of bed, my clothes already soaked through with sweat. With the power almost entirely offline, the air circulator doesn't work. It's nothing like air conditioning, but I didn't realize how much it helped with the humidity until we no longer had it.

I showered before bed, so this morning I just brush my teeth, put on clean clothes, and put my hair back in a ponytail. It's so stifling in the housing block that I'm relieved to step outside, where the air isn't stagnant.

On my walk to the Hub, I see that the bodies of the men we killed yesterday are gone. A woman is riding one of the laundry bikes through camp and two men are pushing wheeled carts past the tower.

I glance up to find Stella in the enclosure at the top of the tower, monitoring the long view of the camp's perimeter.

It's business as usual here, but also ... not. There are no kids out here. No one standing out of the main traffic area, carrying on light conversations. Everyone wears a serious expression, the events of yesterday still fresh.

When I walk into the Hub and get in the breakfast

line, Amira sees me from her place near the front, her face lighting up.

"Hey, how are you?" she asks as she comes to stand with me at the back of the line.

"I'm okay."

"How'd you sleep?"

"Not great."

I was tired, but I could tell from his breathing that Marcus wasn't sleeping, so we both lay there alone with our thoughts. We've spent days on end together, sharing intimacies both physical and emotional. But the wall between us now only seems to be growing bigger. It's left me feeling adrift, like a boat that came untied from a dock and is now floating aimlessly in the ocean.

I speak softly, so only she can hear me when I ask, "Can I stay in your room? At night? I'll sleep on the floor."

Her brows drop in question, but she says, "Of course. I'll see if I can find a cot."

I nod my thanks, the savory scent of cooking meat making my stomach rumble with hunger.

"Did the kitchen get power back?"

Amira shakes her head. "Their ovens are wood-fired. I think we're having bacon and eggs and pancakes."

I groan, ravenous after not eating anything yesterday. "What's the occasion? We usually have fruit and oatmeal."

"I guess surviving the coup attempt? And everyone's really hungry because we only had breakfast yesterday."

"How are things with you?"

Amira and I catch up over dinner and often spend the

rest of our evenings together after that, but we've both been gone from camp a lot, searching for the flowers.

"Not bad." She sighs softly, looking away. "I went and saw Chance. Ellison had to amputate his left arm beneath the elbow. He lost a lot of blood, and when they dragged him out yesterday and tied him to the tower, I was afraid it would kill him."

"Is he okay?"

She shrugs. "He's eating and drinking. Sleeping a lot."

"I can't imagine. I'll go see him soon."

"He's pretty down. He thinks his life is basically over because of the amputation."

We've reached the front of the line, Vadim turning his bright smile on us. "Eggs?"

Amira gives him a grateful look. "Please. This looks and smells incredible."

He tells us about his egg scrambling method—combine the eggs, but don't make them frothy—and his recipe for cooking them in butter with salt and pepper, chives sprinkled in at the end.

We've both gotten eggs and bacon on our plates, and Amira is about to get a big pancake piled onto her plate by a kitchen server when a woman comes running into the kitchen.

"One of the prisoners came back!"

Chatter buzzes through the line of people waiting for breakfast. I step out of line, Amira following. Just in case shit's about to get bad again, I shove a piece of bacon in my mouth so at least I get something to eat.

"Should we barricade the Hub entrance?" Amira asks, reaching for the bow at her back.

"Let's see if we can get a look at what's going on."

We walk out of the Hub, our plates still in hand. I squint to see who's gathered in a cluster by the front gates to camp, my chin dropping when I see him.

"It's McClain," I murmur, walking toward him.

Marcus and Niran are standing by him, Marcus glancing at me as I approach.

"You came back," I say to McClain.

There's a ghost of a smile on his lips. "I want to help."

Marcus says to Niran, "Go help Nova get us back online so we can see if it's fixed." He glances at me then and says, "McClain says he fixed our solar panels."

Relief floods through me. If it's true, it's the first good thing that's happened here in a while.

"It's not my specialty, but I think I did it right," McClain says.

A sheen of sweat covers his skin, his gray hair hanging on both sides of his face in frizzy strings. He's so fragile looking, his face too lean and his shoulders slighter than most anyone in our camp, including the women.

"Eat this." I offer him a piece of bacon from my plate.

His smile grows slightly. "Thank you, but it's okay."

I push it closer to him. "Just eat it. You need it."

He gives Marcus a questioning look and says, "I may be going back to my cell."

Marcus shifts, scowling slightly. A few seconds of silence pass and then a voice sounds over the radio.

"Athena to Ares, we are up and running. Fully online."

Nova's happiness comes through in her rich, warm voice. Marcus sighs deeply, looking like a weight has been lifted.

"Thanks," he says to McClain.

A thought occurs to me. I face McClain. "If you feel like it, can we talk? Maybe over breakfast?"

Marcus frowns, disapproval etched into his expression. "We need to get back out and search."

I'm not letting him call all the shots anymore. He's used to everyone doing what he says all the time, but this conversation with McClain is important to me, and I'm not letting him put me off.

"I'll be ready within an hour," I say, not even looking at Marcus.

He groans. "Fine. We'll meet in the Sub."

"I didn't invite you." I give him a sharp look.

His brows fly up to his hairline. "Are you fucking for real?"

"Do I sit in on every conversation you have?"

Amira backs away and the two gate guards suddenly need to check something out of earshot, leaving just me, Marcus and McClain.

Marcus is about to unload when McClain speaks up instead. "I think it should be all of us. I left Marcus in a bad position when I went to search for the flower and never returned. I understand his reluctance to let us speak alone."

I shrug, my aggravation with Marcus flaring. He

holds my gaze, his eyes narrowed. Then he gestures to one of the gate guards, who comes over.

"Take McClain to get some food. Then bring him to his old office."

The two men leave, Marcus and I still locked in a stare-down. I'm not flinching this time. I cowered inside a hive of vines at his command and came to his rescue when he stupidly offered himself up to Ray yesterday. If he doesn't see how capable I am, that's his problem, not mine.

"I'm staying with Amira," I say.

He scoffs, his gaze darkening. "The fuck you are."

"Either I'm staying with Amira, or you can put me in a cell. Your choice."

He rubs the scruff on his jaw, looking away. "Look, I know I've been a dick—"

"You mean even more of a dick than usual. A massive dick instead of a regular one."

Something flares in his gold-flecked eyes. "Yeah, fine. But we're still ... it doesn't change anything between us. You stay in *our* room. With me."

"Are you going to tell me what's been going on with you?" I fire the question at him like a bullet. "Why you're so distant?"

"I'm getting there. Give me time."

I shake my head, holding back angry tears. "Take all the time you want, but I'll be staying with Amira while you do."

I turn and leave, the tears spilling over. I let them trail all the way down my cheeks to my chin, because I'm not letting him see me raise my hand to wipe them away.

———

"It's bare in here," McClain says as he walks into the office where we talked to Olin yesterday.

"I burned most of your shit," Marcus says tightly.

McClain doesn't react. He just takes a seat in one of the chairs facing the desk, leaving the one behind it open for Marcus. When I sit down next to McClain instead of Marcus, I get a low-key scowl from the man who brought me to tears a few minutes ago.

I'm hoping to ignore him for the entirety of this conversation.

"Did you eat?" I ask McClain.

His eyes brighten a notch. "I did. It's been ages since I had pancakes and bacon."

"Thank you for fixing the solar panels. That was dangerous for you, but now we don't have to worry about the shield going down."

He nods. "It was the least I could do."

"That's a fucking fact," Marcus mutters.

I shoot him a glare before saying, "Dr. McClain, we have to get back to searching, but there's something I need to understand. Can you tell me more about the different strains of aromium?"

He uses his spindly arms to pick up his chair by the back, turning it so he's facing me and then sitting back down. "What do you want to know?"

"I'm sure there's a lot, and I'd love to know everything at some point when we aren't on a tight schedule, but for now, I need to know more about how aromium is affecting me." I shake my head. "I still can't believe this, but somehow aromium has connected me to vines."

A crease appears between his brows, his glasses perched low on his nose. "Vines? Can you tell me more?"

"At first, I didn't even know I was doing it. When I felt strong emotions, like when someone was about to kill me, vines ... responded, I guess? They flew out of the jungle and wrapped themselves around the person trying to kill me, so she couldn't do it. They saved me."

Awareness dawns on his face. "You're the first I know of to link with a plant. I wondered how that would work."

I have so many questions; it seems impossible to narrow them down and keep this conversation succinct. "How many people have gotten the same strain I did? Marcus said he can call wolves and I can call vines because of the strains we were given."

McClain looks at Marcus, whose expression is completely closed off.

"Well..." McClain shifts in his chair, frowning. "Are you sure you want to go into this right now, Briar? You may find it ... disturbing."

"I want to know. I *deserve* to know."

He nods, his eyes meeting mine. "Tell me your full name."

"Briar Hollis. Juniper, if you need my middle name."

His eyes widen, what little color his cheeks have draining away.

"Hollis?" It's almost a whisper. "Are you Lucy Hollis's daughter?"

My heart thunders in my chest, pounding so hard and fast I'm a little lightheaded. "Yes."

McClain's shock unsettles me. I can't even wait a few seconds to let him process it.

"Did you know her?" My voice breaks.

He pushes his glasses up on his nose, his expression turning sympathetic. "Yes. Lucy was an expert in her field. No one knew more about plant biology and pathology."

"How did you know her?"

It's all I can do not to jump out of my chair and shake him—I want to make him tell me everything he knows about her, right now.

"Soren Whitman hired me to assemble a team of the world's greatest minds to figure out how to engineer a compound that improved upon human DNA. Your mother was one of those people."

I stare at him, not breathing. It's not true. My mother was a good person. She never would have been part of the experiments on this island.

"No." Tears fill my eyes.

"You have to understand," McClain says softly, "that we didn't know what aromium would become. None of us had any idea. There were two teams, and I led the aromium one. We were told our work was for the betterment of humanity. We were in the dark, as was the other team. Most of the scientists on the other team had no idea they were actually creating the virus that would wipe out billions of people."

My jaw drops, and I look at Marcus. His expression is stoic, unreadable. But his eyes swim with sympathy.

"The virus?" I can hardly even take a full breath. "You guys created it?"

"The other team did. But we all worked under the same roof. The team I assembled thought we were working for a billionaire who wanted to use his vast resources to genetically engineer cures for diseases."

"But then ... how am I able to control vines just because my mother worked on the project?"

A second passes before he responds. "Because the team I assembled used their own DNA to create aromium. They, and their blood relatives, can do things no one else can with aromium."

I have to put my feelings about this in an invisible box for now. I can't break. After a deep breath, I steel myself.

"It's started happening even when the aromium is off."

He shakes his head. "That's not possible."

"It happens. Marcus has seen it."

McClain looks at Marcus, who gives him a tight nod.

Rubbing his forehead, McClain slumps in his chair. "We unleashed hell on this island. A hell that can't be undone."

44

Dr. Malcolm Lowe was attacked by people at the Rising Tide camp today. His injuries are significant. It's no longer safe for us to enter the camp for monitoring. As the number of soldiers grows, our control over these experiments diminishes.

- Excerpt from the journal of Dr. Randall McClain

"Briar."

"Hmm?" I turn my face toward Amira.

"Did you hear any of that?"

My gaze shifts to Niran, then Marcus. We're at the switch point, the four of us about to go search for the flower after having our aromium switched back on by Nova. It was supposed to be just me and Marcus, but I asked him if we could bring extra help.

He was quick to agree, probably because things are so

tense between us. I had to suddenly leave our conversation with McClain yesterday because I got sick. Learning that not only was my mom involved in creating aromium, but that her DNA is part of it, made me physically ill.

I stumbled to the housing block, holding back tears, until I made it to the bathroom and threw up. Then I sat on the bathroom floor and cried until my head ached.

It's not really a betrayal, but it feels like it. My mom had government security clearance and she consulted on top-secret research that she couldn't discuss with anyone. I understand why she didn't tell us what she was working on.

But I can't stop thinking about all the times I've yearned for her since getting here, wishing I could tell her about aromium. Knowing she'd be blown away. The joke's on me, though, because not only did she know, she helped make it. She helped create the compound that turns women into breeding machines and children into mindless soldiers.

I stayed in the bathroom for more than an hour before dragging myself to the garden to work. I pulled weeds and divided plants, no one questioning what I was doing.

At dinner, I couldn't tell Amira about my mom. It was still too raw. And though I'd planned to stay in her room, I found myself drawn to Marcus. I'm so angry at him, but I also see him more clearly than I did before. This is why he's so cold and bitter toward McClain. McClain sparked a fire that became an inferno and then turned his back on it, washing his hands. I'd be just as furious with him as Marcus is.

I couldn't talk to him last night, but I still curled into his side and cried, his hand smoothing down my hair and his arms wrapped around me. Eventually, I fell asleep.

It's time to return to our search for the flower. But at least Amira and Niran are with us, so we won't be able to argue or rage fuck when we're supposed to be in stealth mode.

"No, I missed it," I say absently.

"We're heading to the volcano," Marcus says, his steely gaze locked onto me. "We're going to climb it again and check for cracks where something could grow."

"Yeah, okay."

After all the crying yesterday, I'm numb today. I want to know everything McClain knows about my mother and her involvement in aromium, but not until the shock of her involvement has worn off.

I can imagine my mom eagerly agreeing to help with a project that was billed as an effort to help prevent and treat diseases. She was passionate about how undervalued plants are in medicine. And if she changed her mind when she found out the project's true mission, I shouldn't hold any of this against her.

I don't really. I was just blindsided by the news. Completely unprepared to find out my mom was partially responsible for what's going on here, even if she didn't intend to be.

Niran leads the way, Amira behind him. I follow Amira, and Marcus walks behind me.

It's raining. Not one of Virginia's superstorms, but a regular rain shower, rivulets of water pouring onto us from tree branches. I don't mind it; it's actually nice to cool off.

We trek through the jungle in silence for more than an hour, the usual bird calls and monkey chatter quieter due to the rain. Even though I know we need to stay quiet in case there are Tiders nearby, I don't like it.

I'm alone with my thoughts, and none of them are good. No one but me and Marcus can see the vines sliding along the ground beside me. I'll tell Amira about the vines soon, but not yet.

We're stopped at a small stream for a water break when Amira asks, "Is there any way you could reverse engineer the aromium? Like work backward from it to create one of the flowers?"

I shake my head. "No. I'd need a seed."

"Jerk me?" Niran offers Amira a piece of beef jerky from his pack, grinning over his quip.

"Pass."

He turns to me and I shake my head. Marcus just flips him off.

"Damn." Niran bites a chewy end off the long stick. "You guys are like a commercial for depression medication."

Marcus catches my attention and angles his head to the side, asking me to follow him. He leads me about fifteen yards away, where we can talk without being overheard.

"You okay?" he asks.

I shrug. "I guess?"

"Is there anything I can do?"

"No. I think I just need time."

He's wearing a gray T-shirt and dark-green canvas pants today, my eyes roving over his chest and arms. There's not a single part of the real me that wants to be in the mood right now, but aromium doesn't care how I'm feeling. It's making me want to drop to my knees and unfasten Marcus's pants.

Use him. Fuck him. Take his power.

I furrow my brow, looking at him and speaking softly. "Does the aromium just make you want sex, or is it ... more? I feel urges to use you and ... I guess, take advantage of your desire."

"It's the aromium. It tells me the same things."

I glance at Niran and Amira. "And you never feel any of that about Amira?"

He shakes his head. "Only you. It amplifies real feelings, and you're the only woman I want. Why, are you drawn to anyone else?"

"No. Just you."

He takes my hand, his expression solemn. "I know you're mad at me, but if you need something, tell me."

"You mean sex?" I glance at Niran and Amira again.

A smile quirks on his lips. "No, but also ... yes. It's not what I meant, but if you say the word, we'll find a place and make it happen."

"You meant like moral support." I fight a smile.

"I meant like anything. If you need someone to yell at—"

I roll my eyes. "If I yell at you, it's because you deserve it. Not because you're my benevolent punching bag."

"That's fair. What I'm trying to say is I'm here if you need me."

"Marcus."

We look over to Niran, who's giving us a questioning look; he and Amira both packed back up and ready to go.

Marcus exhales through his nostrils. "Why'd we bring them?"

"To keep us on track."

I bend and fill my canteen from the stream, looking up at Marcus. "So it's not just me who has a relative who helped make aromium. You, Virginia and Pax do, too."

He nods. "But that's a conversation for another time. Niran's right, we need to get moving."

We resume our walk, Marcus and Niran checking to our right and Amira and I watching to the left for any sign of the bright-blue flower. There are orange, red, yellow, and even purple flowers, but not a blue one in sight.

"Oh!" Niran points, all of us turning.

There's a flash of bright blue, but it's moving.

"That's a fucking bird," Marcus said.

"Oh."

Amira reaches for her bow. "Is it a regular bird, or is it like those mutant mantises?"

"Regular bird," Marcus says. "Keep moving."

We only stop when we need to pee or refill our canteens, and we reach the volcano late in the afternoon. Our boots are still wet from the rain. We have to slowly climb the volcano, our shoes slipping on the wet rock. On days like this, the bottoms of our boots are never fully dry.

"What do you think the temperature is?" Amira asks as we walk up an area of the volcano without a steep incline. "I'm saying a hundred and three."

"Ninety-nine," I guess.

"Remember chilly fall walks? And scraping off your icy windshield in the morning? I honestly can't remember what it was like to be cold."

My foot slips, but I catch myself. We only make it halfway up the volcano before Marcus tells us we have to go back down, so we aren't walking down the uneven surface in the dark later.

It's dusk by the time we set up camp for the night, which isn't much. We can't risk a fire, so it's just the four of us sitting on blankets and eating dried meat and fruit, a thick swarm of mosquitoes surrounding us.

"People used to spend a shitload of money to vacation in a place like this," Niran says.

"In a luxury resort, though," I say. "With walls and air conditioning and fruity drinks."

Niran groans softly and looks at Marcus. "I could go for an ice-cold Modelo right now."

"Wouldn't say no." Marcus leans back on his elbows.

Even though I'm still mad at him, I lie beside him,

staring up at the clear, star-filled sky. The long day of hiking through the jungle mellowed me. I'm no longer worried I'll burst into tears out of nowhere.

"I'd do just about anything for an ice cream sundae right now," Amira says. "With whipped cream and hot fudge and caramel."

I smile, trying to imagine the taste of warm, salted caramel sauce. It's been my favorite since I was a kid. Mae and I would fight over whose favorite it was first, because we didn't want to share a favorite.

"What the hell is that?" Amira jumps a foot closer to Niran, pointing at the sky.

"Just a couple of bats," Niran says. "Probably looking for some bugs to eat."

I shiver. "In the cave I found McClain's knife in, we ran into about a hundred thousand bats."

Amira gasps. "Are you serious?"

"It was awful. You could feel the vibrations of all those wings, and the sounds they make ..."

"They're nocturnal," Niran says, bumping his shoulder against Amira's. "Maybe they'll give you a goodnight kiss later."

"Ugh, no. I'll send them your way, since you're clearly the one in need of affection."

"You noticed my footlong? I can't help it, it's the aromium."

His erection is tenting his lightweight pants, and he's making no effort to hide it.

A thought flickers through my mind, my smile sliding away. I sit up, my heart racing.

"That's it," I say softly

"What?" Marcus bolts up, putting an arm on my back. "What's wrong?"

I look at him, excitement racing through my veins. "I know why we haven't found the flower." The words tumble out of me. "Bats are nocturnal. They mostly pollinate flowers that bloom at night. That's the one thing we never thought of. The flower must only bloom at night."

45

It's hard to sleep here. I'm lying awake right now while everyone else is resting, thinking about Stanley Milgram's words:

"Ordinary people, simply doing their jobs, and without any particular hostility on their part, can become agents in terrible destruction."

Excerpt from the journal of Dr. Randall McClain

"What is *that*?"

Amira points to something in the sky, her tone laced with fear.

Niran looks up. "Raven."

She balks. "Since when do ravens weigh ... that thing has to be at least fifty pounds. It's huge."

"It's a Blue Arrow raven."

For once, Niran spares her a wisecrack. Probably because we're all exhausted. We've spent every moment of darkness on the island searching frantically for the flower for two nights now.

Even though Marcus doesn't need much sleep when his aromium is on, Amira and I haven't been able to sleep much during the day. Niran seems to be able to sleep whenever and wherever he wants. Yesterday, he took a nap on a boulder.

It's evening, and I'm ready to get back to the search. We narrowly avoided a couple of Tiders yesterday when we were searching close to their camp. I've been sticking as close as I can to Amira, because if she gets attacked—by an animal or by a Tider—I want to be there to defend her.

The jaguar attack on Chance has reminded us all that we're not the only apex predators on this island. And our competition has the same aromium advantage we do.

Now that I know more about the aromium experiments, I'm not just leery of the animals here, but also the plants. Vines seem to be my ally, but what about the other plants? An aromium-enhanced jaguar attacked Chance, and I can't dismiss the possibility that plants could turn on us, too.

"Marcus." Niran looks up, and Marcus follows his gaze.

There are three giant ravens now, my heart rate kicking up despite my fatigue. Marcus said Virginia can call ravens. I should've known they'd be genetically enhanced ravens.

My vines can grow rapidly, build protective structures, and immobilize prey. What can the ravens do?

Marcus's expression is impassive, but I know by the set of his jaw and the flare of his nostrils that he's concerned about the birds.

"Can she see us through them?" I ask.

He shakes his head. "Not directly, but they're circling to tell her where we are."

"Wait, who?" Amira asks.

Marcus cuts his gaze to mine. I'm not seeking his permission to tell Amira about the ravens, but I feel him asking me if I'm going to.

He's been distant again since our talk at the stream. Earlier today, he didn't even wrap his arm around me while I tried to sleep. He was right beside me, but he stayed in a sitting position, elbows on his knees.

I told myself it was so he could have a better view of any approaching threats. But it felt like a rebuke. We searched for the flower around Rising Tide and through the swampy section of the island last night, and it was tense, unpleasant work. My aromium never stops begging me to run to him and tear his clothes off, but we hardly even touch anymore.

I was looking forward to that few hours of quiet closeness with him. Of feeling him locked protectively around me. But I didn't even get that.

"Virginia," I tell Amira. "Her aromium connects her to the super ravens on this island, because they have aromium, too."

She sighs, rolling her eyes in exasperation. "Right. Of course. This island is basically an obstacle course designed by Satan. Behind this door"—she gestures to one side—"death by spear-wielding savages! And let's see what's behind door number two—" She holds her hand out to the other side. "Oh! Mauling by a mutant insect or animal."

I put an arm around her, not sure if my smile is sad or amused. "But at least we're not alone."

"Sorry," she mutters. "I'm just tired of being tired and smelling like a dirty sock."

"We need to move," Marcus says tightly. "We should split up for a few hours. The ravens won't know who to follow and they're not all that smart, so they might get so confused they don't follow any of us."

We work out search areas, agreeing to meet back up at the island's tallest waterfall in three hours. Marcus leads the way into a dense section of jungle, where the ravens won't be able to see us.

"You feeling okay?" he asks, throwing a quick glance over his shoulder at me.

"Other than whatever's happening between us, I'm fine."

His shoulders rise and fall in a sigh. "I've got a lot on my mind."

"I know. It's you not wanting to tell me any of it that's the issue."

He spins around to face me, anger pooling in his narrowed eyes. "You think it works like that? Just because we start fucking, I'm supposed to tell you every fucking thought I ever have?"

I raise my chin, not letting him see how hurt I am by what he just said. "My mistake. I won't ask again."

Hands on his hips, he avoids my eyes and looks over my shoulder, doing a double take.

"Hang on," he snaps.

He slashes his machete through something on a branch behind me. Part of a lime-green snake's body drops to the ground with a thud.

"What was that for?" I ask.

"I didn't like how close it was getting to you," he mutters.

"Right. Like when you assumed I wanted to fuck Olin and told me you don't share."

He glowers at me. "I don't."

He's fast-tracking his way to the top of my shit list. It's hard enough being out here scouring an island we've been over time and again on hardly any sleep—I'd rather partner with Amira if he's going to be like this.

"So let me make sure I understand," I say, my pulse pounding with anger. "You want us to share a room and fuck when you feel like it, and you get to decide we're exclusive fuck partners, but I don't get to ask for or expect anything more."

He runs a hand through his hair, his exhale deep. "No. I'm here for anything you need. If you need to talk, I'll listen. But that's not me. I'm not someone who talks about my shit."

I hold his gaze, fighting the lump in my throat. "Then how can I ever really know you?"

Shaking his head, he says, "You don't want to know me. Trust me."

"Yes, I do." I put a palm on his chest, the contact sending a spark of warmth and arousal through me. "I know you've done bad things—so have I. I tried to poison Lochlan once and he blamed it on his cook. They sent her away and I—" I swallow against the shame. "I knew what was going to happen to her, but I still didn't admit what I did. I'm responsible for her death."

His eyes soften with sympathy. He puts his hand over mine. "It was her or you. The real fucked-up part of that whole thing was you being held prisoner in his house."

"I know, but ... I could have been smarter about what I did. And that's not—"

A wolf howls nearby, and Marcus puts a finger over his lips. Then he closes his eyes, seemingly lost in his head for around fifteen seconds.

When he opens his eyes, I ask, "What did you just do?"

"I checked in with Flavius. That was his howl."

I lower my brows, his ability to exchange actual information with Flavius news to me. "And everything's okay?"

He nods. "The pack is hunting. That's all it was."

I dive back into our conversation, our unresolved issues bothering me too much to leave them like this any longer. "I'm going to stay with Amira when we get back."

"No, you're not."

I huff out a bitter laugh. "Am I a prisoner?"

I get his classic scowl. "No, but we're better when we're together and you know it, B. I need you with me."

"But you won't tell me what's on your mind?"

His voice rises with aggravation. "You want to know what's on my mind? I spend most of my time thinking about what an asshole I am for being with you. For letting you think I'm some good guy when I'm really—" He rubs his jaw and scoffs, looking away. "I'm not even close."

"I think you're better than you realize."

His sage-green eyes are shadowed with doubt. "I want to be a man you're proud of, but—" His voice breaks with emotion as he presses my palm harder to his chest. "I've got demons chasing me, and you're the only thing that makes me feel like ... like I'm something more than I really am, even if it's not all the time."

Tears well in my eyes. I've never seen this side of him. He's torturing himself, and it's tearing me apart to see it.

Just as I'm about to respond to him, there's a sharp crack of breaking branches and snarling sounds, something heavy crashing through the undergrowth to our left. Marcus puts his hands on my shoulders, moving me away from the approaching animal. He leans close, speaking in my ear in a low tone.

"Go."

I run, slowed by the density of plants and trees. I can feel Marcus's warmth behind me, a low, rumbling growl on his tail.

"What is it?" I ask, keeping my eyes trained on what's in front of me.

It should be dark as ink in this part of the jungle, but I can make out a lot of things because aromium is improving my night vision. I take a flying step over a rotting tree stump.

"Lion, I think. The pack's on—"

His words cut off and I stop, turning. A massive male lion just knocked him to the ground. The breath whooshes from my chest, the beast's darkened eyes like twin pools of deep, endless darkness.

"Go, Briar!" Marcus commands. "Run!"

He's on his feet, crouched with a machete in hand. The lion dips his head, letting out another deep growl.

I reach for the vines with my mind, begging them for help. They've only ever helped me, but if Marcus was able to get his wolves to help both of us when we were so cold, I can find a way to get the vines to help him.

It's our best option. A single shot from a handgun won't bring the massive lion down, and then he'd be so enraged he'd attack.

Come quickly. I need you.

"Briar, get out of here," Marcus says, his tone low and commanding. "I don't need your help."

Leaves rustle. I know that whooshing sound. It's the vines flying through the air toward me. I keep my breathing steady and continue summoning them.

They come from every direction. Thick, thorny vines swiftly twine themselves around all of the lion's legs. He tries to move, snarling when he discovers he can't.

Marcus wastes no time. He comes to me, gratitude in his eyes as we take off again.

I don't know how long the vines can hold the lion, so we run and run and run. We've covered well over two miles, my breathing hard from pushing myself to my top speed.

"There's a clearing with a stream to the right," Marcus says from behind me. "We can cut through the water and he'll lose our scent if he's trailing us."

When we exit the line of trees, I stop abruptly, throwing my hand over my mouth.

I've never seen anything like this. Water softly murmurs down the wide stream, a warm, honeyed fragrance filling the night air. And on both sides of the stream, hundreds of waist-high stalks boast bright-blue, iridescent, bell-shaped blooms. Their glow illuminates the space, which feels magical.

Marcus huffs out a cry of relief. He sinks to his knees, his hands on top of his head.

"You did it, B." His voice is thick with emotion. "You did it."

"It was us," I say softly. "All of us."

46

This week we'll dive deeper into research I was part of in the Galapagos Islands. We made extraordinary findings about island plants separated from mainland ecosystems. Many of those plants developed new chemical defenses. Some of those defenses were so potent they could alter the neurochemistry of any organism that encountered them.

- Excerpt from a lecture given by Dr. Lucinda Hollis in her Plant Evolution course

"Where have you fuckers been?" Niran demands when we reach him and Amira at the waterfall almost an hour later. "If you've been getting in on while we were here thinking you were dead, I'm—"

I pull a flower from the canvas bag at my hip, silencing him.

"You found it!" Amira launches herself at me with a hug.

"They glow." Niran admires the flower Marcus took from his bag. "Wow."

Marcus shakes his head. "They're everywhere in the clearing we took Des to when he got that snakebite. In the daytime, they're just green bush-looking things, but at night, they bloom."

"This could change everything," Niran says. "We've got McClain *and* the flower. Damn it, I'm getting kind of emotional."

"We won't tell anyone about your soft underbelly," I assure him.

He grins. "We could really use those beers right about now to toast, couldn't we?"

Amira pulls out her canteen. "Canteen cheers! It's better than nothing, right?"

We clink our metal canteens together, all of us taking a swig. I know we still have an uphill battle ahead, but our days of trekking through the rainforest and over the beaches in a search that feels hopeless are over.

I smile, thinking of my dad's reminders to me that pressure builds diamonds. He'd be proud of our tenacity.

"I'm taking the longest shower and sleeping for twelve hours," Amira says. "And the air circulators are back online, so I won't have sweat pouring off me." Her happy expression turns sheepish. "I don't mean to make it sound like I didn't want to be here doing this. I loved it, but I'll also love getting back to camp, if that makes sense."

"We get it," Marcus says. "We should make it back pretty close to sunrise."

We're closer to the west side of the island, where Rising Tide is, than we are to our side. But I don't notice my aching feet or the voracious mosquitoes as we make the hike.

I'd bet money the flowers we found are pollinated by bats. I should've thought of it sooner, but at least it came to me eventually. The nerdy scientist in me is giddy over finally figuring it out.

The quiet of night has settled over the jungle. We have to watch our footing carefully so we don't accidentally step on a venomous snake, but other than that, traveling through at night is peaceful.

I'm hoping McClain will let me assist him in studying each of the flower's components and trying to make a stabilizer. It's possible we could find other ways to fight aromium's effects.

I don't know what kind of doctor McClain is, but from what I know of him, he's very capable. If we work this problem hard, we can hopefully come up with something soon. It's just another one of science's riddles waiting to be solved.

The dark of night turns to gray as we get closer to camp. We leave the dense jungle, following a well-worn dirt path that winds through a clearing, only a few palm trees dotted around it.

Excitement swirls in my stomach as I imagine showing McClain what we found. He played a big part in a lot of death and destruction, but now he has a chance to do something good.

"Niran!" Amira cries.

I turn, finding Niran crouched on the ground, an arrow lodged in his bicep. Marcus, Amira and I run to him, shielding him and arming ourselves, our backs to him.

Another arrow lands on the ground by my foot, the shaft vibrating with force.

Marcus's voice is laced with fury as he roars, "Come out and fight us, you fucking cowards! I'm right here if you want me!"

Amira's heavy, rhythmic breathing is the only sound until she fires an arrow and it whooshes through the air, hitting someone I didn't even see at the edge of the tree line.

A guttural caw sounds from above, and I don't even have to look to know it came from one of Virginia's ravens.

"These flowers have to get back to camp," I say in a low tone. "No matter what, that's the mission."

"I'm not leaving here without all of you," Marcus says.

Niran stands up, blood running from the hole in his arm where he pulled the arrow out. His usual playful expression is gone, replaced with a furious sneer.

"What are you guys up to?" Pax's arrogant drawl grates on me as he walks toward us. "You're not having fun without me, are you?"

Amira fires an arrow at him, and he veers to the side to dodge it so quickly I don't even see the movement.

"What the fuck?" Amira mutters, nocking another arrow.

Marcus's heat disappears from my other side. He crashes into Pax, knocking him to the ground.

Marcus gets on top of him, punching him in the face. An arrow whizzes past Marcus's head, so close my heart nearly stops.

"Amira!" I cry.

"Got it."

She fires, knowing where the other archer is from the trajectory of the arrow that narrowly missed Marcus. Her arrow is no sooner airborne and she lets another one loose.

A body drops to the ground from the tree line.

Pax roars, his arm muscles straining as he holds Marcus's wrist, trying to prevent Marcus from sinking a knife into his chest.

We have to find a way to draw out anyone else who's with Pax. I suspect Virginia is one of the Tiders hiding in the tree line.

"Amira, can you reach the ravens?" I ask.

She looks up. "I think so."

"Take them out."

I shield her body with mine as she takes aim, going for the lowest raven circling the clearing. It barks out a deep caw of pain when her arrow hits it in the chest. The bird is falling to the ground when an enraged Virginia flies out of the jungle, a raised spear in her hand.

Three more people follow her, and I steel myself. We're outnumbered, but they only have spears. Amira quickly takes one of them out with her bow and arrow.

"Niran, she can't fight hand-to-hand!" I yell.

"I've got her!" he says, racing to Amira's side.

She lands another arrow in a man's stomach, but he snarls and breaks it off, not slowing.

Virginia is coming for me. My heart races with worry. I can't risk a glance at Marcus to see how he's faring against Pax.

She stops about ten feet short of me, going still. I'm going for the gun holstered at my waist when another gunshot sounds. Niran just took one of the others down.

A vicious caw near my head makes me turn. It's one of the ravens, its dark eyes wild.

I call my vines, begging them to hurry. But within a second, the raven opens its beak, and I'm looking into a cavernous, black abyss. Its black tongue is the last thing I see before it snaps my shirt into its massive beak, taking hold of me.

"No!" My gun drops from my hand as the raven takes flight, something sharp cutting into my left ankle.

Frantically, I turn my head and find a second raven has my lower leg clutched in its sharp, polished talons, the pointed hooks tearing my flesh.

"Briar!" Marcus's roar of fury cuts through all the other sounds in the clearing.

I reach for him with the same mental pathway I have with vines, calling out to him for help. He's getting smaller as the birds fly higher. I thrash, smacking at the birds.

My vines are on the ground, writhing and winding into towers in an effort to reach me. There's a loud humming in my head that I somehow know is them, frantic to reach me.

The tallest vine tower reaches almost twenty feet into the air before it collapses, unable to get any higher. I feel the terror of the plants, their raw fear for me pouring through my body.

Marcus's wolf pack races across the clearing, their bodies low to the ground and streamlined. They're practically flying, their shoulders and back muscles rippling with each stride they take.

We're so high in the air now that I've stopped fighting back, because if the birds drop me, the impact with the ground will kill me instantly. Pure terror races through my veins as the people and wolves on the ground get smaller and smaller.

When the wolves reach the spot beneath me, they snarl and jump, trying to reach the birds even though they can't.

Blood drips from my ankle, the red drops descending from the sky like rain. Marcus calls for me again, my name a primal cry that tears from his chest.

The branches on the palm trees below start quaking. The wolves tear off toward the woods. The ground is shaking now, trees and bushes vibrating. The air is charged with something warm and still.

Something bright and orange in the air steals my

attention. A new fear races through me when I realize what it is. Giant globs of molten rock and ash are shooting out of the top of the volcano. It's the start of an eruption. Lava could quickly destroy this entire island, eradicating everything aromium has touched here, along with everything else.

Niran is standing in front of Marcus, his hands on Marcus's shoulders. He's saying something to him. Marcus's broad shoulders heave with exertion, his face turned to the ground.

As quickly as it started, the ash and magma stop erupting into the sky. Nothing but steam is there now, the palm trees on the ground still.

I stop breathing. It was Marcus. He made the volcano do that. Niran calmed him into stopping it. Realization washes through me. I remember what he said about not deserving me, about being a terrible person. What has he done with the powers aromium has given him that I don't know about? Whatever it is, he wears the guilt of it like a lead vest.

Virginia and Pax are gone. They seem to have escaped when Marcus, Niran and Amira were distracted.

My canvas bag of flowers isn't more than a dot on the ground now. It fell from my shoulder when the ravens grabbed me. At least Virginia won't know we found the flowers and were bringing them back.

Hopefully. What if they've been following us this whole time and we led them right to the flowers? They could destroy all of the remaining ones.

The raven with my leg in its talons clamps down and

I yelp, pain searing all the way to my bones. It's my only distraction from the terror of what's happening to me. My life depends on these two birds, who may be carrying me out to sea and dropping me. Or dropping me a quarter of a mile to the ground to the Rising Tide camp, where my body could be dinner tonight.

I close my eyes, fighting a powerful wave of nausea. At least my aromium is on. It's not much, but it's an advantage.

Virginia might put me back in that deep hole, where I was helpless. She could let me die there slowly. Or she could kill me in front of everyone.

When the Rising Tide camp comes into view below, I swallow against the bile in my throat. I see the skulls and bones outlining the circle, and the roofs of the camp's buildings. The birds start to descend, the camp getting closer.

Nothing good is waiting for me down there. I steel myself, knowing I may have to start fighting for my life as soon as I reach the ground.

47

President Whitman,

I'm pleased to report the birth of the first baby born to aromium-enhanced parents. The girl weighs nine pounds, three ounces and is healthy in all measurable aspects. At just three days old, she already shows neck control and motor skills that measure in the nine-month range for human infants.

Peace, Order and Prosperity,
Dr. Randall McClain

"No one's here to save you this time."

Virginia's icy tone sends a tremor from the tip of my spine to the base, my breathing the only thing I'm completely in control of right now.

Emaciated Tiders in numbered bracelets are gathered on both sides of the main pathway through the camp. Rona is there, her expression calculating as she watches us.

527

"You've been lied to!" I look from one side of the path to the other. "Look at me. I'm not starving. We have—"

"Shut up." Virginia walks closer to me, her fingers wrapped around a spear with a tip that looks razor sharp.

I ignore her. "She doesn't want you to know the truth. You're all being used by her and Whitman."

"Briar." I turn to find Pax, one of his eyes blackened and swollen and his nose crooked and bloody, holding his hands out to me in a calming gesture. "It doesn't have to be like this."

"Oh yes, it does." Virginia narrows her eyes at me in a murderous glare. "She was on the beach that day when eleven of our people were shot. They didn't even fight fairly. They just shot them."

"It was them or us," I say. "They were running toward us. We didn't attack first."

One of her ravens dips and dives down, the tip of its beak spearing me in the back. I slash at it with my knife, but it's gone before I can get to it, the fresh wound in my back burning.

"Don't worry." Virginia's tone is sickly sweet. "You aren't dying yet. Even though I'm eager to wipe that smug look from your face forever, I have to wait until Marcus gets here."

My eyes widen, my pulse pounding with worry. I so badly want to tip our hand. To tell her we just found the key that will help us keep people sent here from becoming mindless killers.

"Cut her head off!" someone yells.

"Great idea." Her toothy grin is evil. "But not yet. Marcus will come for her, and then we're going to kill them both."

No, I won't let her do this. Marcus is protecting more than a hundred people in our camp. He means too much for me to let him sacrifice himself just to save me. I'm only one person.

"He won't come." I shrug, acting nonchalant.

Virginia's laugh is a shrill cackle that grates on every nerve in my body. "You saw what he did to the volcano. That's a new one. Honestly, I didn't realize he could do that. If he can control the volcano, he's too powerful to live. He's not one to leave anyone behind, and he seems to like you for some reason. He'll come."

The raven returns for a second pass at me, but this time, I swipe my knife at it, striking its beak so hard pain shoots up my forearm. It squawks in protest, flying back upward.

"So no one's here to save me, but the birds are here to save you?" I ask lightly.

"You got help from vines last time. I didn't see that coming. Who are you related to from the original twenty-six?"

I give her a blank look and say, "I have no idea what you're talking about."

"Cut her fucking head off!" a woman belts out.

"For now, she's going back to confinement." There's a rumble of disagreement, and Virginia scans the faces of everyone gathered. "She'll die soon. Just not yet."

My head spins with sickness at the idea of being used

as bait for Marcus. I can't let him walk into their trap, even though he'd be doing it willingly.

An idea bursts out of me before I have time to even think about it. "Let's settle it in the circle."

The murmurs quiet, a second of silence passing before Virginia says, "What?"

I keep my chin raised, not letting her see how nervous I am. "You and me. In the circle. No weapons, no ravens, no vines. Just the two of us. The victor walks away."

Virginia's eyes light with something, but she doesn't respond.

Pax shakes his head. "There's nothing to be gained from that. We're waiting for Marcus."

"Are you scared?" I ask Virginia, taunting her.

She laughs bitterly. "Hardly. But Pax is right. I want Marcus to watch you die."

I lower my brows and raise my voice. "I didn't think refusing a call to the circle was allowed here."

A vein pops out in Virginia's forehead as she yells, "I can do whatever I want!"

Judgmental hums and whispers race through the bystanders lining the path. This might not have been my wisest idea ever, but it's putting her on the spot in front of everyone.

By refusing me, she's saying she's above the rules here. By accepting, she can't dump me back in the hole in the ground.

"The circle is sacred," a man says, every one of the rib bones in his shrunken frame outlined.

Liquid fire pools in Virginia's eyes as she hisses, "Fine. We'll settle it in the circle. And it won't be quick or merciful."

I dip my chin. "I'll make it quick and merciful, because I'm not a savage who feeds on the pain of others."

She flashes a nasty grin. "Only the strong survive here. If that makes us savages, then we're proud to be savages."

Several people holler out their agreement, pumping their fists in the air.

"It doesn't have to be this way." I look around at their angry sneers. "You don't have to starve and train yourselves into the ground. We have something better at our camp."

"You think you're better than us, bitch?" Marcelle glowers at me, her arms folded as she stands in one of the groups of people.

The rumble of discontent is louder now, most of the onlookers giving me disgusted glares.

"No! That's not what I'm saying."

Pax hooks my elbow. "Let's go before you get yourself killed."

He walks me down the path, deeper into the camp. When we reach their training area, he sits down on one side of a wooden table with built-in seats, gesturing for me to take the other side.

"What are you doing?" he whispers, his brow furrowed. "She'll make you suffer just to prove a point."

Conflicting emotions swim around in my head. I

trusted Pax. I liked him. The aromium skewed my feelings for him, but there's a part of the real me that still can't bring myself to hate him.

I don't trust him, though. My lips pressed into a thin line, I look away, refusing to answer him.

"Briar," he says softly.

There's a tug inside me, but I ignore it, shaking my head.

He's not evil like Virginia, but there are two sides on this island, and he's on the wrong one.

Hopefully McClain has the flowers now. Even if I don't make it out of the circle, there's hope of ending the games being played with people's lives here.

48

Plants have their own form of chemical warfare called allelopathy, where they release chemicals that inhibit the growth of nearby plants competing for resources. They can even release chemicals that make herbivores less likely to graze by affecting their nervous systems.

- Excerpt from a lecture given by Dr. Lucinda Hollis in her Plant Evolution course

"Don't do this." Pax's tone is pleading, his gaze jumping from me to Virginia and then back to me again. "If you two could just get past your anger, you'd see how alike you are. This island needs both of you."

It's midafternoon, the burning torches placed around the circle flickering even though we don't need their light. Dark eye sockets in the hundreds of skulls that line the space stare out at us vacantly.

They were people once, with beating hearts and dreams. They loved people and were loved in return. But then the virus came, and life became a battle of survival. I have to believe most, if not all, of the people whose bones rim this space deserved a better death than the one they got.

"I'm nothing like her," I snap. "Nothing like any of you. You eat your own people. You kill for sport."

Gasps sound from the people gathered around the outer ring of the circle. Pax is standing between me and Virginia at the circle's entrance, trying to talk us out of going through with the ritual.

I gesture at the Tiders watching us, many with spears in hand. "Why don't they know what was injected into them before they were brought here? Or that one of the mystery meats here is human flesh?"

Pax's eyes flash with anger. "That's outrageous and untrue."

"She lies," Virginia says. "She wants to divide our people so she and Marcus can rule over us all."

I scoff. "That's so far from the truth."

"Stop stalling and let's do this."

She's dressed in a fitted black sleeveless shirt and canvas pants, her arms too thin but still lined with muscle. Her blond hair is pulled back in a tight bun, the lines on her face making her look older than thirty-five.

My heart thunders in my chest as I move to step inside the circle, Pax calling out, "Briar, don't!"

I'm my father's daughter, and I don't back down from what I know is right. Someone has to stand up to Virginia. If I don't leave the circle, at least the people here heard what I said and saw that someone challenged her iron authority.

The gleam in Virginia's eyes is feral as she follows me into the circle, the bystanders letting out deep cries of approval and slamming the bottoms of the spears to the ground.

This shouldn't be anyone's entertainment. But this island is a merciless mistress, no brutality or sacrifice ever enough to sate it.

The bonfire in the center of the circle crackles as a log drops, the flames blazing more than six feet into the air. Black smoke wafts from the fire, the air still tinged with the smell of burning flesh from the last time people fought here.

"I'm going to enjoy your screams," Virginia says in a low tone.

I'm crouched in my fighting stance. She wants to rattle me, but I won't let her. I keep my breathing controlled and my mind on what I need to do.

"Do you know why I was chosen as one of the original twenty-six?" she asks.

"Were they in need of a psychopath?"

She scoffs. "I worked in Army black ops. I spent my entire career training to kill people and killing people."

"So you volunteered?"

She arches a brow. "Proudly."

"Bullshit. You're here because Whitman's holding your niece hostage."

She narrows her cold eyes at me and advances, throwing a left hook. I dodge it, quick on my feet even in the sand.

"You think she'd be proud of you?" I taunt her, hoping she'll make a dumb move.

She fakes another hook with her right hand, her left punching me square in the gut when I misjudge her intent.

Damn, she's strong. I cringe and recover quickly, but not soon enough. She hits me with a jab and a cross, momentarily stunning me.

I feign a punch to her stomach, instead kicking her knee. She stumbles back, scowling. Then she lunges for me, reaching for my neck and trying to wrap her hands around it. I pivot my shoulder and use my arm to break her hold, driving a knee into her stomach.

My dad's training kicks in. I've gotten a feel for her fighting style; now it's time to catch her off guard. I drive the heel of my hand into her face and kick her other knee as hard as I can.

Right before my foot is out of range, she grabs it, spinning me and shoving me to the ground. Then she jumps me, throwing punches at my face. Sand flies into my mouth, my eyes, and my nose.

I grab a fistful of her shirt and try to push her off of me. She's thin; it should be easier than it is.

"Briar!"

The sound of Marcus's voice infuses me with the

extra shred of strength I need to get Virginia off of me. I throw her to the ground, drawing my fist back before driving it into her nose. There's a satisfying crunch, followed by blood flowing from her nose.

I get to my feet, stumbling slightly, and get enough distance from Virginia that I can safely look over at Marcus. It's not just him standing there, though.

Nova, Amira, Niran, Wyatt, Olin, and Adele are all with him, everyone strapped with knives and guns and holding stun sticks. Marcus's pack of wolves is there, too, Flavius growling and baring his teeth from his spot beside Marcus.

They came for me. I'm not surprised, but I still feel a flicker of gratitude.

"Release her now and no one has to die," Marcus says, his voice lethally calm.

He's a fortress—shirtless, sweaty and still dirty from our trek through the jungle to find the flower. The hard angles of his face and the storm raging in his eyes take my breath away, making me grateful we're on the same side.

"I called her into the circle," I tell him, Virginia on her feet now.

His expression darkens further. "Step out, Briar."

In a very short time, he's come to mean so much to me. I care deeply for him and part of me wants to obey his command, if only to satisfy him. But I can't.

"We're not done. Only one of us is leaving this circle."

A muscle in his jaw tics, Flavius snarling. The ground

hums beneath my feet, a low rumble shaking nearby trees.

"He's breaking the rules," Virginia says.

I hold a hand up, meeting Marcus's steely gaze. "Stop. Please. I agreed to the rules of the circle. No weapons. No help."

The ground still shakes slightly as he says, "No. It's not a fair fight."

Aggravation flares because no matter what I do, he still underestimates me. "This is my choice, and I made it."

The skulls and bones lining the circle rattle as the vibrations in the ground intensify.

"Marcus!" I'm more forceful this time. "It's my choice."

Nova leans over to say something to him, and he closes his eyes, looking pained. The bones stop rattling and the shaking in the ground slows to a stop.

I lock my gaze onto his, silently thanking him. His eyes widen, and I sense Virginia coming for me. I can go high or low, but I have to decide quickly.

I go low, turning, crouching and driving my fist at her. It works perfectly, hitting her squarely in the throat. That's an effective spot to land a hit on someone you don't mind killing.

She drops to her knees, making a choking sound. I use the opening to twist my hips and get the leverage I need to kick her in the face. Gasps sound as she flies onto her back, still struggling for air.

The gashes on my ankles and calf from the raven are

deep, and the wound in my back hurts, too. My face aches from the punches Virginia landed, but energy still surges through me. It's the aromium, lending me strength that's not really mine.

Virginia is getting up when I rush her, knocking her to the ground. I hate that I've been reduced to this, but I didn't see any other way.

I straddle her, digging my knees into the sand and wrapping my hands around her neck.

"Let us offer everyone here a chance to turn off the aromium," I say. "I'll let you live."

She's clawing at my arms and writhing beneath me, but I'm stronger. She's weakened, probably from lack of food. Even on aromium, people still need to eat, just not as much.

Her nails open up gashes on my arms, but I don't let go of her neck.

"Fuck you." She launches the words at me, her eyes dark and hate-filled.

"Virginia, get her off of you!" Pax yells. "Use your legs."

She's trying, but I'm like a dog with a bone. Nothing, absolutely *nothing* short of death would make me release my hold on her neck right now. This has to be as swift and merciful as possible.

I'm too tall for her to reach my eyes. I press my hands into her windpipe as she struggles beneath me, her hands clawing absently at my face.

Emotion wells in my throat, because there's no thrill in this win. There won't be any celebrating. Killing a bully to save others is still killing, and I loathe being in this position.

Her eyes bulge, Pax's frantic yelling at her just static noise I can't make out. A mournful wail breaks free from my chest.

"I won't burn your body." I press harder, willing it to end. "And I'll find your niece. I'll help her. I promise."

Her lips part, awareness of what I just said lighting in her eyes before they fade to lifelessness. Her body goes limp and still and I crawl off of her, the dam of emotion inside me breaking.

"Virginia!" Pax screams and runs into the circle, his devastation cracking something open inside me.

"No one burns her," I say, my voice breaking as I get to my feet. "Give her a respectful burial."

He looks up at me from beside Virginia, the fury in his expression taking me aback. "You're not leaving here."

I feel Marcus's warmth beside me. "Yes, she is." He puts an arm around me, his palm on my lower back, and says, "Let's go."

We walk out of the circle, my gaze straight ahead as Amira draws her bow, aiming an arrow behind us.

Marcus and I both turn to find Pax stalking toward us, his hands trembling with rage.

"I'm calling you into the circle," he says to me. "Right now."

Marcus answers. "No. It's over, Pax. No one else dies tonight."

"Who the fuck do you think you've become?" Pax

sneers at Marcus, disgusted. "You've got her convinced we're the killers and you're some sort of avenging angel, but that's a load of shit."

"We're leaving." Marcus steers me over to our group of people.

I'm still reeling from what I just did. It hurt more than I expected it to. Amira's warm brown eyes meet mine, silently telling me it's going to be okay.

"Tell her who you really are," Pax says from behind us.

Marcus's shoulders tighten and he stands straighter. We both turn around. Pax is unhinged, his fists balled at his sides and veins corded at his neck.

"I already know," I say softly. "He told me everything. About the aromium strains and the reason you and I and he and Virginia can call on other living things."

"He did?" Pax gapes between us, genuinely shocked.

"Yes. I know we all have relatives who contributed DNA to aromium. None of us asked for this."

He scoffs, narrowing his eyes. "That's not totally true."

"Pax, don't," Marcus cautions.

"Fuck you, Marcus." Pax meets my gaze. "My father was one of the original twenty-six. But Virginia didn't have a family member who was in it; she *was* one of them. And so was Marcus."

Marcus stiffens beside me, his cold gaze locked onto Pax.

My heart races and bile rushes up my throat. "What do you mean?" I look at Marcus. "What does he mean?"

It's Pax who answers. "Marcus helped make aromium. He was one of the first ones on this island. He and Virginia were the original leaders of Rising Tide. Isn't that right, Marcus?"

Marcus says nothing, but I don't need him to answer the question. The answer is all over his face. There's fury at Pax for telling me, but also shame. Guilt. Disgust.

It hits me harder than any of the punches Virginia threw. What a fool I've been.

49

The shred of humanity left in me is outraged at the carnage I've caused. The arrogant cynic I'm becoming, though, asks if there's even any significance to adding a few more people to my list of casualties.

- Excerpt from the journal of Dr. Randall McClain

Marcus

Niran and Nova are yelling at me. Briar's pained expression flashes through my mind, lasting only an instant. Then Ellison is there, her brow furrowed with concern. I want to ask them what's going on, but I can't seem to move.

Everything is so heavy. My limbs. My eyelids. My secrets. I can't fight any of it anymore.

"Marcus." Ellison's voice is sharp and insistent. "Wake up. I need you to wake up, Marcus."

She's the only one who knows what I've done. We did it together, as members of the original twenty-six. And somehow, she doesn't hate herself. Or me.

When my leaden eyelids open, her outline beside me is fuzzy. I blink a few times and she comes into focus. Everything rushes back in a sickening wave of realization. The ravens taking Briar. The volcano. The circle. Virginia's death.

Briar knows who I really am.

I jolt, trying to get out of bed, but I'm strapped down.

"Easy," Ellison puts a hand on my shoulder. "The restraints are for your safety. Stay calm."

My heart pumps hard as I struggle against the straps around my wrists and ankles, confining me to a bed. This can't be fucking happening. Ellison would never turn on me.

"Take them off," I command.

"I'm going to." She levels a serious gaze at me. "You listen to me for the next two minutes, and then I take them off. You have my word."

I'm in one of her patient rooms, and the heaviness I feel has to mean I've been drugged. None of this makes any sense.

"What the fuck is this?"

"You got very sick at the switch point when your

aromium was turned off. You had a seizure. Nova and Niran carried you back to camp."

The yelling. They weren't angry. They were begging me to hold on while they got me to Ellison. I threw up all over Niran. He was a wreck, on the verge of tears.

The tension pulling at my muscles fades slightly as I look around the dimly lit room. There's the bed I'm in. A light. Some machines. An empty chair. A small side table. And Ellison.

"Where's Briar?"

Ellison's brows drop a fraction. "She's been here. It's been almost a week. She's working with Dr. McClain; they're studying the flowers and trying to make a stabilizer."

My fury ebbs, my shoulders relaxing against the pillow. I'm not the one who has anything to be furious about—she is.

"I think the aromium switching caused your brain to swell," Ellison continues. "I thought we were going to lose you. Dr. McClain was the one who—" She clears her throat. "He saved you. You've been heavily sedated while we waited to see if the brain swelling would go down."

"Briar hates me."

There's no fight behind the words. I'm a broken, defeated man; the house of cards I built so I could have a chance with her is in ruins at my feet.

"She's angry." Ellison's voice is gentle. "But hate is a strong word, my friend. Give her some time and space."

There's already a chasm between us. Her expression when she turned to me after Pax told her the truth about me is seared into my memory. She didn't even ask if it was true—she knew. My betrayal hurt her so badly that she could only look at me for a couple of seconds before she had to turn away.

Ellison starts unfastening one of the restraints at my wrists. "You have to keep resting. I don't care if you feel like it. You haven't eaten in a week and your body is still recovering."

I don't respond because I don't care whether I'm resting or doing what I usually would. Briar won't ever trust me again. I ruined the best thing I had.

Even though I knew I didn't deserve her, I let her believe I was someone good. Someone she could trust. I'm no better than Pax or Virginia.

"I wanted to surgically remove your aromium implant," Ellison says. "Dr. McClain talked me out of it. Both of us believe that even one more aromium switch will probably kill you. This last one came very close."

I shrug. "It had to be done."

Her eyes meet mine and I find the determination I know her for. "Nova, Niran and I all agreed that if you try to turn your aromium on again, we'll sedate you and I'll remove it."

My brows drop. "What the fuck? That's my decision."

"We made it ours. The aromium switch has been moved to a secure location you won't know about."

I shake my head, disgusted that my closest friends were conspiring against me while I was laid up and drugged.

"We'll revisit that later." I sigh heavily, struggling to keep my eyelids open.

"Get some rest. You need to eat when you wake up next."

My mind is a pretty fucked place to be at the moment, so it's a relief to slip into the peaceful oblivion of sleep.

———

The next time I wake up, McClain is sitting in the chair next to me, a book in his hands.

"Good to see you awake," he says, closing the book and setting it on the small table.

He stands, removing the stethoscope from around his neck, and says, "May I?"

I shrug, because who gives a fuck. He listens to my heart and lungs, seeming satisfied as he wraps the stethoscope around his neck again.

"You're doing much better. The swelling seems to have subsided. Ellison told me about her conversation with you."

"I'm not doing this." I'm less groggy than I was the first time I woke up, and I get into a sitting position. "You fucked me over, and I'm not acting like you never left and everything's like it was before."

He looks about twenty-five years older than he did when I was first introduced to him by one of my college professors eight years ago. He was a guest lecturer in my premed program, and my professor wanted to get me on the radar of one of the leading research physicians in the world.

I was starstruck. He was maybe five feet, nine inches and a hundred and sixty pounds, with thick glasses and salt-and-pepper hair that always looked like it needed a trim. Soft spoken. But to me, he was a giant. A pioneer in his field. Any university in the world would have hired him in a heartbeat, but he was too passionate about his research to teach full-time.

"I know things are different now."

He sits back down and I study him, his body still almost as emaciated as those of the Tiders I saw at the circle. The skin on his face doesn't hang quite as much as when we first found him, which must mean he's put on a little weight.

"What do you think of the flower?" I ask him.

He pushes his glasses up on his nose, his intent expression matching the one he used to have when we were working on the aromium project. After I interned with him the summer after my junior year, he helped secure my place in my top choice of medical schools.

I fell hook, line, and sinker for his bullshit. Basked in his compliments about my intelligence and strong work ethic. When he told me my genetic makeup, including my physical size, made me an ideal candidate to be part of the most exciting project he'd ever worked on, I jumped at the chance.

It landed me here. If I could go back, I'd do things very differently.

"There are a lot of promising components in the

specimen plants and flowers. Briar has been a tremendous help studying them."

The sound of her name is like a knife twisting in my chest. "Can you make a stabilizer?"

"I'm going to do my best. Testing it will be a challenge, but we'll cross that bridge when we reach it."

I loathe him, but part of me is relieved he's here. I'm not carrying all the weight of finding a way out of the disaster we created. Not that I was ever qualified to figure out the things he can.

Deep down, I thought he was dead. Hoped so, even. I didn't want to think he was a big enough asshole to leave our camp and never look back. I figured his guilt became too overwhelming and he threw himself off a cliff or something.

It would've been a cowardly way out. The worst punishment, which we both have to endure for the rest of our lives, is seeing the destruction we caused.

Not that it's even over. Aromium is far from contained. The compound was created on this island, and since it only takes a very small part of the flower that's key to its makeup, we made a lot of it with the flowers we had and sent it to the mainland so Whitman's people could inject test subjects. We don't know if it was used on people in other places.

"I'm pretty sure I made the volcano start to erupt," I say flatly.

He crosses his arms and sits back in his chair, studying me silently for a couple of seconds. "We saw it happen. I thought we were on the verge of a full eruption. But then it stopped."

I nod. "The ground shook before it started erupting. Niran saw me and figured out that I was the one making it all happen. It wasn't on purpose. Virginia's ravens were taking Briar away and ..." I run a hand over the stubble on my jaw. "I've never felt so ... I mean, there was fury, but also helplessness. Agony. I was sure she was about to die and there was no way for me to help her."

There's warmth in his gaze. "It's nice to know you finally care about someone enough—"

I cut him off with a sharp glare. "Don't. I'm only talking to you because you're the only one who might know. We're not having a tender moment—just tell me how the aromium made me do it."

He pinches his brows together, considering. "Are you familiar with endoliths?"

"Not really."

"They're organisms like bacteria, fungi, and lichens that live in rocks and soil. They can absorb dissolved nutrients like iron and potassium from rocks."

"It's ringing a bell. I probably studied them in a bio class. But what's your point? They're alive, so ... did you put aromium in them?"

He shakes his head. "Not directly. But there are plants all over this island with aromium. They could have spread it into the soil through their roots and rain runoff."

"I don't remember the team having any conversations about that possibility."

His shoulders fall slightly. "That's because we never had any. I'm shocked that this is even a possibility."

"I made the ground shake again at Rising Tide. It's just like the wolves—the ground is responding to my emotions."

McClain's face shutters in a grave expression. "You can never use aromium again, Marcus. You're too powerful. And after what happened, I'm afraid the next time will kill you."

Ellison opens the door, brightening when she sees I'm awake. She glances between me and McClain, brings me a tray of food, and departs immediately.

The tray has a plate with buttered toast, a bowl of bean and vegetable stew, and a bowl of fruit. My mouth waters from the savory scent of the stew.

"I never wanted to use it again," I say. "But Flavius even follows me when my aromium is off, and Briar's vines sometimes do the same to her. So what if I connect to the endoliths even without it?"

McClain's expression clouds with worry, though he says, "Don't borrow trouble. You were able to turn it off both times it happened and no damage was done."

His reassurance falls flat. I could be one horrible mood away from destroying this entire island and everyone on it.

Including Briar. She's not mine anymore, but I'd still do anything to protect her. It's what I've been trying to do this whole time, but now reality is setting in, and it's a gut punch: the biggest danger to her on this island is me.

UP NEXT

The next book in the Blue Arrow Island series is Crimson Shore.

I listened to this playlist many times while writing Blue Arrow Island. Every song on this list was chosen because it relates to some aspect of the story.
Art inspires art.

AUTHOR'S NOTE

The idea for Blue Arrow Island first came to me around ten years ago. I couldn't get it out of my head. I'd written a handful of Contemporary romances, and I dove into the challenge of a dystopian sci-fi. The story was a little different then, but the main ideas were the same. I ordered a cover from a designer and wrote a couple of chapters. The chapters frustrated me, because they didn't fit my vision for the book. I couldn't move forward, so I shelved the idea.

Many Contemporary romances later, the idea for Blue Arrow Island reemerged. It had whispered to me over the years, but this time it was louder. I decided to hire a great developmental editor who has helped me outline books in the past. We went back and forth a lot over about a month until I had a solid outline and I knew my structure was in a good place. Then I started writing.

This time, I loved the book. I became a little obsessed. I thought about it constantly when I wasn't writing. I wrote a lot more hours per day than usual. I wrote on the weekends. I loved every minute of writing this book.

My author voice is fast-paced and dialogue-heavy. I'm light on worldbuilding. My hope is that I gave you just enough to envision the island and the story for yourself. Whether or not you loved the book, if you made it all the way to this note, thank you so much for investing your time in my story.

I just finished writing Blue Arrow Island about half an hour ago, and already I can't wait to go back to the island for the next book, Crimson Shore.

ACKNOWLEDGMENTS

It was a big leap to create an entire world like I did for Blue Arrow Island. It wouldn't be what it is without the help of Jenn Sommersby of Plumfield Editing. Jenn is a creative force who helped me answer questions, create new ideas, and build an outline. My process was slow, but it worked for me, and Jenn leaned into it and made what was challenging feel possible. Beta readers Jess and Christina encouraged me and helped shape this book with their feedback—I'm so grateful to you both. My author friends Sara Whitney, Genevieve Jack, Skye Malone, Kate Bateman and Chelle Bliss were everything I needed and more, as always. Rose Puls, my longtime editor, made this book shine. Reader Jamie jumped in to read the first act immediately when I asked her, which I needed a lot in that moment. My agent Stephanie Phillips didn't even blink when I decided to jump into a new genre – she's always there to lift up whatever stories are inspiring me. Erika, Nikki and the entire Hambright PR team got behind this book with enthusiasm that became the wind in my sails. Every like and comment of excitement from influencers and readers meant a lot to me. My husband Dan listened and encouraged me, which made me feel like I could really do this. My boys are my reasons, and their presence in and out of my office as I wrote this book is a core memory I will always treasure. Thank you to every reader who takes a chance on this book. You're the reason I get to have this dream job, and I will never take you for granted.

ABOUT THE AUTHOR

Brenda Rothert lives in Central Illinois with her husband, children and three dogs. She loves to hear from readers through her website or her Facebook Group, Rothert's Readers.

Keep up with all the latest on Brenda's books and get bonus content by signing up for her newsletter at brendarothert.com/subscribe.